GHOSTS ON THE OXBOW

A Novel

Kathy Rhodes

"Every valley shall be exalted, and every mountain and hill shall be made low: and the crooked [places] shall be made straight . . ." Isaiah 40:4 (KJV)

Hummingbird & Heron
KINGSTON SPRINGS, TENNESSEE

Hummingbird & Heron
P.O. Box 605
Kingston Springs, TN 37082
www.publishedbywestview.com

This book is a work of fiction. Names, characters, places and incidents either are products of the author's imagination or are used fictitiously. Any resemblance to actual events or locales or persons, living or dead, is entirely coincidental.

ISBN: Hard cover: 978-1-62880-308-2; Perfect bound: 978-1-62880-309-9; ebook 978-1-62880-310-5

First edition, February 2025

Good faith efforts have been made to trace copyrights on materials included in this publication. If any copyrighted material has been included without permission and due acknowledgment, proper credit will be inserted in future printings after notice has been received.

Digitally printed worldwide on acid free paper.

"To write honestly and with all our powers
is the least we can do,
and the most."

— Eudora Welty, *On Writing*

For my sons

Todd Ellison Belt and Corey Bennington Belt

who work to pull the low places up and strive to make the crooked places straight

AUTHOR'S NOTE

I was born in the Mississippi Delta, grew up during 1950s Jim Crow, and came of age during the 1960s Civil Rights Movement. I lived in Mississippi for thirty-five years and was an absentee landowner in the hill country of Kemper County until 2024.

I witnessed two parallel cultures—Black and White, separate but not equal. I heard things, saw things—bad things I needed to tell.

This novel is a work of fiction: a fictional town, made-up people, an imagined story. But the story is based on snatches from real life, snapshots of this Mississippi girl's memories, images imprinted on my brain that, like a ghost haunting an old graveyard, linger and beg to be seen.

IMAGE #1. *August 1964.*
**Newspaper headlines in the window of a coin-operated news rack
at a motel in McAlester, Oklahoma:
BODIES OF THREE SLAIN CIVIL RIGHTS WORKERS
DISCOVERED IN AN EARTHEN DAM OUTSIDE
PHILADELPHIA, MISSISSIPPI.**

My grandparents lived outside Philadelphia, Mississippi.

I was fourteen on a church youth trip from my Mississippi Delta hometown to Glorieta Baptist Assembly near Santa Fe, New Mexico. We spent the first night in Oklahoma. The next morning, I saw the headlines as I walked into the motel restaurant. The civil rights workers, registering Black voters during Freedom Summer, had been missing since June. The FBI found their burned car two days after they went missing. All summer, Mississippi lied, denied, said it was a publicity stunt, that the workers were up in Chicago laughing at the fuss they caused.

It was a shock seeing the word "Mississippi" connected to the murders. *Bodies. Slain. Buried in Mississippi red-clay dirt.*

It was an epiphany.

Because I was far away from Mississippi, from hometown commentary and home state slants, fabrications, and justifications, I saw the act for what it was—a horrific hate crime.

IMAGE #2. *November 1964.*
The blackened burn circle where the Ford station wagon of the three civil rights workers was torched.

All my father's people lived in Kemper, Lauderdale, and Neshoba counties in Mississippi, and we were visiting my grandparents for Thanksgiving. My father wanted to see the site of the burning, so he, my grandfather, and I drove to the spot where the local chapter of the Neshoba-Kemper-Lauderdale Ku Klux Klan committed criminal atrocities.

I stepped into the car-sized circle in the brush and trees, scorched branches drooping, some weeping, and leaves still singed five months later, and wrapped my hand around a blackened branch hanging down. I stood on the char. I felt the burn.

IMAGE #3. *April 1976.*
A forgotten classroom in an abandoned, red-brick school.

I walked across a weedy field to the low-slung public school building deserted seven years earlier. Its windows were dirty, scummy. I stepped up close to a filmy pane, cupped a hand between my temple and the glass to block the sunlight, and looked inside. Wooden desks were lined up in straight rows, dust and open workbooks on the desktops. Yellow pencils lay across the pages, as if the children had paused work to go outside for recess, soon to return from play.

What really happened was, one school day in 1969, when forced integration was imminent, students in that classroom and every other classroom stood up, left all their books, pencils, and belongings on and in their desks, and marched out of the building. They never went back.

Statewide, children were pulled out of public schools and plunked down in hastily built private Christian segregation academies. In 1964, the state had twenty private schools. By 1971, that number had skyrocketed to 236.

This book has been a long time coming. Because it is about race, I held on to it for decades, edited to water it down, later added material back, did a dozen kindness readings, and still worried what people would think. The message I grew up with in Mississippi and still hear is: "Sit down, shut up, and don't rock the boat." I was inspired by Wright Thompson's *The Barn* (2024) to stand up and tell the truth in this age of erasure of history and denial that systemic racism exists.

I did my best to capture my *own people*—all of us—in our incongruities, complexities, and contradictions arising from our Delta upbringings. I tried to capture all voices.

This would not be an authentic representation of the state of Mississippi without the use of the offensive word "ni—." I chose to use only the first two letters of *that word*. I use it twice as a noun and once as a verb. Sadly, it is a word I heard almost every day in my first twenty years of life in the Delta.

The late Doug Marlette, Pulitzer Prize–winning cartoonist and novelist, who lived in Laurel, Mississippi, during his youth, signed for me a copy of his book *Magic Time*, also about the 1964 murders of three civil rights workers. "To Kathy, Mississippi girl, you'll know these folks!" With that, he gave me authority to write this book.

COGHLAN FAMILY BIBLE
The Line of Evelyn Bounds Carlyle

Andrew Coghlan
1809-1861
married 1828
Eirinn Lafferty
1810-1859
↓

↓ ↓

+Catherine Deering Coghlan
1844-1911
married John Amason
↓

+Victoria Dove Coghlan
1846-1890
spinster

↓ ↓

++Annah Rachel Amason
1862-1934
married Joseph Tanner

++Erin Rose Amason
1863-1890
married Thomas Robbins

+++William Patrick Tanner
1911-2000
married Brenda Smith

+++Emmaline Robbins
1889-1951
married William Bounds

++++Gerald Tanner
1953-
married Jo Taylor

++++Evelyn Bounds
1910-2010
married Lewis Carlyle

+++++Edward Carlyle
1929-1959
married Lucille Doak

++++++Eva Clare Carlyle
1953-
married James Roan

+++++++Lara Coghlan Roan
1978-

PROLOGUE

THE CATALYST

Friday, December 11, 1970
Erin High School
Erin, Mississippi

Fifth-period senior math class, Eva Clare sat staring at the blackboard filled with trigonometric equations. Who the heck wanted to think about math? She squinched her eyes and blurred those white-chalk numbers, variables, and symbols to oblivion. Math was too precise and predictable, with patterns, formulas, and unlike life, equivalent expressions on each side of the equal sign.

Out the window, the sky was low and gray. The empty oaks and chinquapins extended their branches, posing as the hands of winter.

Rain ran in crooked rivulets down the windowpanes. She studied the swirling shapes, dreamed about blending black and white oils with her palette knife, whipping up a creamy mix, and painting on canvas the wavy flows and worn-wood muntins.

The intercom speaker box mounted to the front wall crackled on. Someone at the other end blew into the microphone and executed a series of taps on it. She looked up at the tan mesh screen that emitted static, wheezing, the clearing of a throat.

The calendar page under the intercom box showed December 11—her birthday. Finally, she was seventeen and officially old enough for twelfth grade, where she'd been anyway for three months. Taped to the wall, a *Life* magazine cover—the *Eagle* reflected in Buzz Aldrin's visor—read TO THE MOON AND BACK. The clock above the door displayed one-thirty.

Two more taps on the mic. "Lemme have your attention," the principal said.

"What's goin' on?" Eva Clare whispered across the aisle to Anna Laurel Wood.

"Beats me. Maybe a moon rocket exploded, or another president got shot." With the eraser end of her yellow No. 2, Anna Laurel pushed a strand of long, black hair behind her ear. Eva Clare had to iron strands of her hair to get the stick-straight look Anna Laurel had.

"There'll be three short bells," the principal continued. "Put your books in your locker, get your coat, and go to your homeroom. Your teacher will make an announcement."

The bells sounded in staccato before anyone had a chance to ask what about. Students headed to the door and crowded into the hallway. Eva Clare stopped at her locker, dumped her math book, slammed the metal door, snapped the lock. She fell in with Anna Laurel, Sunny, and Meredith, and they pushed their way into the noisy flow toward Mrs. Cleary's room. They had big plans for her birthday tonight. They'd drive to Greenville in Anna Laurel's daddy's baby-blue Thunderbird to eat at How Joy, the new Chinese restaurant. Then go to the picture show. She rehearsed their plan again over the din of the swarm.

Someone behind her pulled her back bra strap and snapped it against her skin. She recognized his witchy cackle. Her creepy cousin Gerald Tanner constantly flitted about, annoying people with his silly antics.

"Stop it!"

"Oh, shut up, you little goody-goody." He laughed harder.

Students funneled into the classroom at the end of the hall and sank to their seats in a jumble of chatter and laughter that stopped when they saw Mrs. Cleary's stern walk to the lectern—head down, brow crimped. She gripped the sides of the worn pine stand.

"Class," she oozed out in a broken whisper, then squeezed her eyes shut.

Something was terribly wrong. Worse than a moon rocket explosion or an assassination.

Mrs. Cleary's chest heaved with a deep breath. She stiffened, lifted her chin, feigned a professional face. "This is our last day at Erin High School."

"Whaaat?" some yelled above an echo of gasps from others.

"You mean we're getting out early for the Christmas holidays?" Anna Laurel asked.

Everybody seemed relieved. Some started yippeeing.

Eva Clare wrapped her arms around herself and bunched the cold crepe of her blouse sleeves in her fists.

The teacher's rapid claps called them to attention. "At fifteen of two, the bell will ring five short times as it does for a fire drill. We'll stand, leave everything—except coats and purses—walk silently down the hall in single file and out the front doors. Our class will be the last one out of the building. We'll keep walking instead of forming class groups on the football field as we do in a drill. We'll go to the church parking lot that backs up to campus, where car pools and buses are waiting to take you home. We'll never come back."

Students barraged the teacher with questions about ballgames, banquets, and graduation.

Mrs. Cleary held up her hands to quieten them. "They're closing the school. You might've heard your parents talking—"

"Mine told me all about it," Gerald Tanner bragged. Others nodded, said, "Mine, too."

"Even though they were told to keep it quiet so no outsiders would know." Mrs. Cleary frowned at Gerald as she picked up a stack of handouts from her desk.

Eva Clare let out the breath she'd been holding and pulled in another. She'd heard Grandpop Binky and Grandmomma Sweet Evelyn talk about switching from public to private school, but didn't know when, and never in her wildest dreams did she think it could happen to her class in the middle of their final year at EHS. It was Grandmomma who did most of the talking about segregation.

"Your parents attended a planning meeting last month and got preliminary information. I'll pass out the final instructions now." Mrs. Cleary gave the handouts to Judi in the first seat, first row, who took one, sniffed the purple mimeograph ink, and passed the rest back. "There's a town gathering tonight at the church."

"But my birthday party!" Eva Clare blurted.

"On January fourth, we'll resume classes at the Beulah Lake church until the new school on Highway 1 is finished. In May, you'll graduate from Steele Bayou Christian Academy."

Eva Clare's stomach tightened. Right before her eyes, the walls of that new, flimsy metal building had gone up in a muddy cotton field—a beige box in a patch of last year's crop, the remnant stalks fallen, partially plowed under, some sticking up askew. She never imagined being snatched up out of this stately brick school and plunked down in a cheap prefab metal one. "We can't give up this beautiful school for that hideous tin matchbox."

"We're five months from graduation," Anna Laurel said. "Why now?"

"You girls know why," Gerald snapped. "Y'all are cheerleaders. Y'all know the cheer. 'Two, four, six, eight. We don't want to in-te-grate.'"

"We don't want to leave our school," Eva Clare fired back.

"Ain't no ni—"

"Shut up!" She plastered her hands over her ears but heard *that word* anyway.

"Ever comin' in this building!" He shook his finger at her.

Then he said *that word* again with *lover* attached to it. He called her that name. She hated when people used *that word*. Grandpop Binky wouldn't allow it to be spoken in their home. Her face fell forward, chin to collar bone. She didn't like offensive slurs or being the target of them. From now on, she'd keep her thoughts to herself because of loudmouthed bullies like Gerald.

"This isn't a solution." Pete Wong shook his head.

"There's nothing we can do," Mrs. Cleary said. "The town leaders have spoken."

So they all sat there like bumps on a pickle and let it happen.

"Leave all textbooks and supplies in your desk. Notebooks, workbooks, pencils, pens—"

"My own pens and notebook binder?" Eva Clare asked.

"Leave everything. That's what I was told to do."

Anna Laurel sneaked a pouch of magic markers, an avocado green steno pad with daisies on the cover, and two pencils with happy-face eraser tops out of the binder on her desk and stuffed them into her purse.

Eva Clare followed suit, subtly reaching inside her pencil case to get her blue-marbled, monogrammed fountain pen.

"My cheerleading uniform!" Sunny screeched. "I left it in my locker."

"You won't need it," Mrs. Cleary said, provoking Sunny to let out a wail.

"Oh, crud!" Eva Clare left hers, too. Also, a birthday present—a gold pendant she brought to show her friends. She should've worn it, but instead, she wore a jade necklace to match her green worsted wool jumper. She should've grabbed it when she dropped off her math book, but she didn't know then that in fifteen minutes they'd be forsaking their school and everything in it. She'd have to get that necklace, or Grandmomma would pitch a hissy fit.

Her stomach lurched at the loss this walkout represented. There would no longer be an Erin High School. No more Erin Eagles. Her grandmother graduated from here. So did her father. Her chest squeezed, pushing up silent sobs from that tight place below her throat.

"What'll we be at the new academy?" Anna Laurel asked. "Saints? Separatists?"

Mrs. Cleary hurled a scowl at her.

On the round wall clock with bold, black numbers, the big hand clicked forward a notch. Eva Clare's heart ticked and twisted in response.

She studied the faces around her as they sat out the last moments in this microcosm of student society they had created, owned, and loved. A few, including Gerald, grinned and appeared eager to go. Most were crying. They couldn't keep their beautiful, red-brick school building because they didn't want the Blacks in it.

Five bells sounded. Mrs. Cleary motioned the class to rise. Distant footfalls hit the floors. Eva Clare's legs tingled and went weak like they were about to fold.

The stamps of soles leaving got louder, closer. The class next door went. This new wave was coming at them fast.

Mrs. Cleary turned toward the door and walked, flipping off the light switch as she exited. The class followed—Judi Lane, Bonnie Sillers, Pete Wong, Charles Nichols, Bob Neal, the rest of the row by the side blackboard, the next row, and then it was her row's turn.

As she entered the hallway, she stepped out of line and nabbed Anna Laurel, Sunny, and Meredith. They went to the end of the march, held hands, walked four abreast, the senior cheerleaders, and belted out their school song—words that would have no meaning whatsoever in one minute.

Approaching the front doors, the four friends released their hands and walked out singly—Eva Clare last—down the sidewalk into the cold drizzle and winter fog. Students ahead, marching toward a cross on a spire, dissolved to specters in the mist and disappeared into the gray unknown. She followed, looking down as she stepped, right, then left, at her chestnut leather buckle shoes rain-soaked a darker hue, embarking on this course she didn't like or understand, but was born to.

She swore to God, come graduation, she was leaving this place.

1   Goin' Home

Friday, June 18, 2010
Nashville, Tennessee

The morning sun burned so hot and humid, a fog lifted out of the nearby Harpeth River and draped a haze over the crapes and tulip poplars. Eva Clare stood slumped in her driveway, phone to an ear, staring at the dogwood she and her husband planted when they bought this house thirty years ago. The Easter-pink flowers always stood out, showy against the brown brick. This Easter, though, after a late cold snap, after his lies and betrayal, he left, and those satin-blush blossoms fell limp to the ground.

A warm stream ran from her eye and pearled above her lip. She smeared it away.

"I'm packed and loaded," she told Anna Laurel Wood. "But I don't want to go. I don't want to move back to the Delta. I left there for a reason."

"You don't have a choice," Anna Laurel countered. "My professional lawyer advice to you, pro bono and bluntly offered, is 'You have nowhere else to go.'"

Eva Clare's eyes prickled and filled.

"Besides, all your old friends are living here in the Delta again. Me, Meredith—both of us moved back. Sunny never left."

Eva Clare forced a smile.

"So, put on your big-girl panties, get in the car, put your foot on the gas pedal, and come home," Anna Laurel said.

Eva Clare glanced at her Outback, the remains of her life in a U-Haul trailer behind it. An aching hole burned in her chest, padded with resentment and anger. She took a long last look at their house, its arched windows, brick steps, and hollies lining the front of the home where they raised their daughter. A thin layer of flood-silt coated the bushes, as new, shiny leaves emerged.

"By the way, what happened with your house up there?" Anna Laurel asked. "What did your cheatin' husband say about the damage? It's been seven weeks since the flood."

Eva Clare blew out a grunt. "You don't have to remind me." How could she ever forget the Great Nashville Flood, the thousand-year event that took her city to its knees? "He didn't call to check, and he blocked me from calling him." She began to pace.

"You did your best to reach him. It's his problem now."

"Four inches of muddy river water sat in this house for two days."

"It's up to him to deal with insurance adjusters and restoration companies."

Eva Clare's shoulders wilted. Her husband had put his name alone on the house deed, as many men did at the time of their purchase. His religion taught him the man was the head of the household—in charge of big decisions, major purchases, and bill paying—and the woman was created to be a suitable companion. In other words, God built her bone by bone to be a fit mate for a man who cheated, left her, and rose again on Easter morn with a new woman. Thirty-four years of marriage, and her name was on a piddlin' nothin'. Her cheeks burned.

"Silt's covering everything. The drywall needs to be cut out and replaced. Floors are buckled. Rugs, ruined. And we've got no flood insurance." Eva Clare stopped pacing and smacked her thigh. "I'm mad, I'm tired of staying in a hotel, and I'm running out of money."

"You'll get a settlement."

"Our street is still lined with damaged furniture, sheets of drywall, flooded-out HVACs, carpets, padding. Piles eight feet high. It's awful, it stinks, and all our moldy stuff is still inside the house. I can't bear to go in there."

"But did you? Were you able to get some things out? I advised you to."

"I did what you told me. Packed a few items I bought and paid for myself."

"Did you throw away the personal possessions you don't want?"

"I stayed up all night cleaning out my stuff. Bagged it, put it on the curb. I'm done here. Nothing of mine is left." Eva Clare coiled a lock of hair around a finger. "Nothing!" She pulled the strand of hair till her scalp hurt. "And nobody." Not only did she have a flood-ravaged house and a failed marriage, but her grandmomma down in the Delta died night before last. She went limp, bent over, couldn't hold herself up. Couldn't get a breath. Her losses, too many. Her grief, too heavy.

"You hurry on home now," Anna Laurel said. "Take care of your grandmother's funeral, then settle in at the family house she left you and put your life back together. I'm here to help."

Eva Clare straightened, fiddled with the gold pendant necklace at the hollow of her throat—a dime-sized disc engraved with a dove and the word HOPE, a seventeenth-birthday gift from Grandmomma Sweet Evelyn. It was warm against her skin. The dove as a symbol of new beginnings came from a Bible story, Grandmomma had explained, when God caused a great flood to punish the sins of mankind. Noah sent forth a dove from the ark he'd built to determine if the floodwaters had receded, and it returned with a fresh olive branch, a sign of dry land. The pendant was supposed to remind Eva Clare that when she felt she was going under, there was hope of rising and walking out of the deep.

She merged onto Interstate 40 going west out of Nashville toward Memphis, headed to her hometown of Erin on a Mississippi River oxbow lake. A tug and wobble in the rear prompted her to check her side mirror to make sure the U-Haul still followed. She'd never pulled a trailer, not even a small one, but the five by eight was a good fit for the possessions she'd kept—three tables from Rooster Tails in Franklin, ten George Murphy hand-decorated birdhouses, an antique wardrobe that sat through the 1927 Mississippi River High Water, and boxes of basics like clothes, a computer, and a Cuisinart coffeemaker. It also held the things most important to her: a passel of oil paintings she'd created since her college days, art supplies, and art books.

Rush-hour traffic poured in from the opposite direction. Maybe she was going the right way for a change. But in the overall sense of things, probably not. She desperately needed a new start, but the Delta wasn't the place to go for resurrection. She left there in 1971, disillusioned, one of the first in a wave of out-migration. In the four decades since, the Delta had lost a quarter of its population, resulting in boarded-up towns plagued by poverty and unemployment. She winced at the thought of returning permanently. It had been hard enough going to visit her grandparents over the years and seeing the Delta in decline. When she grew up there in the 1950s and 60s, cotton was king, fields were abundant, and wealth abounded.

Her homeland now was stagnant, run-down, and still somewhat separate.

She hit the steering wheel with the palm of her hand. "What good can come from a once-thriving, now-failing person returning to a once-thriving, now-failing place?" She tightened her grip on the wheel and looked in the rearview mirror. Wrinkles ran from the corner of her eye to her temple. Back in her springtide, that skin was smooth and taut. What a gutsy gal she used to be—sneaking off, running through ancient jungle trees, swinging on vines, climbing the levee, fearlessly playing in that big, fast river on the backbone of the Delta.

June 1964

Erin, Mississippi

Eva Clare put on her bathing suit, her first two-piece—blue denim boy-legs for the bottom and a madras bra-top that no longer lay flat against her chest. She was budding, Grandmomma said. She'd be in sixth grade when school started after Labor Day.

"Come, play! Come, play!" the mighty Mississippi seemed to say.

The Coghlan family home where she lived with her grandparents was once on a bend of that river, but the river's course changed during the Civil War, Grandpop Binky said. Rebel soldiers hid in the neck of Beulah Bend and ambushed passing Yankee ships. The neck was so narrow, the same cannon could fire on boats entering and exiting the loop. One Northern commander got so angry, he ordered a new, straight channel dug to cut off Beulah Bend. Afterward, Coghlan House sat on what was left of the old river channel—an oxbow lake, a free-standing pool formed when a wide meander was severed from the river.

Sometimes Eva Clare sat on the pier, dangling her feet in that oxbow called Beulah Lake, reading library books. Louisa May Alcott wrote the first story of summer. Eva Clare dropped the four little women in the water and had to dive in and rescue Meg, Jo, Beth, and Amy. They dried swollen, rippled, and stuck together. The family maid, Marthala, kept watch over her because Grandmomma didn't let her play in the water alone.

Today, Eva Clare planned to break Grandmomma's rules and go all the way to the river. She pulled her blonde hair into a high ponytail and secured it with a rubber band from Grandpop's rolled-up *Bolivar Commercial*. She slipped her feet into red flip flops with that new-rubber smell and grabbed her library book about a girl who lived in New England a hundred years before the Revolutionary War. It was written by a Delta State College professor in the nearby town of Cleveland with the same first name as Grandmomma. Evelyn. Evelyn Allen Hammett's book—*I, Priscilla*—came from the diary of her eighth-great-grandmother, who settled in Massachusetts, then traveled with her family to a new land called Connecticut. They had to cross a tumbling stream on a fallen tree trunk, and the children chanted a marching rhyme of nonsensical syllables. "With a hey and a ho," Eva Clare copied as best as she could remember, "and a hey ho ho nonny no."

Maybe *she* had an eighth-great-grandmother—or any number of greats—who did something famous and wrote about it in a diary.

That library book was her ticket to the river. If Grandmomma or Marthala heard her slam the screen door, they'd look out, see her with a book, and figure she was headed to the treehouse she'd built—a five-plank platform in a mimosa tree by the lake. It was crude but good enough for a reading hideout—and for spying on old men fishing or teenagers water skiing. Eva Clare settled for reading in the mimosa after her two other book hideouts failed. Her first, the barn loft, was smothering hot and smelled of moldy hay, horse pee, and wet-swollen wood. Her second, the closet at the end of the upstairs hallway, had the original raw-wood walls and no electricity. She had to shine a flashlight on the print to read. It also got too hot, and the smell of old, dusty wood gave her itchy eyes and a sore throat.

"I'm goin' to the river," she yelled from upstairs, her door closed. "Hey ho ho nonny no."

No answer. Grandmomma and Marthala were busy making coconut washboard cookies for Grandmomma's missionary society meeting. She'd already gotten to lick a spoon of raw dough. It wasn't her fault they didn't hear.

She ran downstairs, yellow book in hand. "Hey ho ho here I go."

Marthala was pressing fork tines on a ball of cookie dough, not paying one bit of attention.

Nobody questioned Eva Clare as she zoomed out to do the forbidden. She left Priscilla at the mimosa, ran past the oxbow, jumped over the crusty bed of Dry Creek bogue, and walked up the grassy levee. At the top, she stood on the dirt lane and looked ahead at a tangle of trees and swampland, then behind at the church steeple in town. Her people settled here before the War Between the States. Why, she might've had a great-great-great-grandmother who stood on this very spot before the levee was built. She lifted her arm high and wrapped her hand around an imaginary scepter. This was *her* land, by golly, and that made her a powerfully important somebody, maybe like a princess.

She ran down the river side of the levee, followed along the bayou that threaded the bottomlands, skipped at the edge of the ash, sugarberry, and honey locust trees, and tiptoed by cypress giants standing in stagnant brake water. "Trees thick as hairs on a dog's back," Grandpop Binky had said. She'd beaten a path through it all.

Grandmomma and Marthala would've torn up her behind if they had a clue she was going to that beast of a river with its deadly sandbars and strong undercurrents.

Eva Clare got to a clearing and stopped abruptly. Straight ahead, there it was, her magical river. Excitement bubbled up from inside her. She giggled it out. Kicked off her flip flops, waded toward a sandbar, looked at the wide expanse of sun-shimmering water. No barges. Nothing but fast-rolling river. The water pushed against her legs. Her feet sank into slimy muck that squished between her toes. She went out into the safe slack water to play and lowered herself under.

It was muddy ole river water, but when white sunlight speared down, it became a mystical, milky green. Her yellow hair floated around her, her arms and hands made slow dance motions, and little beads of her breath rose to the surface. She did somersaults under the water, blew out a spray of bubbles, and pushed herself up from the dark bottom, emerging into the light with her arms held high and river water gushing off her. Cleansed, washed anew, like a baptism.

"Raised to walk in newness of life!" she proclaimed, like the preacher always did after he dunked somebody to save their soul.

Her dolls ended up under the river when they got old—Tiny Tears, Bannister Baby, Chatty Cathy, a slew of naked, messy-haired Barbies. It didn't feel right to throw them away or burn them, so she gave them a water burial and watched the Father take them away.

Before the dolls went with God, real people did: her daddy and mama. Her father came home from the war with shell shock. He fought in the big battles like the Bulge, never was right again, and all he did when he got back was stand on the street curb, watching and waiting for his ship to come get him and carry him home. He went to the Whitfield insane asylum, then died. Her mother nearly worked herself to death on her nurse's shifts at King's Daughters and then finalized her passing in a car wreck on the way home one night when Eva Clare was five. She went to live with Grandpop and Grandmomma.

Not only did the dolls meet their fate and the parents face their destiny, but the old, nearby town of Prentiss, where her fourth-great-grandfather Andrew Coghlan settled, suffered its own demise. Grandpop said Prentiss died three times. First, a Northern Civil War general named Sherman burned it to the ground. The town built back. Next, after the Yankees dug the new, short channel to cut off Beulah Bend, the river flowed with such force, it chewed at the banks and caused them to crumble, taking one building at a time until the whole town fell under. The people moved a mile inland and named their new settlement Erin. Then, when Eva Clare was a baby, the river ran low during a drought, exposing the silt-covered town. Grandmomma went to the site, found champagne bottles and a whiskey barrel. When the river rose, Prentiss died for the third time until only the church steeple stuck up above the water, and slowly, it, too, succumbed.

Interstate 40 from Nashville to Memphis was mostly eighteen-wheelers—a wall of trucks going both directions, east, west, moving commerce coast to coast and points between. Eva Clare waggled around them. One blasted its horn, snatching her to alertness after she edged toward the lane line. She shook off her startle and tensed her hands on the steering wheel.

When did she begin to surrender her little-girl grit?

The water dreams started when she left the oxbow and went off to college, as exaggerations of images from childhood play in the river. She'd swirl under the surface in sunlit water, cornsilk hair purling about her, white sheer dress flowing, tiny bubbles streaming upward.

The dreams came to her so vividly, she started painting pictures of the girl under the water. Early on, the girl appeared playful, and the art was about color and gentle movement. Later, the paintings grew darker in tone. Eva Clare's art suggested story—a woman repressed, restrained. The woman under the water struggled to rise up for air. She lashed about in a frenzy, watching her hands, fingers splayed, go slowly down to her sides to lie still upon cold leg skin. A moon-white lady appeared and reached out a hand in rescue.

The little girl had become a woman, wispy, wan, and pallid, in a gown, lacy, white, and finespun, and the river dreams foreshadowed this woman sitting at the bottom, always with her eyes shut, sometimes her hands over her mouth, and always needing saving.

May 2, 2010
Nashville, Tennessee

Eva Clare flipped on the TV to BREAKING NEWS. A portable building from Lighthouse Christian School was floating down a flooded interstate past lines of cars stalled in swollen, brown water. She opened the kitchen blinds. The streamlet at the back property line was coming at her in a massive, muddy tide. She dashed to the front window. The street, the yards, flooded above the ankles of those outside watching the water rise and enter garages and crawl spaces. She should've paid attention to the stalled storm front and heavy rains, but she'd been holed up brooding the loss of her marriage.

She grabbed her car keys. Had to get out while the water was still low, go to higher ground, so she drove to the neighborhood clubhouse at the top of a hill. All around, widespread flooding. A yellow-ochre sea, houses standing in water, cars partially submerged. Flashing red lights, blue lights. Boat rescues. She breathed in the earthy odor of the Harpeth River, always a tame trickle contained within a tree line, now roiling far out of its banks.

Her hands trembled. She could barely punch in numbers on her phone. After repeated attempts to reach her husband, she finally got an answer.

"We're flooded!" she cried.

"So are we."

A stab to her gut. His "we" once included her. She ignored her hurt. "I need help. I'm stuck in my car at the clubhouse."

"Surely there's a friend you can call."

"No, there's not. Please help me."

"It's flooded everywhere. I couldn't get there if I wanted to. I can't come anyway, Eva Clare. We're getting a divorce. Eventually, you'll find someone to take care of you. You'll have to. You can't make it on your own." He clicked off.

She crumpled against the steering wheel and sobbed. Her whole body shook. He abandoned her knowing her teaching job wouldn't fund any level of lifestyle in the city, and he didn't care. He left her stranded in a flood. His words reverberated: *You can't make it on your own.* All these years, she'd let herself be held down by a man whose religion lifted him to entitlement and eminence.

She spent the night in her car and kept opening the door to see if the flood was coming for her.

The waters got much of Nashville. Every ditch, creek, and river in Middle Tennessee flared up out of their banks. The Cumberland, the Harpeth, every branch of the two. Thousands of properties were damaged or destroyed, and places like the Grand Ole Opry House, Titans stadium, and Opryland Hotel flooded. Water filled the basement of the Schermerhorn Symphony Center, and ten feet of water stood in Opry Mills mall. Lost was the Lighthouse school's portable preschool building called Hope.

In Memphis, green signs split I-40 traffic by destination. Eva Clare looped south, drove past the MISSISSIPPI WELCOMES YOU billboard, and exited onto Interstate 69. Twenty miles west, the road swung her down the ramp onto Highway 61 in the strip of Tunica casinos and into that great abyss of flatness that was the Delta.

It wasn't a delta by definition. It was not at the mouth of a river. Not delta-shaped. It was a crescent plain that stretched one-hundred-fifty miles from Memphis on the north to Vicksburg on the south, from Greenville on the west to Greenwood, east, where a ridgeline ran up to Tennessee.

She always got a tingling in her stomach, a stir, a swell of pride, going down the last, long hill. This place still got to her—this soulful stretch of abundant cotton and glorious sunsets and slow, serpentine bayous. It had melted into her veins, swirled through her, sweated out of her. She was raised to love this place, as was every other Delta-born child.

Her early instilled ties to the Delta pushed aside her dread of coming home. But that feeling was short-lived, for the Delta had a dark side, and the old ghosts had a way of rearing their heads up out of the earth. Old ghosts—traditions of racial hate, prejudice, and separation. Segregation was dead on the law books but lingered in minds, alive and well. Ghosts were dead people who never quite left; ghosts were also practices of the past that persisted as stumbling blocks in the present.

In all the flatness, the fields had a rising and falling to them. Plowed-up places. Furrows. High where the cotton grew, low where the weeds were, the shadows lay, and the wrongs happened. Crooked places. When she was nine years old, Martin Luther King Jr. had a dream that those crooked places would one day be made straight.

Back then, Highway 61 was only a narrow two-lane cutting through cotton fields. Shotgun shacks—one room wide, two rooms long—lined the road and squeezed into the crop rows. Black field hands lived in those shanties and worked the cotton sunup to sundown. Maybe if she looked hard enough, she could still see clusters of them choppin' rhythmically with their chants. Maybe if she listened hard enough, she could still hear them stampin' out their plight, singin' their Blues to the cadenced clank of their hoes.

Back then, Black people lived in a parallel world to hers. They couldn't use the same public bathrooms, couldn't drink out of the same water fountains, and had their own schools, churches, funeral parlors, graveyards, beauty shops, barbershops, cafés, and everything else. At her White church, members prayed for foreign missionaries in Africa to win Black souls to Christ. At the same time, her White church's deacons stood at the entrances to block Black people from coming in to their services.

Whites driving this highway kept their noses pointed directly ahead, looking beyond the inequity. Like Jesus bugs that walked on water, their feet made dents on the surface, and you could see little cupped impressions, but they never fell through.

Eva Clare closed the panel to the window in her car roof. The sun was overhead, bearing down hot and heavy.

Racism came early to Mississippi's children back then. It came with every store's refusal-to-serve sign, every separate waiting room at a doctor's office, every separate entrance to a movie theater, and every instance of thought that the ratty shacks, secondhand clothes, and out-of-date schoolbooks were good enough for the Blacks. Nobody had to tell the children about discrimination. These practices were lived out around them every day—followed them from home to school, to church, to the playground. Children learned to live the contradictions seamlessly—to pledge the flag, read the Bible, and practice Jim Crow at the same time.

All this didn't feel right to Eva Clare. Grandpop Binky said she was a watchful child. If something didn't look or feel right or serve the principle of liberty and justice for all or fit with Bible verses about loving her neighbors, it would hang with her for a long time. Like racism did.

September 7, 1965
Erin Junior High School
Erin, Mississippi

First day of seventh grade, the day after Labor Day, still hot as Hades, Eva Clare pitched a fit to wear her new, baby-blue Bobbie Brooks pleated skirt, houndstooth top, slipover sweater vest, and matching blue tights. Grandmomma declared she was going to burn up.

It turned out that everybody else was burning up, too, and not because of long sleeves and hot stockings, but burning-up mad because of Ruby Mae Reed. Ruby was the first Negro to attend the White school. A few kids called her ugly names, told her to go back to Africa, and held their noses as they walked wide arcs around her in the hallway.

Ruby was assigned the desk across the aisle from Eva Clare. Eva Clare sneaked a sideways peek. Ruby wore a starched, plaid dress with short sleeves and a white Peter Pan collar. She had on white anklet socks and black flats. Her hair was thick, straightened, in a short flip. Eva Clare wore a flip, too. Ruby had on a green double-twist birthstone ring, exactly like the light blue topaz setting on Eva Clare's finger.

Out the window, green leaves on the oaks and chinquapins trembled in a hot breeze.

Ruby stayed six weeks. She didn't return for the second term. People weren't nice to her.

Eva Clare couldn't say she was nice to her either. She wasn't mean. She wasn't anything. When this change came and sat down beside her, she didn't know what to do, so she did nothing.

Eva Clare drove on past Maud, Dundee, and Moon Lake, where a lone crop duster swooped down and sprayed a field. Highway 61 was four lanes wide now, the tenant shacks gone. Cell phone towers rose up out of cotton fields, as did billboards and casinos. They could tear down the rotten shacks and build golden casinos, but the crooked places were still there. The past had a way of superimposing itself on the present.

Two months ago, she read a news article about a federal judge ordering a Mississippi county to desegregate its schools. Fifty-six years after the Supreme Court declared segregation unconstitutional, that county was still grouping Black students into all-Black classrooms and letting three hundred White students transfer out of district to a racially identifiable White school where they were placed in all-White classes. Laws changed. People didn't.

Society's institutions imprinted images of their prejudices onto a child's brain. It happened to all the children—even her. It was the worn-down grooves of handed-down traditions—practices of a caste system in place for so long, it felt right. Like an old, soft, worn-smooth pair of jeans that fit the skin and felt comfortable—the ones you reached for first.

She rubbed her hand over her old, stonewashed jeans, then put it back on the steering wheel as she followed the road past Clarksdale, Bobo, and Alligator.

She judged others for their prejudices. But what about her? Had she fully disconnected from the discriminatory practices she witnessed as a child?

Out the driver window, the cotton was high and green. Should be in the bloom stage.

It was high time for her to bloom, too. To rediscover her grit. To find that brave little girl who broke the rules, ran freely out of bounds, and dipped her whole self under the water.

August 1964
Erin, Mississippi

The last days of summer, Eva Clare didn't bother to hide her plans to disobey and go to the river. Didn't carry her library book to pretend she'd be reading in the mimosa.

"I'm fixin' to go jump in the lake."

"Mm hmm." Marthala was busy dicing a celery stalk on the wooden cutting board. Grandmomma didn't even look up from arranging zinnias in her green milk-glass vase. Nobody gave a hoot what she did.

She let the screen door slap behind her, ran to the pier, tossed her Hula-Hoop in the lake, and jumped into the circle. With no adults watching. Did it five times, got bored, went back into the house without drying off.

"Whatchu mean drippin' water all over my kitchen flo'?" Marthala stirred mayonnaise into cooked potato cubes and kept an ear close to her Silvertone transistor radio.

"I can do what I want, hey nonny no."

"I'll snatch you bald-headed." Marthala pointed the wooden potato salad spoon at her and shook it. "Now, I gots to hear the news at the top o' the hour, so you go on an' play."

Eva Clare stomped into the den and sat her wet butt on the couch. Grandpop Binky's newspaper lay on the coffee table, a big headline above the fold:

Bodies of Three Slain Civil Rights Workers
Discovered In an Earthen Dam
Outside Philadelphia, Mississippi

Her Uncle Billy Pat Tanner and her mean cousin Gerald Tanner lived in Philadelphia, Mississippi, four hours away in the red-dirt hill country.

She picked up the paper, skimmed the lines: The beaten, shot, and badly decomposed bodies . . . missing since June . . . found twenty feet under a pond dam on a farm six miles south of Philadelphia between Highways 21 and 488.

And there you go, hey nonny no. The end of the narrative that had been playing out all summer, the whole reason Grandmomma Sweet Evelyn and Grandpop Binky were on edge, talking in whispers about civil rights workers, church burnings, the FBI, the KKK, and Uncle Billy Pat. Talking about the Tanners maybe having to move here. Many evenings, Eva Clare snuck into the dining room, hid under the table behind the drop of the Battenburg lace cloth, listened to den conversations across the hall, and pretty much picked up the story plot.

I.   A thousand civil rights workers came to Mississippi from the North to register Negroes to vote.

II.   The Ku Klux Klan didn't want 'em down here "messin' in our bi'ness."

III.   Billy Pat was a member of the Neshoba-Kemper-Lauderdale KKK that met in an abandoned schoolhouse on a dirt road outside Philadelphia. They used flashlights and lanterns because of no electricity.

IV.   Early summer, Billy Pat and his KKK torched and burned a Black church where voter registration was held and beat up some of the members.

V.   Three civil rights workers—Michael Schwerner, Andrew Goodman, and James Chaney—went to the church to investigate the burning and beatings, and the KKK set out a plan to get them. Those three workers went missing that day.

Eva Clare remembered her grandparents' conversation almost word for word.

Grandpop: *Looks like Billy Pat's in deep.*

Grandmomma: *But he's a good man, a church-going man, a fine family man. A veteran.*

Grandpop: *They all are, hon. Army, Navy. Home from war to fight here for their values, they claim.*

Grandmomma: *You think he has it in him to hurt somebody?*

> *Grandpop:*   *He's in the KKK. Klan membership is at ten*
> *thousand in Mississippi, and they're prepared to*
> *use violence to maintain the status quo.*

The FBI had been searching for the civil rights workers all summer. It was on the national news every night. Now, they were found. Dead. Not far from Uncle Billy Pat's house.

She called Billy Pat "uncle," but he wasn't. He ranked as Grandmomma's first cousin once removed, and she didn't know what that made him to her.

At the town of Duncan, Eva Clare turned west off Highway 61 and cut across to Highway 1, which paralleled the levee. Thirty more miles to home.

On her left, soybean fields stretched for miles. On the right, a levee stood high to wall off a river that sometimes swelled and fingered out across the land.

A rusty sign at the intersection with Old Wellington Road read ERIN POPULATION 949. A white arrow pointed to the right. Out in a field of beans stood a billboard: JESUS IS LORD OVER ERIN with BEULAH LAKE BAPTIST CHURCH at the bottom.

Down the road past the intersection, sticking out like a sore thumb above a cotton field, was the Christian academy, one of more than two-hundred private schools that popped up across Mississippi during her high school years.

To her right at the intersection sat Pete Wong's Market—general store, gas station, and short-order café, catching traffic between the riverport towns of Rosedale and Greenville. She graduated with Pete Jr., who ran the store now. She pushed up her blinker and pulled in.

"Hey ho ho here I go."

PETE AND LILY

A bell on Pete's door rang a B-flat as Eva Clare stepped inside. She recognized the note. Her liberal arts degrees had served her well, even if they hadn't translated to a job that paid the bills.

Pete sat with a laptop and paperwork at a table in the eating area. The dinging prompted him to look up and dash over to speak—her dreaded initial immersion back into the Delta.

"Hey, girl! How you doin'?" He grabbed hold of her shoulders. "I figured you'd be gettin' into town today, and I was hopin' you'd stop by. I'm so sorry about Sweet Evelyn." He pulled her in for a hug.

Her muscles tensed. She hadn't showered in two days—not since she got the call about Grandmomma. She'd been in a hurry to tie up loose ends at the Nashville house and get out for good. Her deodorant had worn off. So had her makeup. Her hair, the color of a peeled banana, was already frizzy from Delta humidity. Her eyes were swollen from so much crying.

"You holdin' up okay?" Pete released her, held her at arm's length, narrowed his eyes.

"Yeah." That bony bump of cartilage along the bridge of her nose? She hated when people looked at her there.

"It's been a while since you've been in to see me," he said.

Her shoulders dropped. Guilt nagged at her for not coming home more often when her grandmother was sick, for rushing in late on Friday nights and running back to Nashville on Sundays to teach on Mondays. "I haven't been home since the end of March. Didn't realize Grandmomma was going down so fast, but I did call to check on her every day."

A feminine trill of throat clearing came from behind, and a loud voice followed. "Who'd you talk to when you called about Sweet Evelyn?"

Eva Clare jerked her face toward the sound. Standing behind the cash register was a tall, big-boned woman with shiny black hair slicked into a knot on top of her head so severe it pulled her cheeks up and lifted the corners of her mouth and eyes. Silver bracelets adorned both wrists against skin a natural sienna earth color. The woman chewed a wad of green gum, popped it, made a noise like a string of firecrackers.

"I talked to her maid Marthala."

"Well, Marthala's ill."

"And so lately, I've been talking to the homecare nurse." Eva Clare clamped her lips, put out with herself that she'd answered. It was none of that woman's business. "Do I know you?"

The woman opened her mouth to answer, but Pete interrupted. "Hey, I'm carryin' on a conversation over here."

The woman rolled her eyes, waved him off, and plopped down on a stool in front of a wall-mounted cigarette display rack.

"You know Lily, right?" Pete asked Eva Clare. "She helps me a few days a week so my wife Angie can have time off." He put a hand in his pocket, rattled coins, and went on talking before she could answer. "Say, I saw about the Nashville flood on TV. Y'all affected?"

"Yeah, our house had standing water."

"Oh, I'm so sorry." Pete shook his head, then adjusted his Lennon-like glasses. In the pocket of his checkered shirt were a mechanical pencil, a calculator, and a box cutter.

A stinging sensation filled Eva Clare's nose, signaling a letdown of tears. She didn't want to think about the flood. She was free of Nashville. She looked away.

The old country store hadn't changed a bit since Pete's daddy was owner. The shelves held a bit of everything—bread, toilet paper, soup, motor oil, milk, mosquito repellent, crackers, and Vienna sausages. Still there, the same six-cent Coke machine and old metal signs on the walls. *Drink Barq's. 20 Mule Team Borax. Dr Pepper 10-2-4.* A newer handwritten sign: LIVE BAIT. The store smelled of fried fish and stale cooking oil.

"Your grandmother, she's in a better place now, but we're all gonna miss her."

Eva Clare's jaws burned. Coming home put her newest loss at the forefront.

"The church won't ever be the same." Pete pulled out a white handkerchief, made a honking sound into it, wiped his nose, stuffed the hankie back into his pocket. "Before she got sick, she taught ladies' Sunday School, led the Women's Missionary Union, sang in the choir, and visited the shut-ins. She even baked bread for the Lord's Supper with her sourdough starter that was thirty years old. Nobody can fill her shoes. Dementia's a terrible, awful thing."

"Bet her maid baked that communion bread," Lily offered in a low, gravelly voice.

"Don't pay Lily no mind," Pete told Eva Clare. "She's lippy. Got no filters between her brain and mouth."

"Bet that sourdough starter has gone to waste," Lily said. "Ya got to feed it every day."

"Don't ever mention any hot-button issues around her, or you'll get her fired up. She's loud, blunt, brash, and opinionated." Pete leaned closer. "But nobody's got a kinder heart."

"Good to know." Eva Clare looked at her feet. Chipped burgundy toenail polish, purple and orange Chacos—sandals that had walked through a flood. She wasn't free of Nashville. She brought it with her.

"Yeah, Sweet Evelyn, she was a godly woman," Pete continued. "The sweetest memory I have was one time when she and Marthala came over to help Angie with her patio garden. They brought thinnings and bulbs from the Coghlan House beds, even special flowers Sweet Evelyn had acquired over the years, like white irises from William Faulkner's garden in Oxford. I went home for lunch, heard the most heavenly sound, opened the back door, and those three women were down on their knees, diggin' in the dirt and singin' 'I Come to the Garden Alone.' I broke down and cried." Pete pulled out his handkerchief again, wiped his eyes, squeezed his nose. "Still break down thinkin' about it. My Angie, she could sing a strong alto to Sweet Evelyn's soprano, and Marthala, well, she had the power of God in her voice."

"You got that right," Lily mumbled.

"You made Sweet Evelyn's arrangements yet, Eva Clare?"

"By phone. I'll confirm tomorrow when I meet with the pastor."

"Okay, lemme know. I can pass on the day and time of the funeral."

"Town informant, huh?"

"Busybody's more like it." Lily gave him a side-eye look.

Pete folded his hands over the beginnings of a pot belly. He seemed to be intimidated by Lily, but he held his chin high, as though proud of his assigned role as informant. "Eva Clare, you back home for good, or did you only come for the funeral?"

"I'm back for good." He'd probably pass on that information, too.

"I see the U-Haul out the window. I can grab a few other guys and be over to unload it about six-fifteen, if that works for you."

"That's perfect. Thanks."

"It's a good decision to come home now because this town's gonna be put on the map."

"What do you mean?"

"The new interstate—the Canada-to-Mexico trade highway that'll run through this county a mile south, with an exit to Erin and hopefully, a new bridge over the river near Scott. Interstate 69. It's a real big deal." He pulsed his eyebrows.

"I drove on it from Memphis to Tunica."

"Yep. Miss'ippi's got one segment completed out of Memphis and plans for the Delta route. Our county fought hard to get that highway, and we want the bridge, too, so bad we can taste it. No more driving down to Greenville or up to Helena to cross the river. Soon, we'll have interstate traffic—twenty-one thousand cars a day, they say."

"That should give your business a boost."

"I sure hope so."

Eva Clare rested her gaze on a display of miniature antique frames on the counter with a sign in a clear acrylic stand:

VINTAGE EARLY-1900S PICTURE FRAMES
VISIT BETSY'S TRUNK ON MAIN STREET
FOR QUALITY ANTIQUES.

She picked up a wooden openwork oval with ornate half-moon closures and ran her finger around its edges, then put it down. She touched each one as she studied it—a gilt brass engraved with scrolling flowers, a black padded with gold trim, a cast iron double-standing, and an ornate brass cherub oval holding a picture of a baby girl. The child's expression caught her attention. She'd seen that look. She pointed to the collection. "What's this?"

"A good deed your old friend Anna Laurel did to help Betsy Steele with her failing antique store. If Betsy doesn't get business soon, she's gonna have to shut down and shutter up. And speaking of Anna Laurel, she came by this morning. Said she'd just talked to you."

"She's doing some legal work for me."

"I'm glad Anna Laurel has a chance to practice. Lucky her, retiring early from her career as an attorney." Pete made a clicking sound in his cheek. "I won't ever retire—got grandkids in private school and will be working till lunch on the day of my funeral to help pay their tuition. She never got married, you know. I don't know why." He stopped, shot a puzzled look at Eva Clare as if he expected her to explain, then went on. "She was pretty. And smart. I would've been valedictorian if it hadn't been for her. Instead, I was second place. Now, she's opened a fancy coffee shop. Everything I've ever done, she's done better. But I love her to death anyway."

"You were elected Most Likely to Succeed."

"Yeah, and now, me and Anna Laurel are both looking for success in this dyin' town."

Eva Clare picked up the brass oval frame on the counter, looked closer at the baby in the picture. The eyes, the shape of the mouth, the one dimple. Her daughter Lara had a similar expression. She missed Lara, who was in Scotland getting her PhD. Eva Clare shucked off that sad thought and put the frame back in place.

"That's Betsy Steele as a baby. About a hundred years ago."

Eva Clare chuckled at the thought of Betsy as an infant. Betsy was gaunt, old-looking, and wrinkled when Eva Clare left town forty years ago. She straightened the frame. "I heard our old classmate Meredith Weiss moved back home."

"She sure did. Bless her heart, that poor girl, her husband died, and she gave up her advertising career in the big city of Hotlanta."

"I haven't seen her since our thirtieth class reunion the weekend before Nine Eleven."

"She stops in the store every once in a while. Never says much and doesn't go to the church here. She goes to the synagogue in Cleveland." Pete ran his hand through his hair. "You didn't keep up with the girls much, huh?"

"Not really. We went our separate ways after graduation. Went to different colleges, lived in different states. But we've reconnected on social media—mostly LIKES on Facebook."

"I get it. We're all busy. It's hard to stay in touch." He winked. "You remember Sunny Flowers? She never left town. Plays piano at the church. Hasn't changed a lick. Picked up a little weight but still cute as a button."

"Our old Fab Four. Me, Anna Laurel, Meredith, and Sunny."

"Kinda neat the Fab Four is back home, and all of y'all are in your parents' houses, and your parents are dead and gone. It's like fruit-basket turnover."

"Speaking of going home," Eva Clare said, reaching for a basket from a stack in the aisle, "I've got to pick up a few groceries first."

"Uh oh. Look!" Pete pointed to the weather forecast on a TV positioned high in a corner. "They've issued a tornado watch across the river in Arkansas. It's fixin' to storm."

"Oh, Lordy, here we go," Lily said.

"Always comes a storm when the air's so sodden you can drown in your own breath."

"Oh, Lordy."

"I'm tellin' ya, Lily, it's fixin' to storm."

Eva Clare stood in a direct line between Pete and Lily.

"Ain't dunnit," Lily said.

"Is too."

"Is not."

They were using her like a Ping-Pong net, smacking exchanges over her.

Lily directed her attention to Eva Clare. "His cousin was killed in the movie theater that was hit by the 1953 Vicksburg tornado when Pete was a baby."

Pete lowered his head, then changed the subject. "Hey, Eva Clare, if you need a preacher for Sweet Evelyn's service and don't want to use the new pastor at the church, there's a seminary professor on sabbatical from New Orleans who moved here last winter. He's renting a house on the lake, the old Woodward place, and writing his memoirs. He could prob'ly do it for you."

"The new pastor is fine."

"Uh oh!" Pete pointed to the TV. "They've expanded the tornado watch to include us."

Lily slammed her hands on the counter and faced Eva Clare. "The watches, we're okay. But every time they issue a warning, he goes downtown to the bank and gets in the vault. Gerald Tanner gave him the combination to get in. He keeps some pop-top cans of green boiled peanuts, some warm Mountain Dews, and a few Louis L'Amour westerns in there."

Eva Clare studied Pete for confirmation.

He nodded. "I'm friends with Gerald—the bank president, chairman of the deacons, mayor, and so on. You know how it is in a small town."

"Oh, I know." Gerald was her distant cousin, the one who'd called her and left a come-home message, that Sweet Evelyn was in her final hours, prompting Eva Clare to clear her possessions out of the moldy house and escalate her leave—the reason she was up all night.

"The bank vault is the safest place in town. Helps to be friends with the bank prez."

"I didn't think Gerald was friends with anybody." He was a brat. He'd cut the fingers off her doll when she was eleven, stolen book reports and copied her homework, and told the whole school she got her period when she was twelve after he heard Grandmomma tell his momma. All his trespasses during high school wouldn't fit in a narrow-ruled, five-subject composition notebook. The only thing that had ever brought a smile to her face where Gerald was concerned was the time he was twelve and fell headfirst into a full drum of spent motor oil behind Old Pete Wong's. He would've drowned in it, too, if a truck driver who'd stopped to get a Nehi Grape hadn't pulled him out.

"We're friends on a level Gerald's comfortable with."

"They have a back-scratchin' relationship," Lily said. "Gerald gave Pete the code. Pete gives Gerald the latest gossip."

"Well, I wouldn't call it gossip," Pete countered. "It's more like current events."

"It's gossip." Lily sucked air between her two front teeth, made a whistling sound.

"Anyway, me and Gerald eat lunch here twice a week and catch up. He distances himself from everybody else—"

"He thinks he's better," Lily clarified. "He thinks the sun came up to hear him crow."

"But I'm different. I'm a business owner, and we have history—graduated from high school together, both went to Ole Miss, both returned to Erin to work in our hometown."

"The only reason Tanner ran for mayor is because Pete did," Lily interjected.

"True. I ran to bring change. Half our businesses have closed. It affects you after a while, weighs down on you." Pete cleared his throat, widened his eyes, lifted his voice an octave. "But Tanner didn't want no Chinaman bein' mayor."

Eva Clare bit her lip and tightened her hand around the green, plastic grocery basket she held until she could feel pain in the joints of her fingers. Chinese people in the Delta had to deal with discrimination like the Blacks did. The county schools had assigned Chinese children to Black schools almost up to the time Eva Clare was born. "And he won, of course."

"Of course. He's the banker." Pete patted the wallet in his hip pocket.

"So, you're friends with him, and he gave you the means to get into his bank vault, but he wouldn't support you for mayor."

"That's how we roll." Lily leaned both hands on the counter. "We all know our places. White's right, and Pete ain't White."

"I don't care," Pete said. "I'm proud of who I am. I've worked in this store since I was old enough to see over the counter." He frowned, popped the knuckles on his right hand, then the ones on his left. "My people have been in this county a hundred forty years. Came to work the cotton when the slaves were freed but found out real quick there was no money in it."

"Most Chinese I've ever heard of owned grocery stores like you, Pete," Eva Clare said.

"Yep, we've made a good living at it, too. At first, we lived in the Black communities and served the Blacks 'cause the Whites wouldn't, and we lived in the back of our stores 'cause like the Blacks, we couldn't own property."

Lily gave a nod to Pete. "And like the Blacks, y'all couldn't go to White establishments, like restaurants and hospitals." She turned to Eva Clare. "You know, to this day, we got White cemeteries, Black cemeteries, and Chinese cemeteries. People take their division to their graves."

"They always have, and they always will," Pete said.

"How do you do it, Pete?" Eva Clare's frustration gushed out. "How have you lived all these years in a place still ingrained in the old ways?" Her face burned with the mention of issues that had prompted her to leave Erin years ago.

"It's okay, hon. It's okay. We've made strides. My oldest sister was the first Chinese to attend the White school here when she started first grade. When I was growing up, my family of six lived in three rooms at the back of this store. Now, I've got a nice brick home behind the store. Why, if I was any happier, I'd drop my harp right through the cloud."

"But how do you put up with Gerald?"

"He's always been nice to me, Eva Clare. You gotta deal with what comes to you in life. For me, it's this store. Daddy expected me to stay in the Delta and run it, and I'm makin' the best of it. Change comes slow here. And sometimes not at all. Sometimes it's small changes. Sometimes you gotta poke and push and make little indents here and there. Most times, you lose. But you keep on."

Eva Clare wrestled her tone into neutral. "I'm sure there's a lot of wisdom in those words." She stepped over to the nearest aisle, reached for a box of ginger snaps, put it in her basket. Maybe she expected too much of people and maybe to a fault. Nevertheless, it was incredibly sad that the second-smartest in their class and their Most Likely to Succeed stayed in Erin with little ability to trigger change. She snatched up a bag of jelly beans. Grandmomma's favorite candy. Lots of orange and purple ones in this bag. Her favorites.

"Look, Eva Clare, there's some good people in this town, some fine folks who think right and do right."

"I got a good mind to run in the next election," Lily said.

"You got two strikes against you, girl. You're a woman, and you're Black," Pete said.

"And we all know that in Erin, Jesus rules, like the billboard at the edge of town says, and by divine order, men are over women and Whites are over Blacks," Lily said with a roll of her eyes. "Some people really believe that." She blew a bubble, made a series of pops and crackles, and set her gaze on Eva Clare. "So, what about you?"

"She's only got one strike. She's a woman." Pete clapped his hands together, proud of his quick comeback.

Lily made a checkmark of approval in the air with her pointer finger, then looked again at Eva Clare. "You gon take over the house?"

"I—" Eva Clare pinched her lips. Why was Lily asking this? What business was it of hers? "I am. How do you know about the house? Do I know you?"

Lily stood hipshot. "Naw, you don't know me. How could you? Pfft." She pfft'ed the gum right out of her mouth but reacted fast enough to catch it and put it back.

"Then, how—"

"Wait!" Pete interrupted, waving his hands like windshield wipers. "Eva Clare, you do know who Lily is, right?"

"She will," Lily butted in, then faced Eva Clare directly. "My warning to you is it ain't gon be like you think it is."

"It's gon be better." Pete jumped to the rescue. "We're gonna all get together, grill us some steaks, talk about the good ole days at Erin High, and laugh us up a storm."

Ready to be out of there, Eva Clare excused herself, grabbed a few more grocery items, and unloaded her basket on the counter. Lily rang up the stash, gave a price, and held out her hand. Eva Clare filled it with the correct change, then hurried to the door, but not before she noticed Lily grabbing her phone and purse and scurrying toward the back exit.

Eva Clare headed toward downtown Erin on Old Wellington Road, a narrow blacktop that took her past white asbestos-shingled bungalows and red-brick ranch houses with fields of cotton behind them and run-down sheds with rusty farm implements in their side yards.

On her right was the concrete foundation of the old public high school. Past the remnant of Erin High was Beulah Lake Baptist Church with Ionic columns and a white steeple standing tall with the sycamores. She cut her teeth there on her grandparents' pew—fifth row, left side. She spent her youth going to Sunday School and Training Union there, listening to her teacher present the plan of salvation, watching him draw a circle on the blackboard and tap on it with a stick of white chalk. "Once you're saved, you're in the middle of this circle *(tap tap tap tap tap)* and nothing can ever take you out of it *(tap tap tap tap tap)*. Once saved, always saved *(tap tap tap tap tap)*." She wasn't in that circle anymore. The church folks in Nashville had shoved her out of it because she was getting a divorce and God hates divorce, they said. That hurt. Hurt her way down deep where the spirit meets the bone. Hurt her to tears and sobs and scars.

Off to Eva Clare's left was a sprawling house with a swimming pool, tennis courts, and a golf driving range—Gerald's place.

She crossed the bridge over Steele Bayou at the entrance to downtown's retail district. On both sides of the street were storefronts running one city block. Six on each side. There were some empty storefronts, but the Piggly Wiggly, Harper Hardware & Feed Supply, and Betsy's Trunk were still open. At the end of town, on opposite sides of the street, stood the brand-new Laurel's Coffee House at Levee and Main and Erin State Bank—Gerald's bank.

She drove toward the levee, the outskirts of town, the old house where she grew up and where all her people before her were born and raised.

When she got there, she turned into Grandmomma's long, tree-lined driveway a little too fast for pulling a trailer. The U-Haul whipped and bounced, and her tires slung up gravel like drumfire. A plume of dust blossomed behind her. At the top end of the drive at a turnaround parking area sat an old green Taurus with rust spots on the back panel. Lily leaned against it.

Hammered into the ground in front of Coghlan House was a large FOR SALE sign.

3

Gerald Tanner

Eva Clare skidded to a stop, flung the car door open, and stormed toward Lily, inhaling the dust she'd sent up. "What're you doing here? Why's that sign in my yard?" Her heart beat robustly against the bones in her chest. She'd rightly inherited this house from her grandmother.

"Whoa!" Lily threw up both hands.

Eva Clare jabbed a finger toward the Davis Realty sign. "Did you put that sign there?"

"Me? No."

"Then who did?" Eva Clare smacked her hands to the sides of her head. Every whichaway she turned, life came down on her. "Nobody has the right to put this house up for sale!"

"I had nothin' to do with that. Nothin'. I promise."

"Then *who* did?" Eva Clare dropped her hands and took in a deep breath. Her head still hammered.

"Think about it. It's only one person in town who'd do that." Lily held up a long finger. "Only one."

Behind Eva Clare, car tires entered the driveway and crunched the gravel.

Lily's finger lowered to a point. "And there he is."

Eva Clare turned to see a black Cadillac SUV approach under the canopy of old oaks.

"That's where your battle is, missy." Lily set her fists on her high hip bones.

The car stopped. A man slid out the driver's door and started toward them with a swagger.

"Gerald," Eva Clare whispered.

He wore a navy-blue suit, starched white shirt, and Ole Miss tie in red and blue stripes. He came uncomfortably close, thrust his chin out, looked down his nose at her. "Well, well. The prodigal daughter returns. I guess artists work off a different side of the brain than the rest of us. The rest of us are practical and present for the important things, like when our grandmas die."

Blasts of rage fired off inside her head, boiled through her, and simmered out like lava. Her lips struggled to say words that refused to form.

Lily folded her arms across her chest. "And how many times were you here to help when Sweet Evelyn was sick? I mean, what with her being kin and with you livin' in the same town."

He didn't acknowledge Lily but leaned closer to Eva Clare. "I figured you'd have questions about the real estate sign, so I came right over when I heard you were home."

"Wha' . . . how'd you hear . . . wait . . . did Pete call and tell you I was here?"

Lily muffled a laugh.

"Oh, whatever. Yeah, I do have questions. Did you put that sign in my yard?"

Gerald patted the air. "Calm down."

"Don't tell me to calm down!"

"Yes, I put the sign up. I called a realtor friend to try and get a head start for you. I figured you'd be busy with funeral details and getting rid of Sweet Evelyn's possessions. I thought it'd be good to see if there's any interest in the house—"

"You had no right to do that. I don't want to sell." She stared at him straight in the eyes until she shriveled and looked away. Gerald pretended pure motives, but he always seemed to have something up his white, starched sleeve that benefited him only.

"You don't have to be ugly about it. It's not officially listed. The realtor put the sign up as a favor, targeting people who come here to use the lake for recreation." He waggled his finger in front of her nose. "But I have a question for you. You're listed as sole heir in Evelyn's will, but I'm not sure her will is valid. The original Last Will and Testament of our ancestor, Andrew Coghlan, progenitor of our oxbow Coghlans, is in conflict with Evelyn's. This house and land should fall only to rightful heirs."

"I *am* a rightful heir."

"But in his will, Andrew Coghlan stated that the house and parcel of land it's on were set apart for his youngest daughter, Victoria Dove Coghlan, with the stipulation that if she never had issue, which means if she never had children—"

"I know what 'issue' means."

"Then the land would go to the oldest daughter, which was Catherine Deering Coghlan, and her oldest descendant. We know, based on the family Bible, Victoria Dove never married."

"So? I'm a descendent of Catherine Deering Coghlan like you." Her bold comeback belied her fear. Gerald always got his way. He could talk fast, manipulate, make any dumb thing sound right, make you act on it before you had a chance to think. Surely, he knew better than to mess with a current legal document, but probably, he'd try to plot and push his way through the outdated points of whatever old paper he possessed to convince her to sign some new land transfer deed. He'd try to finagle her out of her inheritance legally.

Lily opened her mouth to speak, but stopped and flattened her lips. She was a tall woman, taller than Gerald. And the way she held her head high made her a tower to his little turret.

"I worked hard documenting the family genealogy," Gerald said. "Andrew Coghlan's oldest daughter, Catherine Deering Coghlan, had four children. Two died as babies. Of the two girls that remained, my grandmother, Annah Rachel, was the oldest. She had a son, my father, William Patrick Tanner, or as you knew him, Uncle Billy Pat. This land was rightly his, and what was rightly his is now rightly mine."

"This land has always been in my line—Catherine Deering Coghlan, her daughter Erin Rose, then Emmaline, Evelyn, now me." Her words faded in intensity. She could've sounded stronger, more confident, but she was never sure of herself around Gerald. She had a history of backing down. She'd have to find a copy of that original will and go over it with a fine-tooth comb.

"Your great-great-grandmother Erin Rose was a year younger than my Annah Rachel."

"Yeah, that's in the family Bible. But there's a legal will in place."

Lily stepped forward. "I could tell you both somethin'—"

"It doesn't matter," Gerald interrupted, again ignoring Lily. "Victoria Dove didn't have children. Catherine Deering did. The oldest descendant gets the house."

"Your stubborn self will face the truth sooner or later," Lily muttered.

"You've lost your senses in the heat, Gerald," Eva Clare said. "Your grandmother Annah Rachel sold her inheritance here and moved back to Neshoba County, where you and your daddy were born. You didn't even move here till sixth grade. All my greats owned this tract of land, and my grandmother inherited it legally."

"You got documents to prove it? I figure we got out of line for a while. I'd like to straighten things up. I'm sure we can work something out." He patted her arm.

She jerked it away.

"I'll let you know if there's any interest in the house." He started toward his Cadillac.

"Gerald, are you contesting the will?"

"No, no, not at all. I'm hoping you and I can come to some kind of favorable agreement."

"Forget that," Eva Clare said, too low for him to hear. "I'm calling Davis Realty to come take this sign down."

Was he bluffing? Surely, the most current deed superseded the will Gerald had. But then again, he was a bully and would lie to get what he wanted. And besides, he was a prominent and wealthy bully, and money speaks, and power entitles, and lies fool people, and they would listen and follow him, no matter what, right or wrong.

"Yeah, girl, you gon have a fight with that one," Lily said. "What're you gon do?"

"I don't know."

"Well, you better think of something."

Gerald stopped beside his SUV, put a foot on the running board, and shifted toward Eva Clare. "All I'm sayin' is, if you're down on your luck and have nowhere else to go, don't be comin' back here to make a life for yourself in *this* house." He got in and slammed the door.

She squinted at the sun glaring through a parting in the thickening clouds.

"That's what you're doing, isn't it? Comin' here to make a new life." Lily shook her head. "Well, don't worry. Tanner shows up, spreads his wings, and cock-a-doodle-doos orders, but he ain't got a leg to stand on."

Eva Clare pushed out the breath she was holding, then turned to look at Lily. "And *you*? Why are *you* here?"

"I came to——"

"He'll pound me down trying to get what he wants."

Gerald made a wide U-turn, leaving ruts in the grass on both sides of the driveway, and sped away. They watched him go under the low-hanging branches of the old oaks standing like specters with their arms out, gnarled and angry, their leaves aquiver. If only the limbs would grab him and squeeze him senseless, gutless, and silent.

Lily put a hand on Eva Clare's arm. "Don't pay him no mind. He throws his weight around. 'Cause he can. Folks are scared of him because they're beholdin' to him. These farmers live on credit. They take out a bank loan at the beginning of the year and pay it off when the crop comes in. If it's a bad crop year, he loans them more money to live on." Lily smirked. "Don't worry. Just because a chicken has wings don't mean it can fly."

"What are you saying?"

"Either he doesn't know everything, or he wants to make sure you don't."

"I don't have a clue what you're talking about, but thanks for taking up for me. At least somebody in this town is brave enough to stand in Gerald's face and speak up."

"Yeah, but he doesn't listen to a word I say."

The sun slid in and out of dark clouds approaching. The wind picked up. Faint thunder rumbled way off in the distance. Eva Clare flicked her hair, then stomped over and pulled the realty sign out of the ground. Flung it under a magnolia tree. For a woman in her fifties, she had some strength and entitlement, and it was high time she learned to use both.

"There ya go," Lily said, rolling her eyes. "That oughta teach him, for sure."

Eva Clare looked at Lily standing beside her old Ford Taurus. That Ford made her think about another Ford—an old, burnt-out Ford

Fairlane station wagon that made national news headlines in 1964. That burnt-out Fairlane wagon represented a hate-filled Uncle Billy Pat Tanner and a young Gerald Tanner practicing the character he was to become.

November 1964
Philadelphia, Mississippi

Thanksgiving came four days after the first anniversary of the assassination of President Kennedy. Grandpop Binky drove their family of three over to Uncle Billy Pat's in the red clay hills of Neshoba County. Said he wanted to check on things, get a pulse on the situation—the intensifying FBI investigation in Philadelphia. A holiday dinner was a good excuse to go.

Between Erin and Kosciusko, Grandpop and Grandmomma sat in the front seat of their Buick LeSabre named Mamie and talked at length about what was happening. Eva Clare lay in the car's rear package tray under the curved back window, pretending to be asleep, but soaking in every word. She had to fold her legs at the knees because she was too tall for the ledge. This position gave her a view of everything around her, and she was elevated to the level of her grandparents' mouths. She clearly heard all the new details.

The FBI had questioned Uncle Billy Pat about the murders of the three civil rights workers: Schwerner, Goodman, and Chaney. Uncle Billy Pat had told Grandpop he was at work that night. He drove a laundry truck, picking up dirty uniforms and delivering clean ones to businesses. He also told Grandpop it looked bad for his friend Jimmy, who drove the three civil rights workers' car to the place they were killed. Jimmy was at the murder scene, and that made him a conspirator to murder.

"Billy Pat's got a lot of hate in him," Grandpop told Grandmomma. "He was likely involved."

"But he's a hard-working, church-going man."

"They're all fine churchmen, hon," Grandpop said. "Deacons, preachers, choir members, Sunday School teachers. And they're all in the

KKK. They believe the Bible teaches segregation. They don't believe in race mixing and see themselves as protecting their schools and churches and children and families. These men can beat and kill on Saturday night and teach and preach the Beatitudes on Sunday morning and not bat an eye. They see no conflict in it."

How could they do that? How could they hurt or kill someone and then go to church and worship God? Apparently, a whole lot of people in this world—folks who sat on church pews every Sunday—didn't connect the teachings in their Bibles to their own words and actions and didn't follow what they claimed to believe.

At the Tanner home in the hills and pine-woods of Neshoba County, Aunt Brenda cooked a big dinner of turkey, cornbread dressing, and vegetables boiled to mush with fatback. After they ate, they went outside and threw the football up in the pecan trees to shake the nuts loose and send them falling to the ground. The kids—Eva Clare, Gerald, and Bubba—gathered the pecans and put them in brown paper sacks, so Aunt Brenda could use them for her Christmas baking. She gave Grandmomma two bags to use in her holiday cakes and candies. Gerald made sure he picked up the most.

Then Grandpop announced he wanted to go see the spot where the old, burnt-out Ford Fairlane station wagon of the three civil rights workers was found back in June.

"I saw it on the national news," Grandpop said. "I want to go there and see it for myself."

Uncle Billy Pat scratched his head, hocked up some phlegm, and spat it on the ground. "Uh, yeah, okay. Sure you don't wont to stay here and have some punkin pie wi' whip cream?"

"I want to go." Grandpop made his serious face that you don't mess with. Even Billy Pat didn't fool with Binky. He knew Binky was above him, smarter, doctor in front of his name.

Eva Clare and Gerald tagged along, sat in the back seat, looked out opposite windows. She saw the Highway 21 sign before they turned onto a dirt road that got more rugged the farther they went into the mix of woods and clearings. It ended up being two narrow wheel tracks with weeds growing in between. They got out of the car and walked to where scorched tree branches hung down around a charred circle. It was obvious some big object had been burned here.

Grandpop rubbed his whiskers from his cheekbones down to his chin like men do—thumb on one side of the lips, the other four fingers on the other side, pulling the mouth open. "So, this is the crime scene."

"Naw, they wasn't kilt here. They was kilt on Rock Cut Road off o' Highway 19."

"How do you—"

"That's what I hear anyways." Uncle Billy Pat patted the pack of cigarettes in his shirt pocket but didn't get one out. "Billy Wayne Posey drove the car to Olen Burrage's, where they was buried, and old man Burrage gave 'em the gasoline to burn the car."

Five months after the fire, the remaining summer leaves were still singed, wilted, black. Eva Clare walked into the burn circle of sweetgums, looked at the black hanging all around her, and wrapped her hand around a small, drooping branch, becoming one with the awful thing that happened here. She shivered.

Gerald saw. "They asked for it." Snarly and red-faced, he kicked at the dry ground and scattered loose dirt. "We didn't need them troublemakers comin' down here stirrin' things up."

"They were here to help colored people register to vote, Gerald."

He narrowed his eyes, looked at her mean-like, wrinkled his forehead. "They got what they deserved."

He must've heard that from his daddy.

She put her fingers in her ears so she didn't have to hear anything else Gerald said and squeezed her eyes shut. Blood rushed through her head and sounded like ocean waves.

Someone tapped her arm.

"Hey, you all right?" Lily said. "Your ears hurt?"

Eva Clare opened her eyes. The tips of her pointer fingers were still in her ears where she'd put them to block the memory of the sound of little-boy Gerald's mean talk. Lily stood in front of her. A burnt-motor-oil smell from Lily's Taurus drifted by. "I'm fine."

"I need to talk to you."

"Okay, sure, what?" Eva Clare turned and started up the sidewalk to the two-story, red-brick house built in 1861. Sturdy and stately, it had survived war and natural disasters, like the 1927 flood, when the levee broke and the swollen river spanned sixty miles. Could the house survive Gerald?

Original stained-glass windows were on each side of the door, and above the transom, a long panel of glass. There was a center row of tall, milky-white rectangles beaded in, with colorful, lead-lined triangle shapes at the top. At the bottom of the panel was a row of squares with colors in a pattern. The mistake was still there. Nobody had ever bothered to fix it. Blue, brown, blue, brown, blue, brown, blue, blue. Two pesky blue squares disrupted the pattern. Now that she was in charge, by God, she'd get it fixed.

"It's wrong. It's just wrong."

"Why sure it is," Lily said.

Lily was obviously still talking about Gerald. She poked Eva Clare's arm again. "I need to tell you something."

Eva Clare's head buzzed with frenetic tangles of confusion. She was back at home where she didn't want to be but had to be, and now Gerald was threatening to take home away from her, so she'd have to fight to stay here where she didn't want to be. Insanity. She reached for the doorknob.

"Wait!" Lily screeched.

Eva Clare jumped, jerked her hand away from the door. "What?"

"It was me. It was me on the phone calls to you. I was Sweet Evelyn's nurse. I took care of her those last weeks, and when she passed, I was the one holding her hand."

"You? What about Marthala?"

"Marthala was too sick. She has cancer, and I had to bring in hospice a few weeks ago."

"Oh no. I knew she'd been sick, but I didn't know she had terminal cancer."

"A couple years ago, Sweet Evelyn got a vision of her own fate and Marthala's. She paid my way to nursing school at Delta State and gave me a lump sum to be her future caregiver. She knew she and Marthala would both need full-time skilled care at some point, and she wasn't about to go to a nursing home or send Marthala to one."

"I didn't know. Grandmomma never told me."

"Sweet Evelyn was the type to take care of matters quietly in her own way. She didn't want to bother you with it. Didn't want to put that burden on family."

"Well, that explains it. I'd call to check on Grandmomma, and I'd always talk to Marthala. Then Marthala stopped answering, and I'd leave a message. So it was you who returned my calls with the medical details. You're the nurse. You're Ms. Greene."

"Yes, I am. Lily Moselle Greene. I was here those last days and nights with Evelyn."

Eva Clare pushed a swoop of bangs out of her eye, looked at Lily, held her gaze. Lily had given up her plans and direction in life to start anew at the request of Sweet Evelyn. Sweet Evelyn, all through her long years, had gone along with separation and exclusion. Yet when it came to the reality of living and dying, she chose integration and inclusion. Or maybe, people as people.

"Sweet Evelyn has gone to be with Jesus, and Marthala is preparing to go," Lily said.

"Lily, I appreciate you caring for them. I grew up with Marthala taking care of me. She was here in this house every day since I started first grade."

"Yeah, she was. And she still is. Marthala and I have been living here for a month."

"What? Here? In my grandmomma's house?" Apparently, this was going on while Eva Clare was dealing with marital troubles and a flood.

Lily nodded. "Marthala's hospital bed was right beside your grandmother's until Sweet Evelyn passed on Wednesday. I've been in charge of caring, cooking, feeding, cleaning, giving meds, doctor visits, and hospice arrangements. Doing the job I was paid to do."

"But I'll be living here. What will you do now that I'm home and Sweet Evelyn is gone?"

"I'm planning on carrying out Sweet Evelyn's wishes, that both she and Marthala could go on to glory right here in this house."

"But . . ." Eva Clare didn't intend to sound selfish or uncaring. She wasn't a mean person. It was just that the losses had piled up on her, and she needed to be alone. Couldn't deal with people and their problems right now.

"I'm planning on staying right here." Lily pointed to the stoop floor and waited for Eva Clare's response.

Eva Clare didn't have one. She twisted the knob, pushed the door open. A shaft of golden light went in before her. She stepped on the yellow rectangle the sun threw against the hardwood floor of the foyer. Why hadn't Gerald said anything? Did he know about the women—of different colors—living together? Surely not. Because he would have minded. Once, when they were eleven, he showed his true colors on race. It was a holiday night six months after the three civil rights workers were murdered, one month after she stood in the burned-station-wagon spot.

December 1964
Erin, Mississippi

Eva Clare sat on the den floor, mesmerized by the colors moving across the aluminum Christmas tree. The needles were shiny, silver foil, and illumination came from a rotating color wheel that purred as it turned. It was Christmas Eve, but it wasn't a holy night.

The household had grown more tense over the past few weeks. Grandpop Binky had learned new information about the murders of the three civil rights workers. Eva Clare hid outside the kitchen door and listened as he told Grandmomma and Marthala.

The Black civil rights worker was beaten with chains, his testicles were cut off, and he was shot. The second worker was shot in the heart. The third tried to run away, but he was also shot. Their bodies were taken to the Old Jolly Farm, where they were buried in an earthen pond dam. One of them was likely buried alive, as an autopsy showed red clay dirt in his lungs and fists. He'd tried to dig his way out, Grandpop said before whispering a cuss word. Grandpop had never said a bad word before.

Uncle Billy Pat, Aunt Brenda, Gerald, and Bubba had picked up in a hurry and were on their way to the Delta. Uncle Billy Pat was moving here to get away from the FBI investigation. Agents had been closing in on KKK members. They had already questioned him. Eva Clare didn't want Gerald in her class at school. Grandpop didn't want any of them here. Grandmomma said they're family and you do for family.

From outside came the sound of gravel pinging off hubcaps.

"They're here," Grandmomma announced. "Binky, get the eggnog out. Marthala, pour some Kool-Aid for the boys."

Grandmomma opened the door, and in came the Tanners. After hugs, Grandmomma said, "Y'all come on to the kitchen. I know you're hungry after that long drive."

A Wonder Bread wrapping lay empty on the counter. Marthala was putting lettuce on roast beef sandwiches. Grandmomma set out bowls of potato chips. Eva Clare climbed on a bar stool, and Grandmomma pushed Gerald to the chair next to her. When Marthala put a sandwich in front of Gerald, he lifted a corner of the top slice of bread and peeked inside. "I don't like lettuce nor mayonnaise." He flicked his hand at Marthala and shot her a snarl. "Fix it."

Marthala pushed her lips forward till her chin looked like a walnut, stretched her neck long like a crane, and raised her eyebrows in that way of hers that said, *I'll cut me a switch and wear yo' hind end out.* You didn't talk bad about Marthala's food and get away with it. But she held herself and reached for the plate. Grandmomma touched her hand and said it was okay to leave it. Gerald picked off the lettuce and ate the sandwich.

Grandmomma shot Eve Clare a frown punctuated with a hard nod toward Gerald, meaning she should be polite and invite him to play. Eva Clare asked him if he wanted to see her Nancy Drew collection. He didn't know what that was. She asked him if he wanted to play Rook, and he said he might. They'd try it with two players.

They sat on the floor of her bedroom, and Eva Clare dealt the cards and put one in the middle. After his fourth turn, Gerald said, "I hate havin' to move here. Wudn't like nothin' bad happened."

"Three men got murdered." She played a card face-up on the floor.

"They was troublemakers. 'Sides, it ain't against the law to kill a ni—"

"Go, Gerald! It's your turn."

His face turned red, and his eyes went cold and empty, and it scared her that he could harbor that much hate in his heart for another human being. What else could she say to teach him that murder was wrong—a sin, a crime, both in the Bible and in the law books? Nothing. He would keep getting madder. So she did what she'd seen people do all her life—kept her thoughts to herself and her lips zipped. Marthala always said the fish that kept its mouth shut never got caught. Nice people stayed quiet. They never spoke out against anything, and they never stood up for anything. They sat on the fence between good and bad. Those people didn't amount to much. They maybe never did anything bad, but they didn't do anything good either.

Eva Clare and Gerald finished the game and joined the others in the den, where Grandpop was talking about the little Mississippi town of Philadelphia. "I once heard it said that the store owners around courthouse square were afraid of losing business to big-city stores when automobiles were first built, so they kept the county highways unpaved, and those roadways washed out in every rainstorm. Most of those dirt roads were old Choctaw trails and are still there in the outlying parts of the county."

"And I know 'em all," Uncle Billy Pat said.

Grandpop lurched forward, arms slung out, fingers splayed. "It's different here. In the Delta, Whites are a minority. We've got rich planters who need the coloreds to work the cotton. You can't grab somebody you don't like and take them out on a dirt road, and you know full well what I mean."

Eva Clare had never seen Grandpop so angry and animated, his eyes so fierce. She pulled her knees up, wrapped her arms around them, buried her face against her legs, peeked at her grandfather between them.

Grandpop put his hand on his chest, sat back, gulped for air. When he calmed down, he said, "I got you a job at Howard Farms overseeing a crew of field hands. You got to follow the way they do things here. Tomorrow, we'll have a nice Christmas, and then we'll get you settled in the overseer's house."

Eva Clare fixed her eyes on the metal Christmas tree, lighted bright amber, as the color wheel rotated and changed the silver branches to a tranquil blue.

She studied the shaft of golden sunlight under her feet on the chestnut foyer floor of Coghlan House.

People were like those colored pieces of plastic in that rotating color wheel of her twelfth Christmas. The same light shined through each plastic piece. But each one filtered the light differently. One reflected amber across the room, one blue, red, green. It was the influence of love shining through some people, but in others, the influence of Jim Crow refracted the light of good.

Jim Crow, statutes that legalized racial segregation, dictated beliefs for a hundred years. Those laws ended with the Civil Rights Act of 1964, which was passed between the murders of the three civil rights workers in June and the discovery of their bodies in August. Even though the Jim Crow laws weren't on the books anymore, they were stamped on the minds of people. A few of them were still stamped on her mind. She remembered them, but she didn't like them.

Separate schools shall be maintained for the children of the white and colored races. The marriage of a white person with a Negro or mulatto or person who shall have one-eighth or more of Negro blood, shall be unlawful and void. Negroes and white families could not live in the same home. Cohabitation of a white and black is a felony; penalty is imprisonment for a month to a year. It is a misdemeanor to rent any part of a building to a Negro when such building is already in whole or in part in occupancy by a white person.

Jim Crow, Gerald Tanner, the color wheel, and two women, one White, one Black, lying side by side on their sick beds, one gone on to glory and one still bedfast—she'd hold these images inside, stuff her thoughts down, and keep her mouth shut like the fish that lived.

4 GHOSTS OF PAST AND PRESENT

Eva Clare stopped in the foyer to look at her ancestors' pictures hanging on the wall above the serpentine-front sideboard. The oxbow's first three generations—solid, upstanding stock, reminders of the stature, strength, and virtue that built this place. An oval tiger maple frame with convex glass held a picture of Andrew and Eirinn Coghlan, her fourth-great-grandparents. Eirinn died before the family's trek to the Delta in 1859. To its right, a tintype of their daughters, Catherine Deering and Victoria Dove. On the left, a portrait of Catherine's daughter, Erin Rose.

Grandmomma was nothing more than a picture for the wall now.

The house still harbored that familiar aristocratic smell of antique furniture and old wool rugs, but a new odor filtered out—a mix of bleach and Lysol.

In the parlor opposite her, everything appeared the same—sofa with carved wooden trim and tapestry fabric, velvet chairs, cherry secretary in Twelve Colonies design, and mahogany tables. Grandmomma didn't have a stick of wood furniture in the house under a hundred years old, except the hardrock maple kitchen table, and it was forty-five.

Eva Clare ran her fingers over the sideboard's flame mahogany wood, then faced Lily. "Wouldn't Marthala be happier in her own house, or yours?"

Lily shook her head. "Not an option. Her old shack has been torn down, and I let go of my lease to come care for these two women when Evelyn asked me to."

Eva Clare bit the insides of her cheeks. She needed to self-isolate and paint peaceful oxbow scenes and cry out loud when she felt like it.

"I want Marthala to have a comfortable place and good care, but maybe not here, since I'll be living here now." Toying with the lion's head drawer pull on the sideboard, she spoke in barely a whisper. "Surely, you understand."

Lily spread her long fingers on the fronts of her hip bones. "So, you bring your privileged self home and the world bows down to you?" She fast-tapped her foot.

"Yeah, I think that's how it's supposed to work. I own the house now."

"Well, you wouldn't if Sweet Evelyn hadn't died."

"Well, I know." Finally, overwhelming tears of grief and frustration came.

"Oh, goodness, I'm sorry. I didn't mean to upset you." Lily winced. "But I've got a dire situation here. Listen. These two women grew old together. Society's rules didn't matter anymore. When they were able, they quoted scripture, held hands and prayed for each other, and prepared to meet their Maker." She laid her hand over her heart. "In nursing school, I studied geriatric care. I understand the emotional and physical aspects of the aging process, exacerbated by disease and dementia."

Eva Clare wiped the wetness from her face and looked at Lily. In her manner of speech, Lily could slide in and out of her life roles as circumstances warranted—from rural girl with common dialect to educated health care provider with knowledge of medical terms.

"I was the only one here for Evelyn during her end stage. Even Gerald didn't come until I called to tell him her body was shutting down. I called you first, but didn't get an answer—"

"I was busy packing. I knew I missed a call from this area code but also knew I was coming home." Eva Clare cleared her throat. "I had a dire situation there."

"I know."

"You do? Oh, of course, you do. Anna Laurel told Pete I had marital problems, and Pete told you and Gerald and everybody, I'm sure. I guess I have no secrets, and more than likely, people have already passed judgment on me for my failed marriage and for not being here when my grandmother was dying." Eva Clare mopped her eyes with her fists, then took a few steps to the kitchen door. Three little pots of African violets sat on the window sill above the sink.

"You did the best you could, given the hand you were dealt. Your marital status is for nobody to judge, and it's nobody's damn business where you were or weren't."

Eva Clare bit her bottom lip. "Thanks." She tiptoed down the hallway to the master bedroom, Lily behind her. The spread on Sweet Evelyn's bed was rumpled on one side. Lily must've slept there. In a hospital bed, head raised thirty degrees, lay a tiny, raisin-like woman with white hair. "She's gone down a whole lot in two months. Last time I saw her, she was up and around, taking care of the house and Grandmomma." Eva Clare walked to the bed and touched Marthala's arm—thin, skin like crepe, cold. "She's so still."

"That's what morphine does. I administered her meds and went to help Pete while he placed orders. I've got relief. Hospice comes by, and Bolivar Homebound Health sends someone to stay with her a couple hours. The caregiver texted me that she needed to leave as I was ringing you up at Pete's. That was my cue to come home. Besides, I couldn't let you walk in on this."

Medical supplies sat on the table by the bed—sublingual drugs, swabs, antibacterial wipes, adult diapers, moisturizing lotion. The room was neat with minimal light.

Marthala coughed, then smacked her lips.

Lily got a glycerin swabstick and wiped Marthala's mouth.

Eva Clare's nose stung. It always happened before crying. She distracted herself by looking at the details of the patchwork quilt that covered Marthala—stars pieced together. It was a work of art, and art always either took her out of reality or put her in the middle of it.

"Marthala will soon transition to heaven," Lily said. "Please let her stay a short while."

They held each other's gaze until Eva Clare looked away. She couldn't give much more of herself. Couldn't keep turning over her needs to the needs of others. She fingered the lines in the design of the quilt, detouring around the guilt trip Lily was putting on her.

"This is a pretty pattern." The quilt had five rows with four blocks on each row. Each block featured an eight-point star with a multi-pointed star around it. The patchwork pieces were in paisleys, solids, and flowers of pastel color combinations—pink, green, dandelion, lavender, and robin's egg blue. As she focused, three-dimensional cubes and parallelograms appeared in the points of the outer star. "Great depth, nice detail. Did you make it?"

"Yes. It's what I call the Carpenter's Star pattern. Some call it the Wagon Wheel—wagon, chariot, swing low, comin' to carry me home, like the song says. The Carpenter's Star refers to Jesus, the Master Carpenter, building a stairway to heaven, or the Promised Land. I put a Carpenter's Star quilt on Evelyn before she died, too."

Eva Clare got a visual of her ill grandmother and teared up again.

It was strange how a room where an old woman died and another was in the process of dying could make one repentant.

She noticed that the bottom two triangular points of each star block were shades of blue in solids or patterns. Blue. Blue. Like the stained glass above the front door. An artist, she noticed things like shape, color, symbolism, repetition. The repetition here bothered her.

Lily straightened Marthala's pillow and took her temperature.

"With all this going on, how do you find time to sew quilts?" Eva Clare asked.

"We find time to do what we gotta do. My grandmother sewed quilts. She learned it from her mama and taught me. She also passed down stories about the quilts that her mama had told her. I've got to keep it up. I can sit here by the bed and stitch blocks, and I sell my finished quilts on consignment at the antique mall in Cleveland." Lily took Marthala's wrist in her hand, checked her pulse, and recorded it in a notebook by the bed.

A flash of lightning filled the room with a white glow that turned to electric neon blue, and it was followed by a loud crack of thunder. They startled.

"Guess Pete's done left for the bank vault by now," Lily said, eliciting laughter from both.

Eva Clare turned her attention back to Marthala, her chest in a slow rise and fall.

Lily rested her hand on Eva Clare's arm. "As I said, my mamaw will soon go on to glory. I beg you, please have mercy on her sick, old soul."

"Wait, what? Your mamaw?"

Another lightning flash. Thunder. BOOM! Windows rattled.

"Marthala's my grandmother. I thought you knew."

"Shootfire! How would I know?"

"When we were kids, I stayed with my mamaw, too, here, at this house, in summers."

Eva Clare shook her head. "I don't remember that. Did we play together?"

"Naw, not back then. But there was this one time that we played paper dolls together."

Eva Clare frowned and focused. "Paper dolls . . . paper dolls. I do remember another girl at the kitchen table with me and my new box of paper dolls from Mr. Ashford's ten-cent store in Cleveland." She pulled up one fragment of the paper doll story, and another came up. "We got in trouble, didn't we?"

Erin, Mississippi
August 1963

Eva Clare sat at the yellow Formica kitchen table with a stack of paper, pencils, and a box of forty-eight crayon colors, designing paper doll clothes for the Lennon Sisters. She swung her legs. Her feet didn't reach the floor.

Marthala walked by with a basket of wet clothes, headed out to the line. She let the screen door slam behind her and reprimanded the Black child playing jacks on the patio before the girl even had a chance to do anything wrong.

"Girl, you sit right here. Don't move nary an inch, else I'll cut me a switch."

"Yessum."

But when Marthala walked away, the girl with the dozen little braids and plastic barrettes of different colors got up, came to the back door, and pressed her nose into the screen.

"Hey! What're you doin' out there?" Eva Clare said. The child was about her age.

The girl didn't answer.

"You wanna play? Come on in."

The child pulled the handle, stepped inside, and proceeded to the table.

Eva Clare went to the counter, lifted cellophane from a plate of rainbow cookies Grandmomma had made for her meeting, and took one. She put the square of three cake layers—red, yellow, green—in front of her newfound playmate. "These have raspberry jam between the layers and chocolate on top." She wiped chocolate from her fingers on her shorts, sat down, and picked up an eight-inch cardboard doll. "I'm designing dresses for Janet Lennon. Have you heard of the Lennon Sisters? They sing on *The Lawrence Welk Show* on TV every Saturday night." She put the doll down, then laid a dress from the box on a sheet of paper and ran her pencil around it. "What you do is trace a dress that came in the set. Draw tabs on the shoulders, color it, cut it out, and fold the tabs down over the doll's shoulders to hold the dress on. See?" She demonstrated with a dress she'd made.

"Yessum." The girl's braids bobbled with her nodding. The barrettes clicked together.

"I'll be in fifth grade when school starts," Eva Clare said. "What grade are you in?"

"Fourth."

"You don't go to my school."

"No'm."

Eva Clare reached in the box. "You can have Kathy, and here's a dress to trace." She set out a blue, belted frock with a full skirt, along with a pencil and a handful of colors. "Don't forget the tabs."

The girl outlined the dress with the pencil, then concentrated with her tongue stuck out the corner of her mouth to draw intricate patterns— eyelet lace, ribbons, flowers.

"Where'd you learn to do that?"

"I seen my mamaw do it."

"Saw. I saw my mamaw do it. Your mamaw makes paper doll clothes?"

"No'm, she makes quilts."

"Oh." Eva Clare watched the girl color and cut out the dress, including tabs. "You did a good job." Eva Clare held up the paper doll for her guest to fit the dress on.

Down the hall, high heels clattered on hardwood, louder with each step toward the kitchen. Grandmomma appeared in the doorway in an orchid-purple dress, pearls at her throat, her hair beauty-parlor fixed with spitcurls at her ears and two curls looped like ram horns at the top sides of her forehead. She looked at the Black child, grabbed the door frame with one hand, and slapped the other hand against her chest.

"Eva Clare, what's going on in here?"

"We're playing paper dolls."

"What is *she* doing at my kitchen table?"

"Cutting out a dress for Kathy Lennon."

The screen door opened with a screech, and Marthala walked in, the empty clothes basket propped on her hip. Her eyes fell on the disobedient child. "Girl, I tol' you not to move off that patio and here you sit. Now you get—"

"Marthala, why is she in here?"

"I invited her in, Grandmomma," Eva Clare said.

"I'm sorry, Miss Evelyn, e'rybody choppin' cotton and cain't look after her. It's my grandyoungun, and she s'posed to be outside."

"She draws real good," Eva Clare said.

"My word." Sweet Evelyn looked at the ceiling and shook her head.

"Get on out this house, Lily Moselle!" Marthala shook a finger at her granddaughter. "I'm 'on wear yo' tail out once I catch up wi'chu."

Lily slid off the chair and ran.

"It's okay, Marthala." Sweet Evelyn waved her hand. "What's done is done. Wipe the table and chair. Use some of that disinfectant under the sink. I've got to run to my meeting." She rummaged for her car keys, hung her pocketbook in the crook of an arm, and picked up the silver platter of rainbow cookies for the church ladies to eat after they prayed for missionaries in foreign fields. "Eva Clare, I'll talk to you later."

Eva Clare sighed. This was one of those things she'd get in trouble for and not know why. And even when Grandmomma explained it, she still wouldn't understand. Because "Jesus loves the little children, all the children of the world. Red and yellow, black and white . . ."

The odor of bleach in the bedclothes assaulted Eva Clare's nostrils. A dying Marthala slept under a stark white sheet and star quilt in Grandmomma's bedroom. Eva Clare sniffed—the same smell as Grandmomma's old disinfectant, a chlorine dilution she kept in a bottle under the sink.

The day after the paper doll episode, Lily Moselle sat far out in the yard on a blanket under a shade tree with her dolls, colors, and coloring books. Eva Clare didn't see a thing wrong with going out there and sitting down to play, too. But she chose to follow the fifth commandment in the Bible that said to obey your parents. Grandmomma had told her, "We don't do that."

The next day, however, Eva Clare went out to the blanket and asked Lily Moselle if she wanted to go to the river. The two of them sneaked off over the levee and alongside the jungle trees to the water's edge. They took off their shoes and tiptoed where the waves lapped in, and they waded out in the slack water, and they laughed and danced and splashed and sang songs like "Three Little Fishies." She got a spanking afterward— not so much for going to the big river alone, but for playing with Lily. She never saw Lily after that day.

Until now.

It shouldn't have been that way. She flattened her lips and twisted her mouth.

In her childhood she had witnessed the hurt of prejudice. Now, home again as an adult, she had the opportunity to do better. As for Marthala's status, how could she stop what her grandmother had started? How could she say no to her beloved Marthala?

She couldn't. She couldn't turn down Lily's request. She'd have to brace up and do the right thing, even though it meant sacrificing her need to hole up and heal from her hurts and losses. She faced Lily.

"Okay, here's the deal. Marthala's a longtime part of this family, and Sweet Evelyn apparently wanted her here, and I'd like to do right by my grandmother. Then after, if you don't have anywhere to go, there's a guesthouse out back."

"I know about the guesthouse."

"You can live there, if you want, until you find something better. It used to be nice, but I haven't been inside that cottage in twenty years. I don't know what shape it's in."

"I understand. Thank you. I appreciate it."

"But. And it's a big but. You've got to help me get rid of Gerald so we can both stay. I don't want to have to deal with him and all the commotion he creates. I can't take it right now."

"He does inspire disturbance." Lily slid off her bracelets and laid them on the end table. "You know," she whispered, "us living together will be a bit awkward. Don't you think?"

Darkness fell, and rain pelted the windowpanes—a hard rain, hail mixed in, accompanied by strobe lightning and a continuous undercurrent of thunder. The wooden door of the upstairs bedroom rattled in its casing when Eva Clare closed it behind her. Moving boxes filled with her clothes were stacked against a wall. They'd gotten rained on during unloading, and their wet-cardboard smell filled the room. She pulled a nightshirt out of her suitcase and put it on.

The room was hot, stuffy, and stale. Her face was steamy, her hair damp with sweat. She turned on the window air conditioning unit and flipped the fan switch to high. It rumbled, moaned, and churned, caught up with itself, and came on full force. She let the blowing air cool her. Grandmomma had never bothered to install central air. She'd relied on window units. She and Grandpop Binky had added a master bedroom suite and den downstairs to the original structure when Eva Clare was a little girl. Eva Clare would occupy that space after Marthala was gone, but for now, she'd stay in her childhood bedroom.

It hadn't changed. Built-in bookshelves, white yellowed to cream, still held her collection of Nancy Drew mysteries, Childcraft encyclopedias, and her Louisa May Alcott favorites: *Little Women*, *Jo's Boys*, and *Lulu's Library*. The furniture was the same cherrywood bed, tables, and dresser, now layered with dust.

She collapsed on the bedspread, curled into a fetal heap, and cried herself to sleep. At some point in the night, maybe during a second round of storms when thunder cracked loud enough to rouse the dead, she got up and flipped off the light switch, then pulled the bedcovers back, crawled under them, and put her head on the pillow. A light on a pole outside cast a glow that silhouetted the furnishings in the room.

The storm settled on top of the house like a July fireworks finale. Despite loud booms and light displays coming through three tall windows, she went back to sleep. Sometime later, she startled upright. Someone had sat down on the bed. She felt it. Felt the mattress sink in. But no one was there. She glanced around the room. No one.

She lay back with a groan, but positioned her face so she could keep an eye on the spot where that someone had sat. Her breaths were fast and ragged. Her own heartbeat hammered in her ears. Then came a remnant flash of lightning, and the woman appeared. Eva Clare stopped breathing, didn't move a muscle, didn't even blink. Sitting at the foot of the bed in the exact spot Eva Clare knew she'd be was a woman with luminous skin, pale gold hair pulled back in a blue ribbon, and a white, gauzy gown. Like the woman in Eva Clare's water dreams. A familiar soul. Did Eva Clare know her? The woman didn't speak, yet her words filled Eva Clare's head.

Rise up.

The water-dream woman stood, walked across the room to the window on the east side. Her dress was filmy, flowing, with a blue-ribbon sash. At the tip of her hem was a pale-blue fluorescent glow. Then she disappeared.

Rise up? What did that mean? Eva Clare couldn't go back to sleep. She flopped, flailed, finally gave up. Got out of bed and went to the window, drew back the drapes, looked out over the patio, down the dirt lane to the guest cottage, the barn, and at the end of the narrowing trail, the family graveyard. The storm had ended, a slight moon came out, and the pole light gave definition to the objects out back. Inside a chain-link fence were eleven graves, dating from 1890 to 1995. Most of the stones were old slabs of granite—some tall, some short, a few ornate and beveled, one obelisk with a decorative finial.

Sycamores stood tall behind the graveyard. Their branches threw shadows across the stones. Wisteria draped the elms, red cedars, and sweetgums, formed an awning over the graves, shielding the corpses beneath the earth from daytime's sweltering heat.

Eva Clare grew up watching real ghosts. About nine o'clock every night when the sky got good and black and the birds settled in to roost and the woods got quiet, the spirits came out of the graves. She could see them better in winter when the sycamores were only white skeletons and everything held close to the earth.

Summer nights, she and her friends, and often some kids from town, would walk down the lane, sit on the wood rail fence by the barn, and wait for dark. She always felt goose bumps rise on her arms when it was about to happen. When all the objects went black with their shadows, and the line between ground and air dissolved into pitch, and form and definition disappeared, the kids quieted, sat still as the gravestones, and stared into the blackness. They waited, like molded vinyl dolls with eyes fixed wide open. Every time was like the first time.

A filmy white apparition would come up from a grave, then perhaps another ghost would follow, and float and flit around, between the obelisk and beveled slabs, up to the wisteria blossoms, to the blackberry bushes on the western fence, to the gate on the barn side, among the stones, flickering, slowing, dissipating. Spirits of her ancestors. Ghosts on the oxbow.

Grandmomma said young'uns down the generations had watched the ghosts—even her as a girl. But as a grownup, she called a chemistry professor at Delta State College and got a scientific explanation. Something about the phenomenon of spontaneous combustion of methane gas originating from decomposing remains in marshy ground, creating the appearance of misty, phosphorescent swirls. Will-o'-the-wisps. Nobody believed him, though. It was far more exciting to believe in ghosts.

Had the ghosts come out tonight?

5   REVENANT

She's back. She's home.
She's here for the reckoning, the healing, the liberation.
One hundred twenty years have come and gone,
and so have I, but not truly gone,
for she is here, and she is me.
I course through her veins.
I dwell in her matter.
I see hope.
Hope that she will carry on what I could not.

6   THE PATRIARCH AND THE PROFESSOR

Saturday morning, Eva Clare sat fidgeting in the pastor's office at the Beulah Lake church. She kneaded her hands together, then rubbed the tops of her thighs. She crossed her legs, shifted, crossed them the other way, rocked, forward and backward. The new preacher had a bedhead hairstyle and wore jeans. Old Brother Shurden never even owned a pair.

"I'll be glad to read the eulogy you prepare for Mrs. Carlyle's service," Dr. Loring said, his elbows on the desk, forearms folded and stacked.

"I'd like to do it myself." It was the third time she'd told him. "When I was a little girl, my grandmother stood in the pulpit of this church and gave the eulogy for my father. Now, I want to do it for her."

Dr. Loring leaned back and swiveled in his leather chair. It creaked, as did other things that were set in an unfitting groove, dried out, warped, or antiquated—like old wood floors, barn doors, and assorted religious beliefs. In front of the preacher were an open Bible and a few commentaries. The screensaver on his computer monitor was black with red wavy lines scrolling—the only thing moving in the room, for this man certainly wasn't budging. He was adamant about doing the entire service himself.

"I've got a manual with funeral sermons in it," he said. "I'll read some scriptures about death—one in Revelation, one in Romans, and all of Psalm twenty-three."

Eva Clare raked her bangs back. Her fingernails scraped against her forehead. She swung her crossed leg as she listened to the preacher prattle on.

"At her service I'll share the 'good news' of eternal life with everybody there," he said.

Those people had already heard the plan of salvation—once a week for eighty years, because they were old and they'd presumably been to church every Sunday of their lives. One service a Sunday for eighty years was more than four thousand sermons. Two services a Sunday, eight thousand. How many times did a person need to hear the gospel before they believed, accepted, and acted on it in their everyday lives? If they hadn't gotten it by now, they likely weren't ever going to get it. Besides, her grandmother's funeral wasn't the place to preach to sinners. And also, Eva Clare didn't want the canned service everybody else got.

She cleared her throat. "I want her service to be personal."

The preacher smiled, wrinkled his nose, shook his head. "You shouldn't have to worry about the details. This is your time of mourning. I'll take care of everything for you."

He was separated from her by the massive desk and by the way he talked down to her. Was he patronizing her?

She was taught to respect the clergy. Taught not to question authority. But shootfire! If her grandmother wasn't worth standing up for, nothing was. "Honoring my grandmother will help me heal. I want to do this."

"I'll be glad to read the words you write."

She was getting to the point of frustration and outright exploding. "Did you ever even meet my grandmother?"

"I haven't been in Erin long. I haven't met all the shut-ins yet."

"Did you know her ancestors founded this church? Gave the land it sits on? Built this sanctuary brick by brick? Did you know she sang in the choir, taught Sunday School, led the Women's Missionary Union? Gave above her tithe?"

"She was assuredly a good servant of the Lord." The preacher blinked repeatedly.

Eva Clare's chest pinched. She watched Dr. Loring thrum his fingers on the desk a couple of times, watched the discomfort in his posture, watched his youth and inexperience melt over the leadership he tried to display. She looked at his degree on the wall. He'd recently completed his doctorate. Beside the seminary name was a blue shield with a white cross, an open Bible at the juncture of the bars. She tightened her lips, wrinkled her brows, started to see the light. What was happening here was a literal translation of the Bible. She snarled, shook her head. Over the last forty years, her denomination had gone through a slow shift from a moderate to a conservative stance. Churches now promoted a more subservient role for women, and some congregations were strict about it. Women were not to usurp authority over men. Women were to keep silent in the church—sit on the pews like plastic dolls that didn't open their painted mouths or blink their glassy eyes.

This man wasn't going to let her stand in his pulpit and speak because she was a woman.

What authority on earth or in heaven or hell did he have to deny her the right to pay tribute to her grandmother in her family's church? She grew up in this church. Got baptized here. Learned about the priesthood of the believer, that every person—man *and* woman—had direct access to God and equal potential to minister. She didn't believe women were inferior, even though she was married to a man who did. She'd already been betrayed by one disingenuous religious patriarch, and by golly, she wouldn't take it again. She got up and headed for the door.

"Oh, but wait, we haven't agreed on a day or time for the service," Dr. Loring said.

She quickened her pace.

"Kiss my butt," she whispered once she was out of his range of hearing.

Eva Clare trudged up the town side of the levee which was maybe fifty feet high with a steep grade. The sun pounded down, and she struggled to breathe the heavy air. She forced herself to keep moving, one foot in front of the other. Her leg muscles ached. Reaching the apex, she looked behind her at the rooftops of Erin. She crossed the narrow, newly graveled road that spanned the width of the levee, then hustled down the other side. Her old childhood pathway was covered up with volunteer trees and saplings, as well as noxious weeds—greenbriers, alligator grass, spear grass. Eva Clare could tell which way to go by the ancient, gigantic jungle on her left between the levee and the river. Her old path had once grazed the edge of it.

Briers pulled at her pants, snagged the leather of her boots. She stumbled, pulled free, moved forward. Sweat ran down her face. It was hot, too hot to walk to the river, and the brush was too grown up to navigate, but she was mad, hurt, and hell-bent on going. She needed her childhood comfort place, needed peace at the water.

The forest, shady and cool, covered her as she stepped into its shade. Virgin hardwoods with thick trunks and woody vines towered over her. Their branches dripped last night's rain. A clamminess lay on her skin. The soft, damp carpet of past seasons' leaves and needles smothered unwanted growth, and she walked easily and unencumbered, taking in the sweet scent of wet evergreen. She tiptoed around painted pools of stagnant water holding circles of colors—emerald green, yellow florescent, and bright lavender. She pushed through low-hanging branches and stepped over tree roots. The entire Delta was once like this, Grandpop Binky had said—a wilderness—before settlers like her people and their slaves came to clear it and plant cotton.

The jungle opened to sky and water—the wide expanse of the Mississippi River. Choking back snivels and glad tears, she claimed her old secret spot at Prentiss Landing, a jutted-out place, where she used to come, think, watch barges, and figure things out. She sat down on the dirt, bent her knees, the toes of her boots touching the wake nibbling in. The sun was high overhead yet lay across the sparkling, golden water. The breeze off the river cooled her.

A tow of thirty barges glided down the channel. Counting was easy. Six rows of five barges.

The strong-rolling, ever-coming water hypnotized her. The river was constant and dependable—exactly what she needed right now. She squinched her eyes, pictured it carrying away her troubles and emptying them into the great gray gulf far south. Maybe she should bring Grandmomma's ashes here and not fool with a funeral and that snooty preacher.

Plink.

The sound of a pebble hitting water.

Someone else was out here in the middle of nowhere. She hunched, tightened to a ball, no longer felt safe. Someone could have boated over from Big Island to check on a whiskey still they'd hidden in the woods. Only bad people lived on Big Island, Grandpop used to say—lawbreakers, murderers, bootleggers. Maybe a new generation Perry Martin moonshiner.

Plink. Plink. Plink.

Someone was hidden behind the stand of cane south of her, skipping rocks.

Then, a whistle. A man's whistle—loud, strong. The line of a song. Four blaring syllables: *Ol' man ri-ver.* He kept whistling, and she could tell he was moving toward her. She stiffened, froze, held her breath. The only people nearby were the riverboat crew, and they were too far away to help.

She looked in the direction of the whistle-sound, waiting for the man to appear. Nothing but cane and the jungle trees: some leaning, a few dead, some with big leaves and white trunks standing higher than the others. The sycamores, tallest of the deciduous, trees of protection and favors. Grandmomma called them "ghost trees" because their whitish bark stood out strong in the woods, notably at night under a big moon. Their branches looked like arms outstretched, especially when bare of leaves. *Help me,* she pleaded.

The man appeared on the path from behind the massive canebrake. He didn't look so scary. He was clean cut, dressed in khakis and a blue polo. Hair short, darkish, graying. Cleft chin. He was looking at the river, likely here on a clearing-of-the-mind walk, as she was. She was confident he wasn't a bootlegger—wasn't going to kill her to protect his whiskey still.

He got nearer, saw her, and stopped, seemingly startled at her presence.

She quickly glanced away at the river, tried to make it look like she hadn't seen him, but caught movement in her peripheral vision.

He took a step closer, held up a hand in a wave. "Hey there," he called out. "I don't mean to frighten you."

She looked, gave a nod, but no smile.

"Are you alone out here?" he asked.

"No." After all, there were the riverboat men.

He looked around. "Your husband must be fishing nearby."

She shrugged, shook her head. "I live close."

"Yeah, me, too. I come here every day. It's peaceful." He started walking toward her.

"I grew up here. I don't know you." The wind whipped her hair in her face. She pushed it back and held it.

"I'm Roy Winslow. I moved here in January to do some genealogy and writing."

Pete had mentioned a seminary professor on sabbatical. "From New Orleans?"

"How'd you know that?"

"It's a small town." She smiled, which Roy appeared to take as an invitation to move closer.

"I'm learning about that," he said. "I can't grill a steak without the whole town knowing if it's sirloin, rib eye, or T-bone. I'm not sure if the butcher spills the beans or if the townsfolk smell it charring or if they all have binoculars watching me."

"All of the above, I assure you."

They both laughed.

"I'm Eva Clare Carlyle. My grandmother died, and I just arrived home."

"Sweet Evelyn?"

"Of course, you would know that."

"She was on the prayer list at the church I sometimes attend. Easy deduction." He closed the distance between them. "I'm sorry for your loss."

"Do you teach at the seminary?"

"Yes, an Old Testament history class. But I'm a tenured professor at a university."

"You preach?" she asked.

"I teach. I'm not an ordained minister. I'm licensed, I speak when asked, but I don't call it preaching."

"You do funerals?"

"I have."

Something about him—maybe his kind smile, his compassionate eyes—made her want to tell him all about how the young minister had made her feel a little while ago and the fundamental wrongness he'd exhibited.

Roy tossed a rock into the water. "Look, if you want me to lead Sweet Evelyn's service, I'll be happy to, and you don't have to explain why."

"Why?" The muddy river showed white caps as it rolled by. The tow was way on down. "*Why?* It's that young preacher. That's why."

"You don't have to explain." Roy held up a hand.

"He's . . . he's a backward literalist."

Roy clamped his lips, pinched a smile.

"I only want to say some memorable words about my grandmother at her service. It's not like I want to preach a sermon. The reverend wouldn't hear of it." She caught herself and stopped. Maybe Roy was new wave, too. "Would you? Would you let me give her eulogy?"

He nodded. "Of course."

"Thank you. I want you to do her funeral, please, if you will. How do I set this up? I don't want to talk to that preacher again."

"Call the funeral director. Set the time. Tell him I'm doing the service. We'll have it in the chapel there, if that's okay with you. I'll also call. It's Mr. Rawl over in Cleveland, right?"

"Yes, thank you. There's only a viewing and service—no graveside. She'll be cremated. I'll take care of her ashes later."

That was easy. She didn't have to fight. She'd been all geared up for a fray. Now, a letdown, and the tears of reversed emotion spilled onto her cheeks.

Roy leaned over and gave her shoulder a squeeze. "Are you going to sit here a while, or shall we walk back?"

She smiled at him through the glaze, wiped her eyes, and stood as he caught her arm to lend support. She started over toward the ancient jungle trees.

"Where are you going?"

"Back to the levee, to town, home."

"Why're you going into the brush? There's a path straight ahead." He pointed.

"A path?"

"Yeah, I asked when I moved here about walking to the river, and I was told that the hunting club due north keeps the equivalent of a one-lane road mowed along their fence row all the way up to the levee. Easy walk. I believe it's always best in life to seek, find, and follow the path that is cleared before you, Eva."

"Eva Clare."

"Eva Clare. How come they don't call you Sweet Eva Clare?" He tilted his head and looked at her teasingly.

"That should be obvious." She laughed.

He did, too.

They walked back to Beulah Lake and Eva Clare's house.

"Wanna come in for a cold drink?"

"Sure."

She opened the back door to smells of down-home comfort food—the same smells that used to fill this kitchen when Marthala cooked. Lily, mitts on her hands, lifted a dish out of the oven, looked at Eva Clare, then Roy, and pushed the oven door shut with her foot. "Wha's up?"

"I ran into Roy at the river. Lily, have you met Roy?"

"Yeah, at Pete's. How you doin'?" She nodded in Roy's direction and set her dish down.

"Hot and thirsty right now, but otherwise, well."

"Smells so good," Eva Clare said. "What are you cooking?"

"Baking catfish fillets coated with buttermilk and crushed cornflakes. Also, butter beans, cornbread, and fried squash with onions. Y'all want some?"

"Maybe later for me. Roy, you?"

"No, thank you."

"What would you like to drink? Water, Coke, tea?"

"Water's fine."

Eva Clare reached into the cabinet for a glass. "Roy's doing Sweet Evelyn's service."

"Didn't go favorable with the new pastor, huh?" Lily's eyes lit up. "He ain't gon let you get up in the pulpit and speak, is he? 'Cause you're a woman." She slapped her leg and cackled.

Eva Clare set the tumbler down hard on the counter and jerked her face toward Lily. "How'd you know that?" So far, Lily had always been one up and right.

"Uh huh, struck a nerve." Lily's expression soured. "Seems like some things don't ever move forward, and some things move backassward."

Eva Clare dug a handful of ice cubes out of the freezer bin, dropped them clinking into the glass, filled it with water, and turned the tap off with excessive force. How primitive of that preacher for silencing her! Like the Mississippi River girl in her water dreams, her paintings—eyes shut, hands over her mouth.

"Everybody's not like him," Lily said. "I know people in every one-stoplight town around here because of sellin' my quilts and doin' home-health visits. I've seen preachers move into these small churches and try to tell folks that women are to be submissive. I've heard the church women fuss about it behind the preachers' backs." Lily took the glass lid off her baked catfish and set it on the counter. Steam lifted from the pan. "But those old women are gon keep on livin' like they always have." She shed her mitts. "They ran their households like Army sergeants and told their husbands what to do, when to do it, what to eat, and what to wear. Even picked out their clothes. They ran the church, too. Soon, they'll all be dead and gone, and that church won't have a membership, except for a few young people that believe like the preacher on account of it's all they've ever heard."

Roy nodded in agreement. Eva Clare handed him the glass of water, then sat down with a long sigh and nothing to drink. Her grandmother was dead. Her town was dying. Her growing-up church was going backward toward elimination. What was wrong with this place?

"What some of them preachers don't take into account is that the man was asleep when the woman was created," Lily continued. "The son of God came out of a woman's womb, and no man put him there. It was a woman at the foot of the cross, and women were first to the empty tomb. Men had no part in creation, salvation, and resurrection." Lily spooned servings onto her plate. "Y'all are sure welcome to have some."

"I couldn't eat a heavy meal right now," Roy said.

Lily scowled at Roy. "So, what brought you here? Nobody ever moves to this town, 'specially from the North."

"The North? I thought you were from New Orleans," Eva Clare said.

"I live there now, but I'm from Illinois. I'm doing genealogy for my Winslow surname. I believe my people lived in this area at one time. I'm here to find out."

Lily stuck a fork in her cornflake-crusted catfish and shook her head. "Winslow? No. Uh uh. You ain't ever had family to live here. I mean stay here, own land, plant cotton. Not in this town. I don't recognize that name."

"Lily!" Eva Clare's face turned warm.

"Well, he hasn't. My family's been here, with yours, since the beginning, and we passed down the names and stories. We kept a record of all the families—White, Black, Chinese, Indian. My people do that." Lily clapped her hands like it was a punctuation mark to end the thought, picked a crumb from the catfish, and popped it into her mouth.

Eva Clare patted the air to tamp Lily down. Lily needed to pile some butter beans in her trap and shut herself up.

Lily looked at Roy. "You want to know anything, you talk to me." She waggled two fingers from him to her, then picked up her plate, mumbled something about her show being on TV, and left the room.

"I hope she didn't offend you," Eva Clare said.

Roy shook his head. "No, not at all. She makes me wonder if I'm on the wrong track. I might've come here for nothing. She's right. The Black culture passes down oral histories. Some know who their family slave owners were, perhaps their whereabouts before slavery, the churches in their past, even the White churches before the slaves became freedmen. They also know former neighboring landowners and slaves." Roy looked out the windows toward the oxbow lake. "She emphasized 'live here, stay here, own land, plant cotton.'"

"They're oral stories. Details could've gotten confused or embellished."

"True, but there have been studies conducted on the Black culture and their slave narratives. Those who couldn't read or write oftentimes drew pictures that told their story. Those who could read and write kept diaries. They've even quilted history to preserve it."

"Lily does quilt."

"I need to talk to her."

"I've known her grandmother all my life, and she told stories but never said anything about her history."

"She wouldn't have told you. She would've told her own children." Roy drank his water. "Some children are interested in stories of bygone days, and some don't care. I remember my grandmother pointing out names on tombstones and telling me a tale about each ancestor. I've studied genealogy for years, and all I've accomplished is to find documentation for the stories she told."

"Maybe down here in the South we're inherently ashamed of our family stories. We're defined by religion, but many families have closet sins they never bring to light."

"That's true everywhere."

"Yeah, but my Southern ancestors were slave owners and civil rights violators. My fourth-great-grandfather owned slaves in the 1860s, and in the 1960s, an uncle got blood on his hands from civil rights murders. And Grandmomma Sweet Evelyn, pure and religious as she was, and she was as devout as anyone I've ever known, was no saint. She cut a niche for herself on the wrong side of history."

"What do you mean?"

"During the civil rights movement, she went with the status quo like everybody else, meaning she aligned with a subtle systemic racism. She wouldn't have called it that, didn't even know the term, and didn't have a clue what she was doing."

"People have reasons for their quirks and behaviors. And some are shrouded in mystery. I've got a gut feeling there's something I don't know about my Civil War ancestor," Roy said. "I think my grandmother felt it, too. We found a reference to Mississippi in his papers—a poem he wrote about a Delta girl. We know he came down the river during the war."

"You've been here for six months and haven't found anything meaningful yet?"

"Part of my sabbatical includes writing and publishing history, so I've been busy with that. I'm researching old Mississippi ghost towns, once-thriving river ports made extinct due to the river's changing course—Port Royal, Princeton, Leota, Victoria, and Prentiss. Also, Napoleon, Arkansas, across the river from Prentiss."

"I might like to sit in when you talk with Lily."

"I might like to come back here and talk with both of you. But first, we'll take care of Sweet Evelyn's celebration of life."

7 "Sweet Evelyn" Bounds Carlyle

Eva Clare eased into Rawl's Funeral Home, its lobby full of floral sofas, reproduction Queen Anne cabriole-leg tables, and pastel Monet prints on the walls. Kleenex boxes everywhere. Old folks started to assemble in little clutches. Roy Winslow set down the Styrofoam cup he was holding and came to greet her.

"I'll go with you to the viewing room," he said. "You should see your grandmother before others file through to pay respects." He pointed the direction with one hand and put his other hand on the small of her back.

A shiver ran through her.

"But first," he continued, "I want you to come to the chapel with me. I have something to show you." He guided her to the open double doors.

She looked in, drew a quick breath, put her hand to her heart. A mantle of warmth spread over her. Someone had draped quilts over the backs of the pews. "Lily's quilts." The words melted out of her mouth.

"Lily did this for you. She gathered all the quilts she had on consignment. Wanted to honor Mrs. Carlyle in an artful way that might be meaningful to you."

"It's such a kind gesture. I'm touched."

Sweet Evelyn lay in Viewing Room Three. Her hair was teased, fixed in a bouffant reminiscent of the early sixties, and she never wore that godawful shade of pink lipstick. Eva Clare sucked in a breath. "I didn't know it would be this hard to see her."

Roy folded his arms, tightened his lips.

It was only a viewing today for friends and church folks, and sometime after her celebratory service, cremation, with her ashes dispersed in the oxbow lake, as she'd requested in her final wishes.

Eva Clare steadied her feet, steeled herself. The sweet, sweet smell of lilies was about to suffocate her. Her growing-up memories pelted her like winter sleet. She had to hold back her feelings for now. In one hour, she'd stand at the podium in that quilt-filled chapel and eulogize Evelyn Carlyle—talk about her mid-twentieth-century beliefs, mightily defend them, and praise this woman who was a good Christian in the way Christians were good in Evelyn's time. With genuine fervor, Sweet Evelyn had prayed every single day for missionaries, home and abroad, witnessing to native souls. Yet at the same time, she'd kept her Black maid "in her place"—a degree of separation that inferred inferiority. She'd pulled Eva Clare out of public school on the cusp of integration and put her in a segregated academy. She'd believed in Blacks staying in their own churches because they had their own lively music and lots of congregational responses.

Eva Clare touched Sweet Evelyn's cheek, then quickly withdrew her hand. Her grandmother's face was hard and cold. But it seemed Evelyn had softened and warmed at the end of her life. As she got older, maybe she realized that equal was not separate and separate was not equal, for she took her aging Marthala in declining health into her own bedroom.

Doesn't it all eventually come home to us? It's more like a return of what we've sown. We have to face the effects of what we've done to others, and maybe even what our beloveds before us did, so our souls can rest for eternity. Eva Clare would speak to this in her eulogy, and she'd do it in a lyrical way so the old folks would dwell on the beauty of her words over the truth in her message.

She pointed to an old piece of Victorian jewelry pinned to Sweet Evelyn's dress—a cameo of brass and pink shell with a white dove on it. "She's wearing the brooch handed down from her mother and grandmother. It's special in our family."

Who gave it to the funeral director? Lily? It had to be Lily. She must've brought it when she brought the quilts.

"I'd like to keep that."

Roy reached into the casket, unpinned and removed the brooch, and put it in Eva Clare's hand. She tightened her fist around the oval piece and stepped back from the casket. Then pinned it to her dress.

Silver-haired ladies with hunchbacks in black dresses and bald-headed men with paunches in black suits entered the door one by one and stood in a long line. They all filed by to say nice things to Eva Clare and look at Sweet Evelyn.

Pete and Angie Wong stopped to share a memory, but Gerald Tanner, next in line with his wife Jo, waved them on to keep the line moving. Then Anna Laurel, Sunny, and Meredith walked in together, bringing a sweet assurance with them.

While greeting other visitors, Eva Clare watched the three women inch toward her. Rekindling the closeness they once had gave her hope for the coming days. She'd already given in to Sunny, who called yesterday, wanting to set up a girlfriend supper-gathering at sundown after the funeral on the Carlyle pier at the oxbow lake. The girls would take care of everything.

Pretty much all of Erin attended the funeral. Except Lily. Where was Lily?

From the

EULOGY *for* EVELYN BOUNDS CARLYLE
by Eva Clare Carlyle

God brought forth this place of Evelyn Carlyle's pride—Mississippi Deltaland. He sculpted river mud, smoothed and shaped it with His own hands as a potter creates a precious vessel, then sparked it to life. He planted his own people here to put seeds in rich earth, to dandle a cradle of cotton, to consummate a harvest of hard work, to fill this crescent basin with livelihood.

He put his people here to labor and love. Coghlan family hands down the line worked this land, wore it on their skin, breathed it, became one with it, returned to it—Coghlan flesh pressed into Delta dirt. That's what you do when you take pride in a place—you carry it on you and in you, you toil for its potential, and you bear its traditions forward.

Right or wrong, you do not know, yet you carry the traditions onward like your people before you did, until your eyes are opened to a more honorable way. God has no hands on earth but ours. Evelyn Carlyle toiled diligently with her hands. She planted, sowed, and reaped. She looked at her handiwork, perceived a need for transformation, and with an open and humble heart, she planted and sowed again and fixed her sights on a plentiful harvest. Evelyn Carlyle's hands altered the course.

"To every thing there is a season, and a time to every purpose under the heaven: A time to be born, and a time to die; a time to plant, and a time to pluck up that which is planted . . . a time to heal . . . a time to build up . . . a time to keep silence, and a time to speak. . . . I perceive that there is nothing better, than that a [woman] should rejoice in [her] own works; for that is [her] portion: for who shall bring [her] to see what shall be after?" Ecclesiastes 3:1-8, 22 KJV

Evelyn Carlyle went before me, and I stand poised at the end of the oxbow Coghlans. I commit to bringing about an honorable "after" to Evelyn Carlyle's works and to finishing her course transmogrified into an inclusive kingdom of love and acceptance.

8

THE FAB FOUR

Carrying a sack of flashlights, citronella candles, and matches, Eva Clare walked the scantily graveled path from her patio to a clearing at the oxbow, passing Marthala's neglected tomato and pepper garden and a tall pole that held painted-gourd purple martin houses.

The sun slid behind the cypress brake on the western side of the oxbow and backlit the trees. Feathery branches filtered lacy shadows across the water. Thick heat hampered activity. Hopefully, her sleeveless linen top would be cool enough for this girlfriend get-together.

The pier ended in a hexagonal deck with posts at the angles. The platform held a circle of six Adirondack chairs and a center cypress table, all old and timeworn. Tiki torches were attached to the posts. As she lit the first torch, she heard music blaring from a car—the Beach Boys, "Fun, Fun, Fun"—and turned to see her friends zooming up the driveway in front of a cloud of dust. Anna Laurel was driving the antique Thunderbird convertible that had belonged to her father. They took the left fork in the lane and ended up lakeside.

Anna Laurel, Sunny, and Meredith trundled down the pier carrying canvas tote bags bulging with food and wine. Their feet pounded against the planks and shook the decking.

"Hey, y'all!" Eva Clare waved. She got a gaggle of heys back.

The girls dropped their bags on the table and gave her tight hugs and vows for renewed friendship, then chattered away as they set up dinner.

Eva Clare lit five more tikis. Yellow flames licked the sky against a fiery sunset. Fishy-smelling water lapped at the base of the pier, and a familiar warm, evening breeze off the lake brushed against her face.

She closed her eyes. She was home. Home on her family's pier, where she and these same girls took sunbaths as teenagers, sat on weekend nights with flashlights and told ghost stories, lay under the stars on summer nights and wondered out loud how far away in this big wide world their lives would take them.

"C'mon, Eva Clare. Sit down." Meredith pointed to a chair. "Have some wine. You've had a hard day." Meredith gave her a napkin and set a stack on the table.

Eva Clare eased herself into an Adirondack.

Anna Laurel poured a glass of red and handed it to her. "Good job on your grandmother's eulogy, E. C. It's noble that you're committed to bringing an honorable 'after' to Sweet Evelyn's works."

"Yeah, but I didn't understand the last sentence." Sunny set out serving spoons and took a sip of Perrier with lime. She always believed it was a sin to drink wine. "Mog . . . mogrified? What does that word mean?"

"Transmogrified. Means change," Anna Laurel said. "She could've said change, but some people don't like change. Right, E. C.?"

"Right."

Anna Laurel picked up a paper plate and handed it to Eva Clare. "Here, help yourself."

Eva Clare fanned her steamy face with the plate before she plopped chicken salad on it. The other women took their seats in the circle and piled food on their Chinets.

"Y'all, try some of this black-eyed-pea paté." Sunny smeared the paste on crostini. "It's got country ham and shiitake mushrooms in it."

Even though she was divorced, Sunny still wore her humongous diamond engagement ring—on her right hand.

"What's in this chicken salad, Anna Laurel?" Meredith winked approval.

"Grapes, green onions, pecans, pineapple, basil, chicken, and mayo, a recipe I've had for forty years. I'm no cook. This is my go-to."

"It's delicious." Eva Clare leaned back and looked out over Beulah Lake as the sun surrendered and the land and water went gray with splashes of pink. Purple martins circled the gourd-houses, and starlings settled in the trees to roost.

"Remember we used to practice cartwheels on this pier? You, Mere—" Sunny pointed at Meredith— "went crooked one time and wheeled right into the lake. We laughed so hard, we almost fell in, too." Sunny still found it funny and inspired giggles in them all. "Those were the good old days."

"We had so much fun on this pier," Eva Clare said. "I wish we could've stayed here forever, young and innocent."

"It was the best of times," Sunny said.

"Oh, no," Anna Laurel protested. "It was the best of times, but it was also the worst of times. Of course, the opposite of best is not worst, but the absence of best, which includes second best. You know, like second place is first loser."

Anna Laurel still had her quick wit and proclivity to disagree and debate.

"Well, I don't get that," Sunny mumbled.

"Of course, you don't," Anna Laurel said. "The worst of times? We were second graders when Khrushchev pounded his shoe on a podium and said he'd bury us. We were fifth graders when Kennedy got shot."

"You're too negative." Meredith shook a finger at Anna Laurel. "I'd say it was the age of wisdom. We went to the moon the summer after tenth grade. Best of times, worst of times, age of wisdom. Like it said in that novel we read our junior year. Remember? *A Tale of Two Cities.*"

Anna Laurel waved her off. "Everybody knows it was a time of foolishness. Hippies, drugs, protests. Radical change in progress." She leaned forward. "And we were so naïve. Wrapped up in our teenage-girl world of cute clothes, records, ballgames, dances, and parties."

"And boys," Sunny said with her mouth full.

"Honestly, I think it was a frightful time back then," Anna Laurel said. "We grew up with the H-bomb, the Vietnam War, civil rights marches, sit-ins, the fight over integration—"

"We were separate but equal!" Sunny said.

Everyone got quiet and averted their eyes from Sunny.

Anna Laurel held out a bottle of Storyteller Merlot. "Anybody need more wine?"

Meredith offered some pepper jelly palmiers. "Chives, Parmesan cheese, and hot pepper jelly on puff pastry."

Anna Laurel crinkled her brows. "You want a palmier and a glass of wine, Sunny?"

"You know I don't drink."

"And I also know we were never separate but equal." Anna Laurel teetered the bottle in front of Sunny.

Everybody went still and silent.

Two mallards flew over, sending out raspy, quacking calls.

"It's so peaceful here." Eva Clare looked at the water reflecting a lone streak of pink in the deep gray of dusk. "Except for Sunny and Anna Laurel and the ducks."

"Yeah, this feels good," Meredith said. "Us being together again. Like we always were, with Sunny and Anna Laurel going at it." She picked up a palmier and handed it to Anna Laurel. "Here, hon, put this in your mouth. Chew and hush. We're back together for the first time in a long time. Don't screw it up. Y'all be nice."

They harked back to the fun days of their youth in a sheltered hamlet, where they slid down the levee on cardboard squares, skied on the lake, and smoked grapevines in the woods. Old stories whirled about Eva Clare's head. Their unabashed laughter echoed out over the lake.

Eva Clare watched the pale streak in the water thin. "Hard to believe this quiet lake was once a busy river." She pointed to her old brick home. "When my ancestors built their house on the riverbank, they had to use a boat to get in and out. No roads inland. The jungle, too thick."

"Then the Yanks changed the river and cut off the oxbow from the rest of the world," Anna Laurel said. "Made it a narrow loop of lake." She made a backward C with her right hand to depict the shape of the oxbow. "Loop of lake."

The oxbow . . . cut off . . . from the world. Eva Clare looked at the plate of food on her lap and crunched her napkin in her fist. The crushing burden of loss settled down on her. Gave her a pain unlike any she'd ever felt. "I am this loop of lake. Cut off from my world, too. Had a family, job, home, grandmother. Lost them all in a two-month timeframe."

The water showed no pink now, only gray.

"I'm so sorry, E. C.," Anna Laurel said. "I guess we're all like that river. Our lives had callings that took us far off. Except for you, Sunny. You stayed in Erin. We've all had tough losses—death, divorce, and financial devastation—that ripped us out of our worlds and brought us back here." She slapped a mosquito on her leg, wiped the blood off with her napkin, wadded it up, and deposited it in a garbage bag. "After graduation, we went our separate ways. Me? I had to get out of this town. After I earned my law degree, I left Mississippi, moved to South Carolina, joined a law firm in Columbia. Owned a condo in the city and a house on Folly Island, the Edge of America. Nobody lived out back of me. Only nature and a mighty ocean with waves rolling in and out, and those waves washed over every grain of sand with the same force. It was freeing and healing, and I came to myself there."

"I had to get out of this town, too." Eva Clare opened her napkin, smoothed the wrinkles. "I felt squashed here. Held down, held back. All my life I was taught to sit down, shut up, and don't rock the boat. To take whatever came to me. I couldn't do it anymore."

"Me? I left because of color TV." Meredith scooped chicken salad with a wheat cracker.

"Huh?" Sunny said.

They sent puzzled gazes Meredith's way.

"Really! I did. We had a black-and-white TV till I was ten, and when we got our first color set, I saw a whole different world out there—a big, beautiful world in living color. I wanted to be part of *that* world." Meredith held up her wine glass and eyed the deep burgundy. "I'm sad to lose my world, but it helps that we're all back together here in Erin."

"Back here in Erin? It's an echo of high school," Anna Laurel said. "I'm driving the same car, living in the same house, sleeping in the same bed, sitting on the same pier with my BFFs."

Sunny smiled. "It shows how much y'all love our sweet little town."

"No, it shows how desperate we are." Anna Laurel poured more wine. "Most kids don't come back after college. That's why downtown is dying, and I hear there are only nine seniors at the academy for fall semester."

"Yeah, what's up with that?" Sunny said, picking up a basket. "Here, y'all, have one of my lemon-filled croissants. I baked them from scratch.

It's my own recipe. I even laminated the dough and made my own lemon curd."

Meredith and Eva Clare reached for a croissant, as Anna Laurel replied. "Do the math, Sunny. Young people go off to college, marry, get jobs in progressive cities—"

"And the old folks die off, leaving ghost towns all over the Delta," Eva Clare interjected. "I drove through many of those dried-up hamlets on the way home. It's sad."

"It really is sad," Meredith agreed.

Anna Laurel stuck a meatball with her fork, put it in her mouth, and ate it without spilling sauce on her white pants. "I'm a small business owner. I keep up with local population stats so I can plan for success." She wiped her mouth with a napkin. "Success. Pfoo. That's a joke. The population of our county is sixty-five percent Black, and surprisingly, many towns are still, for the most part, segregated. In Erin, the old unspoken tradition of no Blacks living in the city limits still exists, which means a large portion of the population won't shop in our stores. They don't feel welcome. We limit ourselves with this practice."

Eva Clare choked on her croissant and coughed. "They're living here now," she whispered. Lily, Marthala, living in her house. Her confession went unheard.

"Thirty-seven percent of our county lives in poverty," Anna Laurel continued. "They can't afford my nice coffee blends."

"So that means you need to offer plain, cheap coffee, too," Sunny said. "Which I do."

"Tell me more about your business," Eva Clare said.

"I bought what you'll remember was the old Downtown Diner that closed ten years ago. Fixed it up, made it into a destination coffee shop."

"It's cute, what she's done with it," Meredith said. "It's an updated nook with crisp colors. I go there, drink coffee—her *nice* blends—and work on my laptop when I've got copy to write for a client. I'm usually the only one there."

"Damn." Anna Laurel huffed. "I wish you wouldn't say that."

"All around her, stores are boarded up or going under, like Betsy's Trunk."

"I don't understand why that's happenin'," Sunny said. "I've lived here all my life, and this was always such a cute, little lake town with a variety of shops and friendly people."

"You didn't see the change happening because you never left, and the decline took place slowly over time," Eva Clare said. "Coming back to visit Grandmomma over the years, I watched Erin—and the whole Delta—go down. All I know is that we used to have a strong cotton economy with planters depending on their field hands, and to keep that system in place, local leaders had to keep out industries that might lure laborers away from the fields. Then the farms became mechanized, and the laborers had no jobs."

"So, to sum it up," Anna Laurel interrupted, "this place went down because machines took over the hand-hoeing and hand-picking of cotton, but also because town leaders put all their efforts into keeping a large segment of the population poor and uneducated with no options but farm work. And then, no farm work." She turned up her wine glass for a big gulp. "It begs the question: Why did I start a business here? And why in the hell did we all come back?"

"Don't say that word," Sunny said.

"Hell," Anna Laurel repeated.

Eva Clare looked down and picked at her food. Meredith stopped chewing, looked away.

"Okay, I'll go first," Anna Laurel said. "Y'all are my girlfriends, and you deserve the truth. I'll tell you the real reason I'm here. Not the euphemized one. Financial devastation. Yes, that's it. I admit it. The downturn in the economy last year caused my firm to fail. The trickle-down of our clients' failures got us. I lost my job, both houses I owned, and my BMW. Even lost some of my investments. My parents had died, so I came to live in the old homeplace—on Daddy's money. I needed to recoup some of my losses. And my pride. For six months, I scouted the area—bigger cities like Cleveland, Greenville, Vicksburg—but couldn't find a job as an attorney. Got tired of looking. Tired of dead ends. So I decided to invest in Erin and do something different for a while. Now, I own this fancy coffee bean shop in a decaying river town where nobody gives a damn about coffee—and don't tell me not to say that word, Sunny

Louise. Give them a cheap, charred, firehouse brand under a dollar, and they're happy as pigs in shit. I'm struggling. I don't know what I'm going to do."

"You're gonna go straight to hell," Sunny said.

"I was anyway, even before I cussed," Anna Laurel confirmed.

"I'm in the same boat," Meredith said. "Not going to hell, but going under. My ad agency lost our two biggest clients because of the recession and had to close. The next week, my Roger died. My parents are gone, too. I've got random copy work for three of the old agency clients in Atlanta. It helps, but I'm living mostly on savings."

"You live in your daddy's house, too, Mere. Alone," Anna Laurel said.

"I'm not alone. I have a cat."

"A cat? My God, you don't want a cat. You live alone, you die alone. Cats'll eat you. Somebody will finally check on you after a week or two and find your rotting, nibbled-on body." Anna Laurel cackled at her own crass response.

They glared at her, and then six eyes landed on Eva Clare.

"My turn? Well, all right." Eva Clare took a flashlight from the table and shined its beam upward on her face. "I married a man who earned a degree in theology, then got his doctorate and became a psychologist. He counsels people on saving their marriages or putting their lives back together after abuse or loss. He cheated on me with a woman he was counseling, and he didn't want to save his own marriage. You know, rules are meant for others."

"Jerk," Sunny said. "I remember him from your wedding. He had one brown eye and one blue eye. Y'all married in July of the bicentennial year and used a patriotic blue and red in your color scheme." She shook a finger at Eva Clare. "Everybody knows summer weddings use only pastel colors." She shrugged a shoulder. "Didn't y'all meet at an Elvis concert?"

"Yep. At the Mid-South Coliseum in Memphis. The time Elvis bent over to kiss a fan and split his pants. Split. That was a sign. A red flag. It was the summer of '75, and the following Christmas, he gave me an engagement ring with a quarter-carat diamond, along with a biblically based book on how to be a good wife. Another red flag. Smack in the middle of the Women's Liberation Movement, church ladies were proclaiming their job was wifely submission. The husband came first, and the wife devoted her days to cooking good food for her king and planning creative ways to fulfill his sexual needs."

Anna Laurel smacked her forehead with the heel of her hand. "Kill me now."

"That book was supposed to teach me how to put some sizzle into my marriage: how to dress up cute—like a sexy cowgirl or a chorus girl—how to take off my clothes and seduce my husband. I once wore pink baby-doll pajamas and white go-go boots at dinner."

"Oh, my Lord!" Sunny squealed. "I had that same book. One time I greeted Donald at the door, naked as a jaybird, wrapped in Saran Wrap, with a big, red bow *down there*." She pointed to her lady part.

Eva Clare tilted her head. "It finally came to me that I was submitting to my husband in a way that was demeaning."

"Ya think?" Anna Laurel said.

"As predicted by Elvis's pants, we split. We're separated. Grandmomma gave me her house. That's the reason I'm here." Eva Clare turned the flashlight off and set it down.

"You're better off with that marriage ending," Anna Laurel said. "He's weak, needy, and can't keep a vow. You deserve better."

"Anna Laurel!" Meredith said.

"Well, he is, and she does."

"Men." Sunny fluttered her lips. "Donald left me for a younger woman. He wasn't kind or fair in the settlement. I'm tryin' my best to get my life together, too."

"The good ole South where we were born and raised." Anna Laurel waved her hands with a flourish. "Where men are rewarded for being manly men. Cowboys with white hats and guns. Lords, warriors, conquerors. And philanderers."

As the tiki torches flamed around her, Eva Clare looked up at twinkling stars pasted to a black Delta sky. She squinted her eyelids into slits, and all the stars faded. Then she blurred them away. Sometimes she wished she could blur the whole world and make it go away.

She studied the other women sitting in the firelight, talking, laughing, flames in their eyes. They all had stories of hard times and hurt feelings, of unfairness, loss, and life change. In their growing-up days, they shared good times mostly, but also some tears and tough times. The school walkout their senior year was one of the bitter experiences—that cold, drizzly December day in 1970, when they walked out the front doors of Erin High and never returned. The old school building stood there empty and abandoned for eighteen years before it was razed.

Now, all that was left of their old public school was its concrete foundation—like a scab for people to look at every time they drove by. Weeds grew through the cracks, and the sidewalk's broken, jagged, concrete shards pushed up by tree roots served as a reminder of how hate can shred a heart.

All that was left of her, too, was a shattered foundation. She had learned all the right fundamentals as a child growing up in a good home, small town, small church. But she didn't always get to see them practiced by the adults who taught her. Religion aligned with racism—that's what disturbed her the most, what she has carried with her all the years. Because of segregation, she and these girls graduated from Beulah Lake Baptist Church. The new private school wasn't completed during their senior year, so they sat in the church sanctuary in front of a stained-glass image above the baptistry. Jesus, with outstretched hands—savior to all— looked down on them. In front of the son of God, the church and the public school were in cahoots to keep the people divided and separated.

"Y'all remember the day of the Erin High walkout?" Eva Clare asked.

"Yes," Anna Laurel said. "Like a fire drill, we marched out. Then they shut down the public school."

"We walked to my house and sat on the front porch and cried," Meredith said. "I'm sure I cried more than y'all. It was a terribly sad day for me. Y'all never understood. We were leaving *public* school that was for everybody and going to *private Christian* school that was not. I'm not Christian. I'm Jewish. My family has always been Jewish. But I had to sit on a Baptist pew every day, pledge loyalty to the Christian flag, and pray to Jesus as savior. It was *not* my belief, *not* my family religious tradition. I was groomed by our teachers in *their* tradition. I was forced to learn and practice *their* faith, *your* faith. I felt pulled, traitorous, punished for who I was. I had stomachaches the rest of that year. Something in me died that semester. I think it was my free soul. My people came to America for freedom of religion. We no longer had that freedom." She ran her hand through her short, brown curls. "Oh my gosh. I'm so sorry. I didn't mean to go off like that."

Only silence came from the other three of the Fab Four.

The hard coldness of Meredith's concrete porch came back to Eva Clare. The wetness—rain, tears. The sidewalk leading to the porch—a crack ran the length of it.

December 11, 1970
Erin, Mississippi

After she was all cried out and the drizzling rain stopped, Eva Clare walked to the school parking lot, refusing to look at the brick building. She got into her green Karmann Ghia and drove home.

She flung the back door open. Grandmomma and Marthala were in the kitchen putting pink icing and sugar-flower decorations on her birthday cake. "Why, Grandmomma? Why'd y'all do it? Why'd you close our school?"

Grandmomma laid down her spreading knife. "It's what we had to do." She walked away, left the room, left the cake for Marthala to deal with.

Marthala held out her hands. "C'mere, baby." Marthala's stout arms pulled Eva Clare in and closed around her. "I'm so sorry, baby, you in your senior year." Marthala reached into her white dress uniform pocket and pulled out a Kleenex to wipe Eva Clare's tears. "It's yo' birthday. You need to hush all this cryin'. It gon be alright."

Eva Clare snatched the tissue. "No, it won't. Things will never be right again." She looked at the cake with colorful sugar-letters spelling HAPPY BIRTHDAY EVA. "I don't want only EVA on my cake."

"I know, baby, I'm 'on fix that. I'm 'on make CLARE go down the side. Mm hmm. Sit down at the table. Lemme getchu somethin' sweet."

"I don't want anything sweet." Eva Clare plopped into a chair. "I don't even want my cake. This is a horrible day."

Marthala sat down beside her, pulled the chair close, and listened to her go on and on about the protest. Eva Clare bawled and blubbered as she spewed every detail, reliving the footfalls of that final walkout from Erin High.

"And for what? Nobody's even tried to integrate, except for one girl five years ago, and she didn't stay but six weeks. The parents are acting on what *might* happen. Why is there so much hate for the Negroes?"

"I don' know, baby. People's scared things gon change. People's scared a what they don' know." She took back the Kleenex and dabbed her own eyes. "Been this way a long time. Ain't likely to change."

"I hate these people."

"Hate makes you jes like 'em. Let that hate go."

Eva Clare rested her head on Marthala's shoulder, and Marthala hugged her, rocked, hummed a hymn, and put an occasional line of words with the melody.

> *Love lifted me,*
> *When nothing else could help,*
> *Love lifted me.*

"Our parents wanted us safe in private school," Sunny said. The pier-party torchlights created dancing shadows on her face. "Wanted us to be with our own kind. But that was a sad day, for sure. That old school had character, history, and tradition. It was built in 1908, and my great-grandfather helped plant the oak trees in the schoolyard. There was a bench with his name on it."

"My people helped, too," Anna Laurel said.

Meredith nodded. "Mine supported the school, as well."

"And mine," Eva Clare added, looking out over the shadowy, spooky oxbow. "Hey! Y'all remember the night of the school break-in?"

They laughed, leaned in close together, and rehashed the story.

December 18, 1970
Erin High School
Erin, Mississippi

Friday night, one week after Eva Clare's birthday and the school walkout and one week before Christmas, the girls planned a sleepover at Meredith's house because she lived closest to the school. They were all in to help Eva Clare rescue the birthday gift she'd left behind in her locker on the day of the walkout. *Omnes pro uno.* They'd break into the forbidden schoolhouse to get the HOPE-charm necklace.

At midnight, when they were sure Meredith's parents were asleep, the girls got their flashlights, climbed out a bedroom window, and ran up the road to the school. Not a soul was out that time of night. Nobody could see them anyway because a fog was thick as split pea soup.

They took cover among the oaks, then sprinted toward the back wall of the building, inching toward the window of the boys' bathroom. Most of the time, that window stayed unlocked. The boys were always forgetting books needed for homework assignments and knew they could get in there and retrieve their materials.

The bottom of the window was over their heads, thus too high for the girls to easily slip in. Two of them would have to make a "basket," like they learned as cheerleaders forming a pyramid, by each grabbing their own right wrist with their left hand and clasping the other's left forearm with their right hand. Another girl would place her foot in the basket and be lifted to the brick ledge of the hopefully still-unlocked window.

"You're the tallest, Anna Laurel," Sunny said. "You climb in."

"No, you dope. Not me. I'll make the basket with Meredith. E. C., it's your necklace. You go."

"Fine," Eva Clare whisper-spat. "I'll go. I'll let the rest of you in through the janitor's door." She pointed to the west side of the building.

"What if we get caught?" Sunny said.

"Don't think about it. Shut up and follow us," Anna Laurel said.

Anna Laurel and Meredith stooped and grabbed wrists. Eva Clare stepped on their arms, and one, two, they dipped and lifted on three and raised her up. She held onto flat, rough concrete and brick with one hand and pushed open the heavy window with all the strength she could muster in her other hand. She put both forearms on the window ledge and levered herself up and in, making all kinds of straining noises as they hushed her from below. She slithered to the floor. Closed the window. Took the flashlight out of her jacket pocket and flicked it on. Ran to the side door, let the other three in.

They stood in the dark hallway. Grabbed arms, clung to each other. Inched down the long hall toward Eva Clare's locker. Held their breaths. A squeak came from upstairs, like a door opening. They stopped and pinched down on each other's arms.

"What was that?" Meredith said in a low voice.

"Don' know," the others whispered back.

They inched farther.

Then, a groan, a creak, maybe footsteps on the floor above.

They stopped again.

"I think somebody's in here," Anna Laurel said.

"Oh, Yahweh," Meredith muttered.

"We're dead," Eva Clare whispered.

"'What time I am afraid,'" Sunny quoted a Bible verse, "'I will put my trust in thee.'"

"Let's hurry to the locker." Eva Clare was desperate to get her necklace. "Turn off your flashlights. I'll use mine."

The group moved forward as one unit, clutching each other. They hobbled quickly, quietly, past classrooms, principal's office, chained front doors. Thud! Eva Clare stubbed her toes on the metal base of the water fountain. "Dang!" she cried. "Shh!" they responded. "Ouch!" she said.

Then, a low *oooooh*. Like a moan. From above.

They stopped, dug fingernails into jackets down to near flesh.

"Y'all, I've got to get that necklace," Eva Clare whispered. "A few more steps."

They made it to locker ninety-eight. Anna Laurel aimed and shined her flashlight and said, "Get it!" Sunny started to cry. Eva Clare turned the lock dial.

Slam! A door. From upstairs.

"Oh, Jesus!" Sunny whispered.

"Hurry! Hurry!" Anna Laurel said.

"Okay, okay." Eva Clare opened the door.

Then, a footstep on the stairs at the end of the hall. And another.

Anna Laurel squeaked out, "Hurry, hurry!"

Another footstep.

Eva Clare reached in, grabbed the necklace box, slammed the locker door, and they took off running to the janitor's door at the opposite end of the hall. They pushed it open, ran out, and panting and groaning, raced back toward Meredith's house.

Up a ways, as they crossed the highway, they heard the janitor's door slam again.

"That was so scary." Sunny slid a cracker through crab dip and looked around the pier-party circle at her friends. "I thought we were goners."

"We never did find out who else was in the school that night, did we?" Anna Laurel's face glowed orange in the torchlight.

"I'm sure whoever it was had a big laugh at our expense," Meredith said.

"Whatever happened to that necklace?" Anna Laurel asked.

Eva Clare reached under a slope-side of her V-neck linen shirt and pulled out the gold disc with a dove and the word HOPE engraved on it. "I'm still seeking hope and dry land."

"Oh, Eva Clare, you've been through a heartbreak, you poor dear," Meredith said. "And now losing Sweet Evelyn. What are your plans? What can I do to help you?"

"Do you need a job?" Anna Laurel leaned toward her with a concerned look.

Eva Clare nodded. "Honestly, I do. I've got to survive, and that means a paycheck."

"Go to Betsy's Trunk. Betsy's got to be ninety-nine by now. She can't run that store. Can't clean or manage the inventory. Can't remember to turn the lights off at night. I swear to God, she's going to burn down the town—and my coffee shop—by leaving those old lamps on."

"Bless her heart," Sunny said.

"Is she wanting to retire?" Eva Clare asked. Betsy was old, for sure—a gruff, hard-dealing, bold-spoken woman who took on estates when people died and sold some nice antiques. She'd been doing it all Eva Clare's life.

Furrows gathered between Anna Laurel's brows. "I don't know. She needs to. Go down there and tell her to. Tell her you'll be glad to take over the store. Work out a deal."

"I can't do that. That would be too pushy." Eva Clare tipped her head to one side. "Um, what kind of deal?"

"Hell, I don't know. You'll figure it out. I'll help with the legal stuff."

"Wait. Downtown is dead. You're running the coffee shop in the red and griping about it, and you want me to take over a business? Why?"

"Because. It's all there is. Don't choke hope." Anna Laurel swirled her wine. "I've had some thoughts about growth, and I've talked to Pete about it, but we need more support." She held up her glass. "Here's to us. Four souls who have had life-altering changes, walked through the fire, and been burned. The Fab Four. Home again. Let's stir this place up."

The girls clinked their stemmed glasses and Perrier bottle and drank.

Car lights and the crunch of gravel signaled a coming car—Lily rushing home to Marthala. The caregiver had sneaked away during their school break-in story.

"I've got something I need to tell y'all." Eva Clare shined a flashlight up to spotlight her face. As Anna Laurel, Sunny, and Meredith sat like statues with their mouths wide open, she told the story of Lily and Marthala living with her. "I'm already stirring things up. Don't y'all choke hope."

9   Betsy Steele and the Trunk

Eva Clare pulled into a parking slot in front of Harper Hardware & Feed Supply next to Gerald's bank. She stepped out of the car, shaded her eyes with a hand, and looked across the street at Laurel's Coffee House at Levee and Main and her destination two doors east. Betsy's Trunk. She'd follow Anna Laurel's advice and check out the possibility of working there.

She squinched her eyes shut, saw sun-yellow-electric on the backs of her lids, and when she opened them, Gerald stood in front of her, wearing a suit and a smirk.

"Hey, Eva Clare."

He had the characteristic lightning-blue Coghlan eyes, but that was the only thing they had in common. Somewhere down his line, an ancestor's seed spoiled while waiting to be deposited in someone's womb, and the offspring that grew out of it was affected.

"Hey, Gerald."

"A man from Greenville wants to look at Evelyn's house."

"I told you I'm not—"

"Wait." He held up his hand, palm out. "Listen to me. We can get a good amount. We're talking five acres, an antebellum house, a guesthouse, and a barn. It's an easy four-wheeler ride to the river on the huntin' club trail, and it comes with lake access. We can split the proceeds, and it's still enough for you to buy a nice little house outright in Nashville."

"I'm not going back to Nashville."

"Then somewhere. You need to do the right thing and honor the Coghlan will."

"Don't tell me what I need to do."

He manufactured a fake smile and a satin voice. "I'm trying to help. I'll bring you a copy of the will. It states who should own the tract of land and the appurtenances and hereditaments pertaining to it. It's what the family wanted."

"I have the only family will that matters."

His face turned red. "You messed up your life, and now you've brought your sin home."

She flinched. An old, rusty truck went by, spewing bad exhaust. She couldn't help but breathe it in.

"You're a woman alone now, and you're not able to take care of that property by yourself. Sell it to someone who can. I'm going to set up a time for this potential buyer to look at the house. I'll let you know when."

"You can't do that. I've got a dying woman there."

"She's already dead, Eva Clare. You missed the dying part."

"I don't mean *her*. I mean Marthala."

"Marthala, Sweet Evelyn's maid?"

"Marthala is ill, living in the house with me, and Lily Greene is providing care for her."

"Lily, the cashier at Pete's? Does Pete know?"

"It's none of his business. Or yours. Excuse me." She set her gaze on Betsy's door, swiveled around Gerald, and crossed the street.

She stopped on the sidewalk in front of the store. Looked down at her shoes—Grandmomma's navy-and-white spectator pumps from the 1960s. They worked well with her navy pencil skirt and cropped, pin-striped jacket. Grandmomma was always doing good deeds—volunteer work, church activities, community service—and succeeded at everything. Eva Clare needed that confidence. Maybe the shoes would bolster her.

Betsy's Trunk was a narrow, brown-brick, two-story structure with three tall windows upstairs and two display windows on the lower level, one on each side of the entrance. A sign in the front window said BRING A BIG STRONG MAN TO CARRY YOUR HEAVY PURCHASES. Eva Clare shuddered that thought away.

The doorknob was loose and rattled as she opened the door.

Betsy stood in front of the checkout counter—a tall, frail woman with a dowager hump, toothpick legs, and uneven hips. Her hair looked like it had a box strawberry-blonde rinse on it. Her white roots showed.

Betsy looked up, an unlit cigarette smeared with red lipstick hanging out of her mouth. She shuffled toward Eva Clare and extended a liver-spotted hand.

Eva Clare shook it. "Hey, Miss Betsy, I'm Sweet Evelyn's granddaughter."

"I know who you are." The cigarette bobbled. "Can't remember your name but remember you bought my Scherzer pink-flowered Bavarian sugar bowl for your grandmother for Christmas about 1968, when you were a young'un." She pointed to Eva Clare's feet with a crooked, arthritic finger. "Besides, I recognize Evelyn's shoes." She coughed little breathless laughs.

"I'm Eva Clare Carlyle."

"I closed the store for the funeral, but couldn't get there. Cleveland is too far for me to drive nowadays. Too much traffic, too much farm equipment on the road. Why, I'm liable to run smack into the back of a John Deere tractor, as slow as they go . . . and as slow as I am gettin' my foot to the brake."

Betsy was about to launch that cigarette right out of her mouth.

"Sweet Evelyn had a nice service with old hymns and beautiful flowers. She would've liked it."

"I'm sure she would've. So, what can I do for you today? Are you here to put some of Evelyn's belongings in the store? You know, I take estates, especially fine things like she had."

"No, Miss Betsy. I've moved home, and I need a job. I was wondering if you could use some help here in the store. Maybe with the inventory or bookkeeping. Or with anything. I have an art degree. I know how to arrange, display, and put colors, fabrics, and textures together."

Betsy's eyes widened. A mix of relief and hope?

"Oh, mercy me. I could use some help. Let's get a cup of coffee, sit a spell, and talk about it." Betsy laid her unused cigarette beside the old, black National cash register. Straight-legged, she scuffed her red pumps across the wooden floor, leading the way to her private space at the back.

Display shelves held some nice antique pieces—a silver three-piece Victorian tea service with containers shaped like quails, a collection of carved breadboards from the 1800s, and cherry mantel clocks.

An avocado green curtain covered the opening to the back room—a work and break area with long inventory tables, a couch and chair, and a kitchen cart. Betsy poured two cups of coffee from a stainless-steel percolator—the old kind with a glass bulb on top, an antique itself. The coffee pot jittered in her hand.

Eva Clare seated herself on the sofa positioned on an oval hooked rug. On a tatted doily atop a wooden steamer trunk being used as a coffee table sat a tarnished silver tray holding creamer, sugar, and a silver spoon, along with a vase of faded-pink plastic roses covered with dust. The powdered creamer and sugar crystals were probably covered with dust, too. Fusty and musty smells and cigarette smoke assaulted her nostrils. Her eyes and throat burned.

She sniffled and coughed. "This looks like an old, sturdy trunk, Miss Betsy." Perhaps a family possession stuffed full of memories. Maybe dresses or cloth from a previous century—lace, muslin, taffeta. Antique jewelry—brooches and lockets. Maybe love letters from two happy souls somewhere down Betsy's line.

"You take anything in your coffee? I got real cream over here."

Real cream. No refrigerator. "No, ma'am."

"Yes, that trunk is a treasure chest filled with photographs and journals and important memories—a trove of history somebody's gonna have fun with one day when they have time to go through it. For now, I keep it locked." Betsy straightened her shoulders and smiled. "My family was among the first settlers here, you know."

Eva Clare nodded. "Yes, ma'am."

Betsy poured thick milk into one cup from a vintage floral creamer. "They came shortly before your Coghlan ancestors. Our people gave the land for the town of Erin, you know. The Coghlans and Steeles owned all this property. My ancestral home was once down the street behind the post office." Betsy stirred, tapped the spoon on the rim of the cup. "My great-grandfather Rufus Steele lived in that house during the Civil War. He said when the Yankees came, the family put their prized possessions in this trunk and hid it in the woods. Those invaders stole most everything. Burned the home. But they didn't get the trunk." She positioned her fingers under a cup and saucer and used both hands to carry the black coffee to Eva Clare. "This trunk supplied the name for my store—Betsy's Trunk. Grandmother gave it to me. Said it belonged to Grandfather's grandmother, Esther Steele, who passed it down to her son's second wife, who added her own family treasures, and also her wedding dress. God knows I never needed that." She huffed out little breaths.

Eva Clare was amused with her funny laugh.

Betsy got her own cup of creamy dark roast, teetered over to a ladderback chair, and sat down with a groan and a splat of coffee on the rug. She let her cup and saucer rest on top of her legs at the knees while she rubbed her gnarled hands together. Even her knees were shaky, and the cup rattled against the saucer in incessant jabber.

"My shop doesn't have much business. People go to Cleveland to the antique malls. I don't make enough to pay help. I do have a lot of inventory. Been thinking about retiring for a long time, but I can't close my store until I sell my merchandise." Betsy leaned over and set her cup and saucer on the trunk. "Can you help? Maybe we can work something out."

"Well, yes ma'am, I can try. What if I come in and work a couple weeks, maybe even for free, to clean up, rearrange the inventory, and make the shop more inviting?" A plan began formulating in Eva Clare's head. "I'll concentrate on attracting customers."

"And I'll pay you a cut of what sells?"

"Perhaps." This didn't sound promising or permanent. She needed a job that lasted more than a couple of weeks or months. "Or maybe if we can bring some life back, you can include me in a bigger way." Full-time employee or manager? "Do you own this building?"

"Yes, I own this building and the empty space beside it."

"May I ask . . . as an exit plan, what do you expect to do with the two spaces?"

"As a what?"

"When you close your store, um, retire, who will take over your properties?"

"I had a nephew I hoped would, but he's gone to Florida."

"Perhaps we could get my friend Anna Laurel to come and talk with you. She's a lawyer. She could help with a will or an exit plan. Something legal. Maybe at no charge."

Eva Clare drew in a deep breath, inhaling stale air, and blew it out. The risks loomed large. If she was going to be doing a lot of free cleaning, arranging, and fixing up, it might behoove her to choose broadly and go for all. "Maybe one day, I could take over Betsy's Trunk. Maybe even purchase it."

Did she really say that?

"Well, I don't know. It won't be Betsy's Trunk if you buy it."

"I wouldn't change the name. It's perfect for an antique shop." What was she getting herself into? The store was a filthy mess, a ruination. Could she manage this by herself? She looked down at Grandmomma's spectator pumps. "I'll come up with a business plan."

"Why do you want to buy my store?" Betsy asked.

"I see potential. Value in the merchandise." Truly, it was a Hail Mary—the only thing in town she could work at and feel good about. The only thing related to art—her first love.

"You got to make me a good offer."

"There's not much business. You said so yourself. No regular customers. And there's a lot of work—*a whole lot of work!*—to get this place in shape."

"But there's some valuable merchandise," Betsy said. "These antiques are left over from the day when I did purchasing the right way. No junk. Only fine antiques."

"Yes, ma'am. But they're not selling. Your valuable acquisitions are sitting on a shelf. I'll try to find each one of them a home. Think balance—new life for old things."

"I guess I'm one of those old things. Where will I go all day? I'm used to being downtown and seeing people."

"You'll still come here. Greet shoppers. We'll put a TV in, and you can watch soap operas. But how about if we don't smoke in here? Shoppers don't like cigarette smoke."

"If I do agree to this, I'm bringin' my bottle o' scotch."

"Okay, sure."

"Hah. Well, I'm left a few of life's little pleasures. Soap operas and scotch."

Eva Clare smiled. "You can tell me old stories about Erin. I think we all need to know our past so we can go into the future informed."

"Hmmm. We'll see." Betsy rubbed one of her hands, then the other, nervously, as if she was putting on lotion. "I know I'm too old and tired to keep up the store. But I'm not set on selling. I'm gon take this slow, and we'll see what happens."

Even if she appeared hesitant about selling, Betsy seemed ripe for change.

"Okay." Eva Clare tugged at the lapels on her jacket. "Let's figure this arrangement out in a way that's fair to you and fair to me and helpful to us both."

"We'll see."

Eva Clare sat at a small, black table by the front entrance of the coffeehouse. On the wall beside her hung a framed quote: AND ALL THE GODS GO WITH YOU! UPON YOUR SWORD SIT LAUREL VICTORY! AND SMOOTH SUCCESS BE STREW'D BEFORE YOUR FEET!

Except for her, the place was empty. Nobody frittered away their time drinking hot brews in Laurel's Coffee House at Levee and Main. The only customer, a man in tan leather work boots and a John Deere ball cap—a planter, which was an old Delta word for "wealthy farmer"—exited with his Styrofoam cup in one hand and a white paper sack in the other. Maybe she could grab a few minutes with Anna Laurel. She needed to strike while the iron was hot, as Grandmomma always said, while her offer sat fresh on Betsy's mind. Grandmomma also said: If you want something, you have to do something to get it.

Anna Laurel made a beeline for her table. "Can I count on you to have the exquisite taste of a city girl?" Then she frowned and stamped her shoe on the oak floor, re-stained a matte gray-black. She rubbed the back of her neck, threw up her hands. "My elite bistro might as well offer a bunch of fried-up breakfast items you'd find at the front counter of a gas station. Greasy sausage biscuits, bacon biscuits, and ham biscuits with yellow-plastic cheese and rubbery eggs."

"Give 'em what they want." Eva Clare looked at the back wall painted charcoal gray with three words on three lines in big white letters: BUT FIRST, COFFEE.

"My biggest customers are farmers," Anna Laurel complained, then pointed out the window at the planter carrying his stash across the street to a fancy, hundred-thousand-dollar, mud-splashed truck. "They'd be here at four a.m. if I was open. And all they want are three sausage biscuits and a house coffee."

"What's wrong with that? It's business. Money coming in."

"Yeah, well, I had a vision that this place would be more upscale, where people would come, read a book, and eat a fresh-baked cinnamon roll, maybe write a poem."

"Yeah, well, remember where you are. A farm town."

"I know I had misplaced hope. But I wanted a little more than these farmers with their maroon Mississippi State T-shirts and mud-caked farm boots. Look at the tracks on this floor!" Anna Laurel propped her hands on her hips and shook her head at the dirt so visible on the dark wood. "Sorry for the rant. I get frustrated sometimes. I don't think anyone here even gets the double meaning of the name of my business—the 'Laurel's' part."

Laurel—honor, distinction, achievement. Eva Clare glanced at the framed quote. LAUREL VICTORY! Shakespeare.

"You're a class act, Anna Laurel."

"Yeah. Act One, scene three. *Antony and Cleopatra.* I know it, you know it, nobody else knows it." Anna Laurel wrinkled her nose and pinched the air with her pointer and thumb. "Let me get you something." She went to the counter, stuck something in the toaster oven for a minute, put it on a white dish, and headed back to the table with a smile and a fork.

Eva Clare cut into the pastry and put it in her mouth. "Mmm. Sweet, almond flavor. Melts in your mouth."

"I don't have a big menu—only seven items, and I rotate those so I don't waste food—but what I've got is superb."

"It's divine. Where'd you get this?"

"Yeah, uh huh, you like it, right? You'll never believe who bakes for me."

"Pete Wong?"

"Oh God, that's an insult. He only cooks chicken and catfish and fries them in the same stale peanut oil for years on end."

Eva Clare laughed, then took another bite.

"Sunny," Anna Laurel said. "Sunny bakes specialty items for me. She loves to bake, so I gave her a venue for her pastries."

"This croissant is fabulous." Crispy, buttery flavor, sliced almonds, and confectioner's icing on top.

"I've got almond croissants, orange mascarpone fig muffins, blueberry scones with clotted cream, lavender lemon raspberry muffins, lemon croissants, bacon chocolate muffins, and cinnamon rolls. On weekends, Sunny makes a fried biscuit dough ball topped with mascarpone lemon cream with a blueberry compote." Anna Laurel clapped her hands together. "Today is almond croissant day."

"Heavenly."

Anna Laurel waved her arm in the direction of the freezer display case that held pastries wrapped in cellophane. The labels were a cobalt blue background with a yellow sunflower and a big letter S. In the below-the-counter display, fresh pastries were lined up. "Sunny also does the country biscuit and sausage staple for farm workers. That's what keeps us in business. She packs each biscuit individually and puts a strip of paper with a handwritten Bible verse on it in the bag. These Baptists get a high off of that. Anyway, I get a cut of what she bakes, and she gets a supplemental income to her church piano job which doesn't pay squat. And when the items pass the sell-by date, I eat them. I've gained five pounds since she started baking for me."

"I've seen pictures of her pastries on social media, but I didn't realize she baked for a living," Eva Clare said. "So, Susanna Louise Flowers has her own business, too."

"Yes. Sister Sunflowers Fresh Baked Daily. She's a wannabe pastry chef."

"Looks to me like she's an already-accomplished pastry chef."

Eva Clare chewed in slow motion, absorbing the sweet, delectable flavor. She put her fork down. "You got a business. Sunny's got a business. I need a business, too. I need your help with Betsy. She's agreeable to the idea of me working for her—cleaning the place, arranging items, advertising, selling antiques, and getting a percentage. She's not sure about selling the place. I don't want to do all that work for nothing. I don't know the next step."

"Okay," Anna Laurel said and took the other chair at Eva Clare's table. "What can I do to facilitate this?"

"First of all, can you make sure she has a will? She's got land and real property and assets. What's going to happen if she falls out dead before we strike a deal? I mean, I don't want to sound crass, but it's a possibility at her age. I told her you'd help her."

"No problem. I'll go see her this afternoon."

"For free."

"Oh, God."

"I also need you to sit down with Betsy and me and help us come to some kind of work agreement—whether I'm an employee or whether she wants to make me manager or sell the business to me. Some type of fair arrangement."

"Okay, I'll take care of both at the same time. You come with me this afternoon—"

"This afternoon?"

"Yes. The will won't take long. Then we'll talk about the business."

"Can you get away from the coffeehouse? Do you have help?"

"I can't pay help. Don't have enough income. I work seven to four. Feel like I'm the only spark of life in downtown, which brings me to a question. Do you have ideas for bringing business in? How do you plan to succeed? Why do you want to *buy* the store?"

"Because you told me to! And that's three questions."

"All legitimate."

"Sure, I have ideas." She didn't. She was making this up as she spoke. "I have a plan taking shape. I'll need to own that shop so I can make strategic decisions. Expand, add a few art classes, maybe art supplies, draw in folks from the surrounding area. I don't want to end up an Erin kid coming home to a dead town."

"Okay. Later, we can put our heads together and talk about turning the town around."

"So?"

"Meet me at the Trunk at four."

Meet me at the Trunk. Had a nice ring to it. So did being an entrepreneur. And having success "strew'd" at her feet. The idea had set well with Eva Clare since Anna Laurel brought it up at the pier party. But a nagging truth wiggled into her positive vibes: the store was failing.

Betsy must have been dozing in the back room when Eva Clare walked in through the rattly door. She stood at the front and assessed the space. Valuable pieces sat on the shelves, but it looked like junk piled on top of junk—old furniture pieces, fine china, and keepsakes most likely gathered from every estate in the area from as far back as the 1950s. What to do? First of all, air the place out. Get rid of layers of oily grit and dust. Bring in light and color. Place items individually and not in piles. Draw shoppers' eyes to beauty and value—items a customer couldn't do without. Impulse pieces.

Anna Laurel walked in at two minutes of four, slinging her hands. "There're only four cars on the main street right now, all over at the Piggly Wiggly. Probably working women buying those fifty-cent hammered beef patties to fry for supper with some skillet milk gravy to sop up with white bread. How are any of us supposed to make a living here?" She spoke loud enough to wake the dead, and sure enough, Betsy came shuffling out of the back room all weak-eyed and wobbly. She must've been into the booze and fallen into a snooze.

Anna Laurel stood up straight, held her shoulders back, and took on a serious expression. "Keep in mind," she whispered to Eva Clare out the side of her mouth, "that I've got to assume an impartial position in my representation of you both." Then she launched into the business at hand. They stood beside a musty-smelling, dark-wood china cabinet full of pink-flowered dishes and re-capped the earlier visit between Eva Clare and Betsy, and then Anna Laurel moved on to the future of the store.

"Eva Clare says you might be agreeable to letting her work here to clean and update the shop. I'm an attorney, and she has engaged me to help negotiate an arrangement fair to both of you. I'll be working on your behalf, too. Are you agreeable to talking about this?"

Betsy folded her arms across her chest and nodded.

"Okay, first of all, do you have a current will that lists the beneficiary of your estate?"

"My will was done in 1960 by the lawyer Blackburn in Cleveland. Everything goes to my nephew, Jamison Steele. He lived in the apartment upstairs. At the time, I had hopes he'd stay in Erin and run my store. But he left Mississippi in 1975 and now lives in a retirement village in Ocala. He's never coming back. As it stands, I don't have anybody else."

"We need to think about this," Anna Laurel said. "I'm sure you have assets other than a house and downtown property. Do you have savings and investments?"

"Have some left. Had to dip in to cover repairs for the house and store, like a new roof."

"You might want to divide up your assets. For example, you can leave your money to your nephew. You can also choose to leave your house and personal property to him—"

"I haven't talked to him in twenty years. I guess I do need a new will."

"I'll be glad to help with that. You can choose a charity or church for some of your assets. Think it over, and I'll call you later. But you do need to name someone to inherit your business—either to close it legally or to run it or sell it. If you want Betsy's Trunk to have a future and leave you a legacy, you might want to consider Eva Clare being the avenue to that."

Betsy nodded. "My family and her family founded the town of Erin. I think it would be fitting to bring us together again."

"You don't have to decide right now. You've already agreed to have Eva Clare work in the store and make it showroom ready. We'll see what Eva Clare can do and how well you like it. We'll see if you are comfortable putting your trust in her. Why don't we sit down and talk over Eva Clare's work agreement, and then I'll prepare a document for us to review?"

Anna Laurel and Eva Clare stood on the sidewalk in front of Betsy's Trunk. At five forty-five, Main Street was deserted. The still-hot sun sent sweat running down their faces, tracking through their makeup, like streams through desert sand.

Eva Clare pushed her long bangs off her forehead. "I don't know how I feel about this."

"What do you mean? I thought you wanted this. You came up with the idea."

"I know, but I'm working for nothing. I need an income. I've agreed to work for a few weeks for free and clean up this store that would obviously take six months and a good scouring with a fire hose. What have I done? I can't do this. I thought you were on my side."

"Pull yourself together, E. C. I'm representing you both. I told you that. I don't want this to appear as collusion, that you and I are trying to take her money and property. This has to be fair. It must be right for her. You said that yourself. We've got a skeleton arrangement in place. Bob Ed Blackburn is deceased, but has a grandson, Milton, practicing law in Cleveland. I can work an updated will through him, probably gratis, because of Betsy's age and history with the firm and my professional status."

"But what about me?"

"You'll be listed as the Trunk's responsible party. We'll work out a percentage of the store's income per month for Betsy in the sales agreement. You're going to have to work hard to make a go of this. You'll have to hang in financially for a few months. You got enough money to tide you over?"

"I don't know. Maybe. I'll have to sell some of my paintings. I'll set up a table in the store for them. This is insane. What was I thinking?"

"You're going to have to dig deep and draw in help. You'll have to bring in some customers and sell some shit." Anna Laurel grinned. "And while you're at it, promote my business, too. And Sunny's. We're riding on your shoulders, E. C."

Eva Clare slumped over like a rag doll, her arms hanging limp. She needed to hold her own self up. Not the whole town. Something good better come out of this in the end.

"Pick it up, Carlyle. Your chin's dragging the concrete." Anna Laurel gave a wink and turned toward her T-Bird without saying goodbye.

10   Trunk Revival

The smell of scorched coffee filled the kitchen. Eva Clare staggered to the counter, poured the last burnt-bitter half cup, turned off the pot, and sat back down at the table. She'd been slouching in the breakfast nook looking out the wall of windows since four—first into black nothingness, then at the faint gray outlines of dawn, then to definition of trees and lake.

Her shoulders sagged and curled. Her head was a battleground of competing ideas. How would she navigate the dying Trunk back to life?

Outside, gravel crunched as Marthala's caregiver arrived and Lily departed in her squeaky-belt car.

Eva Clare picked up a pen and doodled on the pad in front of her. Number one. Consignment booths. It was all the next hour gave her that made sense.

Her heart raced. It was all the coffee. Also, it was because she was in over her head. She'd been here a week, was in a self-imposed time crunch to redo the store, and knew of only one local artist besides herself to consign goods.

The back door whooshed open and slammed against the baseboard stop. Lily stumbled in with a bunch of fat, plastic bags. She toed the door edge with a sneaker, pushed it shut, and plopped the sacks of fabric pieces on the table.

"Where've you been?" Eva Clare said. "It's not even seven o'clock."

"To Cleveland to pick up scraps of material from a seamstress friend for my quilts." Lily began emptying the first bag, folding and stacking the pieces in separate columns of solids and prints. "Why're you up so early?"

"I couldn't sleep. I've got myself in a jam with that antique shop job. I have to clean out the entire store, rearrange things, and find a way to make money."

"Well, it ain't gon happen with you sittin' here."

"I need your help."

"I got my hands full. I can't be down at that store scrubbing floors."

"I don't mean that kind of help."

"What then?"

"Your quilts. I want you to sell them in the store."

Lily put her hands on her hips. "I'm listenin'."

"Consignment booths. It's the way to go. I need to make money right off the bat with new merchandise while I clean up the old stuff and figure out how to display it. I'll start with a small area up front and put in booths for local artisans."

"Yeah?"

"I'll have a booth for my river paintings. I've got enough for a large display. In the next booth, your quilts. Will you do it? Will you sell locally?"

"You offerin' a good percentage?"

"What split do you want?"

"I know the standard, and I know what I want. Eighty/twenty. Me, eighty."

"What about seventy/thirty?"

Lily shook her head. "I said I know what I want."

"Want is one thing, but let's be practical. I want sixty/forty. How about we settle on seventy-five/twenty-five? Me, getting twenty-five percent. I've got to eat, too."

Lily threw up her hands. "Fine."

"For everybody else, it'll be sixty/forty." Eva Clare wrote the amounts on her notepad and started sketching a layout. "I've got two display windows, one on each side of the front door. The checkout counter is an enclosed station that faces the door. For consignment, I'm thinking, as you come in, off to the left of the checkout counter will be three booths, and to the right, three booths. So I need six artisans to sell their wares."

"Yeah, okay. You. Me. Ya need four more."

Ideas began to sprout. "One front display window can show a sampling of all the artists' work, and the other window can show some fine antiques set up around the real Betsy's trunk—the old steamer trunk that belonged to Betsy's great-grandmother. I hope to get this going in three, four weeks. You okay with the timing?"

A grin grew on Lily's face. "Yep. I've got a supply, and I can use the quilts I pulled from consignment for the funeral. I'll start with maybe thirty. I've got extra display quilt stands and tables. You'll make a hundred to a hundred fifty dollars off each quilt I sell. How you gon separate the booths?"

"I don't know. We need them cordoned off so each artist's goods stay inside a specified area, all booths numbered, with accompanying tags on the artwork."

"I've consigned at other stores, so I know how this works," Lily said. "I've got some old quilt backing—bolts of wide-width cotton broadcloth in a natural color. A fellow quilter gave me her supply when she got old and couldn't see to do the stitching. It's been stored too long to use on my quilts. I'm afraid some rot has set in. But we can attach it to wooden frames to use as booth dividers. It'll work fine for that."

"There's some scrap wood for the frames in Sweet Evelyn's barn. I saw it last week when I moved my furniture in for storage."

"I could get Pete to build some simple booth frames."

"Oh, great, thank you, you're a lifesav—"

"I figure I owe you for letting my mamaw stay here."

"Well, you don't, but the booths will help us all." Eva Clare scratched notes as her mind formulated next steps. "I'll go to the store this afternoon and measure off the spaces. You and Pete can build the frames. I'll get in there Sunday when the store is closed and start clearing out the front area. I can stash some of the antiques in my barn while I clean and—"

"Pete's got a flatbed trailer you can use."

"Perfect. I'll mop and wax the hardwood, and I'll paint the walls a soft melon color, maybe the front wall butter yellow. I'll buy paint this afternoon."

"How 'bout the butter yellow color for the frames, too? It'll look good against the old dark hardwood floor and also with my broadcloth."

"Yeah, sure." Eva Clare wrote it down. "I want the room to be filled with light and energy. I want color-warmth to inspire people to buy."

"What other artists will be consigning?"

"I remember a watercolor artist who had a booth at the Crosstie Festival in Cleveland a few years ago. His name was James something. I can't remember his last name. He paints farm scenes, like shanties in cotton fields, barns, sunsets over cotton fields, old trucks in turnrows—"

"Uh huh. McGovern's the name. I've seen his work. He's got sharecropper shacks and Black folks choppin' in the cotton fields and other horrid stuff that White people seem to love and feel nostalgic about. I hate that crap. It's offensive."

"I get it. But we need stuff that people love and buy, so can you maybe hang with it?"

"I have been all my life."

"Yeah, I know. I'm sorry. But we all make compromises when it benefits us." Eva Clare pointed her pen at Lily. "I'll google, try to find and recruit him. I guess I need your help with other artists, too, if you know anybody. I've been away from here too long. Not familiar with the local arts community. I want vendors that promote the area and items consistent with the town and its history. Do you happen to know any other artists who might fit in?"

"There's a potter in Scott—a Black woman. Got dishes, cups, chip and dips, Miss'ippi-shaped trays, and other things in earth colors, hand-painted with a distressed look. She gets her clay from the river. Called Mud River Pottery."

"Sounds like a perfect fit. I'll go see her work and try to pull her in. I need two more."

"Talk to your friend Meredith."

"I will. Her background is in advertising. I'm going to ask her to do a campaign to get customers here from nearby towns."

"How come is it that I know more about your friends than you do?"

"What do you mean?"

"You know Meredith does artwork?"

"No."

"There was a mudbug festival here back in the spring, with craft booths. Meredith made pebble art pictures, using tiny river rocks and little pieces of broken river glass. She glued pebbles and chips of colored glass to canvas and framed them. Designs like a man fishing, a couple canoeing, clothes on a clothesline. Called herself Merry River Rocks. Like Merry from Meredith."

"A new hobby for her? She'll have to join us. That's five. We need one more."

"I can't think of anybody else."

"We've got time." Eva Clare finished her notes about Meredith's art, then put her pen point back on number one of her list to flesh in details. "My booth will be called Ghosts on the Oxbow, my longtime label. What about you?"

"Star's." Lily leaned in and watched Eva Clare write it down. S-T-A-R-S. "No, no. Put an apostrophe after the R."

"But it doesn't need one."

"Hey, if I say it does, it does. I know what I'm doing."

"Okay, fine." Eva Clare groaned.

"And hush that grumbling." Lily chuckled and shook her head so that her earrings swung and tapped against her cheeks. "Oh!" She reached up and touched them. "I know! See these earrings?" She used both pointer fingers to show off the wavy, long-line, hammered wire jewelry. "They represent the Miss'ippi River. A man from Cleveland named Oren, who lives out of state now, makes copper jewelry, some Miss'ippi themed. He might do a booth for you, and he'd sell well 'cause people here know him and love his designs."

"Oren Bagley? I think Meredith had a date with him to a Cleveland High homecoming dance in tenth or eleventh grade. I'll call him." Eva Clare wrote his name on her pad, stood up and danced circles in her yoga pants and Titans T-shirt, then sat down again. "There you go. Six booths of Mississippi Delta art. This could work." She drummed her fingers on the tabletop. "We can't change the name of the store because I promised Betsy, but we can give it a subtitle: Art and Antiques of the Mississippi Delta."

Lily kept her eyes on her material pieces as she sorted and stacked. "Pull in Roy."

"Huh?"

"Pull in Roy Winslow."

"Why?"

"He ain't got enough to do. He can mop and paint and haul junk. He's a live body. And a fine-lookin' one. I could eat him with a spoon. Mm hmm, don't tell me you haven't noticed."

"I haven't noticed." But she felt a ping in her abdomen when Lily mentioned his name. "All right, I'll ask." She pictured a spoon with Roy in it. Wondered what it would be like to have him close for days on end. She shook her head, chasing away that thought. "We've got a start. The store should make a little money, and it will also help the artists and bring good change to downtown. We're in business."

"No, you ain't done the footwork. You haven't got a soul lined up but me. You need to talk to these artists and sign them on before you lay your eggs and count your chicks."

"I know." Eva Clare took the last sip of cold coffee. This had to work. There was no plan B. She'd have to take a risk and contact these people. Beg and grovel. She winked at Lily. "You watch me go."

"Yeah, yeah, and I'm right there with you, pushin' and naggin' and draggin'."

Ten o'clock. Eva Clare stood at the red front door of Meredith's blond-brick ranch house, unannounced, and rang the bell. Meredith answered, barefooted, wearing navy and pink floral lounge pants and a navy T-shirt, coffee mug in hand.

"Eva Clare, what's up?"

"I need to talk to you, now, if you can." She rushed in past Meredith, planted her feet on the shag runner, and turned to face her old friend.

"Why, sure. C'mon in. Oh, well, I see you already have. Coffee?"

"No, God, I've had a pot." Eva Clare walked into the living room. Meredith had some new furniture, while also using old stuff from her parents—her console stereo from 1965 under the picture window, her mama's Pinkie and Blue Boy in gold frames, and the family's silver

Kiddush goblets on the coffee table. "I need to talk to you about the antique store."

"What's wrong with it?" Meredith pointed Eva Clare to an overstuffed chair in bold fabric with a matching ottoman, and then she plopped on the leather sofa facing her, sitting in yoga lotus position. "Did Betsy burn it down?"

"I start working there tomorrow. I may eventually buy Betsy out."

"But Eva Clare, people don't shop there anymore. Everything's covered with dust. The store's filled with cigarette smoke because Betsy sits in there puffing all day, and nobody wants to go inside and breathe that. The floor's filthy. I doubt it's been mopped in thirty years—"

"I'll mop it, and she won't smoke anymore."

"Why're you doing this?"

"We talked about it at the pier party. I need a job." Eva Clare's chest tightened.

"Go to Cleveland."

"No. This is home."

"You won't make money here. My daddy was a store owner, and—"

"I know. WEISS CLOTHING STORE, SINCE 1904."

"I know how hard Daddy worked to keep it clean, presentable, and stocked. Now, he's gone, and it's one of Erin's boarded-up buildings."

"I've got to find a way to make Betsy's a productive business. I'll clean it, air it out, paint, and organize things—"

"It looks like a bunch of junk in there."

"It's got some nice merchandise. It's . . . the only thing here that's related to art. Art is my life. God, Meredith, please, I need your help."

"What, advertising?"

"Well, yes. But first, pebble art. I hear you make river rock designs and sell them."

"Occasionally, for the fun of it."

"Do you like it enough to keep doing it?"

Meredith's face softened to a smile. "I love doing it." She picked up a spiral olive wood candlestick on the table next to her and toyed with it. "Unlike the advertising business, where you're never sure if something you create will work until you test it over time to see if people buy the product and reward your efforts, pebble art is an impulse purchase. People see it, love it, buy it on the spot. It's got instant good results."

Ah, a pleasant expression on Mere—her mouth like the pinkish, curved-up, plump lips of a bream fish. The hook seemed to pierce Meredith's skin. Time to reel her in. "I want to install consignment booths, where people sell their art. I'm here to ask you to be a vendor."

"Me? A vendor? Oh gosh, it would take so many designs to have an effective display." Meredith put down the candlestick, leaned forward. "I don't know if I can do it."

"You won't know till you try."

"I have a dozen or more designs left from a festival I did in May."

"That's a start. Maybe you could have another couple dozen finished before I open."

"Maybe. They're quick and easy to do. But this would require a lot of walks to the river for pebble and glass gathering." Meredith shook her hands out, as she waffled to the negative side. "A lot of canvasses, paint, brushes. Glue, easels, ink pens. That means money."

"You're giving me a whole lot of gloom, Meredith, and reasons why not. You could make a small investment in supplies. Set a goal, say, two dozen pictures. In the meantime, you can complement the designs by including in your booth some rock displays and old cobalt bottles or old medicine bottles, like those the river glass comes from—whatever you need to do visually to make the booth look full. You can do it."

Meredith's eyes brightened. "My parents had a collection of old bottles and jars I can sell. Yeah. People love to decorate with those—for holidays and wedding receptions."

"I'm sure the store has some, too, and we can pull a few for you to sell." Eva Clare needed stuff flying off the shelves. She'd sold Lily on becoming a vendor, and now, Meredith was coming on board, too.

"So, do you want me to do some advertising, too, to bring people in?"

"Yes. Whip up a plan to bring new life to the Trunk and to Erin. Maybe other downtown stores will chip in for an ad campaign." Eva Clare stretched her legs out on the ottoman, flinched, and pointed to her feet. "Look. I've got two different socks on." She pointed to a tie-dye in reds and oranges on the left foot and a tie-dye in greens and blues on the right.

Meredith laughed at the faux pas. "You can't match your own socks, yet you expect to run a successful business and bring growth to the town of Erin?"

"Oh, shut up." Eva Clare pressed her lips into a grin.

"You're a nut." Meredith giggled, then took on a serious look. "Okay, here's the thing. We're a tiny river town set to explode in traffic and tourism. We're on the precipice of opportunity. It takes only a few people to actively drive growth. I can steer the wheel."

"Pete mentioned the new highway coming through here. Is that what you mean?"

"It's part of the NAFTA superhighway," Meredith said. "My cousin who works for the Mississippi Department of Transportation told me about it. NAFTA is the largest transportation pact in the world. Between Canada, the United States, and Mexico. It took three presidents—Reagan, Bush, and Clinton—to get it going. The interstate will come through Bolivar County, run west of Cleveland, east of the Port of Rosedale, and a mile from Erin."

"With a new bridge over the river?"

"That's the plan." Meredith gave a thumbs-up. "We'll be a superhighway town with transport trucks running to countries north and south of us. We're near a port on the Mississippi River that connects to global ports. We're waking from our backward river-town status."

"What about a billboard pulling traffic off the interstate and pushing it into downtown?"

"Or an economic development organization and a marketing plan. People need a reason to come here."

"I want the Trunk to be one of those businesses pulling people in and giving them something to be excited about."

"The Trunk needs me," Meredith said. "Not only for pebble art, but to plan and promote."

"So, you're in?"

"Of course, I'm in. I mean, it's not like I have anything else to do."

"You wanna go downtown to Anna Laurel's and get a fancy coffee and talk with her about this?"

"I'm in my pajamas."

"They look like leisurewear."

Ten minutes later they walked into the modern, monochromatic ambiance of the coffee shop and pulled out chairs at a table by the front window.

"Hey, Anna Laurel, bring us some coffee and something sweet and come sit with us," Eva Clare directed. "We'll pay."

"Let me make sure all my customers are set for a while." Anna Laurel made a wide sweeping gesture with her arm over an empty room. "Okay, I'm good." She'd been removing out-of-date shelf pastries. The next three, she put on a plate for them, poured three cups of coffee, and made her way to the table with the tray of food. "Meredith, why are you wearing PJs?"

"Eva Clare wouldn't wait for me to change. Besides, these are palazzo pants and fine to wear in public. Nobody will know. Nobody's here to see. It's like being home alone."

"Damn," Anna Laurel snapped, clattering plates on the table at each setting.

The chime on the door jingled, and in walked Sunny with more baked goods.

"Drop those on the counter, grab yourself a coffee, and join us," Anna Laurel said.

Once they were all settled and moaning over heavenly lavender, lemon, and raspberry muffins with lemon zest icing, Eva Clare pulled out her notepad and pencil. "First item of business—"

"Business of what?" Sunny said.

"I'm going to be managing Betsy's Trunk. I'm expanding to antiques *and art* and putting in six booths of local artisans. So far, I've got me, Meredith and her river rocks, and Lily and her quilts. Y'all know Lily? Marthala's granddaughter? Works at Pete's? I've got three other hopefuls. One is Oren Bagley and his jewelry."

"I remember him from high school days," Meredith said.

"Also, a potter and a watercolorist. Sunny, we can put a table in for you, if you'd like to bake something special for our opening day, something river or Delta related."

"Oh yeah. Mississippi Mud Cupcakes. That'd be perfect."

"What about me? What am I doing?" Anna Laurel said.

"I want us to work together. There's the one empty store space between us that Betsy owns. I want to get the boards off the windows and use that storefront as an atrium connecting us. We could promote our shops as a destination. This plan is still raw, but has promise."

"Perfect. Sounds like you've been doing some double-time mulling this over."

"You bet I have. So, first item of business is to prepare. We need to scrub and clean the front third of the Trunk and paint the whole store," Eva Clare said.

"*We?*" Anna Laurel said.

"Yes, I need your help. I'll have food in, we can work all night, I'll have wine—"

"Oh, gee golly," Anna Laurel said. "Wine for work and sleep deprivation."

"C'mon, y'all, we can make it fun." Eva Clare tapped her pencil on the pad. "And it's for the town. Reviving the store is the first step to reviving the town."

"I'll help," Sunny said. "And I'll serve refreshments on opening day—cupcakes and cherry limeade." Under her breath, she added, "But I want my own store."

"I'll help, too." Meredith nodded. "Count me in."

"Jeez Alou, the stuff y'all drag me into. Now, I have to do it because everybody else is." Anna Laurel shook her head, wagged her ponytail.

"All right then. I'll close the store tomorrow through the July Fourth weekend," Eva Clare said. "We'll have a Labor Party."

"Labor Day is in September," Anna Laurel said.

"It'll be like an oxymoron."

"Pretty sure that's not what an oxymoron is," Anna Laurel said. "But okay, set the day and time and write it down on your little notepad. Assign each one of us what to bring for cleaning and what to pitch in for food.

This is a good idea, and if we don't do it now, we won't ever do it and nobody ever will. Besides, it'll help me and my store." She laced her fingers on the back of her head.

"We need a Chamber of Commerce," Meredith proposed.

"I think we, the Fab Four, are the chamber," Anna Laurel said.

Friday afternoon, Eva Clare did the footwork—hashed out deals with two artists in person and Oren Bagley by phone. With Anna Laurel's assistance, she fleshed out an agreement with Betsy for a path to shop ownership. She enlisted the help of Roy and Pete, and as the weekend rolled in, the team of seven—the two men, the Fab Four, and Lily—prepared to roll up their sleeves and blow through that shop like a whirlwind.

It was happening fast, too fast. But Eva Clare had to funnel swiftly with it because if she stopped to think about it, she'd chicken out.

Over the next ten days, she stashed Betsy outside on a bench under the porch awning with some cigarettes and a soft cushion to protect her bony back and butt. She propped the front door open, set up fans to stir the air and push the stale out, and with the help of her team, cleared out the front third of the store. They knocked out the wall of Betsy's back room in favor of one big showroom. The team labored on their hands and knees, on tiptoes, ladders, and stepstools—dusted, swept, and bleach-washed the entire store and its contents; scrubbed and waxed the wooden floor; painted the walls pink melon and creamery yellow; repaired, sanded, and stained the checkout station; and washed the windows. Roy did the high work, like polishing the chandeliers and painting the crown molding and trim work in ivory with a touch of emerald.

Eva Clare started work at five in the morning and stopped at ten at night, and had team help most of the time. They broke from labor only to eat, and then they sat on the floor and ate while gulping down iced tea from gallon jugs, sampling Sunny's Mississippi Mud Cupcakes, and approving newspaper ads created by Meredith. They discussed what to do with the upstairs space, the large two-room-plus-bath area—a breakroom or an apartment? Pete and Roy offered to check it out, make sure everything was still in working condition, and hire it cleaned. They would also paint and stain the staircase at the back of the store and prepare a small sitting area at the foot of the stairs by installing a partial privacy wall. After all, Eva Clare had promised Betsy a place to sit. Pete lured a few carpenter and contractor friends to come during the evenings to accomplish the work on deadline by promising them free fried-chicken lunches for a month.

Betsy got caught up in the work spirit and offered to throw in one hundred twenty-nine dollars a month in her final three months as proprietor for the lease of new point-of-sale software and all the needed equipment. At the end of three months, Eva Clare would take over.

Meredith made a sign for the window: PLEASE PARDON OUR PROGRESS! WE ARE REMODELING & HOPE TO SEE OUR LOYAL CUSTOMERS FRIDAY JULY 16. It was an attempt to make everybody feel they were the only ones not regularly shopping at the Trunk.

Meredith also painted a new store sign on the glass front window: *BETSY'S TRUNK: Art and Antiques of the Mississippi Delta. Proprietor: Eva Clare Carlyle.*

"I'm not the owner yet," Eva Clare protested.

"You've got possession and a deal. It's a matter of timing. Three months, it's yours."

Pete built the booth dividers and delivered them on Sunday, July fourth. Lily helped him paint the frames and staple the material in place. They set up six booth spaces.

The checkout station was ready to receive its new iPad and sales software. Eva Clare picked out an antique lamp from inventory for the checkout counter. She chose a few other appointments, too, for brand confirmation—a twelve-inch cedar trunk representing Betsy's trunk; a Victorian porcelain statue of two sisters to represent the Coghlan matriarchs, Catherine Deering and Victoria Dove; and a small figurine of a child to represent Catherine's daughter, Erin Rose.

The real Betsy's trunk took a prime spot in one of the main-street display windows. It was heavy to lift and carry, and Eva Clare determined it would remain in that spot forever. The trunk was locked, and Betsy was adamant about keeping the key. When Eva Clare asked for it, Betsy stomped her foot and yelled a trembly but firm NO.

Everything was falling into place. The store would be ready Friday, July ninth, for the artists to fill their booths. Eva Clare could barely catch her breath.

Tuesday afternoon, Eva Clare stood outside on the sidewalk in front of the Trunk, studying the door. Preparing the entrance was the final step. It was the original glass in a walnut-wood frame with the original brass hardware. She wanted to strip and re-stain it and do it by herself. There was something about a front door—a portal to new possibilities, the gateway to a new life. Hope sprang up and energized her.

Then someone tapped her shoulder.

Gerald. Her good feelings evaporated.

"What's going on?" he said.

"I'm the new owner of the Trunk, and I'm getting ready to stain my door." Well, she wasn't the owner yet, but she didn't mind telling him she was.

"Owner? So on top of everything else, you've got a failing business to contend with?"

"Go back to your marble bank tiles, Gerald. You're a bully. Your words mean nothing to me." But they did. Self-doubt sluiced out every pore.

"Here," Gerald said, as he unbuttoned his sport coat, removed an envelope from an inside pocket, and handed it to her. "I want to give you this. Take a look. I'll be getting back to you."

Eva Clare took the envelope and looked at her typed name on the white linen front.

"Read it." He jabbed his finger at it, then walked away.

Roy came out the front door after witnessing the exchange of words. "What was that?"

"My mean cousin being his mean self." She bent the envelope in half.

"Are you okay? What's in the envelope?"

She looked away so he couldn't see the tears pooling in her eyes, but he likely did because he gave her a quick comfort-hug.

"Let's get out of here for a while," he said. "Let's go get a bite to eat. Everybody's so busy, they won't miss us. What do you say?"

11 MIXING OF THE TWAIN

Eva Clare dozed off on the fifteen-minute drive to Cleveland. She jarred awake when Roy stopped for a red light at Bishop Road. The long stretches of heavy work at the store—bending, lifting, mopping, painting, being on her feet seventeen hours a day—had taken their toll. Her throat was dry. Had her mouth been hanging wide open?

Roy chose a restaurant on Cotton Row, a one-way street with angle parking up against an incline that used to be the Illinois Central train track, but was now a greenway with a walking trail between the stores on Sharpe Avenue and the shops on Cotton Row. The restaurant had a firehouse theme. Pictures of firefighters and firehouse memorabilia covered the walls.

She sat in a booth across from Roy and nibbled on an appetizer of flash-fried crawfish tails.

"I'm almost too tired to eat," she said as she reached across the table and helped herself to one of his fried oysters. "I hope they're not missing us at the store. I feel guilty, but proud we've accomplished so much in such a short time."

"It's all coming together."

"Two more days to finish up the cleaning and painting, and then I'll start re-stocking the shelves with antiques, and on Friday, the consignment artists will come fill their booths." She forked a crawfish tail, dipped it into cocktail sauce, and ate it. She hadn't tasted food this good in months. "Oren Bagley is shipping his jewelry from North Carolina, and I'll set up for him. I can't wait to stock my own booth and get it ready for opening. In *ten* days."

"I'm looking forward to seeing your paintings." Roy pushed another plump oyster to the edge of his plate for Eva Clare. "I admire people who can create something out of nothing, whether it's a canvas or a piece of pottery."

She waved away the oyster offer. "If people will only come and shop. We've got ads running in the *Bolivar Commercial* and the *Delta Democrat Times*. That puts the word out to fifteen thousand people. Word of mouth is also spreading the news of our opening."

"Pete?" Roy grinned. "Is it his mouth the word is coming from?"

"Of course, it is."

The server delivered their entrées and refilled their glasses.

"You ready for this, Eva Clare?" Roy asked.

"What, eating salmon?"

"No, being an entrepreneur."

"I believe so." She took her fork and picked at the pineapple chutney on her grilled fillet. "Everything I've ever done in my life has prepared me for this venture. I have a bachelor's degree in art with a teaching component and a master's that prepared me to be resilient in an ever-changing art business world."

Roy took a bite of his Black Cat catfish entrée but kept his eyes on her as she talked.

"I've run a side business—selling my paintings—for years, and I've also consigned paintings, so I understand the process and know how to keep financial records. I've taught in community college for twenty-five years. Being in a classroom gave me experience in planning, making spot decisions, and achieving results. I think I have a fairly impressive portfolio. And a large collection of paintings." She wasn't one to lay praise on herself or pat herself on the back, but this was all for real. Listing her qualifications out loud gave her confidence, an old feeling that had been sporadically flaring up the last several days. "Yes, I believe I'm ready."

"I've been watching. I've seen you pull this together. I *know* you're ready." Roy ate another forkful. "This blackened catfish has a nice, strong kick to it."

Eva Clare eyed his plate—spicy catfish, rice pilaf, and creamy whiskey crawfish sauce.

"So, Eva Clare, tell me more about yourself. What's your story, if you don't mind sharing? The personal you, not the business you."

Her muscles tightened. She didn't like talking about her personal side. "Not much to tell. I was raised here, went off to college, married. Now, I'm separated and back home. My joy is art. I love the feel of spreading paint onto canvas. I'm inspired watching something take shape. And I loved teaching art—seeing others get a feeling of accomplishment and pride."

"That's why you're enjoying this project. It's the process you like—the organized cleaning, painting, putting things in order, watching the store change and take shape with new purpose."

"I also love team effort—seeing how each one contributes to the whole." With the tip of her fork, she tinkered with the red pepper flakes in her chutney. "This has been good for me. I lost faith in myself the past few months, and the store is helping me build it back."

"What happened, Eva Clare?"

"I lost my marriage, and with it came layers of loss—home, friends, church. All those years, I gave more to my marriage than to myself. I put him first. Mostly did what he wanted or needed to do for his betterment." She set her fork down. Bitterness oozed out with her words. "A woman gives up her dreams and potential for a man, and he fails her and leaves the relationship." She opened her napkin and pressed it out on her lap as in a ritual, running her hands repeatedly over the fabric, then clasped her hands and set them on the table top.

"I'm sorry." Roy reached over and touched her folded hands.

"Honestly, other things fed my lack of faith in self, too. I couldn't get on a tenure track at my job. Adjunct teachers are part-time with no benefits and low pay. It's less costly for a college to hire on a contractual basis than to offer permanent positions."

"Don't sell yourself short. You may not feel it on the inside, but you exude confidence and capability."

"Wish I felt it."

"Lots of wars going on down deep inside?"

"Oh, yeah."

"In the few weeks I've known you, I've watched you tackle situations. You identify, respond, and resolve."

"You see a whole lot more in me than I do."

Roy tapped his finger on the dessert menu sitting to his right. "Look here under the banana pudding and caramel cheesecake. It's the definition of the term that gave this restaurant its name. '*BACK~DRAFT: an explosion that occurs when the heated gases of an oxygen-starved fire mix with oxygen and ignite.*'"

"And . . . so-o-o?"

"Two opposite forces meet to spark combustion," Roy said. "It fits you. You've come home, you've been re-introduced to an old house that lost its matriarch, a faltering business, a dying town, and you stand up and meet them headlong. You're the oxygen. You generate a spark of combustion. You ignite the flames of change."

"Those are mighty impressive words." She laughed at his dramatic interpretation. "But pfft."

"Here's another way to address your lack of self-esteem. Tell me three solid accomplishments you made in your work in Nashville." He held up three fingers. "Only three."

She looked down at her plate, picked up her fork, picked at her food, looked up and met Roy's eyes. "Okay, I can play along." She bit her lip. Her motive for playing slid from simply participating in a conversation to proving her worth. "One. I was selected to be part of the Arts Collective Artistic Associates, which offered artistic services to businesses, and to display my work in their storefront."

"Good advertising. Bet you got a few jobs that way."

"Yes, I did." Eva Clare sipped her wine. "Two. I was commissioned to do a painting for a historic plantation house that was a field hospital for Confederate soldiers. Three. I was the first artist in town to display my paintings in a Nashville bank, with an opening and closing reception. The bank even sent out engraved invitations and had the event catered."

"Classy. Yeah, I'm looking at a woman who can blaze a path."

Her cheeks burned. "You're way too kind. But thank you. I appreciate what you're trying to do—make me feel better." She studied his face, his eyes. "So what about you, Roy? What's your story? Were you ever married?"

"I married when I was a junior in college. We met our freshman year, went through university and grad school together. She died in an accident when she was twenty-nine."

"I'm so sorry—"

"It was a long time ago. I've dealt with it. I've never had an interest in remarrying. Never been with anyone else. Never plan to."

He sounded firm on that decision. Why was he opposed to a relationship? Had he resorted to burying himself in books and teaching?

"Don't look at me like that." He pushed his lips out into a wrinkled smile. "I have friends, a social life, a professional life. Although, I admit, my life is in New Orleans, and I've been pretty lonesome here."

The restaurant lights dimmed to announce the official arrival of the evening dinner hour. "Ooh. Prophetic," he said. "I have to admit, I was glad you asked me to help work on the store. I needed something to do besides read and research all day. Pathetic, huh?"

"Sheer desperation." She smiled. Squirmed and shifted in her booth seat. Didn't want to feel anything for him. "Tell me about your genealogy and how you came to Erin."

"I landed here by doing a google search of 'little Delta towns on the Mississippi River.' One of my ancestors was in Mississippi during the Civil War, based on my grandmother's word and on some poems she had in her possession. I'm looking for him. I decided to live somewhere between Memphis and Port Gibson and branch out to do research. Then I narrowed my location to this county."

"Why?"

"Because during my sabbatical, I'm studying Civil War ghost towns, and there are two interesting ones nearby—Prentiss and Napoleon across the river in Arkansas."

"My people settled in Prentiss."

"You may know this, having grown up here: Mark Twain wrote about the town of Napoleon in *Life on the Mississippi*. He learned from a deathbed confession that ten thousand dollars was hidden behind a brick of a building in town, and he went to retrieve it, but discovered the town had been washed away by the river." Roy made a clicking sound in the side of his mouth. "Said it was astonishing to see the river rolling over a spot where he used to see a big self-complacent town, a town with a United States Marine hospital. A town swallowed up, vanished, gone to feed the fishes."

"Ten thousand dollars. The brick livery stable. At the corner of Orleans and Market. The edge of the building facing the courthouse. Fourth row down from the top, third brick. That's where the money is."

"Of course, you know." He laughed, and his shoulders shook.

She tucked back a smile, proud of the local history and her knowledge of it. "I think you're wise to follow your grandmother's word, but this sounds like a daunting search."

"I remember the day I went with my grandmother to our church cemetery back home to put flowers on the family graves. It was so hot we could've fried an egg on a tombstone, but still, she wanted to linger at each marker and tell a personal story about each ancestor. I wanted to go home and stand in front of the air conditioner with a cold root beer. I was ten. I remember looking down at my black-canvas high tops, letting her words float in one ear and out the other, like any kid would do. You know what I mean? I wish I'd listened better."

"Yeah, Grandmomma told stories, too, about the people buried in our little family cemetery."

"Grandmother got to one old stone, put her hands on her hips, and shook her head." Roy copied her. "She said, 'Now this one's got some mystery about him.' I perked up when she said that. She told me he'd married after the Civil War and had six children, all boys. He wrote poems and tucked them inside his Bible. Many of those poems were about a girl. The family thought he wanted a daughter. But it was a Mississippi Delta girl. I think there's something to that. His unit went south during the war, moved down the river, and crossed the state of Mississippi from Port Gibson east to the capital. I think he met his first love in Mississippi."

"But he didn't marry her?"

"No, he was moving with the war. Later married a girl on the adjoining farm in Illinois." Roy paused to eat. "But I want to know about that Mississippi girl. I'm a sucker for romance—as long as it's not mine. I'm looking for a true story to plant in my historical ghost-town research."

"And the poems? What about the poems? Where are they now?"

"I carry a copy of one in my wallet. The original paper is too fragile." He dug it out.

Mississippi Yazoo Delta Girl
Flaxen, wild and curly hair, the bonnet of a buttercup.
Lips, sweet nectar of a flow'r in pose,
Eyes, delphiniums in Mother's yard,
Skin pink and silky as a rose ~
A single rose abloom at dawn
Where the whip-poor-wills sing
And the wind flickers leaves
And the river rolls on 'til spring.
I carried you south, carried you north, on the river.
I will carry you to heav'n once I lie
Where the blades of my grave grass quiver.

~ W. E. Winslow

"He was smitten, all right," Eva Clare said.

Roy folded the paper and put it back in his wallet, then resumed his Black Cat. "What about that envelope Gerald gave you?"

"Oh, I forgot about that." She reached for her purse. Pulled it out, tore the flap open, retrieved a copy of a will in old-fashioned, hard-to-read handwriting where the esses looked like effs. She and Roy stumbled through it, seeking the pertinent lines.

State of Mississippi, Bolivar County. Know all men by these presents that I Andrew Coghlan for and in consideration of the agreement hereby entered into between my natural daughters Catherine Deering Coghlan Amason and Victoria Dove Coghlan and myself to the effect that my unmarried younger daughter Victoria Dove Coghlan will support and take care of me during my natural life, and in the further consideration of the natural love and affection which I have and do bear toward the said Victoria Dove Coghlan, I have this day and by these presents do give granted and delivered to my said daughter Victoria Dove Coghlan the following property and described parcel of land "to wit." The family home, original and newly built, and the tract of land bordered on the north by the river, east by Steele Bayou, south by Wellington Road, and west by the Dry Creek Bogue, comprising five acres more or less and situated in Bolivar

County and State of Mississippi to have and to hold the same with all the appurtenances and hereditaments, thereunto appertaining and to her heirs and assigns forever. Furthermore, if said daughter Victoria Dove Coghlan never has issue, the land and house shall revert to the oldest heir of my oldest daughter. In testimony whereof I the said Andrew Coghlan have hereunto set my hand and my seal the 21st day of February 1861.

"Who do you descend from?"

"The oldest daughter, Catherine Deering Coghlan Amason."

"Gerald, too?"

"Yes."

"Doesn't make sense. With all the property and wealth he has, why does he want that old house and five acres? Why is he pursuing this so fiercely?"

"I don't know."

"There's a missing piece to this puzzle." Roy rubbed his hand over his face, his whiskers. It sounded like he was scraping on sandpaper.

"Or he's mean and greedy."

"Nope, I'm betting there's a missing piece. What is his motive for wanting your inheritance?" Roy shook his head. "The land was Victoria's unless she didn't have children. Did she? Did Victoria ever have children?"

"No, she never married."

"I didn't ask that."

Eva Clare grimaced. "No. *No-o-o-o-o*, she was from a good family. They were pillars of the church and community. She wouldn't have had a child without being married." Eva Clare splattered words and excuses and tripped all over them as she tried to justify her upstanding ancestry.

12

NETHERMOST AND CREST

Booth setup day! It took three trips for Eva Clare to haul her oil paintings from Coghlan House to Betsy's Trunk. She arranged small canvas boards and larger ten-by-fourteens and twenty-by-sixteens in her booth. Displayed smaller pieces on easels and in baskets on a table covered with a black cloth. Hung larger ones on pegboard affixed to the wall. She stood back and took stock. A lot of work represented here. Lots of strokes. Lots of shades—grays, greens, creams. And black.

Her river paintings represented the story of a watercourse, alive, in motion. They showed change over time in the emotion of the woman in the water—from a girl reveling in play to a woman struggling at the bottom. The paintings were dark and disturbing. Her newer line of paintings, lighter in subject, showed meanderings of the Mississippi River—loops, curves, curls of the riverbed in all its ancient and modern positions based on geology and cartography. The river was dynamic— changing course over the course of time.

She set a thirty-six by forty-eight-inch painting on an easel in a corner, then stepped back to admire it. *Nethermost and Crest*—the last piece she painted before her husband left, when she knew things were terribly wrong between them. It depicted a woman swimming under water, going down to her nethermost point, but leveling out, poised to arch upward and crest.

Her booth was stocked and ready for opening day.

Turning the key and unlocking the door to Betsy's Trunk on that first day under her watch equaled a commitment to this store, this town, this place called the Delta.

No turning back. Only moving forward.

And rising up.

Tired, stressed, she worried nobody would come to the store's opening tomorrow, but she made herself take care of other business tonight. She sat at the rolltop desk in the Coghlan House parlor, raking through drawers.

Lily slogged in, flopped down in a wingback chair next to the desk, and hung a leg over the arm. "My mamaw's not doing well."

"She's not?" Eva Clare kept rummaging. In front of her lay the Coghlan will Gerald had provided and a sawtooth-rimmed crystal bowl full of jelly beans.

"Her breathing's slow, labored. Her pain has increased. I don't think she'll last more than twenty-four hours. I've alerted the doctor and hospice." Lily started to cry.

Eva Clare shut the drawer and turned toward her. "I'm sorry. Is there anything I can do?"

Lily shook her head. "Time to up her morphine. Then wait it out."

Eva Clare's shoulders dropped. "I've never known this house without Marthala. She fed me, fussed at me, cleaned my room, washed and ironed my clothes. Spanked me with one hand and loved on me with the other."

"Yeah, me too."

"Tomorrow's opening day at the store. Your booth is ready. Your merchandise will take care of itself. Stay with Marthala." Eva Clare reached over and patted Lily's arm. "But what about the after-party at Sunny's house at close of business? If Marthala is holding her own, I hope you'll come, even if only for a minute."

"I'll try to stop by." Lily folded her long legs under her and changed the subject. "What're you plowing around in the drawers for?"

"I'm looking for old family papers—wills, land documents, something, anything. I've got to fight that big bully Gerald over this house. You'd think Grandmomma would hang on to important papers, but no, I can't find a thing."

"You got her current will. I don't know what you're so worked up about."

"It's not about being legal. It's about getting Gerald off my back." She picked out a purple jelly bean, popped it into her mouth, and chewed on it. "I need an edge over him—some other document to prove I rightly own Coghlan House. I'm running out of places to look."

"Sweet Evelyn saved everything."

"She did? How do you know?"

"I've seen things."

"What've you seen? What do you know?"

"How well do you know this house?"

"What do you mean? I grew up here. I know this house well."

"I mean Sweet Evelyn saved everything from way back to the 1700s when the first Coghlans—your family and mine—settled in North Carolina from Ireland and got recorded in the first census." Lily arched an eyebrow. "It's all here. You have to know where to look."

"Obviously, I don't. Where, Lily? Where do I look? I don't have the time or patience for endless forays into drawers and cabinets. If you know, please tell me."

Lily stood, hands on hips, chin up, winked. "There might be a nook somewhere—"

"You mean the secret hinged stair? The seventh one up? Because I've already looked, and nothing's in there."

"No, not that. I don't know about that."

"What then?"

"You don't know about the hiding place?"

Eva Clare threw up her hands. "What hiding place?"

"Oh, sakes alive. You *don't* know. Oh, my God."

"How about you tell me?"

"You never explored this house?"

"Sure I did." Eva Clare scrunched her face. "Mostly outside the house, though. The woods, the barn, the river. Are there nooks and crannies inside the house that I may not be aware of? Tell me."

Lily formed a wicked smile. "In due time. Can't now. The light is underneath us. We got to wait for the light of day. And now, I'm goin' to check on Mamaw."

Eva Clare pulled in a breath, huffed a sigh. What had she missed during her growing-up years here in the family homestead? What did Grandmomma hide from her? And where? And why? And how did Lily know?

Sometime in the night, Eva Clare came out of a deep sleep. Someone was in the room. Afraid to move, she lay there under the covers, eyeing the hall door, the closet door, the window seat, the wicker rocker, the dresser mirror revealing the opposite wall. The window across the room was backlit by the pole light outside. The drapes hung straight and still. No one in sight.

Her heart kicked up to a rapid pace. A warm flush approached, wrapped around her, entered her body, and filled her with peace.

She squeezed her eyes shut. Then opened them.

The woman stood between the bed and the window—a figure with long blonde hair, a white dress, a bluish glow around her. She stared at Eva Clare, didn't utter a word, but slowly formed a smile.

Then she disappeared.

Eva Clare sat up, blinked hard, scanned the room.

Was it a dream?

She lay down and pulled the covers up tightly around her. Yes, she'd had a dream. Upon awakening in the morning, she'd see that woman's face, that piercing stare. The image would linger. But it was only a dream.

Wasn't it?

She turned over and buried her face in the pillow. The hum of the window unit lulled her back to sleep.

13 REVENANT

She's here. She's close.
Very close now.
Close to me, close to her past, close to her future.
Close to truth. Close to setting the course straight.
The stars are aligned.
I see hope.
Hope that she will carry on what I could not.

14 LETTING OUT THE STEAM

Eva Clare checked the time on her wrist. Ten o'clock. The date: Friday, July 16. She flipped the OPEN sign around to face the street and unlocked the door. The new Betsy's Trunk: *Art and Antiques of the Mississippi Delta* was ready to meet the public.

Would people come? What if nobody showed up? A sick feeling ran through her. A kaleidoscope of butterflies flickered inside her. She put her hands over her stomach to hold them still, did a half-turn, and studied the store she and her team had transformed.

Booths teemed with ample merchandise and enough variety to keep customers interested: oil paintings, quilts, watercolors, jewelry, pottery, river rock designs. A sign tacked up at the antiques section read: WATCH OUR PROGRESS! COME OFTEN! She'd continue to display old finds for her customers and as needed, bring back stock she'd thinned from the shelves and stashed in her barn.

She breathed in the smell of antique books, a scent from a lighted candle on the checkout counter. Its fragrance came from the right combination of oils creating an interpretation of the smell of aged leather book covers. The leather smell combined with fresh paint and orange furniture polish covered any remnant of the old mildewy stew of odors that refused to air out during remodeling.

Betsy, in a red polyester suit, ruby-red lipstick, and a long strand of pearls, occupied a spot in the checkout area. A table with a white cloth awaited Sunny and her Mississippi Mud Cupcakes.

Eva Clare stroked her gold necklace charm that read HOPE. This was her moment to prove herself. She swallowed her tingling anxiety and took her position beside Betsy.

"It's our big day, Miss Betsy. We'll see the results of our hard work."

"You've earned a good day." Betsy's open smile showed her trust, as well as some ruby-red lipstick smudges on her teeth.

The bell on the door dinged, and a deliveryman from Mistlow Gardens in Cleveland entered with a tall dracaena plant. He put it on the counter by the register, and Eva Clare checked the tag: "Wishing you much success! Pete."

"Aww. Sweet Pete. He doesn't miss a thing."

Roy walked in, came to stand with Eva Clare and Betsy, and as he shut the waist-high door of the checkout station, he said, "I'll help make sure your point-of-sale system works properly, while you handle everything else."

"Thanks." Eva Clare twisted her hands and rubbed them together. "No customers yet."

"You've only been open five minutes. Give it ten or fifteen before you fall apart."

The door whooshed open, and Anna Laurel rushed in. "I abandoned my coffee shop—and all my customers—to check on you and tell you that if anyone asks about lunch possibilities, Sunny made some individual ham and egg pies. If nobody comes, I've got my own lunch and dinner for the next four weeks. Now, I've got to run back. Oh, and it looks fabulous in here."

Sunny pushed in behind her. "I've got it!" Her hands reached toward the ceiling.

"Well, I don't want it. Don't pass it on to me," Anna Laurel said with an eye roll. "I'm getting out of here. Move out of my way." She did a double take of Sunny all dressed up in a white, double-breasted chef coat and shook her head as she exited.

"You've got what?" Eva Clare said.

"I've got a great idea. During our planning meeting a few weeks ago, you mentioned incorporating and connecting the store space between the Trunk and Anna Laurel's coffee shop." Sunny held her hands in front of her, palms out, in a wait-for-it flash. "I've got it. It could be a pie store. We—or I—could bake meat pies and fruit pies. We could sell pies. We could sell whole pies to go, and we could put in a few tables and chairs where people can sit and eat individual slices of pie. Pie makes everybody happy. People love pies, but they don't like to bake them. Lord knows, it's too messy, takes too much time, and it's too hard to make double crusts. I've even got a name."

"What?" Eva Clare asked.

"Pie Bird."

"Pie *Bird*?"

"Do you know what that is?"

"I guess not."

Roy shook his head. Betsy smiled.

"Okay, forgive me. I stole something from your store last week. I mean, I didn't really steal it. I borrowed it to do some research because it caught my eye. Now, I'm returning it." Sunny pulled a small ceramic item out of the pocket of her chef jacket and showed it to them.

Betsy's mouth dropped open, and she lifted a crooked finger to point. "That's an old pie vent that belonged to my family."

"I'm sorry I took it, Miss Betsy. It's also called a pie bird."

"Tell us what it is," Eva Clare said, eyeing the door for customers.

"It's a hollow ceramic tool used for venting a pie." Sunny held up the four-inch gadget, turned it side to side. "Look. It's shaped like an upstretched bird with an open beak. You place it in the center of the pie, and the steam from the fillin' escapes by flowing up and out the hollow center through the mouth. That keeps the pie fillin' from boiling up and leaking through the crust and makin' an ugly mess on the pie top and the oven floor."

Eva Clare took the pie bird from Sunny and examined it. It resembled a bird, all right. Cream-colored with flower decorations—little blue periwinkles, a red tulip, a yellow bloom with sunflower-like petals—and a gold beak and gold feet.

"They date back to the Victorian period, but this one's from the 1940s," Sunny said. "Note the age crazing—the fine lines in the glaze— which is common in an old ceramic piece. This little bird is worth about a hundred and fifty dollars. I can get cheap reproductions and sell some pies with the pie birds and some without. The pie bird symbol gives the business a vintage-sounding name."

"I like pies," Betsy said. "I like the idea. I have several pie vents at the house you can have. And I've got a few ice cream parlor tables and chairs stored in my shed at home from some estate sale years ago. Maybe got three or four old pie safes. You can fix them up and use them."

"Oh gosh, thank you. It's a sign. It's meant to be. I'm excited!" Sunny clapped her hands. "I can bake ham and egg pies from my grandmother's recipe, chicken pot pies, Mississippi Pot Roast pies, strawberry pies, apple pies, blackberry pies. I can bake the world a better place!"

"Is this pie vent thing like 'Sing a Song of Sixpence'?" Roy asked. "'Blackbirds, like blackberries, baked in a pie'?"

"Yes! 'When the vent was placed in the pie, the birds began to sing.' That was the steam coming out of their mouths." Sunny laughed and did a Roger Rabbit hip-hop dance move.

"Oh, Christ," Betsy said.

"We'll talk about it later and put some concrete ideas on paper," Eva Clare said, trying to quell some of Sunny's exuberance. She handed the pie bird to Betsy, who passed it to Sunny.

Sunny squealed her delight. "Yay! I've got to set up my cupcakes now."

The door opened and Meredith walked in as Sunny ran out in loud, triumphant glee. "What's up with her? She's acting like a balloon with the air farting out."

"Sunny being Sunny."

Meredith pointed toward her booth. "I'm going to hang out a while in case any shoppers have questions about my designs or want to place special orders."

Everybody had high hopes about the store opening . . . except Eva Clare. She still had a host of fluttering butterflies.

Fifteen minutes in, the door opened, and in walked a real live customer, a woman wanting to look at quilts. She ended up buying three, one for each of her grandchildren. Then two young women in ponytails and tennis skirts came, apparently after an early-morning game. They browsed, then lingered at the Merry River Rocks booth for a conversation with Meredith and a purchase each.

About every fifteen minutes, someone new entered the arts area and browsed the merchandise. At noon, Eva Clare checked the guest book she'd put on a table by the door and saw that eleven people had signed in, and her records showed that fourteen items had been purchased. Betsy confirmed this totaled more than the shop had sold in the last two years.

Roy left at twelve. Sunny was still passing out free cupcakes and promoting her pastries. Employees of other stores came in on their lunch breaks, got free dessert, and browsed. Some progressed to the aisles of antiques behind the consignment area, and several bought vintage pieces that had been sitting in dust for decades before being cleaned and polished for opening day. Shortly before one o'clock, Gerald strutted through the door.

Eva Clare's stomach twisted.

Why did she let him get to her? She hated herself for that as much as she hated him. She wished he'd leave her alone. But no, he showed up on her special day. He always ruined everything.

He eyed the cupcake table where Sunny carried on an animated conversation with Jean from the Piggly Wiggly and Martha from Harper Hardware. Both ladies had made purchases and were carrying little brown paper Trunk bags. He looked at her booth—Ghosts on the Oxbow— where an art student from Delta State was browsing. Moved on to Star's—Lily's quilts with the colorful star patterns. Put his hands on his hips, stood in a wide stance, locked his knees. Then he went on to Merry River Rocks and listened to Meredith describe to shoppers how she collected her materials from the riverbank and put together her art pieces of tiny, unique rock shapes and bits of colored, broken glass. He scanned the rear antique section, then turned and started back up the aisle, first stopping at the Delta Scenes Water Colors booth where two out-of-town women were comparing prints of cotton fields and old sharecropper shacks to determine which to buy. He lingered at the Delta Strong jewelry booth where four women were examining copper bracelets and necklaces, one an employee of his bank. Then he entered the Mud River Pottery booth and inspected a few pieces. On his way toward the exit, he reached for a cupcake and licked the chocolate and marshmallow icing. Never even looked at Eva Clare, never spoke to a soul, even Betsy, didn't sign the guest book, didn't even thank Sunny for the cupcake. He could've sent a pretty plant like Pete did, he could've congratulated her or at least said hi, but he didn't. Her face heated.

By closing time, the guest book and register listed forty-six shoppers and thirty-nine purchases. Eva Clare had sold six of her small four-by-fours and two ten-by-eights. She'd have to get busy painting again. She'd set up an easel in the back of the store and do all her painting in the Trunk during work hours.

It was a successful day. But something gnawed at her.

Then she remembered.

Gerald.

He came. He looked. He listened.

What was he up to?

Sunny pulled her front door wide open. "Come on in, y'all," she said to Eva Clare, Anna Laurel, and Meredith. "I've got ginger ale punch, pastries by Sister Sunflowers, and other delicacies. Help yourselves." She was host of the after-party that also included Roy, Betsy, Pete and Angie Wong, all the Trunk artists except Oren, local merchants and spouses, and several couples from the church. About forty people showed up to celebrate the town's new business.

After Eva Clare and her friends served their plates, the doorbell rang. Sunny answered, and Lily strolled in, made her way to the food spread, picked from the table, and gravitated to a potted ficus tree in a corner of the living room. Eva Clare, Anna Laurel, and Meredith made their way to her.

"How's your grandmother?" Anna Laurel asked.

"I could barely get a BP reading. I'll stay fifteen minutes, and then I better go home. A hospice nurse is with her now and will stay till the end."

"We understand." Eva Clare smiled at Lily's use of the word "home." She put her hand on Lily's back and rubbed it to comfort her.

"Of course, we do. We're glad you came." Anna Laurel swiveled her punch cup to break up the ice chunks.

"I had to support my friend." Lily gave a nod toward Eva Clare. "I'm proud for you."

"Thanks. And on a happier note, you sold some quilts today."

"I love your quilts," Meredith said. "How long have you been making them?"

"All my life. My grandmother taught me. She also taught me about quilt patterns."

"I've read that quilt patterns were used during the Civil War to communicate information about the Underground Railroad to runaway slaves," Anna Laurel said.

"That's true. Slaves couldn't read or write, so they used a needle, thread, and fabric to make quilts that communicated travel directions and safe places. They understood the meanings in the quilt patterns, but plantation owners didn't." Lily ate a ham-and-pickle roll-up.

"I've also heard there were 'safe houses' in the South, even as the South was fighting to keep slavery." Anna Laurel sipped her punch, bit down on a piece of ice.

"Yeah, that's right."

"How, Lily?" Meredith asked. "How'd they use the quilts to communicate?"

"A plantation seamstress sewed a sampler quilt with twelve blocks. Each block had a different secret-coded message to help slaves plan their escape and travel routes. She'd hang it on a fence, off a porch railing, or out a window, like she was airing out bedding. The slaves studied it. Learned what each block meant by word of mouth."

Meredith and Anna Laurel leaned in to collect every word.

"The first block in the sampler quilt was Jacob's Ladder. It showed the slaves what direction to travel. Dark colors pointed the way out of bondage. Slaves would know the way to go by the angle at which the quilt was placed outside a sympathizer's home." Lily glanced at her watch. "The second block was the Monkey Wrench pattern. The monkey wrench was a tool that blacksmiths used to turn the nuts that held a wagon wheel to an axle. The blacksmith was the most knowledgeable slave on the plantation and could move around and talk to people without anyone being suspicious. He was the one who got things going, the one who turned the wagon wheel, so to speak. The message of the Monkey Wrench pattern was to start gathering supplies they'd need for the journey."

"So much communicated in such a simple design," Meredith acknowledged.

"The third block, the Wagon Wheel pattern—or Carpenter's Wheel or Carpenter's Star, a variation of the Wagon Wheel—was symbolic of a chariot coming for to carry them home, like the song 'Swing Low, Sweet Chariot' says. Home meant heaven to some, freedom to others. Wagons with hidden compartments were used to carry runaways to freedom, so the message was to pack their belongings in a bandana bundle but pack light so it would fit with them in a wagon's secret space under the seat." Lily ran a chip through crab dip. "My pattern is based on the Carpenter's Star variation."

"Tell us about yours," Eva Clare said.

"It has an eight-point star in the center of the block. Each star point has a meaning. The star is symbolic of divine guidance. The message: Follow the North Star to freedom." Lily ate the chip and looked at her watch again.

"We're bombarding you with all these questions when you probably need to go home to your grandmother," Meredith said. "We're sorry."

"But this is history, and it's fascinating," Anna Laurel said. "Are you okay to stay a few more minutes?"

"Sure. I should finish my crash course in quilt history." Lily winked and lifted her brows. "Slaves used the sampler quilt to memorize the codes. Then the seamstress sewed twelve quilts, each in one of the twelve patterns. When the time was right, she'd hang out the appropriate quilt, and the slaves would interpret the code and follow its direction. Like when the Monkey Wrench quilt was displayed, the slaves knew to pack needed supplies, like a knife, a compass, food, coins, something for self-defense. Even mental tools, like alertness."

"That was pretty well thought through," Anna Laurel said.

"There's a tradition of coding with symbols in Africa," Lily said, "and it's controlled by secret societies. To learn the meanings of the codes, you had to prove you could keep quiet. I've kept the code secret all my life.

My grandmother insisted on it, and I respected her wishes. Now, my mamaw is dying, and I'll be talking about my quilt pattern. I don't feel a loyalty to silence and secrecy anymore. I want people to know. Telling is freedom. Knowing is freedom. Truth is freedom." She drank her punch. "One of my ancestors wore shackles. Her name was Star. Marthala's mother Alight remembered seeing the scars on her legs."

"That's why your quilt company is called Star's?" Meredith asked.

"Yes, and also because the stars are sky markers. People have long used the stars for navigation. Even the slaves did. They sang a song called 'Follow the Drinking Gourd.' That's the Big Dipper. The front side of the dipper's bowl faced the North Star, which guided the runaways. They traveled at night. Slept by day. Followed rivers. Stopped at sunrise when they spotted a house on the riverbank with a quilt hanging on its porch rail or out a window. A quilt with a star meant it was okay to stop, that sympathizers lived there. The slaves could get food, sleep, a hideout from soldiers or the law, and directions for their journey."

"Our town's on the river," Meredith said. "Wonder if we had sympathizers here."

"Well, I'm not lettin' all the steam out," Lily said, glancing at her watch. "Runaways walked alongside the river, followed the North Star, got through Memphis, kept walkin' that river till it forked, and they walked the Kentucky line east till they came to a crossing point where they swam or boated or walked across the Ohio River to a safe house. A long time ago, that river wasn't deep like it is now. Then they went on to freedom in the North." She handed Eva Clare her empty plate and punch cup. "Now, I might better go on home."

Lily's phone made a piano-riff sound. She grabbed it from her pocket and looked at the incoming text. Eva Clare stood close enough to see it was from hospice, the message clipped and urgent. "Come home. Come now." Eva Clare put her hand on Lily's arm.

Lily looked up at the ceiling. "She's going. She's going."

15
SECOND CHANCES

After changing out of pajamas into yoga pants and a slub cotton T-shirt, Eva Clare lumbered from her bed to the couch in the pine-paneled den. She curled up under an afghan to watch a Sunday-morning, black-and-white TV movie of *Little Women*.

Whomp! A weighty garbage bag hit the floor down the hall. "Dammit!" Lily yelled.

The noise jarred Eva Clare. She tightened into a fetal position and pulled the blanket over her shoulders. The past few days, Lily had been bagging and throwing out Marthala's belongings, packing and returning medical equipment, and cleaning the master bedroom and adjoining bathroom after Marthala's death three weeks ago. The harder she worked, the more stuff she banged around and the more expletives she spewed.

Eva Clare had offered to help once or twice. But this morning, she couldn't. Working at the Trunk six days a week and cleaning and rearranging antiques on the seventh made every muscle in her body hurt. It even pained her to sit up on the couch. She was worn slap out.

Another *whomp*. Glass shattered. Lily, in the hall outside the den door, followed it with a string of profanities.

"Lily?" Eva Clare pushed herself up.

Lily started to cry, an open-mouthed wailing.

"Lily, what's wrong?"

"It's all too heavy."

Eva Clare winced. Lily obviously meant something other than the heaviness of her load. She meant loss and bone-deep mourning. "I'll help you." Eva Clare forced herself off the couch.

"I miss my mamaw, and I don't want to be throwin' her stuff away." Lily bent forward, clasped her hands to her knees, and sobbed. "She's gone. When I dump these bags, her stuff'll be gone. Like she was never here." She straightened. "It ain't right. I can't do this."

"C'mere." Eva Clare pulled Lily to her and put her arms around Lily's shoulders for a hug. "Maybe it's too soon. Wait a while." She'd gotten used to having Lily and Marthala in the house over the last month and a half. Lily was like family now—someone you looked out for, cared for, would do anything for.

"I know I need to be out of this house."

Eva Clare reached for her hand. "Take a break; sit a minute." She guided Lily to a chair in the den and sat on the couch facing her.

"You don't have to leave, Lily. Stay as long as you need."

"I promised you I'd go when Mamaw passed."

"I've been so busy with the store, I don't even know you're here. And Lord knows, I don't have time or energy to move bedrooms right now. I'm not pushing you to leave."

"I got to find a place. I've also got to redirect my whole future. What will I do without my caregiving responsibilities? First, Sweet Evelyn. Then, Mamaw—now out there in that hot hell of a graveyard."

"She's in a peaceful spot under a shade tree."

Eva Clare had attended Marthala's funeral and burial at the County Road 446 A.M.E. church, surrounded by cotton fields. She'd been the only White person present. People had looked side-eyed at her, but she didn't care. She didn't know a world without Marthala, and by golly, she was going to be at the final service. She'd watched as Marthala was lowered into the ground in the church cemetery inside a chain-link fence that served to separate the headstones from the cotton. One new green boll stuck its face through diamond-shaped wire.

"I don't have anywhere to go." Lily's shoulders dropped.

"I mentioned the guesthouse out back."

"I went and took a look. It's in pretty bad shape. Some of the floor boards are rotten. You could walk across the floor and fall through. There are holes, and in some places, you can see the dirt ground."

"I didn't know—"

"I know you didn't. It was kind of you to offer, but it would take too much money to fix."

"Yeah, and I'm sorry, I don't have the money."

"I understand. It's not your problem. It's mine. I knew this day was coming, and I didn't want to face it. I don't know what I'm gon do." Lily stroked one of her gold-cross earrings. "I'm like you. My life fell apart. Only I don't have a home to go back to."

A pang struck Eva Clare in her chest where the rib bones met. A rush of compassion followed. "Stay here as long as you like. Take your time looking. We'll look together. I'll help you find a place." She put herself right in the middle of the search. "But for now, you've got to keep your head about you."

Lily got up and walked toward the door. "Then I guess I'll haul this stuff to my car and to the dump. The strain of lifting and toting the bags helps me push out the hurt."

"I can help, if you want."

Lily shook her head at the offer of assistance, caught hold of the bag tops, and dragged those heavy burdens down the hallway.

Eva Clare heard the door close behind Lily, went back to the couch, and tried to ease her conscience as the March sisters played out their antics on the TV screen.

A rapping at the door stirred her. She went to the window and peeked through the blinds. Roy. He'd made a habit of dropping by unannounced every few days. She licked an index finger and ran it under each eye to clear mascara residue, raked her fingers through her hair, then opened the back door and wrapped her arms across her chest because she didn't have on a bra.

"I'm warning you, I'm lazing around today and not prepared to meet the world," she said.

"I'm not the world. I'm just one lonely boy."

"Well, come on in, lonely boy."

Roy closed the door behind him. "Want me to make a pot of coffee?"

"Sure. And I can warm up some of Sunny's day-old cinnamon rolls."

Eva Clare took the Sister Sunflowers box out of the fridge, put three cinnamon rolls on a plate, stuck it in the oven on low to warm, and set the timer. "So why aren't you in church this morning?" She watched from behind as Roy filled the carafe with sink water. "I figured church attendance would be a requirement since you teach at a seminary."

"Touché." Roy poured the water in the reservoir of the Cuisinart coffeemaker. "I had my own worship service at the river this morning."

"Didn't gather with the saints, huh?"

He scooped in coffee, snapped the lid back on the canister, and faced Eva Clare. "Nope, gathered alone at the river." He leaned back against the counter and took on a serious look. "I like the people here. They're fine folks. But there's only one church in town, and when it comes to religion, well . . . they're a little too narrow for me."

"Yeah. Me, too."

"They're comfortable with their beliefs, but I'm not." He cocked his head. "I once read of an experiment in which flies were put in a jar with holes poked in the lid and held captive for a time. Then the lid was removed. The flies didn't try to leave. They kept flying around and around inside that jar."

Eva Clare pictured the jar, the flies going in circles, each one watching the little fly butt in front of him.

Roy looked at the ceiling. "There was a bigger world outside the jar. Full of freethinking and openness, reason and wonder, but the flies stayed content in the mindset they'd fit themselves to. Their reality had shrunk to the jar. Life outside the jar ceased to exist."

The coffeemaker sputtered and dripped, and the smell of French roast filtered out.

"People can be like those flies," Roy said. "They feel safe inside their jar—their church, religion, political party, family tradition—and they're fully satisfied with their set of beliefs. All they know is packed tightly inside that jar."

"I understand that mindset. I used to be a fly inside that jar. I held my set of beliefs like a deck of cards, spread them fan-style in one hand, and shuffled them around as I needed to. That's the way I grew up in this small Delta town. But I came to see the inconsistencies in the principles I was taught and the lives lived out by those teaching me. It made me question everything."

Roy walked over to her and put his hands on her arms.

She sucked in a breath, didn't know what to do with the closeness. "Then my husband left me, and divorce was not a belief that was inside our jar. I felt the other flies pushing me out."

"So what did you do?" He slid his arms around her and drew her in. She responded, put her head against his shoulder.

What was she doing? Did she want to be this close to him, to anybody?

She released herself and stepped back. "I left the jar."

"You did what?"

The back door swung open, and Lily barged in.

"I left the jar," Eva Clare repeated.

"You left what jar where?" Lily asked.

Eva Clare and Roy laughed and moved farther apart.

"What are y'all doing?" Lily wagged a finger from Eva Clare to Roy.

"Nothing, and not a real jar," Eva Clare said.

"Well, I ain't got the time to follow that one." Lily sat down at the table and fanned her face with her hand.

Roy got two cups out of the cabinet and filled them with strong-smelling coffee. He handed one to Eva Clare and asked Lily if she wanted the other.

"No, it's too hot out." She wiped sweat off her forehead. "Besides, the caffeine will make my blood pressure higher than it already is."

"Lily, I'm sorry for the loss of your grandmother." Roy took a few steps to the table where Lily sat and leaned toward her. "I hope you're holding up."

"I'm trying. I get depressed and have crying spells. Sometimes, I fall to pieces." She scrunched her face. "I haven't seen you around the last couple of days. Where you been?"

"Down on Lake Washington doing research. My sabbatical includes writing the history of selected Mississippi River ghost towns. I was visiting the extinct town of Leota."

"I've never heard of Leota," Eva Clare said. She wrapped her free hand around her coffee cup and leaned against the countertop.

"Me either," Lily said.

"Key word: extinct." Roy chuckled. "Leota Plantation was established in 1825 by Isaac Worthington. He built a mansion to be their residence and the farm headquarters. The farm became a shipping point for cotton." He took a sip from his steaming mug.

"Was it a plantation or a town?" Lily asked.

"Both. History calls it a forced-labor farm."

"Yeah, and we know what that means." Lily rolled her eyes. "Slave labor. I don't know why history can't say 'slave labor.'"

"As for the town, Worthington built twelve stores, a post office, a school, and a church. In 1900, the population was fifty. The mansion was eventually destroyed by a flood, and in 1930, the entire plantation was taken over by another flood. Seems like every place along this river eventually gets covered up by it. Eva Clare, it's a wonder your house still exists."

"Oh, it has flooded a few times. Especially before the levee was built."

"It's heart-wrenching that a hundred years ago, people lived a full, busy life there that we know little or nothing about," Roy said. "They built houses of timber and bricks fired on the spot, went to a mercantile to buy cloth and candy, went to church, had babies and raised children. Nothing's left of it. It's all gone. Nothing's there but forestland, farmland, and grazing land. And a levee and an old cemetery with some unmarked graves at a three-point intersection north of an oxbow lake. Now, Roy's Store is there." He grinned. "And there's even a Roy's Store Road."

"Is Roy's Store going in your write-up?" Lily asked.

"You better believe it is. That and the cemetery stones and the black cows standing around eating grass." Roy pressed his lips into a fine line and tipped his head to the side. "You know, there's nothing but change up and down this river. Nothing stays the same."

"Wha—?" Eva Clare jerked her head to a tilt. All her life she'd complained about no change. She set her cup on the counter with a thud. Roy brought a disturbingly different perspective to the matter. But he was right.

"There's so much people don't know about what used to be," Lily said. "It's all lost."

"I want to talk to you about your people, Lily," Roy said. "Let's set a time. I'm at a dead end with my personal research. I can't find my ancestor. I need to know what your people knew about this town and its settlers."

"I'm glad to share, but I'm real busy these days."

"I understand. But you have to eat. Come over to my house, and I'll cook for you. We'll eat and talk. Eva Clare, the invitation includes you."

"Sure. I have to eat, too." She winced. What a lame answer.

"Okay," Lily agreed. "Maybe late in the week. Friday? I've still got work to do here. That'll give me time to finish."

Eva Clare's phone rang. She looked at the screen. "Gerald." She pushed the green circle.

Roy and Lily waited as Gerald talked, then listened to Eva Clare's answers.

"No, I'm not interested. Please stop pushing me."

Roy and Lily looked at each other with raised eyebrows.

"No, I will not sign."

Roy and Lily looked at Eva Clare with raised eyebrows.

"Gerald, I said no, I'm not signing anything. I'm not making any deals."

There was a long silence as Gerald talked to Eva Clare.

"No!" she answered. "I said no. I will never agree to give up my land. And I don't appreciate the threat of having to go to court over this. I don't want to talk to you anymore."

She pushed the red circle on the screen and dropped her arm to her side.

"I guess you told him. But what did he tell you?" Lily asked.

"He says he's got a quitclaim deed and wants me to sign it and gift this land to him as the historical rightful owner, based on the original will. He says if I don't sign, he'll take me to court. He says he's got a deal with a land development company that wants to build a hunting, fishing, and recreation resort here on my land."

"He's bullying you," Lily said.

"They'll tear the house down. My family home." Eva Clare's shoulders sagged with the weight of Gerald's intimidation.

"That's the missing piece," Roy said. "He's got a deal in the works."

"He wants to take my past, present, and future away from me."

"He wants to take it away from everybody," Lily added.

Eva Clare studied Lily for the meaning of that remark. "What am I gonna do?"

"Gift. He said gift. That's the word to focus on," Roy said. "He knows he's got nothing. It's an idle threat."

"Okay, that's it. This has gone far enough." Lily struck her palms together. "I've been pussyfootin' around, but now, I'm gon tell you what I know. It'll help you put Gerald Tanner in his place. I've had enough of him and his claim of being the rightful owner of your grandmomma's house. I'm in a mood anyways these days. Let me get a flashlight. I'm gon show you something that'll rock your world." She scrambled to retrieve a light from a kitchen drawer.

Eva Clare set her coffee cup down, turned the oven off, and took the rolls out. "Flashlight?" she mouthed to Roy, who shrugged and shook his head. "What does she need a flashlight at high noon for?" she whispered.

# 16 HIDDEN IN PLAIN VIEW

Lily started down the hallway, flashlight in hand. "Follow me." She led Eva Clare and Roy through the foyer, out the front door, and onto the stoop that faced the oxbow, the old river channel. "Turn around and look at the panel of colored glass above the door. This is what people going down the river in the olden days saw. Anything catch your eye?"

"Yep," Eva Clare said right away. "The stained glass is out of pattern."

"What?" Roy strained to see the discrepancy.

Eva Clare pointed to the leaded-in geometric shapes. "Look at the bottom row of squares above the transom, each one about the size of a cocktail napkin. The color pattern is blue-brown. The row should finish in blue-brown, but instead, it ends with blue-blue."

"Is this important?" Roy scratched his head.

"Keep it in mind." Lily waggled her flashlight. "Y'all ready?"

The crunch of gravel came from behind them as a car turned into the driveway. Eva Clare turned to look. Baby-blue T-Bird, Anna Laurel at the wheel.

"What's she doin' here?" Lily stood hipshot.

They lingered at the open door and waited for Anna Laurel to make her way to the porch. Lily fast-tapped her foot.

"Hey, everybody." Anna Laurel strolled up with a box of Sister Sunflowers pastries. "I brought you some day-olds." She handed the box to Eva Clare. "What's going on?"

"Lily's giving me a guided tour of my house."

"Why do you need a tour?"

"I'm fixin' to find out. Apparently, there are things I don't know."

"Stop being sarcastic," Lily grumbled. To Anna Laurel, she said, "C'mon, go with us." She stepped back to make room. "You're gon need some facts to shut Gerald Tanner up."

"What's he doing now?"

"He's threatening court," Lily answered.

"He wants to sell my house and property to a development company," Eva Clare added.

"He's baiting you, and you're eating the crumbs right out of his hand. Quit falling prey to him." Anna Laurel shook her pointer finger at Eva Clare. "You have a legal will."

"I know," Eva Clare growled. "It goes back to childhood. He always bullied—"

"Okay, let's go back inside," Lily interrupted.

"You let him." Anna Laurel snarled. "It should be: He is rain; you're a duck."

"Follow me." Lily stepped into the foyer and pointed the flashlight toward the staircase to the second floor, making hand signs and arm flourishes to dramatize her commands. "Let's go up." To Eva Clare, she said, "Put those pastries on the sideboard."

Up the stairs they followed Lily. The top tread creaked under Eva Clare's foot as she knew it would. She placed the other foot on the wood of the wide hallway. Under her step the floor had a shoe-sized indention where so many others before her had stepped. The second story had four rooms remodeled in the 1940s, then in 1959 after Eva Clare's arrival, and lastly, in 1995 after Grandpop's death. When the house was built in 1861, the rooms were bedrooms with no closets and no bathroom. The remodels reflected needs of the occupants in their day. Now, to her right was a guestroom. To her left was a big bathroom with a clawfoot tub, wicker furniture, and an antique wardrobe for towel storage. She knew all there was to know about this house.

After turning on the light, Lily led her entourage down the hall, stopping at opposite doorways—Eva Clare's room on the left and what they called the reading room on the right. In front of them at the end of the hall was the door to the linen closet. "Look in Eva Clare's room, y'all, at the back outside wall of the house. Her room had one of the original fireplaces. It was removed in 1959, when the downstairs master bedroom, bath, and den were added, according to my mamaw Marthala."

Eva Clare nodded. Grandmomma had told her about the fireplace.

"Your grandmomma and grandpop put in that window and window seat where the fireplace used to be and had bookshelves built on each side of it. They also added a closet, because in the olden days, people used wardrobes to store their clothes. Those additions took up room space and made the back wall even with the front of the hall closet and the wall in the room to our right." She demonstrated the evenness with a smooth run of her hand left to right, ending in a point. "Let's go in there."

They entered the reading room with its brown leather chairs, mahogany desk, shelves filled with books, and metal-scroll daybed that served as a couch.

"This room still has the original fireplace on the back wall. See?" Lily extended her arms. "And there's a reason for keeping it intact."

"It's a simple fireplace." Roy put his hands on his hips like most men do when they're contemplating the construction of something. "Plain mantel. Brick hearth."

Anna Laurel checked the title of a worn volume on the bookshelf. "*Where I Was Born and Raised.* This is the book with the famous quote about the Delta beginning in the lobby of the Peabody Hotel up in Memphis and ending on Catfish Row down in Vicksburg."

Lily whirled her hands to get their attention. "Y'all, stay with me. I'm losin' you. Pay attention. I'm tryin' to tell you that a new back wall of studs, sheetrock, and bookcases between the fireplace and the hall door was added when Sweet Evelyn and Binky remodeled in 1959 to hide the original wall of long, thin strips of wood." She raised her voice. "Did you get my key word? *Hide.* As in *cover up.*"

"Original wall? Hide? What're you talking about?" Eva Clare asked.

"There's a space behind this wall. You used to could tell. Now you can't."

"I don't understand."

"It's a cover-up."

"Cover-up of what?"

"Only one person in the world knows about this now. Me. Maybe Gerald. I don't know." Lily shrugged. "Behind the wall is a passageway."

"Huh?" Eva Clare screwed up her face. "A passageway to what?"

"To what I brought you up here to see."

"Which is what? Do I have to pull it out of you?"

Lily hesitated, pointed upward, whispered. "A secret room."

"A what? What're you talking about? Where? I never heard of a secret room." Eva Clare splayed a hand against her chest. "And I lived here and played all over this house my whole childhood." Her phone rang. She startled, squealed, fetched it from her pocket.

"Dang interruptions!" Lily huffed.

The screen showed GERALD TANNER. Eva Clare slumped.

Anna Laurel peered at Gerald's name on the display and grabbed the phone. "I'll take this, E. C." She put the phone to her ear. "Mr. Tanner, this is Anna Laurel Wood, Attorney at Law, representing Eva Clare Carlyle. May I schedule a face-to-face with you, perhaps Monday, u-u-um, August twenty-third, six p.m., the office at Laurel's Coffee House?" She squinched her eyes and waited for his reply. The others did, too.

"No, sir, Ms. Carlyle is not available for consultation," Anna Laurel answered. "I'll be handling all questions concerning the house matter and billing you accordingly for my time."

Eva Clare blew out a soft laugh. Lily held up a thumb. Roy nodded approval.

"Because this is a non-issue, that's why. There's a legal will in place, and you're the one bringing up non sequiturs. I'm glad to discuss this with you and will see you on the twenty-third. Hereafter, all calls will go through me, and starting now, you're on the clock. Thank you, sir, and good-bye." She clicked off, then turned to Eva Clare and handed her the phone. "Do not talk to him if he calls again. Make sure I have the needed paperwork tomorrow morning. I'll have two weeks to prepare a document to oppose his claims. This, only for you, out of what little goodness exists in my heart, to shut him up. He has no claim. He's just a rich banker bully."

"Yes, okay, I will, thank you."

Lily loudly cleared her throat. "Now, as I was saying before we were so rudely interrupted, there's a secret room in Coghlan House."

"And as I was saying, that's nuts," Eva Clare said.

"Y'all, look around." Lily stretched her arms out. "This is what I'm tryin' to show you. There are no walls that appear out of line with the others, and the walls also seem to align with the back of the house. Everything's straight and flush and even. There's nothing to make anyone suspect hidden spaces."

"No one ever did suspect hidden places." Eva Clare straightened her posture. Claimed awareness and position. She was the only blood Coghlan present. But apparently left out of the family knowledge pool. "Enough talk. Show us the room."

"Okay, c'mon." Lily led Eva Clare, Roy, and Anna Laurel back to the hallway in front of the closet. "This is the original linen pantry." Lily placed her hand over the white porcelain doorknob, turned it, and pulled the closet door open as far back as it would go.

All the doors in Coghlan House used to have those white porcelain knobs, and Grandmomma said the early women would put an extra one in their hens' nests, so if a chicken snake came looking for eggs, it would eat the knob—which looked like an egg—and choke to death. Yeah, she knew stuff about this house.

She stood shoulder-to-shoulder with Roy and Anna Laurel in front of the primitive closet—about four feet deep, made of hand-sawn, unfinished wall boards, with a simple, two-can-deep shelf-case on the right and deeper shelves on the left, crudely built. Two more shelves hung high on the back wall, and beneath, three original peg hooks. Bed linens, blankets, quilts, towels, and washrags were stored in there now, along with vases, candlesticks, and boxes of Christmas decorations.

The hot, mildewy smell filtered out.

Eva Clare pinched her nostrils. "I always hated this closet. It stinks. It doesn't have a light, and the boards were never painted. I took my Barbies with their slumber party outfits in there to play pretend-campout, and I made a cozy reading hideout once, but abandoned it because the dust triggered my allergies." Her nose burned already.

"You played in here?" Lily asked.

"I tried to, but the smell made my eyes water, my nose run, and my throat burn."

"Sweet Evelyn let you play in here?" Lily said in a high-pitched voice.

"Grandmomma didn't know, and Marthala didn't care."

"I wonder why they never updated the closet," Roy said.

Anna Laurel twisted the wide-band silver and turquoise ring on her finger, glanced at the ceiling, bent to look low under the shelves. "I don't understand what we're looking for. I don't see anything that makes me curious. I'm not following what's happening here."

"I'm fixin' to show you." Lily stuck the flashlight in the waist of her jeans, then stepped inside the closet. She moved stacks of washcloths from the two-can-deep unit to the opposite shelves. Grabbing the side of the empty shelf-case, she pulled. Yanked again. And again.

"Whoa, Lily, what're you doing?" Eva Clare squeezed Lily's arm.

"You need help?" Roy stepped closer.

Lily pulled again. The unit moved an inch away from the wall.

Eva Clare sucked in a breath.

"Oh, God." Anna Laurel covered her mouth with a hand.

Roy laced his fingers behind his head.

Lily heaved again, and the unit responded, sliding farther away from the wall. She kept at it until she pulled the shelf-case open, like a door, short of a ninety-degree angle. Behind the unit was a gaping hole in the wall—crudely cut, at least three feet high and two feet wide.

The three spectators gasped and moaned. Eva Clare's stomach dipped, then lurched. She slammed her palms against her temples. Cupped her head.

Heat escaped from the blackness. The wall-hole belched an earthy smell.

She was about to learn something shocking. She could feel it coming.

"Wha—? What in the world is this?" She staggered nearer.

"It's what I've been tellin' you. A passageway to a secret room." Lily pulled the flashlight from her pants.

"How long has it been here?"

"Since the house was built." Lily pushed the switch to ON and shined light into the darkness. The roughed-in space was eerie, made of uneven widths of planks for the floor and thin, narrow boards with cracks between them for the sides.

"The shelf-unit is lipped on the back, so it's flush to the wall, to keep out the heat and cold," Roy noted. "And so it appears built in and not an individual piece of furniture."

"Lily, how do you know about this?" Eva Clare asked.

"Mamaw showed me one time when y'all were down at the church at Vacation Bible School. My people believe in passing down the old mysteries and true histories." Lily patted the bun on top of her head and pushed wayward strands of hair back in. "Once you go through this hole in the wall, you ain't ever gon be the same. The secrets stashed in here were shameful. The family tried to hide them. Your grandmother didn't tell you, I 'spect, 'cause she wanted them to die with her. Most likely, Gerald knows, and that's why he wants this property. Wants to burn down this house and destroy the truth about the Coghlan family."

"What truth? What could be so bad? It makes me think there's a dead body hidden away. Lily, is there a skeleton in here?"

"Naw, he ain't in here." Lily bent over and pointed the flashlight into the passageway, as Roy and Anna Laurel moved in closer to look. Eva Clare was still stuck on Lily's "he ain't in here" comment. But she shook it off and leaned in with the others. Lily aimed the light at the far back of the space.

"Old bricks," Eva Clare said. "There's an old brick wall."

"It's the fireplace in the reading room," Roy said. "Providing a wall support."

"Right," Lily answered. She shined the light on crudely built, slightly angled ladder stairs that butted up to the brick wall, then moved the light upward. "The secret room's up there."

"Ohhh, E. C.," Anna Laurel said, slowly and gutturally.

Eva Clare's heart throbbed. Her breathing quickened.

"Let's go in," Lily said. "You've got to step over, duck, twist, squeeze, and scrooch to get through this hole, and it's a tight space inside." She leaned down and maneuvered her tall, curvy body through the opening, scraping the sides, and the others followed with groans and complaints about bad knees, stiff backs, and torsos wider than they used to be.

They stood close, cramped in the dark passageway no more than a couple feet wide, heat encapsulating them.

Lily wiped sweat off her face and out of her eyes. "Before we go up this ladder, I need to show you something." She aimed the light behind the ladder and brick wall, leaned over, tugged at a leather handle nailed to a floor plank, and pulled open a trapdoor to a tiny hole and a built-in ladder going down. "This ladder goes to the ground, where there used to be a little door that opened to the butler's pantry off the kitchen, as well as a door to the backyard. It was an escape route. During the 1959 remodel, the outside door was closed up, and in 1995, both doorways were built over."

"Escape route for what purpose?" Anna Laurel asked.

"For—"

"This is crazy," Eva Clare said. "Plain crazy."

"Eva Clare, you didn't know about the hidden door in the butler's pantry?" Roy asked. "I mean, it looks like, something in the kitchen, where people spend a lot of time, you might—"

"Well, yeah, I knew about that. I opened that pantry trapdoor and looked into the crawl space at the dirt ground many times. But the outside door was boarded up then, so it held no fascination. It was only a narrow spot with no wiggle room and too low for comfort."

"The ladder was behind a wall a little ways in. You couldn't see it or get to it without crawling over to it."

"Also, Grandmomma told me cottonmouth moccasins came up from the river and hid in the crawl space, so no way was I going in."

Lily chuckled. "That ain't true 'bout the snakes. She just didn't want you in there." Lily closed the trapdoor.

"Y'all know, all old houses have trapdoors," Eva Clare said. "There's another one in the floor of the foyer closet, and there's also a hinged stair tread."

"C'mon, let's go up." Lily put her foot on the first rung.

One at a time, Eva Clare last, they climbed the rungs through a hatchway in the ceiling and stepped onto a narrow strip of flooring that led to an open area about eight-by-ten feet. A small, round window, held closed with a hook-and-eye latch, could be opened for fresh air. It also let in light.

Eva Clare scrutinized the space—unfinished wood under arching rafters. Cobwebs hung in silver skeins in the corners. A weathered-oak travel trunk, trimmed with tarnished hardware, sat in the middle of the room, a cane-bottomed chair in front of it. The rafters and flooring planks, filled with summer heat and humidity, reeked of a caustic combination of dust and hot air that burned her nostrils.

She rubbed her temples, then laid her hands against the sides of her head, shut her eyes. How could this be? How could she not know about this room? A good part of her life, she slept and played under this hideaway so close to the truth. But a thin barrier, a ceiling, prevented her from seeing it. She groped for words to express her feelings, but they jammed in her throat. Betrayed. That was it. The best word she could come up with.

Grandmomma hadn't trusted her enough to tell her. That hurt. Hurt her to tears.

Anna Laurel patted her on the shoulder. "It's okay, E. C."

"Your history is in this room," Lily said, "and your family's secrets. Right there in that trunk. And trust me, there are secret sins that're going to rattle you to the core."

Eva Clare noted fingerprints in the dust on the trunk top. "The Coghlan history is in the family Bible downstairs. But you say secrets? You know them?" She shot a scowl at Lily.

"I do," Lily said. "They affect me, too. As slaves, my family was attached to your family from the beginning—Edgecombe County, North Carolina, then Neshoba County, Mississippi, then here in the Delta. We were Coghlans, too." Lily staked claim to her position.

"Secrets, pfoo. Like what?" Eva Clare opened the trunk and let her hand grasp the edge of the lid. Curled her lip. Her hurt bordered on resentment.

"That's for you to discover."

Heat radiated off Eva Clare's forehead. Weather heat. Mad heat. A drop of sweat rolled down the back of her neck, tickled, made her shiver. She looked at the trunk's upper tray. A family Bible lay there, where Grandmomma likely put it, its padded cover worn, chipped in places down to cardboard. This Bible appeared much older than the one downstairs in the parlor. She picked it up with both hands, cradled it on a forearm, and opened its fragile pages: *The Family Bible of Andrew Coghlan, born in Edgecombe County, North Carolina, 1 April 1809, died 1861, married Eirinn Lafferty, born 1810, died 1859, seven children.*

Thomas, born 1830, died 1848, typhoid
Andrew Jackson, born 1832, died 1832
Martha Ann, born 1837, died 1848, typhoid
William Lafferty, born 1839, died 1839
Joseph, born 1842, died 1843, malaria
Catherine Deering, born 1844, died 1911
Victoria Dove, born 1846, died 1890

She twitched her nose, sniffed, and glared at Lily. "Nothing new here." The only surviving children of Andrew Coghlan who migrated to the Delta with him were the last two, the Delta matriarchs, Catherine Deering and Victoria Dove. They remained on Erin Plantation—named for their mother—the rest of their lives.

"Girl, that's only one page. One source."

She stared Lily down. "All right, Lily Greene, you think you know so much, so tell me. Why is there a secret room in this house? With an escape route. One short sentence, spit it out."

"They hid slaves."

"I *knew* it!" Anna Laurel punched the air with her fist. "Knew it! I've always heard there was a safe house around here. So, this was it. This was a station on the Underground Railroad." She stomped her foot, clapped her hands, giggled like a child who'd just discovered chocolate.

"Your ancestors. Catherine Deering and Victoria Dove. Hid runaway slaves," Lily said.

A rapid mix of emotions shot through Eva Clare—from the hurt and betrayal of not being told to the satisfying pride of knowing. As a child, she loved reading about the Underground Railroad, loved the heroics. Now, she learned her blood was mixed up in that massive, secretive effort to move human slaves to freedom.

"Eva Clare, your ancestors risked their lives to get people out of bondage in the South," Anna Laurel said. "They could've been killed for protecting runaways. Do you realize what you've got here?"

Eva Clare closed the Bible, nodded slowly, put it back in the trunk.

"Wow," Anna Laurel whispered. "This is huge. *Huge.*"

Eva Clare scraped her teeth over her lower lip, looked at Lily, and lifted her brows. "Nobody knew it was a safe house but the two matriarchs and the slaves, right? How did runaway slaves know this was a station?"

"The color pattern in the stained glass above the front door," Lily said.

"The blue-blue mistake?"

"The blue-blue was a secret code to runaways. The pattern was easy to see at night when the foyer lamps were lit."

Eva Clare sank to the cane-bottom chair. "I hated that window. Wanted to fix it." Her hate began to melt into meaning. Her house was a small part of something big in history.

She looked at the beads of sweat on Lily's upper lip and wiped moisture off her own.

"And the quilts," Lily continued. "The stained glass was hard to see from a distance, and the house didn't have a porch rail to hang a quilt on, so the sisters, Catherine Deering and Victoria Dove, and their slave, Star, my ancestor, hung the safe-house quilt out an upstairs window. Like some baby had peed on it, and it was airing out. Star's quilt pattern. My quilt pattern. The plan to freedom was hidden in plain view."

Eva Clare fixed her eyes on the trunk and stared at what was before her.

"Were there other stations around town?" Anna Laurel fanned herself with her hand.

Lily wiped her moist cheek on the shoulder-sleeve of her shirt. "The Underground Railroad didn't officially exist in the South. It was only a few houses here and there. Slaves hardly ever got help until they reached a free state up north, like Ohio, but even Ohio had laws about slaves coming to the state. Mostly, the slaves had to make it on their own."

"But by the grace of God, people like the two sisters existed," Roy said.

"You always hear it was sympathetic White people helping slaves to freedom." Lily shook her finger at Roy. "That's only a small part of the story. Black people plotted their escape from the time they were captured in West Africa, shackled, and put on slave ships to America. On plantations across the South, they used symbolism out of their own culture to put secret codes in their quilts. Quilts were their maps to freedom. Give them some credit, too."

"Sure, of course." Roy nodded, clamped his lips tight, winked in agreement.

"How did the Coghlan sisters know where to send the slaves?" Anna Laurel coughed, obviously bothered by the dust and hot-damp-wood smell. "You know anything about that?"

"Word of mouth from plantation to plantation," Lily said. "The Coghlan sisters and Star got word of a safe house in Cincinnati through a grapevine of slaves who almost made it, but were captured and brought home to a nearby plantation. The runaways told how they heard of a lantern in a window of a house on the Ohio side of the river on land that belonged to a family named Stallo. When the lantern was lit, it was safe to cross the river and go to the house for food and shelter in the cellar. There was a tall wooden cross on the Kentucky side of the river across from the Stallo house. Those Mississippi slaves made it to the foot of the cross, saw the lantern in the window, but stayed to rest before crossing and were caught. Not many from the Deep South made it to freedom."

"How tragic," Anna Laurel said.

"There were four million slaves in the South before the war," Lily said. "Might've been a hundred thousand that made it to freedom. Most were returned to their owners."

"Why're you sharing this with me?" Eva Clare said. "You don't have to."

"It's your answer to Gerald's threat. You told me your first day home I had to help you keep Gerald off our backs. And besides, you deserve to know the truth. Everything's in this trunk—land deeds, wills, journals, letters, pictures. These are *your* maps to freedom."

Eva Clare slumped. Felt like a fool. Being shown secrets about her house, her people, by someone outside the family. Secrets her grandmother should've told her a long time ago.

"Read these secrets hidden in plain view," Lily said. "Find out who you are and where you came from."

"Yeah, but can you read downstairs?" Anna Laurel said. "I'm about to suffocate."

Roy pulled a handkerchief out of his pocket and wiped his glistening-red face, folded the cloth, and returned it to his pocket. He leaned over the trunk and combed through the stacks of papers, homemade leather books, and scratched-up cardboard pouches.

Lily poked Roy's arm, then pointed to the wall behind him. "You see that cut-out place? That inset shelf in the wall with the board nailed across the bottom of the opening?"

"I see it."

"Put your hand in there on the right side behind that front board."

"Ooh, Lily, there might be spiders," Eva Clare said.

"Naw, don't worry 'bout that."

"Okay." Roy stuck his hand in, feeling around. "Feels like a glass jar."

"Take it out."

Roy fished out a dusty, blue Mason fruit jar filled with little pebbles, wiped and blew the dust off, and held it up. He rolled it sideways, letting the rocks slide.

"The two sisters and Star recorded each runaway they helped by putting a pebble in that jar," Lily said. "Each rock represents a human soul who took a chance at freedom."

"I should count them," Eva Clare said.

"Sixty-nine." Lily rested her hands on her hips. "Sixty-nine slaves during the course of the war. We don't know if any of them made it."

The four friends stood spilling sweat and staring at the pebbles—gray and black ones, tan and reddish, some with spines and skeletons etched into them. Each one stood for a life with a distant hope. The weight of the gold HOPE disc on Eva Clare's necklace burned against her breastbone. On her shoulders sat the weight of discovery.

Lily grabbed the jar from Roy, breaking up the silence with the rattling of rocks, and shoved it into Eva Clare's hands. "Hold them. Hold every life in your hands."

Eva Clare's breath caught in her throat. She held the jar with both hands wrapped around it. This was her jar, her house, her ancestors standing up against the tide. She was responsible for the contents of the jar, for steps she could take to honor every stilled heartbeat and ensure that no more souls were closed up in jars and every crooked place was made straight. The heat, the sweat, the tears covered her.

Lily turned to Roy. "Put your hand back in and run it to the left."

Roy followed directions and poked around until he hit upon something. "Feels like a cardboard box."

"Pick it up, bring it out." Lily made round, forward motions with her hands like she was beating eggs.

Roy pulled out a Florida Queen cigar box thick with dust.

"Open it, open it."

He lifted the lid and read the words out loud: "Florida Queen De Luxe, Made in Florida, Havana Blend, 6 cents." They all peered inside to see a small, thin Blue Horse notebook bent at the top and curled at the spine to fit, along with four yellow pencils in varying lengths of usage, all with points that had been sharpened by a knife. In a corner, a child's ring with a blue stone.

Anna Laurel grabbed the Blue Horse, let it fall open, and read aloud. *August 11, 1963. Dear Diary, I am hot. I am hungry. I hate—*

"Don't read that!" Lily snapped. "It's private. Put it back."

"Oh, I'm so sorry." Anna Laurel fit it back into the box.

"Hey!" Eva Clare said, blinking through tears blurring her vision. "That's my ring I lost one summer."

"Yep, you dropped it on the patio, and I picked it up and kept it. I figured I deserved it for having to play up here in this hell of a hotbox hid away like a slave."

"What?" Eva Clare asked.

"Yeah." Lily made a flourish with her arms. "This was *my* playhouse. Up here in this hot oven, with the little round window open in hopes of a breeze that never came."

"Were you being punished?"

"Yes and no. Mamaw had to look out for me in summers while the others chopped cotton. The summer I was nine, you invited me inside to play paper dolls. Sweet Evelyn had a hissy conniption fit, and after that, my mamaw had to hide me."

"Oh Lily, I didn't know any better. I didn't know we'd get in trouble."

"Yeah, I know that now. But up here is where I had to be. I'm the girl who brought slavery to our generation. I'm the face of what your people did to my people, while those same White folks sat in their pure-White churches and sang 'Blessed be the tie that binds our hearts in Christian love.'"

"Whoa, hey, Lily," Anna Laurel interrupted, stepped between them, her hands up. "Eva Clare was only a child. She's not responsible for what her grandmother or the entire church or the whole South did. Don't lay it on her."

"I don't mean to lay it on her. I do mean to say my piece." A fat tear streaked down Lily's face.

Roy looked down, covered his mouth with his fist, closed his eyes.

Lily smeared her tear, blinked repeatedly, wiped the wetness that spilled. "Every one of those scorching Delta summer mornings, this Black child was pushed through the opening in the kitchen pantry between the bottom two shelves where the Irish potatoes were stored in a bin. I was told to crawl behind a wall and climb up the steep ladder to the slave room out of Sweet Evelyn's sight, amidst Mamaw's warnings of whippings if I didn't shut up and stay put. Here I'd play, separated from the White child. Sometimes I'd lie here on these planks, barely breathing from the heat, look up at the rafters, and wonder if the sixty-nine slaves had looked up at these same boards. I counted those rocks, I played with those slaves, I knew how they felt. Hot, dirty, beaten low down in society, beaten physically—me, spanked for playing with you, Eva Clare."

"Oh Lily. I'm sorry for my grandmother. I wasn't like her. I'm so sorry."

"I know. And I know Sweet Evelyn cared about us. She was good to us. But our relationship was not equal. My mamaw was a maid, a servant. And Sweet Evelyn had to keep us in our place. She had to stop me from being inside her house, sitting my nasty bottom on her kitchen chair, and touching your toys. It's the way it was with everybody."

"Oh God, Lily, I'm so sorry. I didn't understand back then what it was like for you. I lived in my world. I didn't know what you had to put up with in yours." All her life she didn't know. She still didn't know. Not till this moment.

"I grew to see that." Lily's posture crumpled. "Meanwhile, as I was not allowed in the public library to check out a public book bought by public taxpayer money, this was my summer reading." She flared her arms toward the trunk. "Now, I'm passing it on to you. This, Eva Clare, is *your* summer reading."

Handing Lily the jar, Eva Clare knelt in front of the trunk, squelching sobs dammed up, and filtered through the contents. Her hurt spiraled into a new feeling—shame. She was ashamed of herself. She truly was a whole lot like her grandmother. She had privilege because of who she was—rich and White. She never thought she had privilege and never thought about privilege being related to her color. That was the ultimate privilege.

Eva Clare cried as she scooped out some papers and a stack of journals to take downstairs. She wiped her nose on the back of her wrist, wiped her wrist on her pants, and held her summer reading close to her chest as she started back toward her living space with her answers in her arms.

Her posture was bent, her chest curled.

Something had cracked inside her.

AT THE HOUSE ON STILTS

With Lily riding shotgun, Eva Clare steered her Subaru up the levee road to the top and drove over the graveled single lane. She veered right, down the slope, followed the dirt road beside the oxbow, and made her way into Roy's driveway for a Friday-night dinner. His was a rented, furnished cabin inside the Mississippi River levee system—a house on stilts twenty feet high for protection from floods. It had a cypress exterior and a screened front porch that faced the lake. Before getting out of the car, she checked her hair in the rearview mirror, ran her fingers through it, and picked at strands to give it a piecey texture.

She and Lily started up the long flight of stairs. About the twelfth tread, Lily was breathing hard. "Oh mercy, I couldn't do this every day."

"Imagine carrying groceries up here. Multiple bags, multiple trips."

"Glad it's him and not me."

Both paused at the top of the stairs to catch their breath. Eva Clare turned to look at the lake in shades of sunset: rose, orange, yellow gold. The sparkling wake of a jon boat smeared the colors. The fisherman cut the motor and drifted toward cypress knees near the shoreline beneath tall trees, their wide bases with folds like a draping curtain.

"It's beautiful."

"It's hotter 'n a witch's armpit." Lily fanned her face with her hands. She opened the squeaky screen door, they walked across the porch, and Eva Clare knocked at the entrance.

Roy greeted them wearing an apron with red and pink flowers and ruffles up the bib straps. Eva Clare clamped her lips and stifled a laugh.

"C'mon in, ladies. I've got dinner on." His hand caught Eva Clare's arm to usher her over the threshold.

The scent of fresh garlic—and his smile—drew her into his world.

One large room—kitchen and den—held light oak furniture and a black leather sofa and recliner. The wall facing the lake was all windows. The other three walls were bare, except for one big painting of Jesus standing in a boat on the water, preaching to people sitting on the shore. Like in church—one man standing on a platform preaching to congregants gathered beneath him.

Roy hustled toward a platter of raw meat.

"Whatchu makin'?" Lily asked.

"Veal piccata." He dropped a few garlic cloves in a pan on the front burner. On another burner, water was heating to a boil. "With angel hair pasta."

The table was set, a Caesar salad prepared, a bottle of pinot noir open.

"Pour yourselves some wine and relax while I finish. I'll be quick." He floured the veal and put each scallop in bubbling oil to brown.

Eva Clare poured Lily and herself a glass of the dark California wine, then leaned against the counter and watched Roy exercise his culinary skills. He dropped the pasta in the pot and added butter, wine, lemon juice, and capers to the pan of veal scallops. Talked to them and watched the timer simultaneously, then drained the angel hair and plopped some on three plates on the counter. He placed the veal on the dishes, spooned extra sauce over it, and topped it with Parmesan shavings and fresh parsley.

Serving the plates to the table, he tossed his apron and beckoned the women to join him. Dinner talk began with descriptions of various Italian veal dishes—piccata, saltimbocca, Marsala—moved to antique-shop talk, then turned to the music playing. Instrumentals from the movie *Dead Poets Society*. Eva Clare poured more wine. Handel's *Water Music* played softly in the background, a fast piece to eat by. She found herself chewing veal with the tempo. It didn't help that Lily was tapping a foot to the beat.

The first notes of "Keating's Triumph" came quietly, hauntingly, and folded her into the high softs and commanding lows, captured her so fully that she separated from the table camaraderie into her own space of heightening sound and drumbeat. Her heart quickened. Her arms wanted to pound out the beat. She closed her eyes and let the music fill her. If she weren't a visual artist, she'd be a poet and meet in an old Indian cave in the woods with others and lovers at midnight, read poetry, praise rhyme and meter, and suck the marrow out of life. When she opened her eyes, Roy and Lily were looking at her as if she'd lost her mind.

"You okay?" Roy said.

"Yeah, yeah." A tingling swept up the back of her neck and across her face. "Lost in these songs. It's my favorite music . . . and favorite movie. I loved when the new teacher at the strict all-boys' school inspired his students to 'seize the day.' Pluck the day off the vine, squeeze its juices out, use it to its fullest, fill it with their dreams and desires. Do extraordinary, original things instead of merely copying what others do." She gulped a breath.

"I like how the song moves from reserved to confident," Roy said.

"I thought we were gon talk about me." Lily tapped her fork against her plate.

Eva Clare ignored her. "He inspired them to challenge the words of their authority figures who demanded the boys see their leaders' ways as the only ways." She forked a piece of romaine, ate it. "I was also taught to follow the authoritarians in my life."

The music faded out on a flute sound. The cave music came on with notes that sounded like footsteps running through woods, like the boys did in the movie.

Like she used to do on this forestland between the levee and the river. Back when she was young, carefree, innocent. When she didn't have to worry about lovers and others sneaking around behind her back. Before she ever knew what it was like to hurt in the heart. In the dark, tremulous, tingling soprano fingers, passionate bass percussion. He cheated on her.

In tears, Eva Clare jerked her face to look out the wall of windows at dark blue shadows now shrouding the cypress trees along the oxbow. She listened to the sounds in the music—the notes, the night birds, the instruments. She looked at Roy, twirling pasta on his fork. He was calm and in control after preparing dinner in front of guests. She'd be a melted-down hot mess.

Her chest fluttered. Did she have feelings for him? A desire to know him better? To run through the woods with him at night, their steps like the light notes playing in the background? Yes. She wanted a turn at being a lover with another. Maybe it was the music, maybe the wine. Maybe it was being with a man in his own house. She shouldn't be thinking like this. Still, she wanted to be close, put her fingertip in the dimple on his chin. What a great song to play while making love. She looked away, pushed her wine glass back, her face and neck hot.

"So, Lily," Roy said, leaning in her direction, "you're here to tell me what you know about the early days on the oxbow. Talk to me about your people."

Eva Clare fanned her face, pulled her wine glass back toward her, lifted it to hide any blush remaining in her cheeks.

"I'm seventh generation on the oxbow," Lily answered. She put her fork down and set her elbows on the table.

"My oxbow-settlin' ancestor was named Star. She was nineteen when Mr. Andrew Coghlan and his two daughters, Catherine Deering and Victoria Dove, brought her to old Prentiss from Philadelphia in Neshoba County, Miss'ippi. Star was four years older than Catherine and six years older than Victoria, so she was old enough to be aware of what happened in the early years on Coghlan Plantation, and she passed the stories down."

Roy gathered a few capers on his fork and held them balanced between the tines, listening intently.

"Star was a Coghlan. She was born into the Coghlan slave family and given the family name. Not because of any warm blood feelings they had for her, but because they owned her. *Owned* her." Lily raised her shoulders, then dropped them with a sigh. "The Coghlans came here for better land. Neshoba County was red clay and couldn't grow a thing. They came even though they got word about the Delta's thick jungle, its droughts, rains, flooding, its swarms of mosquitoes and diseases and death. The whole world had heard how fertile the Yazoo Miss'ippi Delta bottomland was. There were more slaves here than White settlers. The slaves did most of the work—cleared the land, drained the swamps, planted cotton. They built this place." She thrummed the table with her pink fingernails.

"There're some good books about settling the Delta," Eva Clare said. "You could probably learn more from reading a book than only listening to Lily."

"What?" Lily scratched her jaw, her lips downturned, and shook her head. "Ain't so."

"Yeah," Roy said, "but I have a feeling I'm going to learn things from Lily that I won't find in a book."

"Dang right." Lily jumped into her story. "That first year at Prentiss, 1859, the Coghlans cut timber, dug up stumps, hacked out cotton fields, and dug ditches to drain the evercomin' floodwaters. They worked the fields, wet or dry, hot or cold. Mr. Andrew, he didn't have men slaves or sons. His girls had to do a man's work plus a woman's work. Star, she worked right beside the two sisters in the fields and in the kitchen. She knew everything about those girls—all their secrets." Lily gave a nod as an exclamation point. "Sometimes they traded off work with slaves on other plantations. Picked up a few men that way. Star might've helped the Steele family with quilting or with slaughtering hogs, and the Steeles would send a man slave over to work the fields."

Roy cut his veal, chewed, and nodded understanding.

Lily picked up a Caesar crouton and bit into it, making a loud crunch. "White men knew their lives depended on their slaves, so if they couldn't afford to buy them, they made them."

"Made them?" Roy perked up, his eyes wide, put his fork on the side of his plate, and folded his hands in his lap. "You know about this personally?"

"Yep. You ain't gon like it, Eva Clare, but Mr. Andrew made him some slaves. He made two babies off of Star. The second one died at birth. The infant mortality rate was high. Not even one fourth of the babies born were raised."

Eva Clare drew her shoulders in and shrank down. Did she hear this right? Her fourth-great-grandfather had sex with his slave? She didn't know whether to believe it, to be embarrassed or shocked by it, or to be angry, or who to be angry at. She clamped her trembling knees together. Glanced at Roy. Must he hear this? He put an elbow on the table and leaned in, his fist covering his mouth. She looked down, let her hair fall over her face.

"That first baby of Star's was named Riselle. Riselle begat Ellie, who begat Alight, who begat Marthala. Next, my mother Josie, but she doesn't count 'cause she ran off to Chicago to work in a factory and deserted us. That's my family line."

Lily crunched another crouton and drank some wine. "Come to find out, Star was Mr. Andrew's, too. Uh huh. Her mother was Luvenia. Mr. Andrew had four babies off of Luvenia. This was back in Neshoba County when his wife was alive. By the time Star was born, he'd already lost two of his own boys, and he needed more males for the farm work. Luvenia gave him Star, one stillborn, one boy who died in early childhood after one cotton-pickin' season, and one boy they sold to pay off some debt."

"My goodness," Roy said, leaning back, a red flush running up his neck and face.

"Yeah," Lily said.

Eva Clare looked away, focused on the picture of Jesus in the boat. Holy-white robe. Blood-red shawl. She sensed Lily's eyes burning into the back of her, wanting a reaction. She steeled, determined not to give one. Not here. Not now. What could she say anyway? She moved the story around in her mind. Her righteous, upstanding fourth-great-grandfather left his wife asleep in bed and sought a slave to have a romp in the hay with and had children with her, and Lily was at the bottom of that line. No wonder Grandmomma hid these things. Maybe she should, too. She set her fork down and scrunched the napkin in her hands. Yes. She should hide the truth.

If there was ever any question about it, here was the answer. She was like her grandmother. Couldn't take the truth. Wouldn't do right in the wrongs. Wanted to cover up the bad things and pretend they didn't exist. Wanted to erase history or bend it to her liking.

The food curdled in her stomach. She wanted to go home to her childhood bedroom and crawl under the covers where she was safe and knew nothing of the sexual escapades of Andrew Coghlan. Lily should shut up about all of this.

But Lily kept going. "After his wife died and they moved here to the river, he climbed on his daughter Star and got Riselle. Family legend says he took Star in the field while they were pickin' the cotton. Said he told her he needed a woman in the worst way, and women were as scarce as chicken teeth in these parts. Told her to bend over; it was her duty. He took her reg'lar in the fields. They say the cotton was so high, nobody could see what they were doing, even his own daughters workin' a few rows over. Star once birthed a baby in between those cotton rows, squatted and popped her out, then carried the stillborn and the afterbirth back to the house, blood runnin' down her legs to the dirt, buried that baby in the yard and went on back to work."

Eva Clare's heart reeled. So did her stomach.

"Riselle, they say, was high yellow," Lily continued. "And she had blue eyes. You ever seen a Black woman with blue eyes?"

Eva Clare shook her head no.

"You know how Mr. Andrew died?" Lily asked.

"No." Eva Clare closed her eyes. Couldn't this conversation and this whole night be over and done with? "But I'm sure you're gonna tell me."

"That's 'cause nobody knows but my people. You won't find this in any book. She killed him. Star. Uh huh. He came for her one time too many. She didn't want that White man in her, never did, and she didn't want no more babies. She had a knife ready. When he pulled that swollen thing out, she stabbed him. Ten times, they say. Got blood all over the cotton bolls. Then dragged his dead body over to a clearing where they were building the house and buried him in a shallow grave. She did it with nobody seeing. Then put the bloody cotton in her tow sack. The townsfolk, all disturbed by his disappearance, came to help build that new house right on top of Mr. Andrew. They didn't know. His daughters didn't know. Figured he fell in the river, drowned, got washed away."

"My gosh," Eva Clare said, "I don't know these people, and I don't know who I am anymore. I want to go home."

"Eva Clare, it's okay." Roy clutched her arm. "They were human, flawed like we all are, living a flawed history in a dark time the same way other people lived it. Slave women were considered property, owned, for breeding. Their bodies belonged to their owners. People back then normalized this. Like flies in the jar in the experiment I told you about—people comfortable with their beliefs, even flawed beliefs, not thinking, only following. It was an accepted practice that many participated in."

"I don't want to hear any more."

"Human chattel slavery was legal in our country for almost a hundred years, Eva Clare. Your people were following the laws of their society."

"These are *my* family secrets," Lily said. "They happen to involve your family, Eva Clare. Yes, a lot of landowners around here used their slave women as broodmares. Some owners mistreated their slaves, and those slaves were always running away. They'd flee up the river's edge right through old Prentiss."

Eva Clare crumpled her brows. Not only was this the history of her family, but it was the history of her country. America, land of liberty, home of the free, moral leader of the world.

"Okay," Roy commented, "but this doesn't affect me, my family, my search."

"It sort of does," Lily said. "It's the background for your story."

"How? I don't get it."

Lily looked at him, at Eva Clare, then said softly, "Soon."

Roy rubbed his forehead and looked out the windows where dark was falling.

"Keep your focus on the Civil War," Lily added. "By the way, things changed with Abraham Lincoln and the war to end slavery."

"You know. You know who my ancestor is, don't you?"

"All you need is in plain view."

"Lily, please don't play games and put him through agony. Tell him," Eva Clare said. "He went to a lot of trouble to cook this meal for us in order to learn about his ancestor." Also, it would get the focus off her family.

Lily shook her head. "He'll get there. You'll help him."

"So I'm close." Roy clicked his cheek.

"Speaking of Abraham Lincoln," Lily said, "family legend says that he came to Prentiss. Word was that before the 1860 election, he wanted to see slavery for himself, so he dressed up like a peddler and went undercover to some towns in the South. He came here, went to the old

Coghlan cabin, asked for a meal and a bed for the night, and shook hands with Star who was then pregnant with Riselle. He told her she'd soon be free."

"Oh, Lily, I don't believe a word of that." Eva Clare laughed. "It's way too farfetched."

"Well, hey, it's a family story passed down, and a good one, and I'm stickin' to it." Lily pointed a finger at Eva Clare. "And because of that encounter with Abraham Lincoln, Star became a part of his story. She became a part of the freedom movement. The two Coghlan sisters were sympathetic to the cause, too. The three of them began helping slaves escape to freedom. You saw the secret attic room they built in their house, which was in progress at the time of Lincoln's visit."

Eva Clare shook her head. She was done with Lily's storytelling.

"And I've already told you about the quilt patterns and their meanings. Like my Carpenter's Star. It tells the whole slave journey in the eight points of the star—the struggle between the darkness of slavery and the light of freedom."

Lily paused, cut a bite of veal, forked it into her mouth.

"Well?" Roy said. "C'mon, tell us the slave-journey story."

Lily washed down her food with drink. "I made up a story to go with my star pattern. I call it 'Eight Points to Light.' Picture it—the eight-point star. Two pointy triangles on each side of a square. We'll go around it clockwise and look at the meaning of each point."

Eva Clare propped her elbow on the table and rested her forehead in her hand. This was way too much information, and none of it was about Roy's ancestor.

Lily lifted a finger. Held it in the air at the top of an imaginary star.

"The first starpoint at the top right is Darkness—the sin of slavery. Slaves remembered a past of better times in their old world before they were captured and forced into hard times in the new world. The second point"—she hopped her finger to the first triangle on the right side of the square—"stands for Choice—a crossroads, a time to decide whether to stay down in slavery or not. The next starpoint is Hope—the inspiration to leave where they were and run away to a better place with hope of a better life."

"It's like the jar of flies," Eva Clare said.

"Yes, it is." Roy nodded exuberantly. "The flies were content being closed up inside the jar. When the lid was removed, they chose to stay."

"I don't understand the jar talk," Lily said, "but moving on with my points to light, the fourth one is Pathway to Freedom." She moved her finger to an imaginary point at the bottom of the star. "This is when the slaves gathered their tools and possessions and stepped onto the road to the Promised Land. The fifth starpoint is Guidance—help for the journey from God above, the stars, the quilts, the safe houses, and the sympathizers along the way."

"This is *your* story, Eva Clare," Roy noted. "It's the journey you're on. Life falling apart. Choosing to come home. Making decisions to move forward. Becoming independent, providing for yourself. Getting help from friends."

Eva Clare ran her hands through her hair at the temples.

Lily moved her finger in the air to the next pretend-point at the left side of the imaginary square. "The sixth point is Salvation—saved from bondage. Next, Resurrection—buried to the old life, rising to the new. Last, the eighth point at the top left: Light—hope fulfilled, freedom."

"Lily, this is so meaningful," Roy said. "It's a journey of sin, suffering, and survival. It's everybody's spiritual journey." He looked at Eva Clare. "Your ancestors helped with the Underground Railroad. Your history shows strong, compassionate women, and you should be proud. These women took their places on the right side of history." Roy reached over and patted Eva Clare's hand. "Now, who wants dessert?"

They made a pot of dark roast Community coffee and spooned out their final course. Took their cups and plates of fried biscuits with mascarpone lemon cream and blueberry compote, compliments of Sunny, to the den. Eva Clare looked out the wall of windows into the darkness, fireflies lighting up as night came full on. Like blinking stars. The music ended quietly with "Carpe Diem."

"Look at those lightning bugs," Lily said, pointing out the windows. "You know, legend says that all the lightning bugs along the river are ghosts of the slave souls that didn't make it."

Chill bumps spread up Eva Clare's arms.

Roy sat in the recliner that had a few tears in the fabric with white stuffing sticking out. He held his plate and set his coffee cup on the end table next to him. "Have you made any discoveries, Eva Clare, with the papers from the secret room?"

"With work at the store, I haven't had much time to read—"

"Oh, I don't want to hear that," Lily interrupted.

"But yes, I've found a couple of interesting documents so far. I came across the original will that Gerald gave me a copy of, saying the youngest daughter of Andrew Coghlan, Victoria, should inherit the house and land, but if she didn't have issue, her sister Catherine's issue would inherit the estate. We know Catherine married and had children. The will was in a brown paper pouch, and it appears that every succeeding will to present day is also in that pouch. The second will showed that the youngest daughter, Victoria, inherited the land and house because she willed it to my great-great-grandmother Erin Rose. But that's not the big thing."

"What's the big thing?" Roy asked.

"I found a few pages of loose minutes from the church. I think they're the originals from 1863—the real church record book. I don't know why my grandmother had them and hid them in her trunk and why they're not locked up somewhere at the church. Those were the days when members held each other accountable for their sins. One entry has me intrigued. I'm not sure what to make of it. I took a picture with my phone."

She set her dessert down, pulled her cell phone out of her purse, and went to the chair where Roy was sitting. She knelt and held the phone up. Lily joined them.

She read it out loud.

***"Saturday before the 3rd Lord's Day in June, 1863*. Met in conference. A charge was brought against sister Victoria Coghlan for adultery, the fact being fully known of her case. It was resolved to withdraw the fellowship of the Church from her, and announced by the moderator that the Church be no longer responsible for her conduct."**

"Ouch," Roy said. "What did she do? She was put on trial, judged, and sentenced, with no chance for repentance. That doesn't follow a Biblical mandate. She should've been given a chance to make satisfactory acknowledgment."

"But . . . adultery?" Eva Clare frowned.

"And 'the fact being fully known of her case.' It sounds like she had a baby out of wedlock."

Lily simpered.

Eva Clare breathed out a loud sigh. "The goings-on of my family leave me flabbergasted."

"If it's true, I wonder what happened to the child." Roy took Eva Clare's hand and turned the phone toward him for another look. "It was June of 1863. Let's do some research and find out what was going on around that time."

Lily smirked, wagged her head. "Y'all think you're so smart." She cackled wickedly.

18   REVENANT

She's close. She's poised to act.
She has opened her hands wide
and received the gift of truth:
the knowledge of darkness and light, of past and present.
Children come and go, play and laugh, live and die,
without searching, asking, feeling.
This one is different.
This is the one.
This one is one with us
down the generations to our Delta origins.
She is poised to rise strong with her gift
and show acts of fairness
and deliver evenness over her land.

19   Water Impressions

An undercurrent pulled the woman down the river, darkness beneath, sunlight above. She glided horizontally in the water, went vertical, danced a graceful ballet, her filmy dress and flaxen hair swirling. Her smile expressed her gladness for this milky green where she'd played as a girl—diving to the bottom, rising to the top, swimming fast and felicitous.

Orchestral water music accompanied her, an overture of spirited dance movements. She moved in rhythm with it. The hornpipes, regal. The bourree, double-time dance steps, on pointe, arms fluttering, one lifting above the head, the other following to fifth position, fingers touching in a circle of completeness. The dancing and music heightened.

She whispered breath pearls, myriads of them, like stars coming alive in the nighttime sky. Then, a struggle, and the bubbles slowed . . . stopped. Her chest heaved, then fell still. The dance steps stopped. The music stopped.

She succumbed to the current. Before she gave her whole self, she twisted to look at her dreamer.

Eva Clare bolted straight up in bed with a long sucking gasp. Best she could figure, the woman in the dream drowned.

But who was that woman?

Was it *her*?

No way was she going back to sleep. She needed to let the images settle, so she went downstairs, poured a glass of milk, and stirred in some chocolate powder.

"What the—?" Lily appeared in the doorway, tousled from sleep, hair down from her bun sticking out all whichaways. "Girl, whatchu rattlin' in here at three a.m. for, bangin' a spoon against a glass?"

"I had a bad dream."

"Sweet Jesus, I got to find my own place." Lily slammed her forehead against the door jamb.

"Stay here with me a few minutes." Eva Clare put the spoon on the counter. "You want some chocolate milk?"

"No. Milk makes me pee."

"Please come sit with me." Eva Clare went to the den, sat on the couch, pulled her feet under her, covered up with an afghan against cold air blowing from the window unit.

Lily flopped in a chair. "What'd you dream?"

"I think I will drown in the river." Eva Clare set her glass on the end table. "All my life I've had dreams about a woman under the water. Playful at first. Then she struggles to go to the surface to breathe. But she can't rise up. She can't get out of the undertow." Eva Clare pulled the afghan tighter around her. "You've seen my paintings. You know my obsession with the woman under the water. I think it's me."

"Why do you think it's you?"

"Before the woman in the dream died, she turned and looked at me. She *was* me. Maybe she was giving me a warning. Seems like I've always been pulled by some undercurrent, held down by things I can't change."

"Yeah, well, join the club."

"I don't understand the meaning of that dream, but I do feel afraid and alone here on the oxbow."

"You're not alone. You got the girls. They all jumped in to help you with the store. You got Roy. He looks at you like a man oughta look at a woman. And you got me. Here I sit at three a.m. listenin' to you rattlin' spoons and complaining. You ain't got nobody better than me. I tell you like it is." Lily sighed, her broad shoulders drooping with the exhale. "I swear, if there was a glass of sugar-sweet, fresh-squeezed lemonade in front of you, you'd only see the two seeds at the bottom."

"Probably so. Doesn't change how I feel."

"You want to talk about being held down, we'll start with my people," Lily said. "Here in this place, in old Prentiss, my people wore chains. In our lifetime—yours and mine—my people couldn't vote. Here in our own state, our own county, White people thought freedom was for Whites only. Some still do. Even now, Blacks don't live in the Erin city limits."

"And yet here *you* are."

Lily jerked her head up. "Huh?"

She obviously hadn't thought of that. By golly, Eva Clare got her on that one, a rare happening.

"Ha *ha!*" Lily bellowed. "That's right! I've shattered the glass ceilin'. Gone above my station in life." She threw her head back and laughed hard and loud with her mouth wide open.

Eva Clare looked at the silver fillings in Lily's teeth and laughed along.

"Me? I'm above my raisings. You? You still got to figure your situation out." Lily furrowed her brows. "You haven't read the journals you brought down from the secret room, have you?"

"Not yet. I've been working early to late all week, and I'm—"

"I don't want to hear it. No excuses. You need to sit here the rest of the night and read. You want to know who you are? Know your people? Know what you came from? Understand the dream?"

Eva Clare nodded.

"You gotta read the journals. Quit puttin' it off." Lily leaned forward. "Listen. There *was* a woman who drowned here. On accident. And there was a *second* drowning. Only it was no accident. She killed herself."

"Who? When?"

"She was only twenty-seven. Had a child. Her husband left a month before the baby was born to go off to the Oklahoma Land Rush to get some free acreage and settle there. Said he'd send for her and the child. But he never did. He was never heard from again. She committed suicide a year later."

"Who was she?"

Lily sat back, crossed her long legs, swung her foot. "She found life was a lie. Her mother had lived a lie. All the family behind her had lived a lie. This place was mired in sin and lies, and each generation heaped on. She left this world, this place, even left her daughter. That daughter was named Emmeline. And Emmeline's daughter was Evelyn."

"Evelyn? My Sweet Evelyn?"

"Read the journals." Lily stretched toward the coffee table to the stack of materials Eva Clare had brought down from the secret room, pushed some papers aside, and uncovered a brown, timeworn journal. "Here you go. Start with this one."

"So it was Erin Rose who killed herself? Emmeline's mother? My ancestor Catherine Deering Coghlan's daughter?"

"Read. The. Journal." Lily tapped the cover with each word. "You got nearly thirty years of journal writing to go through."

Eva Clare reached for her chocolate milk, took a drink, and set it back down. She picked up the diary, ran her fingers across the hard, scratched leather of what appeared to be a handmade book. The back cover folded over with a decorative tab and a leather strip to tie and secure the little book. She untied the cord and pulled the tab back to open the journal. Inside were tan, blue-lined pages, and lines of old cursive script with perfect slanting to the left. It was the diary of Catherine Deering's sister: VICTORIA DOVE COGHLAN, 1862 – 1863.

Lily stood and started toward the door.

"Where're you going?" Eva Clare said.

"I'm goin' back to bed. You got your company for the remainder of the night." Lily blew her a kiss and left the room, rocking her hips side to side.

"Shake it, but don't break it," Eva Clare whispered mockingly into Lily's slipstream.

The journal pages were separated by something folded up, so she turned the first portion of pages over to uncover a fragile, sepia-colored square of thin canvas, which she carefully opened. A map of an army outpost. ARKANSAS POST. CAPTURED JANUARY 11th 1863. It showed a section of the Arkansas side of the Mississippi River opposite Prentiss. She recognized the old Beulah Bend before the watercourse was straightened to keep Southern Rebels from firing at Northern gunboats. She recognized the town of Napoleon, once directly across the river from Prentiss. The channel washed it away, too, the same time it got Prentiss.

She knew from studying Mississippi History in ninth grade that Napoleon was once the largest town in Arkansas, except for Little Rock. Her teacher had included Napoleon in the history course because it was so close to them, even if it was in another state. Eva Clare didn't remember much, only the few details that had impressed her. It was a wealthy town, and its planter families went to New Orleans to shop for stylish clothes and host fancy balls. She'd also learned that Prentiss was a thriving port town with a hotel, newspaper, racetrack, and one of the only ferry crossings between Vicksburg and Memphis.

Eva Clare looked at the diary page marked by the map. She scanned a few January 1863 entries about chickens disappearing, fields flooding, and suppers of the last of the turnip greens with salt pork and cornbread. She lingered on the post about General Sherman and General Grant meeting in Napoleon where they conceived the idea of burning all the villages along the Mississippi River. She skimmed over lines and posts until her eyes settled on one in particular, and she read entry after entry.

January 23rd, 1863.

Snow came last week. It was a harsh blizzard, and very cold. A thick blanket of white covered our fields. The ground was frozen, trees wrapped in glistening ice. The sun made it quite a spectacle.

Our neighbor Ellis Steele came to look in on us, what with Father gone, lost in the mad river. Ellis said in Napoleon, now federally occupied, Union soldiers were freezing cold and in such dire need of firewood that they pulled apart the county courthouse plank by plank and used it for burning.

I sit here now in the night, keeping our fireplace stoked so the others can sleep. I must not let it burn down to embers. My front side is warmed at the hearth, but I can feel cold air push against my back. The candle flickers and makes shadows on the wall, what looks like a man's long nose, beard, curls at his collar, and cap.

I think about Teddy. And the warm September sun the day I first saw him in Prentiss. I think how our eyes met, how he took my hand, told me his name. How handsome he was in his blue uniform. How he stole away from Napoleon again and again, by ferry across that wide river, for me alone. I think of the woods at Indian Point as the days grew shorter and cooler and the trees turned time into a season of red and yellow, a season that matched his fiery passion. And I'm warmed inside.

I think of our special place by the river, at the base of an ancient sycamore with a tall, white trunk, holes hammered into the bark by some old Indian hen, limbs dead, missing, flickering leaves of yellow. A sister sycamore was felled beside it, forming a protective wall in the thicket of evergreens and colorful leafy trees, vines wrapping, knitted around us like a shawl. Many afternoons we lay there on the soft needled forest floor promising undying love.

The ferry isn't running now. There's ice in the river, and danger. ~VDC

March 24th, 1863.

Our world here on the river is fire and flood now. First, the Lincolnite commander William Tecumseh Sherman docked in Prentiss and burned much of our town. He tore it to splinters after swearing not to leave a shred or shingle of it and left only the Steele dry goods store, the fag end of a blacksmith shanty, and a few brick chimneys of merchants' establishments. Houses for the most part were spared. The town people fought back by building anew.

As if the Union soldiers didn't bring enough harm to us with fire, they assaulted us again with water. They dug a new channel to straighten the river and cut off the bend. Our beloved farm is no longer on the lively Mississippi.

The new flow is fast, forceful. And higher. Chewing away at its own banks. Ferry traffic has ceased for now until the river carves out its bed and settles.

Sometimes nature makes its own course, to which the intentions and designs of men have no answer. Sometimes a river runs headlong to future destinations and there's no stopping it.

Teddy is not like the other soldiers, for he is kind and considerate, but he is leaving with them and their boorish ways, going south with the war. He may already be gone. He cannot cross the frightful river to say farewell. All of me aches for him.

My dear, dear Teddy, I miss you, and I pray one day you will return to me, for I will love you only and forever. ~VDC

April 20th, 1863.

I catch myself curving my hand under the bulge my belly has grown. At first I thought I was fat and fleshy from feasting on too much ham, biscuits, and soppin' gravy over winter, but I have come to realize the bigness is only under the front pleats of my skirt, beneath the bodice waistline of my dress. I cannot fasten the bottom button.

My work apron covers the roundness that has started to show. Sister hasn't noticed, for she's busy with her infant and field work, now that her husband is gone east fighting with the Mississippi cavalry. Since Father died, Sister and I work the family land together, with her husband when he's not off at war, and with our slave.

I've had an instinct about this bulge all along. I've had the signs, but I've dismissed them. Now I must come to terms with the reality of my condition.

Today I slipped away from the house as Sister suckled her babe, sweet Annah. I walked up Wellington Road through the bottoms to Prentiss town. April warmth wrapped around me. The air was full of birdsong. The earth was adorned in flower color—buttercups, black-eyed Susans, and swamp lilies. Trees were spring green, and the dogwoods bloomed out. New life flourished all around me.

I stood on the bank of the Mississippi and watched it rolling over itself in a rush south to bigger places like Vicksburg. The river was angry and frothy white today. It once was a happy-playing place. Now, it carries a war.

Doc Henry's office is a small room behind Old Man Steele's general store, so that the doctor's door faces the river and not the town's main road. Doc directed me to a table, then put his hands on the bulge. I felt movement under his fingers.

"Miss Coghlan," he said, "you're with child, and your time will be accomplished in a matter of weeks, with the coming of summer." He asked who fathered the child.

I could not tell him. All I could do was push up off the table and run to the door.

I stood on the warfire-blackened planks of the porch with both hands curved around my belly, around Teddy's child. I looked out at the wide waters racing madly by, the same river that takes Northern gunboats and soldiers down toward Vicksburg.

Teddy is gone. And I'll forever have a part of him with me.

But this is a bastard child.

What will people say?

What will I do?

I hope this new life is a gal baby, with Coghlan blue eyes and yellow hair, and my lover's full, curvy lips, and I'll name her Erin, after my young dead mother. Erin Rose, after the soft flowers that grew on the forest floor, the tiny white roses I saw once in a blur as my eyes came open when he was on me, and I smelled their wild sweetness.

This child is a war baby, a tie that binds the sides of disunity in hope. She'll bring light and laughter to a dark world. As soldiers and towns are falling all around me into death, she'll smile on recurring life. She's redemption, and she will mend hearts. She will carry her presence, my presence, through the ages, down through the generations, down to our daughters in all times. Her spirit will be everlasting like this river that keeps on coming and going.

The river sound was intrusive today. Water was throwing itself at the bank, flinging itself high and falling back into a swirling current. The new channel has a great force to handle. I watched as the rush broke off a big chunk of riverbank and washed it away, down toward Vicksburg. The river came a foot closer to Doc Henry's stoop.

Dear God, this whole town could fall into the river. ~VDC

June 8th, 1863.

My gal baby came this morning with the sunrise. There is hope upon my breast as this infant presses her mouth into my flesh and takes sustenance. I will give all of me for this blessing of the love I have for Teddy. I have such joy holding this creation that I could burst. May my love for Teddy always be aflame and always be. ~VDC

July 19th, 1863.

Vicksburg has surrendered. Thousands of Southern soldiers laid down their guns and walked away from war. It was a long and devastating siege. Northern troops have moved onward. Teddy has gone farther away, with no choice but to march on. The system of slave ownership is crumbling before us. On our farm Star has been more like family than one in bondage. We work side by side as sisters.

Four weeks ago, the church removed me from her rolls. Though during my days in waiting, I stayed away from divine service and remained hidden on the farm, except for occasional trips to town, someone learned of my bastard child, told the churchmen, and the old men of God struck me down.

To protect this child and the family name, I must relinquish my daughter. Sister will raise this child as her own. My beautiful gal baby will be known as the daughter of Catherine and her husband

John Amason, and will take his surname, not Teddy's. We will change the birthdate of the child. When Sister's husband arrives home from war, he will have a delightful surprise. Sister will tell her husband the truth of the matter, and he will help cover it up, and the people in town will conveniently forget any truth they may know and go along with the lie he tells because he is the man of the house and a man of God. Sister and Star will go to the church under cover of darkness and tear away the page in the Book of Holy Minutes where my fate was recorded, wiping all written memory away and sealing a holy future for my daughter, Teddy's daughter.

I vow never to return to the church house.

Dear Teddy will never find his way back to this forgotten spot. He is forever gone and will never know of his daughter. One day I will tell her about her father. One day when she is a woman and the world is a kinder place. When the people do not divide themselves with labels of North and South, Yankee and Rebel. When the people do not hate their brother and bear arms against him with no qualm of shooting him through the heart because he believes differently. When the people do not sit under their steeples and judge the behavior of a sister and dismiss her from their midst, with no thought of God's love and mercy, and set her life on a lower course over which she has no control, nor does God have any control over her fate. ~VDC

Eva Clare shut the journal, pressed it to her chest, struggled for breath that wouldn't come. The revelations sank in. Should she cry, crazy-laugh, or what? Victoria Dove Coghlan had a baby. Family history had recorded Victoria Dove as a spinster. Eva Clare's lineage was not through Catherine Deering Coghlan Amason as she'd always been told and as it was written in her family Bible. That Bible was a lie.

A lie.

The truth? Her lineage was through Victoria Dove Coghlan who produced a love child with a Union soldier, never married, and gave up her baby so it would have a name to please society. Victoria Dove, abused by the men of her religion, turned her back on the church.

The sins of the father . . . the mother . . . are carried down the generations.

They, all her people, all in the family line had lived a lie, and the tangled tentacles of region, race, and religion had wrapped tightly around her ancestors and strangled the truth.

The images of these journal people were with her now, the manifest content of her dreams, their truths coming out.

By having issue, a child, Victoria Dove fulfilled the points of the original will of Andrew Coghlan. Should she wag this in Gerald's face? This was all she needed to shut him up.

Or should she keep up the tradition and protect the lies as her grandmomma had? What should she do with the confessions in this little brown book?

She cried. Tears seemed to come out of every pore of her body, involuntarily, the weight on her circulatory system pushing them out, pushing out the pain of deception, secrets, and lies. Like a birth, the sins were coming out with the water. She wept until she slept.

20 BLESSED BE THE TIE THAT BINDS

Smells of bacon frying and coffee brewing nudged Eva Clare awake. Her eyes were gritty and swollen from crying, her head full and tight. Last night's revelations flared up, reminding her that she was a different person today. She pushed herself off the couch and joined Lily in the kitchen.

She grabbed a slice of bacon, poured herself a cup of dark roast, and plopped on a dinette chair. "Victoria Dove is my third-great-grandmother. You know that, don't you?"

"Yes." Lily stirred batter and turned on the waffle iron to heat up. "She's the Delta oxbow line. The other line—Gerald's ancestors—returned to the Mississippi Hill Country."

"Why'd you study and memorize the journals? Why the interest in Coghlan history? What's it to you?"

"Girl, you're so busy thinking about yourself, you're not connecting the dots. Don't you see? Because it's *my* history, *my* family, too. Andrew Coghlan is *my* ancestor—my third and fourth great-grandfather. I told you Andrew fathered Star and Riselle." Lily banged the spoon against the rim of the bowl to knock excess batter off. "We're kin. You and me. Andrew is our common ancestor." Lily poured batter onto a spit-hot grill, and steam sizzled out from the bottom. "Your grandmother would've never told you that. It's way too scandalous."

Lily's assertion swirled around Eva Clare's head so fast she had a hard time holding it.

Lily was right.

She had been too busy thinking about herself to allow the full implications of Andrew Coghlan's sexual escapades to sink in. She circled the coffee cup with her hands, clamped tightly, the mug burning her, but she let it.

Lily lifted the lid to check the waffle. Eva Clare focused on Lily's brown arms. Different race, different color. Kin.

"Also, I read the journals because I wanted to see what Victoria Dove knew and recorded. I know things passed down to me by word of mouth that she apparently didn't know or didn't want to document," Lily said.

"Like what?"

"I already told you Victoria's daughter Erin Rose drowned herself in the oxbow. But I didn't tell you that it was her second try at suicide. During the first drowning attempt, Victoria Dove pulled her out, but was so fatigued from the struggle that she gave up, slipped under the water, and lost her own life. She was forty-four."

"Victoria Dove died trying to save her daughter?" Could her family situation get any more messed up?

"Yes." Lily forked the waffle off the iron, flopped it onto a Fiesta plate, and poured more batter over the hot teeth of the grill. "And what do I know that they didn't know? Well, the sisters, Victoria Dove and Catherine Deering, never knew Andrew was murdered by Star. They invited Star to live in the main house after it was finished and gave her what would've been Andrew's upstairs bedroom. Remember, he was buried in a shallow grave under the house."

The waffle iron hissed and steamed.

Lily adjusted the setting. "They brought Star inside during the bad winter of 1863, when they had a big snowstorm and temperatures went below zero for days. Star would've frozen to death in her shanty. The women were already working together to maintain the farm and to help runaway slaves. Star and her girl Riselle lived in what's now the reading room across the hall from Victoria Dove who had your room."

"How do you know all these details?"

"I've told you. My people tended the legends and passed them down. Your people created the version they wanted the world to believe."

Eva Clare snapped off a piece of bacon. "You're telling me that Catherine, Victoria, and Star, and their children—plantation owners and slaves—lived together in this house."

"That's what I'm saying."

"So these three women, sisters by blood, set a course for the family to live right, yet unconventionally, and to practice that all citizens are created equal."

"I reckon so. They lived in a slave society but changed it in their household, if only for safety and convenience. They changed to what came naturally and worked for them. I always thought it was funny that here in the South, in the Bible Belt, where people believe that men are powerful over women, in our Coghlan family, the man was put down low and the women were walking all over him." Lily laughed as she smeared butter on the waffle occupying the plate. "And Sweet Evelyn? That's what she did, too, in her last years—accepted what came natural for her and Marthala, regardless of color."

Eva Clare put her cup to her lips and drank. That's what she and Lily were doing, too. She had another thought. "Oh goodness gracious sakes alive. I suspect that visual of those three women walking over Andrew Coghlan will stick in my mind forever."

They both laughed, and then it hit Eva Clare. "Oh my God. He's still under us this very moment. We are living here and walking all over him." She lifted her feet off the floor and put them on the bottom rung of the chair.

"Eww." They squealed and shuddered.

"Now another thing—the big reveal. And you ain't gon like this at all," Lily added. "What Gerald Tanner, and even you, don't realize about Gerald's claim that this house should've gone to the oldest descendent of the oldest daughter of Andrew Coghlan: Star was the oldest. Uh huh. If we ignore your grandmother's will and go by what Gerald wants, then Star inherited Coghlan House and the land it sits on, and I'm her descendant and the rightful owner. Not Gerald. And not you. Y'all put that in your pipe and smoke it."

Eva Clare's heart rolled over. "Oh, Lily—"

"Yeah. Uh huh. Me. Lily Moselle Greene."

"Oh, Lily."

"Don't worry. I ain't gon do nothin' with that. I got the sense to know better. And I don't figure these journals would stand up in any court of law. And anyway, Victoria Dove did have a child. And you got a will."

Eva Clare released her breath slowly. It weighed on her that Lily had done so much for Sweet Evelyn, had given up her own apartment and her freedom to come and go in order to be an in-home caregiver, had a genuine entitlement in the Coghlan family, yet didn't have a pot to piss in right now. Her chest clenched tightly with guilt about the unfairness of Lily's situation. She couldn't help it. It's the way she was. She'd offered to help. But what could she do? She, too, was a woman starting over. And they both wanted their own space.

She looked out the wall of windows at the oxbow shimmering in the light of early morning. The sun lay against the tops of the bald cypresses, poplars, and sweet gums. A blue heron flew over the lake. It looked so peaceful. But peace was not what she was feeling. She thought of her unfair privilege. "Star was the oldest," she said in barely a whisper. "Daughter." She cleared her throat. "And I have the house."

"Uh huh. And don't get all bent out of shape over it. I don't. This was your grandparents' home. You grew up here. You've got memories, traditions, and a piece of paper that says you are the rightful owner." Lily put the second waffle on a plate and set it in front of Eva Clare. "Getchu some syrup and some more bacon."

Eva Clare thanked her and reached for the maple syrup. "Gerald will have a fit."

Lily turned off the iron and pulled the plug. "I suspect he knows more than he is letting on, and that's why he's all in your business right now."

Eva Clare groaned.

"One more thing you don't know," Lily said, "is that Victoria Dove was an artist. I remember coming across her drawings in the trunk when I was a little girl playing in the secret room. After I saw your paintings, I went back up there and pulled out two to show you at the right time." She took a bite of waffle. "It's the right time," she said with her mouth full, her words warped. She got up and retrieved her purse from the counter.

"Her journals are artistic, too, from what I've read," Eva Clare said. "Her posts use rich, descriptive words."

Lily set her leather satchel on the table. "Let me show you the drawings." She pulled out a manila envelope, removed two pieces of parchment paper, and held one up to Eva Clare. "Here's one she titled *Lady of the Lake.*"

Eva Clare clasped her hands to her mouth. Though old, rubbed, and faded, the graphite sketch was much like her own river paintings—her theme of a woman submerged—showing a lady with long hair and a full dress under the water, little round breath bubbles, and gracefully poised limbs reflective of dance.

"It's as if I've been copying a mentor." Eva Clare put her finger on the dress and followed its lines. Her world narrowed. She was part of a bigger effort, an expression of feelings on the subject of women gone under, women needing to be rescued.

"See at the bottom, it says 1888," Lily said. "That was a couple of years before she drowned."

"Oh, Lily, don't you see? She felt pushed down, held under. She had visions of something happening in the water. She knew her fate, and she couldn't rise up and overcome it. She transported her hurts and fears down the family line to me."

Lily nodded, laid the drawing on the table, and held up the second sketch named *Lady Rising.* This drawing showed a woman kicking, rising up out of the water powerfully, leaving a wake behind her.

The ghost woman in Eva Clare's dreams had always told her to rise up. Eva Clare knew right then, her dreams, her obsession with the water, the sketches and her paintings, the lady of the lake and the lady rising, were tied together, bonding the generations.

"I must frame this one."

"All right, you do that," Lily said. "Go on and eat now. You got to get up town and open the store. But one more thing. Did you finish reading the journal?"

"No, not yet. I fell asleep."

"Promise me one thing. After work today when you get home, read the end. Read the December entries. It's only a few pages. Tell me you'll read them tonight. Promise me."

"Okay, I will. They're hard to read, you know, in that old-timey script."

"I know, but do it. I mean it. I'll see you in a little while at the store. I've got to re-stock my booth."

Before going to work, Eva Clare walked to the pier. The air was already hot and heavy. A sun-sparkled haze hung over the water, and wisps of fog were lifting from the surface.

Her family secrets were coming out. She stepped onto the old planks and walked out over Beulah Lake, looked down at the wavy water, saw herself. She was the end of the line of generations of women raised here on the oxbow, generations who worked and played and laughed and cried here, and two who died here—one a savior, one a sacrifice.

No matter how much she hated what went on in this place during the time she grew up here and in the decades prior—the wrongs and violent acts people committed in the name of ill-perceived right and religion— this was her home. She was born to this place. It was embedded in her matter, imprinted on her brain.

Those who lived here before her still lived in her. Their monumental experiences and enduring memories were passed down the generations through their DNA. Maybe all children were born with memories held by their ancestors printed on their genetic material. Maybe it was biologically possible for a strong connection to a place or person, a deep passion, or a frightful trauma to stamp descendants with inherent awareness, feelings, and fears.

Her image in the oxbow shimmied. Her chest throbbed. Coming home had unlocked the secret behind her water paintings. She was the recipient of the experiences and emotions of Victoria Dove Coghlan. It was up to her now to be the lady of the lake awakening and walking in the power granted to her by the first female of her line to come to this water, the first to be held under by this place. She had to be brave enough to follow her heart, bold enough to use her voice, and strong enough to be the lady rising above the fray.

Eva Clare parked in the alley behind the store, unlocked the back door of the Trunk at nine o'clock, and walked into the rear foyer behind the dividing wall Roy and Pete had built, which included a wide, center opening to the store. The foyer was a cozy sitting area for Eva Clare and Betsy, with a camel tan leather loveseat, a ladderback chair for Betsy's bad back, and a little TV atop an antique chest. Next to the staircase going to the apartment upstairs were a sideboard, mirror, and a brass, low-light lamp. A burgundy, purple, and oxblood red Moroccan rug complemented the melon-pink walls. The wooden stairs were waxed and shiny.

Store aisles and shelves were clean, neat, and perfectly organized. The booth art was selling well, and antique treasures and heirlooms were starting to move.

She'd left the corner space at the back wall of the store empty. That's where she'd paint. She was counting on kindling some customer interest in oil painting, then offering landscape classes in the fall—a moneymaker, hopefully. Now, after listening to Lily this morning and seeing the artwork of her ancestor, she was driven to paint a scene exactly like Victoria Dove's sketch of *Lady of the Lake*. Next, she'd paint the other sketch of the woman coming up out of the water. *Lady Rising.* Maybe it was what Victoria Dove had hoped her daughter Erin Rose would do—let her inner strength save her.

She set the easel up. Next to it, a wooden butler cart she'd pulled from inventory. She arranged her supplies on it—paints, medium, brushes, palette, jar of solvent. Then she stepped back to check and make sure she had everything she needed. A shaft of light coming through the window gleamed against a polished stairstep and caught her eye.

An idea slid to her off a sunbeam.

She scurried over to the golden-lit tread and walked upstairs to the two-room apartment—living and kitchen combo and bedroom with full bath. It was spacious, clean, move-in ready. Three tall bedroom windows looked out over the main street, and two narrow living room windows gave a view of Steele Bayou, a hardwood forest, and a clearing off to the north with an adjoining field of soybeans. She stood in the middle of the living room with her hands saddled on her hip bones, doing a three-sixty and assessing, when she heard a high-pitched voice downstairs.

"Woo hoo. Anybody here?"

"I'm upstairs. Come on up." She heard footsteps before Lily appeared in the doorway.

"Are there too many stairs for you to climb?" Eva Clare asked.

"Me? No, there aren't as many as at Roy's, and these have got a landing in the middle."

"Come on in and look around. What do you think about this space?"

Lily looked at the ceiling, then the floor, her critical eye geared to doing a thorough review. She walked over to the sink, turned the water on, off, opened drawers and cabinet doors. She looked in the refrigerator and dishwasher. Turned on a burner of the stovetop and waited for it to redden. She went into the bathroom and checked all the faucets, then to the bedroom where she inspected the windows and the big closet.

She turned to Eva Clare and nodded. "It's real nice. It needs some soap run across the rung of the drawer to the left of the sink in the kitchen so it will open and close smoothly. And it's got some rust stains in the bathtub from an old leak that need to be scrubbed with some Bon Ami, but other than that, it's in perfect shape." She pushed her watch around and around her wrist. "So what're you gon do with it? Rent it out?"

"What about you living here?"

"Me?" Lily slapped her hand to her chest, her silver bracelets jingling.

"You."

"You crazy as a betsy bug, girl. I can't live here."

"Why not?"

"It's downtown Erin." She held up one finger. Then two. "I'm not sandy-beach color like you." Three fingers. "Gerald Tanner would dig himself out a white robe and erect a cross on the front sidewalk. How many reasons do you need?"

"Don't worry about him. It's my building. I'll handle him."

"You? You'll handle him? You, the woman who's gon let him cheat you out of all you're entitled to because he intimidates you? Hah!" Lily threw her head back and laughed. "Girl, you ain't got the guts."

"Yes, I do. I can deal with this. I believe—after looking at those sketches you showed me this morning—I won't be standing alone. I've got the power of strong women behind me, in me, and with me." She put her hands on her hips. "Now, first of all, you must answer this: would you like to live here?"

"Oh, sweet Jesus, I'd love it." Lily clasped her hands, held them under her chin. "Love it. It'd be better than anything I've ever had. Girl, I grew up in a shack in a cotton field. This is a dream place. In all my born days, I never lived in anything this nice." She twirled around, tears brimming. "But I can't afford this right now. Not until I get back into nursing full time."

"Money's not an issue. We'll work something out. Already, by contract, I have the right to make decisions about the store and the building, and I will buy both in two months for a nominal monthly amount paid to Betsy until she dies. If you would like living here, we can make this happen."

"Oh Jesus, I'm so touched by this I don't know what to say. Thank you." Lily wiped the wetness spilling onto her cheeks. "But I've got to be on a working team. Paying my way. I can't take charity."

"We'll work up an agreement. Maybe you can help me with the store, manage it at times that fit with your future nursing schedule. We'll figure it out. We'll be a team, like Victoria Dove and Star."

"All right." Lily offered her hand, Eva Clare took it, and they shook on the deal in progress. "Now we best get this store open."

They went downstairs, where Eva Clare turned on lights and equipment, logged into the computer, and unlocked the front door. Lily went straight to her booth. She got busy rearranging her wares, and all the while she was working, she was talking up a storm under her breath, with occasional sniffles and thank-yous to Jesus.

Eva Clare got out her palette and started mixing paints—white and Sap Green. Then she whipped some Oxide of Chromium Green and Naples Yellow Light into the mix. She was going to paint the murky green that took her ancestors. She added a dab of this and a dab of that until she found the exact lake color. She knew it well from being under it.

The first person in the door at ten after ten was Roy. He made small talk as she put a canvas board on her easel and arranged her brushes. Then he caught her off guard with a question.

"How would you like to go out tonight, have a quiet dinner, share company?"

Eva Clare stared at the canvas board and bit the inside of her cheek. Did she want to go out? Did she want to go out *with him*? Start something she wasn't sure she could finish?

Yes. She did.

"I would like that. I close at six."

"You can leave at five," Lily interjected from her booth, not looking up from her busyness. "I can close for you." She sniffled and kept mumbling low.

"Pick you up here at five-fifteen?" Roy said to Eva Clare.

"Sure." She yelled back to Lily, "Thanks!"

"What's up with Lily? Why is she talking to herself? And is she crying?" Roy asked.

"Lily is overjoyed and emotional right now. We decided she's moving in upstairs. She'll be living in the apartment you and Pete checked out."

"Oh, that's a great idea. A good, convenient place for her and a constant presence at the store. But what will your cousin Gerald say?"

"After he has a conniption fit, he'll put on a white robe and burn a cross on the front sidewalk."

21   CHANGING COURSE

"I know where a good river lookout point is." Roy pulled the visor down to keep the evening sun out of his eyes. He positioned his hands at ten and two on the steering wheel. "Can you climb a tower after eating that big steak?"

Eva Clare could still taste the juicy T-bone and buttery, garlic bread she'd had for dinner at Doe's Eat Place in Greenville.

"That depends on how high it is."

"Three levels above ground, but the view at sunset should be worth the effort."

"Let's do it." She'd never pass up an opportunity to visit her river.

They drove southwest down Highway 82 to the Greenville port and Levee Road, then to a riverfront area with trails, a campground, a boat landing, and a tall, wide tower.

After following the sidewalk to the high structure, they climbed the staircase to the first lookout level, the second, the highest. It was a large, roofless, square platform that could hold maybe a hundred people, but they were the only two. They leaned against the rail, side by side, and looked out at the mighty Mississippi, a glistening-white ribbon beginning to show the colors of the sky at setting sun. A barge tow, a long black line backlighted by the red-golden glow, moved north.

A soft wind swept her face.

Roy leaned closer, put his hand on the rail, let his arm rest against hers. "I think I understand your strong feelings for this place—this river, the tugboats and barges that move on it, the history it carries."

The lowering sun painted the water gold.

"This river has always been mine. I belong here." She laid claim to the wide water-strand that formed her Delta. "Growing up here, I was one with it. I took it in every possible way—swallowed it, soaked it through my skin, breathed it up my nose. It's part of me."

"For some reason, I feel like I belong here, too."

"You can't belong here unless you were born here."

Roy frowned, stared at her, seemed baffled at her comment. The breeze off the river blew a clump of hair in her face. He pushed it behind her ear, then let his hand rest against her cheek for a long, quiet moment until she couldn't hold his gaze any longer and looked away.

"Then maybe I lived here in a previous life."

They watched as the sun dropped and touched the water with an explosion of color against the horizon. Then the ball of fire quietly sank into the river, making wavy, moving lines. Something about it was satisfying.

"Eva Clare, you've told me how much you love this place, but you've also expressed some negative feelings about it. How do you explain the contradiction?"

"I'm ambivalent. Love and hate. It's possible to do both, you know, to have both love and hate for a place. With the Delta, everybody should have both. I love the Delta's soul that comes from far down in the fertile earth. I love the tall cotton and the flat landscape where you can see for miles and miles. But I am not deceived. I know this place is troubled. There's a long, conflicted history here, and that history isn't only in the past. People have brought it into the present. They have a great devotion to the old ways, to the Confederacy. I'm not sure they realize the Confederacy was a failed, four-year-old, illegitimate, now-nonexistent nation of traitors to our country."

"Ouch. Those are some strong words."

She winced. "People here would hate me for saying that." Another barge tow approached from the north. She counted nine rows, five abreast, a forty-five-barge tow. "There's a disconnect here between what's real, right, and lawful and what some people glorify and want to be real. It's the alignment of racism and religion that I cannot tolerate."

The sky closed down to dusk, and the river became a silver metallic string.

"This river runs fast and changes course often, but the people who live by it don't."

Roy raised an eyebrow. "Nothing changes till people want change."

"This river, like any force of water, goes where it wants to. It may go around an obstacle or knock the thing down. It makes its way, and nothing can stand against it," she said.

Roy nodded and put his hands in his pants pockets. "We need to start back. They lock the park gates at dusk."

"Oh yeah, sure." Eva Clare turned toward the stairs.

He reached for her arm. She pivoted and faced him. He clasped her shoulders, slowly leaned toward her, and put his lips against hers, briefly. They parted, held the silence, and he pulled her in, wrapped his arms around her tightly, and kissed her long and hard.

It was nine by the time Roy dropped her off at the back alley of the store where she'd parked, and nine-thirty before she got home, after a conversation with Lily, who was carrying clothes up to the apartment.

She dropped her purse on the kitchen table, wrapped her arms around herself, took a deep breath. Wouldn't be falling asleep any time soon. Not after being with Roy. Not after that kiss.

She poured a glass of milk, put a few little powdered-sugar donuts on a plate, went out to the patio, and sat at the black wrought iron table. It was time to figure out her relationship with Roy. The pole light gave definition.

A car came creeping up the driveway. Too slow for Lily. Maybe it was Roy. No, it was Sunny's white-pearl Acura. The car door opened, the interior light came on, and Sunny clambered out.

"I'm on the patio." Eva Clare groaned in her throat. Weaved her hands through her hair.

"Hey!" Sunny walked over to the old-brick surface flanked by monkey grass, azalea bushes, and hydrangeas. "I've been working down at the Pie Bird. Anna Laurel's helping me. We carried in the ice cream parlor tables and chairs Betsy gave me." She shifted from foot to foot. "I painted the tables and chairs white, and they look brand new. The pie parlor will be ready to open soon." She sat down across from Eva Clare.

"Good." Eva Clare crossed her legs, swung her foot. Other things were on her mind.

"I'll have a featured meat and dessert pie each month. I'll also sell slices of other flavors. And whole pies for people to take home for supper. What do you think?" Sunny scratched the back of her head, then fisted her hands and put them in her lap.

Eva Clare didn't want to think about pies right now. But she gave a resigned shrug and went along. "Sounds good." She took a bite of a donut and spilled powdered sugar on her pants. "You want one?"

"Yuck. You're asking a pastry chef about commercial cakes with chemical ingredients? No, thanks."

"Okay, then." Wet chemical-cake stuck to the roof of her mouth. "Sunny, I've been meaning to ask you, I've got some big potted plants from Sweet Evelyn's funeral that need a home. Do you want to use them in your decorating?"

"Yes, I want the space to be like a courtyard garden between your Trunk and Anna Laurel's coffee shop—full of greenery. Big pots of palms, lavender, and spearmint. A bubbly fountain. I love that our three stores are all connected, and we all work together and look out for each other. And that brings me to the reason I'm here." Sunny leaned in, widened her eyes, blinked a bunch of times.

"Which is?"

"Lily is still down there at the store. She's haulin' stuff in, like clothes, shoes, pictures, and an ironing board. Not quilts like you'd expect her to be bringing in for stock. I thought you should know."

"I know Lily's there. I saw her a while ago when Roy dropped me off to get my car. Lily's moving into the apartment upstairs."

"Moving what in?"

"Moving herself in. She's going to be living in the apartment over Betsy's Trunk."

"Living there?"

"Yes, she's in need of a place to live, and I have this space that needs to be occupied. She'll help run the store. We'll all work together."

"Do you really think that's a good idea? We've never had people live downtown."

"Betsy's nephew did."

"You know what I mean."

Eva Clare stared at Sunny unflinchingly. "She's Black." Her shoulders slumped. "She's also nice, smart, educated, honest, funny, a hard worker, a good friend, and a truly gifted quilt artist." Eva Clare raised her voice. "Look, I'm doing what works best for me and for Lily and for the store. Besides, I think Erin is due a change—people occupying space downtown, living above their stores. I think we're bringing change—me, you, Anna Laurel. We've established three women-owned businesses. Because of our example, two other stores are sprucing up. It's good change, Sunny. I need you to be okay with this."

Sunny rubbed her hands over her thighs. After a moment of silence, she reached over and selected a commercial, chemical-laced donut. "You went out somewhere with Roy?"

"Yes." Eva Clare turned up her glass of milk.

"So, is there something going on with you two?"

"No. Only dinner. That's all." Eva Clare changed positions, bounced her knee up and down, raked her hair behind an ear. She gazed at the oxbow—dark, glistening from the pole light. She couldn't look straight on at Sunny. Because she was lying.

They debated back and forth over whether there was something going on or not and talked about ham and egg pies and bourbon pecan pies, and then Sunny left.

Eva Clare rubbed the back of her neck, frazzled from dealing with her longtime friend who hadn't changed her worldview since she was a kid in a training bra. She looked up at the sky. Myriads of stars. Bright ones, tiny specks, the Big Dipper, all in their places across the heavens, even with the pole light diminishing some of them. Looking at the blackness full of distant mysterious twinkles always made her feel small and insignificant—and open-minded.

She heard another car turn in and creep up the drive. She'd never known Lily to go that slowly. She watched as the vehicle appeared at the corner of the house.

Roy. Her breath stopped in her throat.

He coasted in. Got out of the car. She went to meet him.

"I couldn't go home," he said. "I mean, I went home, but I couldn't stay. I wanted to be with you." He took her hands.

Her pulse quickened. "Come sit with me on the patio." She kept hold of a hand and walked Roy to the table. "I'm stargazing."

He pulled a chair over beside hers so he could see the same view of the sky. "They're magnificent out here in the country."

"I'm thinking how I'm only one little star in the middle of nowhere."

"But with a big, bright light."

They talked about the opportunity they had to shine their lights along the oxbow, along the ribbon of silver, sparkling river.

Then Lily's car wheeled in and slung gravel up the driveway, digging in and skidding to a stop two inches from Roy's bumper. He laid a hand on his chest and swallowed hard.

"She drives like a bat out of hell," Eva Clare said, and they laughed.

Lily sauntered over. "What are y'all laughing at?"

"The way you drive," Eva Clare said.

"How?"

"Fast."

"Girl, I got things to do."

"At ten o'clock at night?"

"Well, I'm moving," Lily said. "And look at you. Here you sit, and you didn't read the end of that journal like you promised, did you?"

"Not yet."

"Well, you shoulda done it before you sat out here holdin' hands and smoochin' with Roy in the moonlight and Lord knows what else." Lily strutted inside, shaking her head and mumbling.

"What's up with her?" Roy asked.

"Who knows?"

22 WOMEN'S BUSINESS

Eva Clare walked in from work Wednesday evening, kicked off her shoes, and pulled a baking pan out of a cabinet. She'd invited Anna Laurel for dinner so she could tell her about Lily and Star and the ancestry connections Gerald either didn't know about or was desperately trying to cover up. She'd bake salmon, throw a couple of Irish potatoes in the microwave, and fix a Caesar salad. She put fillets in the pan, poured Jack Daniels whiskey over them, topped the fish with garlic salt and pecan chips, and drizzled maple syrup.

A knock sounded at the front door. Anna Laurel usually came to the back and didn't bother to knock. Eva Clare cussed under her breath, set the oven to four hundred, then hurried to see who was disturbing her at the end of her workday. She didn't have time for surprise visits.

Dr. Loring from Beulah Lake Baptist Church stood on the welcome mat.

"Good evening," he said with a smile. "I hope I'm not interrupting anything, but—"

"I just got home from work. I'm getting dinner—"

"I won't be but a minute. I must hurry to prayer meeting."

"I'm having a dinner guest and—"

"Yes, I heard you and the visiting professor are friendly."

"That's not—"

"That's not why I'm here." Dr. Loring pulled his sport coat together, pushed the top button through its hole, and cleared his throat.

She didn't mind her manners and invite him in.

"I'm here to politely ask for your consideration," he said. "We all want to be sensitive to the feelings of others in the community, especially when it comes to . . . matters of inclusion. You understand."

"Wha—?" She flinched. "You talking about Lily? Staying here? Moving into the apartment above the Trunk? How do you even know? She hasn't finished—"

"I'm sorry. I honestly don't mean to overstep. I'm here on behalf of someone else, a church member who was concerned it might stir up old feelings."

Eva Clare stepped back. Put her hand against her forehead. Who was the church member? Gerald? How did Gerald know? As soon as the question tumbled out, it hit her. Sunny. Her plea to Sunny to accept Lily's move had failed, resulting in the probable scenario of Sunny's tattling to the preacher or more likely, ratting to Gerald, who went to Dr. Loring for the official spiritual warning. Small-town, small-church patriarchs like Gerald used their preachers to push their agendas. "Damn."

"Excuse me?" Dr. Loring said.

"Look, this was a business decision, as well as a personal one. It's a good decision. I stand by it." She stopped short as she saw Anna Laurel's baby-blue T-Bird turn into the driveway. "Would you like to talk to my attorney?"

"Oh, no, ma'am." He flashed his palm in a stop motion. "No, no. This is a friendly visit. I'm only asking you to be mindful of how some people in our peaceful town feel." He steepled his hands, then tipped them toward her, as if to say he was finished with his mission. "We don't want to upset any applecarts, do we?" He turned to leave, then looked back. "Is she your supper guest?" He tilted his head toward the T-Bird.

"She is."

"Oh." Dr. Loring nodded and held the pause. He raised his eyebrows. "Take care not to put yourself in a compromising situation." He made a hard-blink nod and muttered, "Have a blessed evening."

Eva Clare cocked her head and computed his comment. If A equals B and B equals C, then A equals C. Wasn't that the transitive law of mathematics? She wasn't sure. But it was one of the laws. If Anna Laurel equals compromising situation and compromising situation equals lesbian, then Anna Laurel equals lesbian. That last bit of advice was straight from the preacher himself. Not from Gerald. Or Sunny.

She looked up at the stained glass in the transom above the door—the blue-brown, blue-blue messed-up pattern that once designated this as a safe house. "Nowhere is safe." She stepped inside, slammed the door so hard it rattled in its casing, and stormed to the kitchen in time to meet Anna Laurel entering the back door.

"That son of a bitch." Eva Clare picked up the pan of salmon and rammed it into the oven.

Anna Laurel's eyes opened wide. "E. C., you never cuss in front of people. What's wrong?" She pushed the door to. "Who's a son of a bitch? The preacher? I saw him out front."

"How dare he—"

"What? What did he do?"

"And Susanna Louise 'Sunny' Flowers! That little two-faced snitch!"

"What did she do?"

Eva Clare groaned, pulled a colander from under the sink, plopped it on the counter.

"Huh? What did Sunny do? C'mon, E. C. What happened to get you so riled up?"

Eva Clare put her fists on her hip bones. "I mean, it is not okay to waltz in here and tell me how to run my business and live my life."

"The preacher? What did he say?"

"Because he's a preacher, he thinks he has authority to stick his nose in my business."

"Honey, because he's a man, he thinks he has authority. What did he say?"

"Accusations, implications, and plain old meddling." Eva Clare grabbed a handful of romaine lettuce, began tearing it into shreds, throwing it into the colander.

"What accusations?"

"I'll tell him a thing or two." Eva Clare ran the lettuce under the faucet.

"What implications?"

Eva Clare ranted on. Anna Laurel poured herself a glass of Merlot, sat down, and propped her elbows on the table. Finally, Eva Clare got around to the reason for getting together.

"You set up that fake meeting with Gerald for next Monday, the twenty-first, and I need you to keep it for real . . . before I cut his tongue off . . . and maybe one other little organ."

Anna Laurel spat her wine on the beige linen placemat as she choked out a laugh. She frantically wiped at it with a matching napkin. "What in the world happened? Tell me."

"I gave Lily, a Black woman in an all-White town, the apartment over the antique store to live in."

Anna Laurel set the napkin down and put her hand over her mouth.

"Also, I had a date with Roy and spent half the night with him."

Anna Laurel put the other hand over the hand already on her mouth.

"And tonight, I'm having dinner with a . . . lesbian." Eva Clare winced.

Anna Laurel slapped both hands on the table and sat up straight. "Wait. Is that me? Are you talking about me? Did that preacher say something about me?"

"He implied. I knew what he was referring to. I'm real sorry, Anna Laurel."

"How could *you* know? How could *he* know? That son of a bitch. I ought to slap the shit out of him. I never told anyone. You're not supposed to know anything about that. Nobody knows."

"Hell, Anna Laurel. We always knew. Meredith, Sunny, and I. We never said anything. Figured it was your private business and if you ever wanted to talk about it, you would. It didn't matter to us."

"It didn't matter to Sunny?"

"Well, maybe a little, but she tried not to think about it."

Anna Laurel showed a pained expression. "Now I bet the whole town knows."

"Well, yeah, but they always did know. And wait, this is not about you. It's about Lily."

"Right. Okay. It's about Lily. It's about a Black professional woman living in downtown Erin. Okay." She took a deep breath and settled back behind her professional façade. "The three things you mentioned—Lily's apartment, dating Roy, eating dinner with . . . me—there's nothing wrong here. What are you losing your shit over? Why are we having this conversation?"

"Because I'm mad," Eva Clare bellowed. "Mad at the preacher for being a puppet for Gerald. Mad at Gerald for sending the preacher over here to tell me what not to do. Mad at Sunny for blabbing to Gerald."

"You don't know that's what happened, do you? You're making it up."

"Pretty sure it's something like that, and whatever way it played out, I'm mad." Eva Clare got a vintage pink depression glass salad bowl out of the cabinet and poured the romaine into it. "I'm mad about the racism and gender put-downs in that conversation with Dr. Loring. It was ugly, having a pastor tell me to keep our town White and to stay away from gays." She hammered her fist on the countertop. "I guess, most of all, I'm mad at myself for all my submissive cave-ins all my life—to men, to religion, to systemic racism. It was always easier to go along with it than to go against it. I should've been better than that. But in the Delta, we all know a person can't speak the hard truth about race and still have friends."

"I can't disagree with that."

Eva Clare flattened her hands on the counter surface, leaned over, shook her head. "Look at me today. I did nothing to challenge what that preacher said. I stood there, let him talk down to me, talk inappropriately about you, and watched him walk away."

"We're all guilty of that at times."

"I don't want to be that way anymore."

"So, *you* need to change?"

"Maybe so. The wrongest voices are always the loudest ones. Sometimes the only ones. If I see or hear something that is clearly wrong or that I firmly believe is unfair or unjust, I should say so, even if I'm the only one who thinks so. I don't want to take whatever comes at me and pretend it's right."

Anna Laurel poured another glass of wine.

Eva Clare poked holes in the potatoes with a fork and stuck them in the microwave.

"So, the encounter with the preacher happened five minutes ago," Anna Laurel said. "Why did you want me over here to talk in the first place? Oh, and that stuff about me. Never bring it up again." She waggled her hand. "I mean it. It's nobody's damn business. That's all I'll say about it. As my friend, that's all you should say."

"I won't. I promise. Lips zipped," Eva Clare said. "And the reason you're here is that I have new information, and I want you, me, and Lily to meet with Gerald."

"What and why?" Anna Laurel lifted her glass to her lips.

"I need you to tell Gerald that Lily is his cousin."

Anna Laurel spat wine again, this time across the table, staining two linen mats.

"You're ruining my placemats."

Anna Laurel wiped her purple-red mouth with a napkin. "I'm done with wine for this meal. Next time you've got disclosures like this, get white wine. What do you mean 'cousin'?"

"We have a common ancestor. Andrew Coghlan was Gerald's great-great-grandfather, my fourth-great-grandfather, and Lily's third- and fourth-great-grandfather. We're kin."

"How can he be third *and* fourth—? Never mind. I don't want to know. Oh, this is rich. You gotta love the South." Anna Laurel threw her head back and laughed. "Gerald doesn't know?"

"I don't think he does. Or if he does, he's not aware that I know."

"Oh, I want to be in the room when he hears."

"That's what I'm asking you to do," Eva Clare said. "And there's one more gem."

"Oh, God, it can't get better."

"Oh, yeah, it can. Following Gerald's logic, that the oldest daughter should own the house and land if Victoria Dove had no children, well, the oldest daughter was Star, Lily's ancestor. So Lily would be the rightful owner of Coghlan House."

Anna Laurel's eyes widened. "Didn't see that coming."

"But we know now that Victoria Dove had a child. She got pregnant by a Yankee soldier and had Erin Rose, my great-great-grandmother."

"Yankee soldier?" Anna Laurel chuckled, then straightened herself. "Of course, you know, you've got your grandmother's will, and that's sufficient. All this other stuff is insignificant fluff that will whip Gerald into a frenzy. And it's likely the only way to shut him up. He won't want the whole town to know this scandalous information."

"I need to share the truth about my family," Eva Clare said. "And I must deal with the voices that tell me I should submit—Gerald, the preacher, my husband, all those who've always told me to sit down, shut up, and don't rock the boat." Eva Clare opened the oven door and looked in at the salmon sizzling in the whiskey juices.

"So, are you going to tell Sunny about your mixed-race ancestry so she can write it in the town's history?"

"You bet I am. This new info brings me, Gerald, and Lily to equal footing, if nothing ever did before."

Eva Clare poured dressing over the lettuce, added shaved Parmesan, and checked again on the fillets. She heard a car driving in, spitting gravel. "Here comes Lily."

They both looked at the door as she entered.

"What?" Lily said. "Is this about me? What'd I do?"

"Nothing," Eva Clare said. "I've got extra food. You want to eat with us?"

Lily looked from Eva Clare to Anna Laurel. "Sure. If you don't mind."

"I'll get another plate." Anna Laurel jumped up and headed to the cabinet.

"I'm famished," Lily said. "I worked hard today setting up the apartment. Pete helped me carry my bed in." Her forehead wrinkled. "Is everything still good with me being there? I'm planning to spend my first night tonight, if it's okay." She toggled her glance from Eva Clare to Anna Laurel and moved her hand like a metronome between the two women.

"Yes," Eva Clare said. "In fact, I'm going to have a sit-down with Gerald and tell him about this. Anna Laurel is setting it up. I want you to be there."

"Whoa." Lily put up both hands. "Uh uh. No. I don't want any trouble out of Tanner."

"I'd like for you to be sitting in front of him when I tell him you're his cousin."

"Nope, no way."

"You've got to stand with me against him."

"I will. But I'm not gonna sit in front of him when he learns a truth that will topple the rich Delta life he has built up in his mind. I'm no fool."

"C'mon, Lily."

Lily continued to shake her head, while Eva Clare served up the plates. Conversation at dinner moved from the meeting with Gerald to shop talk. They dispersed at nine.

Eva Clare cleaned the dishes, flopped on the couch, and turned on the Greenville news. Victoria Dove's journal that Lily had been coaxing her to finish reading was on the coffee table in front of her, but she was too tired to read. Her sleepy eyes blurred the inch-thick diary sitting there, aged, worn, rustic, tied shut with a thin, leather strip. Were more secrets standing on the lines of those tan, deckle-edged pages, ready to jump out at her when she parted the book?

23 Truth Be Told

She was under cold water. A purple-flowered vine wrapped around her shoulders like a shawl. In need of air, she panicked, flailed, pushed against the current. Gulped. But it was dirty river-water she swallowed. She gagged to bring it back up, but nothing happened against the pressure of the water. She was desperate, aware of the fierce fight she was putting up. She grew weaker, sank lower until her feet touched bottom.

With the last bit of life in her, she braced her feet in the muck, bent her knees, and pushed with all her might, using her arms to propel herself into one big surge upward and out of the river, high into the air, coughing, gasping, water trailing off her. She sucked in air so hard she made this godawful rattling sound that could wake the stone-cold dead.

Eva Clare jarred awake, found herself standing in bed, fists tight from the dream-fray. She realized she was not in a river, but safe in her childhood bedroom. She caught a glimpse of a silhouette and saw a blue glow on the hem of the ghost woman's skirt.

The woman stood across the room, light from the pole lamp outside filtering through the window and over her moon-crepe skin and filmy-white gown. Her blue eyes locked onto Eva Clare's and held the gaze.

Rise up, the ghost woman said, not moving her lips. *Rise up.*

The words came perfectly formed, but with no sound. Eva Clare's finger bones hurt as she clenched her fists. She'd had enough of these dreams and faced off with her ghost.

"Victoria Dove, what do you want from me?"

The woman continued to lock eyes.

"I said, what do you want?"

Rise up.

Again, no sound, but the words were clear.

Then the ghost woman was gone.

Eva Clare was left standing on her mattress, the bedcovers in a rumpled mess. The image in the mirror across the room was that of a crazed woman.

It was her last night in her upstairs bedroom. All week, she'd been readying the master suite downstairs that Lily had vacated—getting rid of Sweet Evelyn's things, moving her own in.

The clock on the table next to the bed showed four.

Her cell phone rang. Who'd be calling at this hour? She picked it up off the bedside table. Caller ID: Roy Winslow. She was still breathing hard when she sat down and answered.

"Eva Clare, I awakened with a strong sense that I should call. I'm so sorry if I woke you, but are you all right?"

"I had a bad dream."

"I'll be right over."

Eva Clare slipped on some yoga pants, rinsed her face and mouth, ran a brush through her hair, and went downstairs to wait. She stood by the back door, trembling, her head still full of the dream, pulsing the image of the ghost with the electric-blue-glowing hem. In the middle of a long, cleansing breath, she heard gravel crackle outside.

Roy opened the door. "Come here." He wrapped her in his arms.

She sobbed. He held her tighter.

Eva Clare clung to him as if he were a last desperate chance for salvation and sanity. Then she loosened her grip and looked at him. "I saw her. I talked to her."

"Who?" He tightened both hands around her arms.

"Victoria Dove. Her ghost. I believe her spirit has always reached out to me."

"Why you?"

"I have her need to survive. It's obvious in my paintings—and in my dreams—that I know her fear of dying under the water, and I feel her need to rise up from the bottom." Eva Clare's mission for being home in Erin was coming to light.

Roy put a hand on the back of Eva Clare's head, filtered her hair through his fingers, drew her closer.

"I have to be stronger than she was." She pushed out of Roy's embrace and stepped back. "I'm not going to let anybody—not a young preacher, a mayor cousin, or an old girlfriend—dictate what I do."

She'd talk to Sunny first. Then meet with Gerald.

She pulled into what was left of the public school parking lot—now full of cracks with tall weeds growing up through them and Bermuda grass crawling forward in a coup to cover it all up. She slid out of her car and walked to the concrete foundation of the old building—the one place in Erin that got to her the most.

Was she the only one in town still bothered by the school walkout forty years ago?

She'd asked Sunny to meet her here after church.

The school's foundation was circled by oak and chinquapin trees. On the adjoining property was Beulah Lake Baptist Church, where Sunny was getting out of worship. These two institutions had stood for generations on the road between Highway 1 and downtown Erin. They were like two sisters, standing by each other, holding each other up, taking care of the clan, raising the children, teaching them the tenets of life. Only one made it and was still standing. The other didn't and wasn't.

Sunny pulled up and parked next to Eva Clare. She got out of her Acura and pushed her way around the taller weeds and Johnson grass, some of it chin high. "It looks like a cornfield out here. Somebody usually brings a tractor and mows once a year. Looks like that hasn't happened yet this summer." She moved a weed out of her way. "Why're we here? It's hot, and I'm hungry."

Eva Clare stood on the old concrete among the horseweed, thistle, and foxtail sticking up out of the cracks. "What are we going to do about this place?"

"Huh? What do you mean?"

"I mean you, me, the town. We must look at this cracked foundation every day, every time we drive in or out of Erin. Parents carpooling to the academy drive past it four times a day."

"It's been like this for years," Sunny said. "What's the problem?"

"You remember what this place was?"

"Of course, I do. The old school. We went from kindergarten to twelfth grade here."

"But we didn't graduate from here." Eva Clare crossed her arms in front of her chest.

"No, we didn't."

"We got up from our desks one Friday afternoon, marched out of the school, and never went back. They chained the doors. We abandoned the building and the public school system."

"I remember."

"Do you remember why?"

"Because of the Blacks."

"What did they do?"

Sunny ran her finger across the purple and green-seedy spike at the top of a stalk of Johnson grass higher than her shoulders and shrugged. "Nothin', I guess."

"Okay, then that wasn't the reason we left this school."

Sunny twitched her shoulders. "We were afraid they might do something."

"Yes, we left this school because the adults were afraid of integration. Their goal was keeping Black kids out of White schools."

Sunny put her hands on her hips. "Everything would've changed with integration."

"Everything changed anyway. Look around you. Look at our decaying, dying town. So, what are we going to do with this place? We shouldn't have to be reminded of the fear and hate this foundation represents. Don't you see? It bothers me, Sunny."

"Yeah, I know it does."

"We fear ways that are different. We fear what we don't understand, what we've never done before, what others have told us will be our ruin." Her shoulders caved. "We're broken."

"You're talking about Lily, aren't you?"

"Yes, I am. I don't know if you spoke to the preacher about her living downtown or if you told Gerald and he complained to Dr. Loring, but somebody told somebody, and that preacher came to my house with unwanted advice."

"Oh."

"Sunny, you know as well as I do that the church always justified racial separation. They used their preachers to perpetuate it from the pulpit because people listen to pastoral authority."

"Well, but—"

"No buts. Please don't deny it or excuse it." Eva Clare threw her hands up. "When we marched out of this school in 1970 and the town shut it down for good, who was in on it, and who took us in?"

"I guess you mean the church."

"That's right. The church. Classrooms were set up in Sunday School rooms and other available spaces, even in the pastor's home. We sat on pews in the sanctuary and completed our education. This was a wrong committed across the South. Can't we do better?"

Sunny shifted her weight to a different foot. Her neck turned red.

"Sunny, you know as well as I do that Gerald Tanner went to Steele Bayou Christian Academy on a scholarship provided by the church because his daddy was a farmhand and couldn't afford tuition for private school."

Sunny lowered her head and nodded.

"Look at that purple flower." Eva Clare pointed to a tall plant. "It's called thistle. If you look at the stalk closely, it's prickly. But at the top, there's a bloom. How refreshing after all the sharp, hurtful quills. It gives me hope for how things can be. In spite of how ugly things are, there's hope for a better outcome."

Sunny looked at the thistle, then down at her feet.

"We need to fix our dissonance." Eva Clare waved her hands like windshield wipers on high. "I don't know how. I figure it's up to you. You started it. You made Lily living downtown an issue. You must end it." She pressed her lips together and paused to think. "I'm an artist. I make shadows, light, and colors come together in beauty and purpose. You're a musician. The different notes you play work together in harmony. We should do right with color and harmony in every area of our lives."

Sunny turned her head and looked off toward the tree line that hid the church.

The meeting with Gerald had been confirmed for Monday at six o'clock at Laurel's Coffee House at Levee and Main. Anna Laurel and Eva Clare set out bottles of water on a big, round table.

"How many do we need?" Anna Laurel asked.

"There'll be you, me, Gerald, Meredith, and Sunny. Five."

"What about Lily?"

"She won't come. I've begged. She won't do it."

"I wish she would," Anna Laurel said. "I'm setting up for her anyway. I'd like the dramatic effect of her sitting in front of Gerald when the news is presented to him."

"I'm surprised he agreed to come."

"I told him there was no charge. I also told him we discovered new information regarding the Coghlan family that he might want to be aware of before it's made public. He couldn't stand not knowing what we learned." Anna Laurel placed two stacks of papers on the table—one containing copies of documents for her and the other with copies for Gerald, supportive material to back up the connections they planned to reveal about Coghlan lineage.

Eva Clare walked to the front door and looked out at the main street of stores, angled parking spaces, and pots of ivy, geraniums, and leggy petunias beside every doorway. In recent days those parking spots had been filled. Traffic had picked up, and there was almost always an out-of-county car in front of the antique store. Harper Hardware across the street had placed new park benches on both sides of their entrance and set up a display of garden merchandise out front to lure folks inside. Martha, the manager, had hauled in five big concrete pots and planted crape myrtles in them to give shade to folks wanting to linger on the benches. The Piggly Wiggly had painted its storefront. It seemed people were proud of their town once again and welcoming visitors, even though the new interstate was nowhere near the beginning phase of construction. Money had not been appropriated. But she was feeling confident that even without an influx of travelers on a new NAFTA Superhighway, Main Street would be okay.

It was five till six. Gerald would be walking into the coffee shop any minute. She rubbed her hands together, like rubbing sticks to start a fire.

Sunny came in through the interior entrance, a rolling, overhead door they left up all day so customers could pass from Laurel's to the soon-to-open Pie Bird to the Trunk without going outside. Sunny and Anna Laurel sat down at the table. Meredith arrived and joined them.

"C'mon, Eva Clare," Anna Laurel called to her. "I want you sitting and ready when Gerald gets here."

Eva Clare looked at the clock on the wall. The big hand moved to the twelve. It was time.

She sat.

They waited.

Eva Clare looked at the front door and the sign with the Shakespeare quote hanging nearby. *Upon your sword Sit laurel victory! And smooth success Be strew'd before your feet!*

She had it. Success. Her store was doing well. After five weeks, new customers were showing up and old ones were coming back. People were hungry for new shopping experiences. She'd have to find ways to keep the momentum. In a few weeks, she'd set up a cotton harvest promotion, then a fall display with pumpkins, and then they'd enter the holiday season with an open house. A spark of confidence flickered in her chest.

Then a pang struck.

Where was Gerald?

"Sunny, when is the Pie Bird's opening day?" Meredith asked.

"September first, for Labor Day weekend. Cherry pie will be the dessert special. The meat pie will be Hamburger Pot Pie, with cut-up chuck roast, cremini mushrooms, onions, garlic, carrots, peas, tomato paste, Worcestershire, and red wine."

"You're killing me," Meredith said. "It's suppertime. I'm hungry."

"I know," Sunny said. "It's so delicious. I can't wait."

They all kept glancing at the door. Then the clock. Nine after six.

"You think he's coming?" Eva Clare said.

They caught sight of him out the window crossing the street in his navy suit, shaking his head. He walked in, pulled out a chair with considerable noise, and sat, with no eye contact.

"Good afternoon, sir," Anna Laurel said cheerfully. "Thank you for being here."

He gave a curt nod.

"Okay," Anna Laurel said. "Let's get on with it." She rested her arms on the table. "First of all, let me explain that we found an old family trunk dating back to before the Civil War in a hidden room in the attic of Coghlan House. In it are journals and other original historical documents. This afternoon we'd like to present a summary of—"

The door whooshed open. Bells banged against glass. In rushed Lily. "Wait! Wait a damn minute."

Eva Clare pushed out the empty chair beside her, and Lily sat and plopped her big purse on the table.

"Ain't nothin' gon get said about me without me bein' here."

Eva Clare bit the insides of her cheeks to keep from laughing.

Gerald edged his chair away from the table.

"Welcome, Lily," Anna Laurel said in a businesslike manner. "We're glad you could join us. To continue, we'd like to summarize—"

"Wait! Y'all wait a minute." Gerald leaned toward Anna Laurel. "Before you say another word, I want to make the point that y'all have ni—ed up downtown. As mayor of Erin, I can't allow that."

"I'm not following your assertion, sir," Anna Laurel said. "And please watch your language."

Gerald pointed to Lily. "She's got blankets hanging out the upstairs windows of Betsy's Trunk. The downtown shopping district is not a place to dry bedclothes." His face reddened. "*We* don't hang *our* laundry out of store windows."

"What are you talking about? I didn't see anything." Eva Clare pushed away from the table, walked to the front of the coffee shop, then outside to the far edge of the sidewalk to look. She tried her best to stifle a smile. Lily must've just hung the quilts out. She stepped back inside, sat down at her place, looked at Anna Laurel, Lily, Gerald. She couldn't stop herself. She started laughing. Laughed hard, loud, uncontrollably. Could not stop. Tears ran down her face.

The others sat with their mouths open. Gerald tried to speak, but Eva Clare's cackling drowned him out. Her face was wet, her eyes blurry, and all she could do was keep on laughing.

Lily pulled a Kleenex out of her bag and passed it down. Eva Clare wiped her eyes and reined in her emotions.

"Okay," Anna Laurel said. "Now that we've gotten that out of the way, we'll continue."

Eva Clare reached over and touched her arm. "Thanks, Anna Laurel. But I'll take it from here." She was stepping outside previously drawn lines to be her better self, and Anna Laurel seemed to sense it, settling back with a smile and a nod.

Eva Clare cleared her throat and straightened her shoulders. Her heart pumped harder than ever, thumping in her neck, her head. "Gerald, the quilts aren't hanging out to dry. They're in the windows to make a point applicable to this meeting. The quilts are symbolic of everything we want to tell you today. Everything we are as a people." Eva Clare paused to let that soak in. "As you know, Lily sews quilts. All the women in her lineage did, and they passed down the skill, as well as the star pattern you saw hanging out the window. In the 1800s, the star pattern was a secret code for slaves on the run, designating a safe house or a station on the Underground Railroad."

Gerald's shoulders sank. His back curled.

"The two original Coghlan sisters—Catherine Deering and Victoria Dove—were sympathetic to the anti-slavery movement. Coghlan House was a station on the Underground Railroad. There's a secret room where the sisters hid runaway slaves. The sisters and Lily's ancestor, Star, would hang quilts out the upstairs window so the runaways would know it was safe to come in, eat, drink, and rest a while."

"That didn't happen in Miss'ippi," Gerald said.

"Let me give you some facts we've learned from papers stored in the trunk. Anna Laurel will provide you with copies proving what I'm about to tell you. This information is also strengthened by family legend passed down by word of mouth. Sunny, this is for you, too, as you write the town's history. And Meredith, as my friend, I want you to hear this from me."

They all leaned in and waited for the revelation, except for Gerald who sat back, lowered his head, and looked down at his watch half buried under a stiff, white sleeve.

"Our ancestor, Andrew Coghlan, brought a slave named Star with him to the Delta. Andrew was not only her master. He was her father. And he also fathered a daughter with her named Riselle. These are Lily's ancestors."

"You're makin' this up," Gerald snapped.

Lily jerked forward, opened her mouth to dispute him, but Eva Clare grabbed her arm, squeezed it gently, and continued talking.

"Andrew Coghlan was Lily's third- and fourth-great-grandfather. Lily is our cousin."

"That's bullshit." Gerald looked directly at her, eyes blazing.

"And the two Coghlan sisters? It was said that Victoria Dove never married and never had children. That's not true. Victoria Dove had a child out of wedlock fathered by a Yankee soldier. He left the area with his unit, and she let it be recorded that the child, Erin Rose, was her sister's daughter. The sisters changed the birth date to make it fit with Catherine Deering's husband's visits home from war. Victoria Dove was kicked out of the church for her sin of adultery. This was confirmed in the church minutes. Later, the family tore the pages out, stole the minutes from the church record book, and hid them in the trunk in the secret room. We found them."

"That's a crock of—"

"You say Andrew Coghlan's oldest daughter and her descendants are entitled to the house? Well, the oldest daughter was Star, who was four years older than Catherine Deering and six years older than Victoria Dove. And her descendant is Lily."

"Aw, come on! Who do you think you are, moving back to this place and spewing all these lies?" Gerald pounded the table with his fist.

Sunny covered her face with her hands. Meredith wrapped her arms around herself. Anna Laurel gave Gerald a threatening glare.

"Listen, Gerald," Eva Clare continued. "You need to understand that you, me, and Lily are blood kin. Our ancestors, Catherine Deering and Victoria Dove and Star, stood for what was right for humanity. So did Grandmomma in her last days. And I'm going to do the same."

Gerald screwed up his face so that his lips looked like something under a dog's tail.

"Lily is living in this building that I'll own October the fifteenth, based on my agreement with Betsy Steele. Lily will help me run the store. I need her, and I think she needs me."

"She—"

"Let it be." Eva Clare stomped her foot on the wooden floor, and the sound echoed. She looked hard into Gerald's fiery eyes and said again with authority, "Let it be."

He tightened his lips and looked away.

"I'm going to carry on the tradition of our family in honor of my grandmother and all those women before her. I'm going to do what's right according to the Bible and the law." She turned toward Anna Laurel and gave a nod. "I'm done." She stood.

"Thank you all for coming. This meeting is concluded." Anna Laurel handed Gerald his set of papers. "These include a copy of the family lineage page from the original Bible—the Holy Word of God, true and infallible."

Gerald snatched them and stood, knocking his chair over. "Y'all can kiss my ass." He stormed out the door. Even with the truth in his hand, he wasn't budging. He wasn't going to change what he believed for anyone in this world, or God, or heaven to come.

"Well, that went well," Anna Laurel said. "Pfoo."

Eva Clare watched Gerald cross the street toward his bank, and his posture said everything. His walk was stiff, his shoulders slumped, head down, a fist clenched. She doubted he'd ever get beyond where he was right now. As a child, he'd known more than most Mississippi children about the ugly violence that came with hate—beatings, burnings, lynchings, murders, the execution of three civil rights workers in Philadelphia, Mississippi, during Freedom Summer. He'd heard the voices of his parents, teachers, and preachers telling him in so many words: Hate those who are different. It started there, early, in childhood, with all the kids, including her.

And for some, it stayed there. And was there still.

Gerald was one of those, and there were hundreds, thousands more like him—people who listened without thinking and thought without discerning.

How could she even have a rational conversation with someone who practiced his religion faithfully yet hated or mistreated his fellow man?

She lowered her head, closed her eyes. Things weren't going to change. Like Pete told her the day she got back to town: "Change comes slow . . . and sometimes not at all."

If she was going to stay in Erin, Mississippi, she'd have to be the one to change. She'd have to get used to the folks who weren't amenable to change, who'd ignore the Bible and the laws of the land and follow their archaic system of handed-down beliefs passed down generation to generation.

Lily put a hand on Eva Clare's shoulder. "I do need you. We all do."

"Thank you, Lily."

"You finished reading that 1863 journal yet?"

Eva Clare winced. Lily wasn't going to let up.

"Damn, girl, do it." Lily picked up her purse. "Now, I got to go home and take some quilts out of windows before it rains on them or before Gerald pees on himself."

24 DARKNESS COMES OUT OF LIGHT

Eva Clare arrived at Betsy's Trunk early Saturday. She set a twenty-four by thirty-six-inch canvas on the easel at the back of the store, turned on the fluorescent tube lighting, got out her palette and box of oil paints, and arranged her brushes. She laid out tubes of blues and whites.

For this painting, she'd create a new hue, and she'd call it Blue Hem Glow, the shade of blue that glowed around the dress hem of the ghost— the spirit margins of Victoria Dove. It was an ethereal blue, the softest, lightest ghostly blue, and as in tune as she was to colors, she had never seen such a shade.

The artist in her knew there must be contrast in the colors, for one cannot know the light if she hasn't experienced the dark. Light comes out of darkness. In this painting, Blue Hem Glow would serve as the darker aspect, and creamy white mixed with Blue Hem Glow, the lighter.

She did a study sketch on paper—based on one of the drawings of Victoria Dove. Next, she'd lightly pencil in the main lines of the composition on canvas.

She'd paint only the shoulders down to the feet of the ghost under the Blue Hem Glow water, as the spirit-woman floated up in a spray of droplets. The painting would be full of swirls and splotches, but with no face on the ghost. The painting was not about the ghost woman, or her, but about all women emerging from where they'd been kept in their places over the centuries, so it was not appropriate to give her a face. Besides, the woman was rising up, and the face was already out of the river. It would be the first time Eva Clare had ever painted a woman whose head was above water.

She'd call the painting *Eva Rising*.

She folded linseed oil into titanium white to make it creamy. Added a dab of phthalo blue. A fleck of Naples yellow light. A little cobalt. More white. Watched the different hues come together. Witnessed a new color emerging. Saw change come about in the mixing process.

Lily dropped a bag of cash on the counter behind her and screeched, "Ooo-wee, my blood's still thin from summer. Time to turn on the heat in this place."

It was September's first cool snap, and the temperature had dropped into the fifties overnight. Eva Clare didn't notice the weather last evening when she was with Roy. They caught a late movie in Greenville and then drove up the levee at the end of downtown's main street to look at the lights on Lake Ferguson and the Trop Casino.

"Ooo-wee," Lily repeated, squeaking out the second syllable.

"It'll be back up in the eighties by noon, Lily."

"I sure hope so, or I'll have to dig me out a sweater."

Eva Clare put her palette knife down. "Let's get all the lights on, and maybe they'll help warm the place." She was dressed in jeans and a long-sleeved flannel shirt.

"How come you're not dressed for work?"

"I'm going to be painting this morning since you're running the store today. And I'm taking off this afternoon."

"Say what?"

"Yep, I'm leaving at high noon." Eva Clare turned on lamps and the computer and pulled up the point-of-sale software.

"Where you goin'? What're you gon do?"

"Because it's cool out, I can go back up to the secret attic room and spend some time digging through the trunk. Thought I'd take the journal and finish reading it up there, you know, with all the historical ambiance."

"Well, all's I can say is it's about time." Lily lit the old-book-smell candle at the front station, fanned the scent toward her, and took a few sniffs once it got to burning.

Eva Clare unlocked the front door.

Saturday usually brought good crowds. Folks had learned they could come to Erin early, have a gourmet coffee and pastry at Laurel's, browse the art booths and mosey through aisles of old treasures at Betsy's Trunk, maybe even walk over to Harper Hardware and stroll through the garden center, looking at the new fairy garden merchandise, then go to the Pie Bird for a lunch of meat pie and dessert pie with seasonally flavored coffee or tea.

Back at her easel, Eva Clare took a soft-lead pencil and translated the study sketch lines from paper to canvas. She selected a size sixteen flat brush and slowly lowered the bristles to the mix of paint on her palette, loading up on one side, then the other, easy back and forth. She was aware of the flow of customers—light, but talkative and complimentary of the artwork in the booths—and couldn't help but hear Lily's loud greetings.

She kissed the tip of her finger and touched it to the ferrule of her paintbrush. Put her loaded brush against the upper left area of the canvas and let the Blue Hem Glow glide against the white nap. It was such a release, much like her voice being put out there for all to hear. Her arms and hands tingled with creation. She was moving into her zone, spawning color and meaning, and letting everything around her fade as she worked.

Lily's cautiously polite voice grabbed her back to awareness of her surroundings.

"Good morning, sir," Lily said. "May I help you?"

Other shoppers had gravitated into the Pie Bird for lunch, and the antique shop was quiet. Eva Clare looked up to see that Gerald stood at the front of the store, taking something from his coat pocket. He shook his head, not looking up at Lily, but looking down at a small paper square he held in his hand. He moved to Lily's booth, selected a quilt, and unfolded it on a table over the other merchandise. He examined the pattern, then the paper square, looking back and forth. Never looked up, never said a word. It got the best of Lily, and she went over to him.

"Mayor Tanner, may I answer any questions for you?"

He didn't look up.

Eva Clare put her paintbrush down and moved closer up the aisle so she could intervene, if need be. She stood near the checkout station.

Gerald held out the paper square—a sepia-toned photograph. He put the picture down on a star of the quilt.

"This is my grandmother, Annah Rachel Amason Tanner, daughter of Catherine Deering Coghlan Amason. The quilt she is holding is the same pattern as the quilts in this booth."

"My quilts are reproductions, you know."

Gerald nodded, looking from quilt to picture. He put the photograph back in an inside pocket, turned, and walked out of the store.

What was that about? Was he warming up to acceptance of Lily's family connection? Could he possibly change his views?

But she knew, in the end, he'd stay in his groove, for he was shaped and formed that way, that spirit deep in the fissures of his brain and the marrow of his bone. He'd hold fast to the hate he harbored in his heart right next to his Savior Jesus.

Eva Clare arrived home at noon, got a battery-operated lamp, grabbed the journal off the coffee table, and proceeded upstairs to the closet at the end of the hallway. The shelf unit was still open from Lily's house tour. She squeezed through the hole in the wall into the dark passageway, where sixty-nine slaves had stepped as they walked the freedom trail. She held her belongings close to her chest with one arm and climbed the ladder to the loft using the other hand to hold on. This venture up, it was chilly. The back of her neck prickled.

What a tangled history the Coghlan family had woven! Secrecy, slave ownership, sympathy to slaves, plotting, deception, lies, love, hate, hypocrisy, adultery, bastardy, suicide, murder, coverup.

She turned on the lamp to boost the skimpy light coming in the window, sat in the ladderback chair with its stretched and torn cane bottom, propped her feet on the top front rung, and put the journal in her lap. There was a folded sheet toward the back of the book. She removed the paper, ancient blue stationery turning brown, and slowly folded back layer by layer of fragile creases until the paper revealed a letter and poem in a fancy cursive slant. It began, **My beloved Victoria Dove . . .**

April 8th, 1863.

May you, my beloved, long remember my embrace, for I must say farewell to my island and you, and return to the battlefield. I waited on Big Island for winter to pass and the river to slow, so I could come deliver my goodbye in person with these words that sprang from my devoted heart.

> *I remember those sweet and happy days*
> *When first thy voice caressed my ear,*
> *When first my throbbing heart confessed*
> *Thou wert of all the fair most dear.*
>
> *Then never, ever from my heart*
> *Can time thy treasured visage blot;*
> *The dreams of other days may dim,*
> *But thou wilt never be forgot.*

~ WW

WW?

Who was WW? Victoria's lover was Teddy. Was there another man?

Her heart quickened. And so did her fingers.

She turned a few pages forward and skimmed short entries from the summer of 1863, mostly about work on the farm, then no entries in September, October, and November. Victoria's world had gone quiet. Eva Clare found one entry for the month of December.

December 24th, 1863.

> *The darkest of all Decembers*
> *My life has ever known*
> *Sitting here by the embers*
> *Forlorn, afraid, alone.*

Tis the holiest night of the year. Silent night. But where is my Savior?

The fire burns warm, yet my heart is like a hard, cold stone.

These Christmas days are happy ones for the others in the family and the little Amason girls: Annah Rachel, nearly two, and baby

Erin Rose, six months. We've made dolls out of old quilts for the girls and in their stockings are fruit and peppermint sticks. For the grownups, horehound drops and nuts and popcorn. Tomorrow we will feast on roast goose with applesauce and light the candles on our cedar tree.

The Steeles, I heard, have told their little ones the Yankees shot St. Nicholas.

My beloved Yankee is far away with the war.

I held our blessed Erin Rose this evening as the others made ready for sleep. I told her the story of a gal baby born during war and how her father was marching across the southland to free those in bondage. I told her to hide three words inside her pretty, yellow head—her name: "You are Erin Rose Winslow. Daughter of Winfield Edward Winslow." ~ VDC

Winslow.

Winslow?

Her heart dipped.

She sucked in a ragged breath, swallowed air, had a choking, coughing fit. Rubbed her eyes and looked at the print again.

"WINSLOW?"

WW? . . . Winfield Winslow?

"Roy Winslow's Yankee-soldier ancestor?"

Her intuitions whirled fast around her. From the chaotic tangles forming in her mind, she pulled, separated, and ordered her thoughts as best as she could. Then they marched out straight and tall like soldiers as she watched their stern steps and even lines.

Her forebear was also Winfield Edward Winslow.

Teddy, Victoria's lover, was a nickname for Edward.

Her father was also named Edward, likely after that Yankee soldier. Following Erin Rose, at least one descendant in each generation was given a name that started with E. Could it be in honor of Edward? Her grandmomma never told her. Never said a word.

They'd all been given jewelry with doves etched in after their true matriarch, Victoria Dove. The family acknowledged this descending line and covered it up at the same time. The truth had been with her all along. She wore it around her neck—the dove charm on the necklace Grandmomma gave her when she was seventeen.

The full extent of the truth? She and Roy were related.

Why didn't she listen to Lily and read the journal sooner? Before she let herself be drawn to him, or maybe fall in love with him. Being able to trace back to a common forefather might kill any romantic tendencies between them, even if their relationship was distant.

Her heart beat hard and fast. Her hands shook.

She reached into her back pocket, pulled out her phone, punched in Roy's number, heard his innocent hello. "You'd better come over." She spoke low. "Now. The back door's unlocked. Come up to the secret room."

He hung up without an answer or a question.

She remained seated with the journal in her lap. Rocked her torso forward, backward. Was empty and full at the same time. Lost and found and lost again.

Within five minutes, she heard Roy groaning entry through the opening to the passageway, heard his feet hit the wooden rungs. His head appeared above the attic floor. He climbed a few more steps and entered the place of secrets.

"It's all here." Eva Clare held up the brown leather book. "All here."

"What do you mean?"

"Your Yankee-soldier ancestor."

"*My* Yankee-soldier ancestor? You found him?" Roy slapped his hand to his chest, and his voice kicked up an octave. "In your family journal?"

"Yes."

"Well, tell me, show me." He hurried to her.

She opened the book and pointed to the place on the page. "Victoria Dove writes to her daughter, 'You are Erin Rose Winslow. Daughter of Winfield Edward Winslow.'"

"That's him." Roy sank to a knee beside the chair. "Wait. Erin Rose? *Your* great-great-grandmother? The one in the picture in your foyer?"

"Yes."

"So . . . *you* . . . descend from my ancestor, Winfield Winslow?"

"He's my great-great-great-grandfather."

"You and I—"

"Are kin."

"But generations ago." Roy put his hand on the back of the chair, reached up to touch her hair, rested his hand on her shoulder.

"Yes."

They both stared at the journal, the bearer of truth. Sometimes, folks were not able to see truth, weren't ready to see it, didn't want to see it, didn't even know to look for it.

"How do you feel about that, Eva Clare?"

"Shocked." She lifted her brows and looked at him. "I'm shocked that the world is this small, that you came here to Erin at this particular time and I came home to Erin and we met and we discover we have a past connection." She shook her head, then paused. "You?"

"I guess it's why I felt led here," Roy said. "I had a calling to return to a place I've never been."

Eva Clare stiffened. Her eyes prickled with tears.

"I don't know about you," Roy said, "but I'm pleased. I've found what I was looking for. Heh! I found my ancestor . . . and a whole new family. You're part of that family, but so far back that I have no qualms reaching for you and kissing you."

"You don't?"

"No, I don't." He put his hand on the back of her head, pulled her to him, kissed her. After they parted, he clasped her hand and let it rest on the open journal in her lap, the century-and-a-half-old book full of names, people, and events they both held claim to. He kept his face close to hers and said what he wanted to say to her through his eyes, and she sensed what he was doing and continued the silent talk, convinced that her uncertainties and aversions were being transmitted to him. They made movements and expressions with their eyes befitting their feelings. It was the most sensual thing she'd ever done.

Eva Clare looked away first. She glanced at the raw, rough-wood rafters made from old timber cut here on the property owned by Andrew Coghlan, and she remembered he was murdered and buried under this house. His bones had fused the foundation.

Roy sat down on the floor. "Let me read that revealing diary post from December."

Eva Clare handed him the journal. She wondered what it would be like to love a man, then have to give up your baby, his child, because people in the church made it an unforgiveable sin to birth the child and keep it.

After he read the page, Roy looked up from the book. "Is there anything else we can learn from the journal? Have you read the whole thing? Was there anything about when Winfield and Victoria first met?"

"I only read her posts from 1863 because that's where a folded map of Napoleon was, and also a mention of her lover, Teddy, short for Edward, who was stationed there. The map separated the 1863 entries from 1862." She took the open journal, turned back the pages, and perused the January entries, running her finger down the lines. "Here," she said, stopping mid-page. "It says here, 'I think about Teddy and the warm September sun when I first saw him in Prentiss.'"

"Turn back," Roy said, motioning with his hand, "turn back, hurry, turn back, and see what she says in September of the previous year."

Eva Clare turned the brittle pages, all thumbs in her haste to get there. She read the first entry aloud.

September 2nd, 1862.

I walked to town today for sugar and cinnamon spice to bake an apple crisp. The apples are coming in now, hanging full on the trees and falling to the ground. Ellis Steele was helping his father in the store. I think he will be the one to ask for my hand.

Yankee soldiers were all about, coming over on the ferry from Napoleon town and the Arkansas Post. I'm sure many work at the hospital there. What a wretched town Napoleon has always been, where every brawl ends in a burial. There are murders among Napoleonites daily. I do not wish for their kind to come here to our peaceful Prentiss. A few soldiers seem mannerly, one in particular. His strong blue eyes gave me a stir. He accompanied me out of the store and carried my package to see me safe to the edge of town. He said he'd be back and hoped he'd see me again. ~VDC

Eva Clare leaned over, held the book so Roy could see, and they traced their pointer fingers over the lines of other posts from the fall of 1862, reading fast, reading some lines out loud in unison. **"'Teddy came to Prentiss today. He is a Lincolnite, a Yankee soldier, the enemy of Mississippi, and it matters not to me. But to others, it would, and I must keep him hidden.'" . . . "'We found a hiding place in the woods near Indian Point, under a fallen sycamore, where he reads me poems, pledges his love, where we are convivial.'" . . . "'The yellow sycamore leaves of November lie on the ground beneath us, and we bear some risk in our fadoodling from lack of privacy provided by the canopy of summer's fully-leafed trees.'" ~VDC**

"Fadoodling?" Eva Clare said, exaggerating the syllables, as a flush crept up Roy's face.

He turned to the next page, stained and torn. "Hey, here's her Christmas post. Come down here. Sit on the floor with me so we can both see better."

Eva Clare sat beside him, their legs crossed in Indian-chief position, knee to knee.

She rested the journal against her left knee and his right and read the diary entry.

December 24th, 1862.

It was a holy day of surprises as Sister's husband John arrived home unexpectedly from Richmond. He slipped away from the hospital where he was recovering from a right leg bone fracture after being shot in battle at Mechanicsville. He thinks he may never straighten his leg and now walks with a limp. But he speaks of their loss of nine thousand killed and wounded, and he saw the dead strewn all along the road, some of them without legs and others without heads. He now holds some bitterness, that some Confederates owning twenty slaves are exempted from war, when others are exposing themselves in the defense of the rich men's property whilst the rich men are at home enjoying their ease. He expects the war will last four or five years longer. Says the Yankees seem as much as ever determined on the South's subjugation and

the South is resolved never to submit. While he spent the afternoon with his wife and baby Annah Rachel, I took leave.

I went to the hiding place at Indian Point and waited at the edge of the forest, hoping Teddy would come, hoping with all my hopes and pleading in my prayers. As the sun's rays began flattening out over the river, he appeared, carrying a brown package. I had my own surprise for him. I had sewn a grey linen cravat and stitched a black cross on it, black for my mourning his departure. I also cooked chinquapin burnt-sugar candy and wrapped some for him. The nuts are rare, sweet, a treasure. Teddy is a treasure, too.

Inside his package was a cameo brooch. It is of brass and pink shell and has a white dove carved on it. Because I am Dove, and he calls me Dovie. I shall treasure it always. ~ VDC

"The brooch!" Eva Clare's heart kicked into high gear.

"The one from your grandmother's dress at her funeral?"

"Yes, yes. Her mother gave it to her. It was passed down in the family." Her eyes teared with her shaky breaths. "Your ancestor gave it to my ancestor. You've held it, and so have I—this jewel they both touched. It's mine now. You removed it from Grandmomma's dress and gave it to me." She pulled in a breath, then let it out.

Roy folded his arm around her.

She melted against him, then spread her hands against his chest and pushed him back. "Wait a minute." She scooted away from him, scrunched up her face, and gritted her teeth. Her lower lip trembled. "He left her."

"What?"

"Teddy left Dovie." A hot flush rolled through her, and her words poured out with madness. "He sweet-talked her, took her to the woods, fadoodled her, left her with a full belly, and she went through the pangs of childbirth alone. After all the fadoodling, he never checked to see if a child had resulted." She shook her head. "He left her."

"It was a war. He had to."

"It's what men do."

"Oh, Eva Clare—"

"No!" She threw up her arms. "No. I can't be with you right now." She pumped the air with her hands, backing him off. "I need to be alone."

Her words were swaddled with the incredible hurt and anger of a woman jilted. A woman not good enough for her man. A woman not worth coming back to. She pushed herself up off the floor and stormed away from that cryptic room of blackness, for while hopefully, light always comes out of darkness, sometimes darkness comes out of light.

25

Changes Up and Down the River

Eva Clare woke up with a heaviness on her—that embarrassing emotional outburst yesterday with Roy in the upper room. How would she move beyond that?

She stole away to her childhood soul-spot on the river, where a narrow strip of land jutted out into the water. She sat on the ground, both feet at the edge of the bank, soft waves lapping at the toes of her boots. A chill wind blew, challenging her fleece jacket. Cold regret ran through her on the inside, too, after the way she'd treated Roy. She'd lashed out, acted rashly, and didn't know why that response came on so quickly.

She warmed her hands in her pockets. It would heat up by late morning, but now, the sun was still low in the east behind the trees and the levee.

The church bell from town rang, beckoning worshippers to Sunday service.

It was here, long ago, on this little isthmus, that she decided to leave the Delta. It would be here now that she'd figure out how to come back and live in this place of longstanding incongruities and newly revealed connections.

Here, at the river, her sanctuary, she could think clearly and examine her reactions to the changes that had come to light about her past. She always talked big on change, especially how others reacted to it, but when change came to her, she got up and walked away. Yes. Walked away. She couldn't take change either. All her life she thought she was different, open-minded, more tolerant than the others, but she wasn't. She was like them, balking at anything new and different. And furthermore, she was a judger of people. All her life she'd looked down on these folks, judging them for not living up to their religion, for separating themselves from those of another color, but she'd separated herself, too—from people of her own faith and her own color. She was flawed in her thinking, wrong in her actions. Thou hypocrite, she told herself, straight from the Bible, *first cast the beam out of your own eye.*

On top of that, yesterday, she put the blame of all unfaithful men on Roy and stormed away from him. He didn't do anything to deserve that. She left him sitting on the hard floor of the secret attic room. Because of what one man did a hundred fifty years ago. *He left her.* That's what she'd told Roy. Teddy left Dovie.

Why did those three words hurt so much? One reason. Her husband left, too.

She hugged her legs to her chest, let her face fall in the gap between her knees, and cried. Her sobs came loud and involuntarily. Her body squeezed them out wave after wave like the pains of labor. She groaned with each contraction as it pushed out a little more hurt and betrayal, blaming of others, reliance on others for help pulling her up from the low places. She wept until there were no tears left. Her chest couldn't expand to let in another breath. Her eyes burned, the lids swollen so plump she could barely see.

She had to stop letting what others did or said pull her down. Needed to put her failed marriage behind her. Needed to fix what she'd broken with Roy. Change how she dealt with Erin and the Delta's struggle with White privilege and Black-not, even change her feelings about Gerald.

She lifted her head and wiped her nose. Shivered in the wind, pulled her jacket tighter around her neck, rubbed away her tears. She'd made physical changes in her life simply by moving back here and figuring out how to make a living. It was time for internal and relational changes.

The sun was warm on her back now.

"Eva Clare."

She jumped, jerked around, hadn't heard anyone come up.

Roy. He formed a meek smile. "I'm sorry to startle you. I knew I'd find you here. I need to talk to you. I found something—"

"I'm sorry." She inched her body around to face him. "I shouldn't have run out on you. I guess I still have some unresolved hurt from my—"

"It's okay. You don't have to explain."

"Oh, but I do. It's baggage I'm carrying. I've been so busy with the store I haven't processed my impending divorce. Wasn't aware I still have feelings about it. I'm so sorry. It's not your fault that Teddy left Dovie, that my husband left me."

Roy reached into his jacket pocket. "I have something to show you." He pulled out a brown paperboard diary with a flap closure, the edges cracked, the binding broken. "I found this in the trunk after you left."

Eva Clare looked at the little book, then at Roy. She let her shoulders sink. Now what?

"It's Victoria's journal from the next year after what we read. There are only a few entries from 1864. It's mostly empty pages." Roy opened the book and held it out to Eva Clare. "Read this entry from July."

She reached for it, but withdrew her hand, turned away, and looked at the river, fast and choppy, moving a long barge tow. Water gurgled at the bank, and mourning doves cooed in the woods nearby.

Once again, she'd pulled back from change. She was afraid of spoiling this place, this magical spot on the spine of Mississippi, by opening up to more new material that might further change things.

"Eva Clare, empty pages are good. Means life is being lived, people have dealt with heartaches and moved on. This entry will change how you feel. You want me to read it to you?"

She nodded and looked down at the innumerable grains of sandy dirt on the ground in front of her. "Yes, please."

Roy lifted the journal and read.

July 2nd, 1864.

Ellis Steele is dead. I went to the mercantile today, and the door was closed and locked. A boxwood wreath with black ribbons hung on the door. His older brother Rufus saw me peering through the glass and came to tell me that Ellis was shot by a Yankee soldier at Indian Point. The Yankee then fled from the other enraged Rebel boys clamoring for his hide. Ellis crawled home leaving a trail of blood and died on the steps of the mercantile. Before he died, he told his brother the Yankee soldier wore a grey neck scarf with a black cross stitched on it. I knew it was my Teddy wearing the

cravat I sewed for him at Christmas. My Teddy, he tried to come back to me. He got into a skirmish with Ellis, who was all the time acting up and ambushing Yankee soldiers at the river, and he mortally wounded Ellis to save his own life.

My Teddy, my love, my heart is overjoyed. ~ VDC

Eva Clare looked at Roy, then behind him at the sunlight filtering through trees, making their yellow leaves pure gold as they sparkled and fluttered in the wind.

She pushed bangs out of her face. "He came back. Victoria was worth coming back to. That changed everything for her."

"And it should change things for you. Sometimes you know something, and it makes you feel a certain way. Then you learn an additional detail or see a fuller perspective, and it sheds light on the situation, and—if you let it—changes the way you believe."

"But he still went home and married someone else. You once told me he married a girl on an adjoining farm."

"What would you expect him to do given the circumstances? Pine away for the rest of his life?"

"That's what you've done." She blurted it out before she could stop herself. "Oh, I'm sorry." She lowered her head and shook it. "I'm so sorry. I shouldn't have said that. But Roy, you have stayed alone."

"Don't, Eva Clare. Don't hurt me because you're having flashbacks to your spouse. All men aren't like him. Some make a vow and keep it. Even Gerald. You've laid heavy judgment on Gerald. As bad as you believe him to be, he has stayed with his wife. He may have other faults and a troublesome history, but he has been faithful to his family. And his job. And his church. He's in church every week. He's got some good qualities. He's done some good things. He has chaperoned youth retreats, and he records the worship services to take to seniors who can't get out and go to church. Also, I've seen Gerald and Pete put together fried chicken buckets for Black farm families after the funerals of their loved ones. There's a morsel of good in that heart of his." Roy held the journal with one hand and turned the delicate pages with the other. His hair ruffled in the wind. His jacket rippled. "There's another thing you need to know."

"What now?"

"Open your heart, Eva Clare, and embrace change. I'm about to give you another detail that will change everything again—your way of looking at Victoria Dove, your family tree, and information you can give to Gerald, however you choose, if you choose. It happened one hundred forty-six years ago today. Today, Eva Clare. It's why I had to find you and tell you."

September 19th, 1864.

Today is a day I dreamed of but thought would never come true for me. For two years I have lived a lie. I have pretended I never loved a man and never had a child, but I did, and I took the consequences. I was an outcast. But I have found a man who will make an honest woman of me, and today, I will wed Rufus Steele and take his name, and change my own, and take the children of his first wife Penelope who died last year to the fever, and take my child to his home. The church will restore me. Today, I will stand by this everlasting river and give my troth. ~ VDC, soon to be Tory Steele

Eva Clare got a fluttery feeling inside. Chill bumps popped up on her arms. "Victoria Dove married?" She spread her fingers like a fan over her breastbone, the protector of her heart. "*Married.* The root reason of why the land passed down my line from Victoria Dove." Coghlan land, the Coghlan ancestral home were hers rightly from the beginning, her current legal will a fulfillment of the original.

She snorted out a laugh. Gerald. He'll have a hissy-pissy fit. She couldn't wait to tell him. Needed to gloat a little, or a lot. Victoria had satisfied the points of the will Gerald had.

Then, another sinking feeling in her stomach.

She was still judging and trying to get even.

And yet another epiphany. She pursed her lips.

Victoria had married a Steele.

Betsy's kin?

Had to be.

She was related to Betsy in some way. The Trunk transition was probably natural and proper. The circle had closed. A sense of completeness settled upon her.

She looked at the wide, rolling river, its life of commerce and growth evident in the barge tow passing by, another coming, change going up and down the river, tons of coal, chemicals, grains, steel, sand, petroleum— change reaching into Erin, into her.

If someone remains in the same hurtful environment, they're inclined to change who they are on the outside. They may change their name, their position in the community, their status, as in a new relationship. But change must go deeper—into heart, bone, and soul. It was time for her to find out who she truly was and what she had inside her.

She had taken back her maiden name, become an entrepreneur, and entered new relationships—Roy, romantically, and Lily, friend and business partner. She kept her longtime beliefs that we were all created equal, we must love our neighbors as ourselves, and we should be kind and fair to all in word and deed. But she must do more than simply believe. She must act on it.

She looked at Roy. *He* came back to *her.* He came to straighten things out between them.

He closed the journal, put it in his jacket pocket, zipped it. "You want to go to Pete Wong's and get some catfish and hushpuppies and eat on your pier?"

"I'd like that." She reached out to Roy who helped pull her up. "But first, I've got some business to tend to."

Eva Clare parked in the alley behind the Trunk, hurried in the back door, and made her way into the Pie Bird by raising the rolling door. She selected an apple pie from the showcase, put it in a colorful brand box with a picture of a pie vent on it, left a twenty on the counter, and set out for Gerald's house.

What would she tell him? She wanted to rub her new knowledge in his face, smear it into every pore. When she thought of a married Victoria, her foot pressed harder on the gas pedal, and the corners of her mouth crept up in an evil Snidely Whiplash sneer.

But she ran into a wall of guilt. She'd already met her judgment and determined she needed to be a doer of good and change her feelings about Gerald. She let her foot up, slowed, and pondered what to say as she drove down Old Wellington Road where little white asbestos bungalows and big brick ranch houses were mixed in with equipment barns, grain bins, rows of tractors, and cotton and bean fields. She steered her Subaru up the long teardrop driveway, parked in front of a gaslight post at the entrance to a wide sidewalk, picked up her pie box, and walked to the front door.

Gerald answered, dressed in tan slacks and a navy-blue golf shirt. He'd already changed out of his church clothes. The smell of a well-seasoned pot roast crept out to the front porch. Gerald looked surprised to see her.

"Hi, Gerald. I thought you and Jo might enjoy a pie on this crisp, fall afternoon." She held it out to him.

He pressed his lips into a thin line, squeezed his eyebrows together, and reached for it.

"It's apple." She stretched her mouth into a wide smile.

"Okay."

"Apple pie and a cup of coffee might be good after your Sunday dinner."

"And what's the reason for this bearing of gifts?"

Here it was. The invite to let loose. *Na na na na na na, Victoria Dove was mar-ried.*

No, she'd take the high road. She wanted the low road so bad she could taste it. But she wouldn't let herself go there.

"Because. You're my cousin. I wanted to bring you a pie."

He didn't invite her in. Didn't ask her to join them for pot roast or a slice of pie. Didn't even say thank you. Gerald would always be Gerald. She studied him, standing there holding that perfect pie, not knowing how to acknowledge a kind gesture.

"Well, bye, Gerald." She didn't wait for a response, but with a wave of her hand, turned and hurried to her car. As she buckled in, she looked at him and waved again. He was still standing there holding the pie. She pulled the car forward. As she drove out toward the road, she looked in her rearview mirror. He hadn't budged.

What a shameful spectacle. He didn't deserve her pity, but he got it. She was glad she'd risen up to do a good deed. Maybe it would make a difference.

The wind died down, and the lake was clear as glass, sparkling in the afternoon sun. Eva Clare and Roy sat in the Adirondack chairs on the pier, boxes of fried catfish tenders, hushpuppies, fries, and corn on the cob on their laps, Cokes on the table in front of them.

"Pete makes some dang good catfish," Roy said, holding a strip and eyeing its cornmeal crust. "Crispy. Not greasy."

"The woman he's got working for him has been doing it a long time. She doesn't have all her front teeth, but she does know how to fry fish." Eva Clare picked off a piece of fillet and put it in her mouth.

"He's getting new signage and having his parking lot paved next week."

"Pete is? Really?"

"Yes, and he planted new azalea bushes yesterday. Spiffing up the landscaping."

"Good. He's the gateway to Erin. He sets the tone for the town." She bit into the buttery corn, juices ran down her chin, and she wiped her hands and face on her napkin.

"Pete asked me if I'm going to stay here."

"Stay here in Erin instead of going back to New Orleans?"

"Yes, stay here permanently."

"What did you tell him?"

"I told him I didn't know." Roy reached over for his soda. "Pete said you should run for mayor next time. Said you've done more for the town than anybody else in the last forty years. Said you've brought *good* change."

She fluttered her lips.

"Yeah, he was serious."

"I don't know anything about being mayor."

"You think anybody else here does?"

She ran her finger over the coating of another piece of fish. "No, I guess they don't. Gerald has a business degree, but he mainly cares about his own interests—the success of the bank and keeping a White person as mayor."

"Person?" Roy said.

"Huh?"

"Person?" he said again, a lilt on the second syllable.

"Oh." She laughed. "Gerald intends to keep a White male as mayor. That's enough of a reason right there to make me want to run."

"Atta girl. You're getting name recognition for the good that's happening downtown. You've already got a team working with you. And you've got a brand expert on the team."

"Meredith. I've got a legal person on the team, too. Anna Laurel. And Sunny, a longtime local, a storeowner now, who's writing the town's history. And I've got Lily." She took a bite of fish. "You think Pete would support me?"

"I think he'd kowtow to Gerald to his face, but yes, in a private booth, I think he'd vote for you in a heartbeat." Roy picked up a fry and waved it like a banner. "And Betsy. She'd get behind this, too. And get the old folks to the polls." He ate the fry. "And she might know things you don't. After all, you know, she has a family trunk, too."

"Ohhh." She hadn't thought about Betsy's trunk. "Ohhhhh. It could hold more about Rufus and Ellis. And Victoria. Tory. Whatever her name ended up being." New details could be sitting right in front of her every workday and right in front of everyone coming into the store. After all, she'd put the trunk in the display window in full view of the main street. "Oh my gosh. I've got to dig through that trunk. I'll look like a fool sitting in the front window rummaging around."

"We'll make you a sign—UNPACKING ERIN'S PAST."

They both laughed.

"It's not a bad idea," she said. "It would be good promotion for Sunny's upcoming book of Erin's history."

Roy nodded and looked at his food box, picking around with his fingers as though choosing his next taste. Eva Clare studied him, this nice and handsome man, this man who seemed to care about her. How much of a fool would she be if she plopped her fish box down and threw every Adirondack chair in the lake to make room for two bodies to lie together in splendor on the pier deck. She wanted to so badly. She put her hands on the arms of her chair, ready to push up, take action. She scanned the horizon. A troll boat sat across the lake in the cypress knees, men fishing. She shook her head—*damn them*—and glanced at Roy. He caught her eye. They held the gaze. She knew he was thinking the same thing. She also knew he'd go with her into the house if she asked. She debated it in her mind. From across the lake came the faint purr of the fishing boat motor as the men started up to move to a new spot. Should she ask? Little waves on the lake came gently toward the pier. Her heart dipped and spun.

She cleared her throat, tried to shake off those thoughts, started speaking before she knew what she was going to say. "How 'bout let's—" She stopped herself and swallowed hard. "Have a big pier party." She wasn't forward enough to suggest making love. "Maybe have a lakeside bonfire, bring food, and invite the whole team of players in the town's renewal. Have music and dancing. What do you think?"

"That's not what I was thinking, but that sounds great. Events that build community are good." Roy closed his food box. "So are indulgences that build a couple."

"You want to go inside the house?"

He nodded.

They stepped off the pier onto the path, and as they walked past a tree line of elms, yellow slash pines, and sycamore ghost trees, Roy stopped and pulled her to him. She responded. They began talking to each other with their eyes.

Then she pushed away. Took his hand. Took the first step. Led him toward the trees, under an awning of millions of summer-old leaves jutting out from the branches above. They eased their way into the woods and lay on a sheltered, pine-needled bed.

They started gently and rhythmically, caressing and nurturing their feelings, enjoying the tender touching, holding that pace until it couldn't be helped, then built the fervor and carried it wildly to completion.

26 REVENANT

She's poised to act.
She's lived her struggle of darkness to light.
She has chosen light. And love.
We've come full course. Another pairing of souls,
of bodies. More splendor in the wilds.
My child. My Teddy's child.
They will walk the path of truth and tell it.
Change is up and down the river and coming to town.
She will lead it with a torch to the skies.
I watch now. I wait.

27   UNPACKING ERIN'S PAST

The last Saturday of September, leaves had started to turn, bolls of cotton had cracked open, and the smell of defoliant hung in the air. The energy of fulfillment billowed up out of the fields.

That same fulfillment energy swelled in anticipation of the new crop of information Betsy Steele's trunk would surely produce. Eva Clare and Sunny arrived at the store at seven-thirty after lattes at Anna Laurel's.

"You ready to harvest?" Eva Clare reached into her purse and withdrew a small brass key with a heart shape at the top. She held it up. "I got the key from Betsy."

"Let's do it." Sunny dug a pad and pen out of her satchel.

For two weeks, they'd been planning to sift through the Steele family's old travel trunk displayed in the front window of the antique shop. Eva Clare had already caught Sunny up on new information she'd learned about the Coghlan-Steele connections. Sunny had copied and re-saved Part One of her manuscript on Erin in the eighteen-hundreds—the founding of Prentiss, the Civil War days, the flooding and resettlement at Erin.

"We've got two and a half hours before the store opens," Eva Clare said. "We'll look like mannequins sitting in the window." She climbed onto the display stage and placed a big sign against the glass facing the street: UNPACKING ERIN'S PAST.

Sunny was right behind her. "Yeah, mannequins that have movable limbs and can talk." She set up her smaller sign: *The History of Erin, Mississippi.*

They sat cross-legged on the floor at the front ends of the trunk.

Eva Clare inserted the key, jiggled it, opened the top. "Keep in mind we're looking for connections between the Steele family and the Coghlan family—new information or information that confirms what I've learned about the marriage of Victoria Dove Coghlan and Rufus Steele."

"Got it," Sunny said. "Where's Lily? I thought she was coming."

"She'll be here shortly, I'm sure."

"It's not like she has far to go. I mean, down the stairs." Sunny reached into the trunk, picked up a cotton infant dress and matching cap, moaned her approval, vowed to make one like it for her grandbaby. "I wonder how far off we are in our knowledge of Erin's past. I always assumed our 1950 benchmark history was correct."

"Based on all I've learned about my family, I believe that old history book is way off."

"So instead of minor revision, I may have to do a re-write?"

"I'm afraid so." Eva Clare reached in and retrieved a stack of documents on top.

"What is that?"

"Looks like copies of old business forms. A plan to start and operate a business. Permits. A copy of Sales and Use tax registration. All dated February 8, 1952."

"Betsy's store?"

"They're related to the startup of a store, but they're all in the name of Victoria's Trunk."

"Not Betsy's Trunk?"

"No. Maybe the store was previously named Victoria's Trunk."

"No. In my manuscript I've got pictures of downtown from every decade in the twentieth century," Sunny argued. "I know there's one from 1953—the year we were born—and the sign on the storefront says Betsy's Trunk. Before it was Betsy's, it was Jo Ann's Bakery, famous for its doughnuts and cream puffs, and the store between Jo Ann's and the old diner where Anna Laurel is now was a shoe repair shop."

"Well, phooey, I don't know. Right off the bat, we've got a mystery."

Sunny reached over and turned the top document toward her. "But why Victoria?"

"Pretty sure this Victoria is *my* Victoria."

"It was a common name at the turn of that century—a queen's name, you know. Ask Betsy. She'll know, and you won't have to sit here and speculate. Keep those papers out to show her, and let's move on."

Eva Clare placed the stack beside her and turned her attention back to the trunk.

"What's that note?" Sunny pointed to a pink memo sheet taped to a stack of folded doilies, the writing in a left-handed slant.

Tatted doilies of Emily Woodward Steele, wife of Josiah Napoleon Steele, circa 1900.

"I guess Betsy labeled things so anyone looking through the trunk would know which one of her ancestors made the doilies. I don't know of Emily and Josiah. But I do know Betsy held her cigarettes, flask, and coffee cup with her left hand."

"No one in the future will have a clue who these people are."

"Unless you put them in your book." Eva Clare picked up a doily, held it up to the light, and studied the handiwork. All the old-timers kept doilies on their end tables, under lamps, vases, or knickknacks. This one had rusty age-stains, and some of the threads were loose.

Sunny voiced approval of the tatting knots. "It's so sad that Betsy has no family to care. When she dies, somebody will have to go through her stuff and will most likely throw it away."

"Sunny, I think that somebody will be me. In three weeks, I sign an agreement with Betsy for ownership of the Trunk and this entire building and the building the Pie Bird is in. Everything in the store is mine. She has said nothing about wanting this trunk."

"Oh, that's heavy. I wouldn't want that responsibility. It'd be hard to throw away somebody's beloved family possessions."

"Everything will stay in this trunk, exactly like it is now." Eva Clare set the doily back in its place, and her hand rustled against tissue paper wrapped around something. She removed the tissue to reveal a dress, someone's wedding dress. She unfolded it and laid it out over the open trunk—semi-sheer material, white turned to antique ivory, with a floral-lace neckline, short sleeves with lace inserts, and a filmy skirt with a scalloped hem.

Her skin prickled. "This dress," she pushed out in a whisper, "is the dress in my water dreams. In my paintings."

Sunny put her hand on Eva Clare's arm. "Oh, dear."

"How can this be?"

"Oh, this is spooky." Sunny rubbed her arms. "Gives me chill bumps."

"Next chance you get, look at my paintings that show the dress details of the woman under the water. All my life, I've painted this dress." She ran her hand over the soft material, shivered, blew out a breath, then folded the dress and put it beside her.

Sunny scooted a little closer to the trunk and dug down beneath a layer of stitchery. "Here's the family Bible." She took hold and began to lift it, when something under it caught her attention, and she pushed the Bible aside. "Look at this big, black book." She pulled it out and handed it to Eva Clare. "Let's go through this."

MEG'S PHOTOGRAPHIC SKETCH BOOK.

The first page identified the author.

> *Diarist and artist—Margaret Steele. I was born the daughter of William and Esther Steele in 1845, Wellington, Yazoo-Mississippi Delta. The pictures and words herein depict my life on our lively cotton plantation beside the mighty waters of the Mississippi. "Let the words of my mouth and the meditation of my heart, be acceptable in thy sight, O LORD, my strength, and my redeemer." Psalm 19:14. Yours truly, "Meg," 20th 2 – 1862*

The book's yellowed pages were full of drawings. Slaves chopping and picking cotton, children carrying long tow sacks, and slave women doing laundry by the river with a tub and scrub board.

A loud popping sound interrupted their viewing. Lily was making her way toward them, chewing a pink wad of gum, and blowing bubbles.

"How's it going, girls?"

"Hey, Lil," Eva Clare said, looking at Lily dressed in pink skinny-pants tight as a tourniquet, white sweater, and glittery silver slides. "Come on up." Lily smelled of bubblegum and vanilla body spray.

"Is there room up there for one more big girl?"

Eva Clare glanced at Sunny, who frowned, seeming to take it personally that Lily might be calling her fat. "We'll make room, won't we Sunny?"

Sunny nodded without cracking a smile.

Lily climbed up, and Eva Clare didn't know how in the world her stretch didn't split the butt seam of those pants.

Sunny whispered to Eva Clare, "Those pants are so tight I can see her religion."

"I heard that." Lily sat with her back against the front glass, making the women three points of an isosceles triangle. She folded her long legs into a twisted-knot pretzel. "What've we got so far?"

Eva Clare pointed to the stacks of papers, doilies, and folded garment on the floor. "Stitchery and some papers of a business being established and someone's wedding dress. We also found a sketchbook of a Margaret or 'Meg' Steele, the daughter of William and Esther Steele. We were looking at the pictures she drew."

"One thing I know is William and Esther Steele were the family's first settlers here. They lived on the plantation next to the Coghlans." Lily pointed at Eva Clare. "You know of Ellis and Rufus Steele from reading about them in the journal. They were the sons of William and Esther. Meg was Ellis and Rufus's sister." She leaned toward the book. "What kind of pictures?"

Eva Clare pointed to a sketch of a round Black woman wearing a full, long skirt and a rag around her head. "Like this one." Beneath it were the words **My Beloved Sally**.

"Sally was the Steele's house slave. Had a bunch of kids until Mr. William sold them."

"Here's another one." Eva Clare turned to a sketch of a dock full of slaves loading cotton onto a boat. "Look at the detail. You can see the rippling muscles of the dockhands handling the heavy bales. Meg was good with anatomical detail."

"Uh huh. Rippling muscles, buff bodies. Let's move right along."

Eva Clare skipped to a page with a sketch of a bunch of men, one lying on the ground and one with a whip. The caption said, **Flogging**. Meg had written,

> **"Father whipped my beloved Sally's eldest boy because he left the plantation without permission to go see a servant girl on another farm. Father left bloody marks on the boy's back. I do wish the boy hadn't broken the rules."**

Eva Clare held the drawing up for Lily to see.

"Yeah, there were slave codes back then," Lily said. "That was one of them. You couldn't leave your home plantation. Slaves were property and treated as such. Another was, you couldn't read or look at any material that was anti-slavery. That put our family in danger. Our quilts were anti-slavery because they contained messages about running away. Our whole family could've been flogged or lynched if those messages had been decoded."

Setting the book on her lap, Eva Clare put her finger to a line of writing. "Here's more."

> **"Now because the boy disobeyed and is a liability to our plantation, Father is going to sell him. He is selling our beloved Sally's four eldest boys. They are twenty, eighteen, seventeen, and fifteen years of age. Sally is distraught. She up and left. Father and the other hands went looking for her, but she was nowhere to be found. I think someone surely is hiding her to keep her safe and I pray to God it is so and I also pray to God that my father never discovers who is giving her safe harbor."**

Could Sally have been given refuge at the Coghlan Safe House? Did Victoria Dove and Catherine Deering and Star hide her?

Eva Clare turned the page to find two newspaper ads unevenly torn out and pasted on the verso leaf, barely clinging to the page due to the failing medium.

**VALUABLE GANG OF YOUNG
NEGROES
BY WILLIAM STEELE**
Will be sold at Auction
ON WEDNESDAY, 11TH INST.
At 12 o'clock, Steele Mercantile,

4 Valuable Young Negroes,

All Men, Field Hands.

Sold for no fault; with the best city guarantees.

TERMS CASH.

Prentiss, Mississippi, June 10th, 1862

RUNAWAY – $20 REWARD

Will be given for the apprehension and delivery of my Servant Girl SALLY. She is 36 years of age, a light mulatto, about 5 feet 4 inches high, of a thick and corpulent habit. Being a good seamstress, she has been accustomed to dress well.

It is probable she designs to transport herself to the North.

All persons are hereby forewarned against harboring or entertaining her, or being in any way instrumental in her escape, under the most rigorous penalties of the law.

WILLIAM STEELE

June 20th, 1862

"Mr. Steele sold her children," Sunny said. "*Sold* them. That's awful. I didn't realize our country treated people so terribly, even if they were just slaves."

Lily jerked her head toward Sunny. "Just slaves? Um, slaves were people, in case you didn't know." She widened her eyes and glared. "And I'm going to venture out and say that our country has never treated all people good or fair or equal, and everybody isn't free." Lily situated her hands on her waist. "I think the Founding Fathers meant 'equal' for people like them only—wealthy, White, male landowners."

"Ohhh. Male. 'All *men* are created equal,'" Eva Clare said. "I'll be damn. Those words weren't meant for *me*. As a woman, I wasn't meant to be equal. I always thought 'men' meant 'mankind.' All people. But maybe that's not what the Founding Fathers meant."

"I guess I wasn't meant to be equal either," Sunny said.

"It changes things when it excludes you, doesn't it?" Lily blew a bubble and popped it.

"I guess. But we've always had inequality and slavery. Even in the Bible," Sunny said.

"The Bible says 'Christ hath made us free' and not to be 'entangled again with the yoke of bondage.' That's Galatians five one, if you want to look it up for yourself." Lily looked sideways at Sunny. "Surely you can decipher it isn't right to own another human being and your ancestors were wrong for doing it."

"I shouldn't be held accountable for my ancestors who owned slaves."

"You should be accountable as a member of the human race for thinking slavery is okay because we've always had it."

"That's the problem," Eva Clare said. "We didn't think. Growing up, we were blind to the injustices our White race was putting upon the other race. We didn't think about it, and we would have never questioned our parents in the wrongs they represented."

"Y'all, give me a break. I'm trying to understand and get this right for the sake of our town's history," Sunny said. "I'm up here in this window going through the trunk with the best of intentions—to get the facts and write the truth. I could be home sleeping."

"Granted. Just so you write the truth and not what you want the truth to be," Lily said. "But there's one more point to be made. Our state of Mississippi didn't vote to abolish slavery until 1995. You hear me? Only fifteen years ago. Put that in your history book."

"I never heard that," Sunny said. "You sure that's right?"

"Wait, no, there was an amendment to the Constitution," Eva Clare countered.

"Yeah, the thirteenth, in 1865, but Mississippi never ratified it," Lily said. "Slave owners wanted to be compensated for the value of their freed slaves, so the state never voted on the amendment until recently."

"Oh, good grief, that brings slavery into our adulthood in the twentieth century. That's embarrassing! Lily, how have you kept your sanity? How do you forgive?" Eva Clare grimaced.

"How does anybody forgive those who show no regret or have no understanding that what they did was wrong? And when told, they don't believe it."

"Well, not everybody is like that."

Lily flinched. "Yeah, well, some people don't believe lard is greasy, even when they got a hunk of it in their hand. And the people who know better and aren't like that don't speak up. White silence is my biggest enemy, and it's hard to forgive that."

Eva Clare's heart flip-flopped. She knew that was true like she knew the back of her own hand. And she had been as guilty as anybody in the state of Mississippi for standing silent and not pushing back in the face of wrong.

The crack inside her widened.

She gripped the sketchbook. Her heart pulsed in ragged beats. She looked out the window at early stirrings on Main Street—a mud-splattered truck turning into a parking slot in front of Anna Laurel's, old Mr. Dakin walking his Jack Russell dog, Sara Alice Neal strolling her baby Robert III and her yellow lab, Martha Harper watering crape myrtles in front of the hardware store.

"Let's get back to our purpose here." Eva Clare turned a clump of pages in the sketchpad. "We don't have time to read this whole book." Flipping a few more pages, she came across a sketch of a young man with big angel wings, looking down at a tombstone with the name Ellis Steele on it—Victoria Dove Coghlan's friend who died at the hand of her lover, Winfield Edward "Teddy" Winslow, after an ambush. On the following page, there was a picture of a bearded man and a young woman in a wedding dress—the same wedding dress Eva Clare had unwrapped from tissue paper moments ago. Beneath the couple: ***"Rufus Steele marries Tory Coghlan, September 1864."***

"Ah-ha!" Eva Clare screeched. "And there it is! Corroboration!" She hammered her fist on the page. "We now have two sources that show Victoria Dove Coghlan married. Sunny, take note. *This* is the town's history. It was surely their union that produced the donation of land for the new town of Erin after the flood destroyed the old town of Prentiss."

Sunny scribbled on her pad, mouthing the names and date.

Eva Clare turned a page of the sketchbook and pointed out a drawing of a soldier holding a newspaper that read LEE SURRENDERS AT APPOMATTOX, April 9, 1865. She thumbed through more pages, looking at dates—sketches from 1865, 1866. A sketch from 1867 of a fat baby holding a rattle caught her attention. ***"Josiah Napoleon Steele, named after the town of Napoleon across the river. My nephew. Son of Rufus and Tory Steele."***

Eva Clare sucked in a breath, and her air went down the wrong pipe! She grabbed at her throat, coughed, choked, struggled to breathe.

Lily lurched forward and slapped her on the back in rescue, skimming her arm across the trunk in the process, raking out a manila envelope, spilling its contents on the floor.

"Breathe, Eva Clare. Slow. Deep." She breathed in as an example. "Relax your throat."

"I'm fine. Quit being a nurse," Eva Clare squeaked out. "That was a shock. Victoria Dove Coghlan—Dovie, Tory, whatever the hell her name was—had another child."

"Wait, what? I didn't know that. There was a child after the bastard one?" Lily said.

"Yeah, here, look. Josiah Napoleon Steele. Like the book says." Eva Clare tapped her finger on the open sketchbook. "I know good and well she named her baby boy after the town her lover, Winfield Winslow, lived in while he was in Mississippi and Arkansas, and I'd be willing to bet on that." Eva Clare threw her hands up and laughed maniacally. "And I bet you a million dollars Betsy knows this. Why didn't she tell me? What's wrong with the truth?"

Sunny was madly taking notes. Lily had her hands clamped to her mouth.

"Funny how you can live your whole life right in the middle of truths and not see or hear or know a single one of them." Eva Clare pushed her lips forward, wrinkled her forehead.

"Hey, what're all those pictures on the floor?" Sunny said.

Eva Clare scowled at the mess in front of her. "Looks like they spilled out of this," she said, pointing to the manila envelope hanging halfway out of the trunk.

Sunny picked up a photograph. "Aww, a baby girl in a pretty white dress with a lace-scalloped collar and hem, and her hair parted and spit-brushed to the side." She turned it over. ***"Dovey Elizabeth Steele, 1924."***

"What?" Eva Clare grabbed the picture and held it up. "Elizabeth? Betsy? Is this Betsy? Our Betsy? Dovey? DOVEY?"

"Oh shit," Sunny said.

Eva Clare started laughing hysterically. First, because she was pretty sure it was Sunny's first cuss word ever, and second, because how could things in her family get any screwier? "Get that Bible out of the trunk and open it to the genealogy page. Let's see how Dovey Elizabeth connects to the other Steeles."

Sunny got the Bible, turned to the family tree, and handed it to Eva Clare.

William Steele   **b. 1817**
                                              m. Esther

+ Rufus Steele   **b. 1840**
                                              m. Penelope d. 1862
                                              m. Victoria Dove, Tory

++ Josiah Napoleon Steele   **b. 1867**
                                              m. Emily

+++ William Jack Steele   **b. 1898**
                                              m. Lizbeth

++++ Dovey Elizabeth Steele "Betsy" **b. 1923**

Eva Clare slammed the Bible shut and dropped it to the floor beside her. "I'll be damned. Our Betsy is the great-granddaughter of Victoria Dove Coghlan."

"What the—"

"H-E-double-hockey-sticks!" Sunny said. "Heavens to Betsy!"

Eva Clare pulled her knees up, feet and hands flat on the floor, and pushed herself to standing. "Betsy better have her bony ass in this store right now. She's got some explaining to do." Eva Clare climbed down off the display stage and stomped across the floor to the back foyer where Betsy spent much of her time watching game shows and old sit-coms.

Sunny and Lily scrambled to get up and follow her.

Betsy was sitting on a straight chair watching TV, an unlit cigarette dangling from her red-painted lips. She wore pink, fuzzy bedroom slippers, a far cry from her former workday pumps. She was drinking a bought bottle of cold coffee latte because Eva Clare wouldn't let her sit on the good rug with a cup of coffee. She shook too badly and sloshed it every whichaway.

"Okay, Betsy, it's time to confess." Eva Clare stood in a threatening position—legs spread, hands on hips. "What's your full name?"

Betsy laughed in small puffs, making the cigarette bob and almost topple out. She started into little cough spasms. "You found pictures in the trunk."

"Yes, I did."

"You put it all together."

"Yes, I did."

"You found the wedding dress of Victoria Dove—the woman they've always called a spinster."

"Yes, ma'am, I did."

"I knew you would. Well, you're right." Betsy reached over to the end table beside her, picked up the remote, lowered the volume on the TV, put the remote down. "My name is Dovey Elizabeth Steele. My grandfather was Josiah Napoleon Steele, son of Rufus Steele and your Victoria Dove Coghlan." She took out her unfired Virginia Slim and laid it atop the remote. "Victoria Dove was my great-grandmother. That's why, when I opened this store, I registered it as Victoria's Trunk. I guess you saw that, too."

Eva Clare groaned, plowed her hair with her hands, held it in clumps, and shook her head vigorously. Sunny and Lily walked silently up beside her. Lily cleared her throat. Eva Clare turned and said, "Don't grab me, Lily. Don't slap me on the back. I don't need a nurse. I don't need saving." Then she looked at Betsy. "Why didn't you keep the store name? Why didn't you ever tell this? You've known the family connection all along. You could've put this in the 1950 town history, but you didn't. I suspect my grandmomma knew, too, didn't she? She could've told me. But she didn't. Why didn't she? Why did y'all hide this information about our families?"

"Neither side wanted it told. Victoria was an embarrassment to the family. They wouldn't let me use Victoria in the store name. They wanted to hide the family sins. These were town builders and church founders. Victoria, a prominent settler, a *lady*, committed sin with an enemy soldier, had a child out of wedlock, got her name removed in shame from the rolls of the church her family founded, then married another prominent settler. No, no. It was a black mark against the families, and they did everything they could to cover it up. They lied, they altered or stole public and church records, they recorded it wrong in their Bibles." Betsy cleared her throat. "Sometimes we write our own history. What we want to believe. What we want others to believe about us."

Lily nodded and pointed a finger at Sunny.

Sunny rolled her eyes.

"Sunny would've had her history written and secured the lies for another generation or till the end of time." Betsy nervously put her hands on her skinny knees and inched her skirt down some. "Why do you think I agreed to give you my store and my two buildings and all the contents? I'm not that poor of a businesswoman. You're family. It's the right thing to do. I knew you'd figure it out. And I figured you'd make it right."

"Gerald Tanner knows all this, doesn't he?"

"He knows. I'm sure he was afraid you'd come home and dig through things cleaning out your grandmother's belongings and discover the godawful truths—the same stories most families have, but that our family was too proud to own. He's been hounding me for years. He wanted me to give him the store and my house. Tried to trick me out of it by getting me to sign some legal deed. I may be as old as the damn dirt this town sits on, but I'm not dumb. And I'm not demented. Not yet."

"I guess position and reputation are more important than truth to some."

"Our families wanted respect as the founders of this place," Betsy said. "Too many ghosts haunted them—family lies, secrets, skeletons in the closet. Those haunts have rolled down generation to generation, like a fire blowin' through a forest burnin' down every tree in its path until one person finds the courage to face the flames. That person is you, Eva Clare."

This was the final thing of things Eva Clare didn't know previously but now had to deal with—her husband's cheating, her ancestors' sins, her ancestors' illegal good deeds of trying to save people from bondage, her ancestors' attempts to hide their sins, her lineage and history, Roy's ancestor's role. She covered her face and started to cry, lathering it into a weeping, a cleansing.

Lily got one of her arms, and Sunny got the other, and they walked her upstairs to Lily's apartment and gave her some nurturing.

Betsy was left to open and mind the store in her fuzzy slippers. The trunk in the window was left wide open, its contents spilling out for all to see and read through the glass.

Eva Clare took some time to gather herself. She came back down the stairs to the showroom and stopped upon seeing her newly finished painting on the easel at the back of the store, the oils still drying. The blue hues of the water were beautiful, the light perfect. The painting showed the body of a woman under water. Her head, not shown, was above the surface. She had risen to the light.

Maybe the ghost woman depicted in the painting, with truth spread out around her now, would be able to rise up to the heavens and look back on a meaningful life.

Eva Clare turned to walk toward the checkout station where Betsy was tending the store, her strawberry hair shining under the pendant lights. Betsy was the real hero here. She could've taken what she knew to her grave, but she trusted it to Eva Clare, and Eva Clare was exposing the facts to the whole town in the window of the antique shop and soon, in lines of black ink straight across the pages of a history book.

28 REVENANT

She has chosen light.
And truth.
She has made the low places exalted.
And the crooked places straight.
I am redeemed.
My time here is done.

29   TRUNK TRANSITION

Friday morning, middle of October, Anna Laurel showed up in front of the Trunk. Eva Clare met her on the sidewalk. Pumpkin pyramids, cotton stalks with open bolls in painted milk cans, wagons full of pumpkins, and pots of chrysanthemums decorated the storefronts.

"We need to talk." Anna Laurel gave Eva Clare a pat on the arm, then reached inside her camel leather tote and took out a folder. "First item of business for today. I've got some paperwork for you." She pulled out a thrice-folded, multipage document and handed it over. "This arrived from the Nashville lawyer. As you requested, he sent it to me, your attorney."

Eva Clare opened it.

IN THE CIRCUIT COURT OF DAVIDSON COUNTY, TENNESSEE . . . FINAL DECREE . . . This cause came on to be heard on the Complaint for absolute divorce by the Husband, signed and notarized Marital Dissolution Agreement . . .

Eva Clare stopped reading, looked at Anna Laurel, and folded the papers.

"Your divorce is final, Eva Clare."

Eva Clare opened the top third, looked at the date. "Four days ago. So easy. I wasn't even there. I was divorced and didn't know it." Her hands shook.

Anna Laurel nodded. "That's the way it usually is."

"It shouldn't be that easy."

"You're moving on, Eva Clare. You've built a good life here. Shed a tear for this dissolution, then be done with it."

A fat, warm tear rolled down Eva Clare's cheek, blurring her image of the baby-blue T-Bird at the curb. It also blurred and compacted the last thirty-four years of her life—her marriage, her identity, the memories.

"Okay, that's enough grief. Let's get on with the second item of business for today. Let's go buy you a store." Anna Laurel gave her a slap on the back. "C'mon, E. C., get in the back seat, and I'll go get Betsy. She can ride shotgun."

They drove to Cleveland to the office of the lawyer Blackburn, as Betsy referred to Mr. Milton M. Blackburn, all of them together in the T-Bird, top up. Betsy carried her little flask of scotch and turned it up every few miles. She was steel inside, and the liquor never affected her.

Highway 8 was lined with what looked like snow, but it was cotton blowing loose between the pickers and the trailers parked beside the road, the end of the harvest. Cotton pickers were combing the white fields, big green and yellow machines that moved down the rows and stripped the cotton lint from the plants.

This was Eva Clare's first harvest back in the Delta. Picking was the climax of the growing season. It was money being picked, the livelihood of this place. It was magnificent, the Delta in all its glory.

All three women in the car lived through the days when these cotton fields were picked by hand, mostly by Black field workers, towing their long canvas sacks, pulling the lint away from dried burrs with sharp spurs that stuck and bloodied their hands. As a child, Eva Clare watched the pickers at work. She heard the spirituals they sang, the field hollers, early blues music.

Once the women reached the Cleveland city limits, they turned onto Fifth Avenue across from the university coliseum and drove by the college. Students filled the sidewalks as they changed classes. All the parked cars had little green-and-white delta-shaped stickers on their back windows. Anna Laurel turned left in front of Delta State's Roberts-LaForge Library onto Court Street. The lawyer's office was between the courthouse and the old Ellis Theater, across the street from a train museum and the old remodeled depot for the Illinois Central Railroad that once ran through Delta towns up to Memphis.

Anna Laurel coaxed Betsy into leaving her flask in the car, and Eva Clare helped get Betsy across the street in her black pumps with a black snap-top purse hanging off her arm.

"I'm transferring my store called Betsy's Trunk to Eva Clare," Betsy told the lawyer Blackburn, "but it was never named this legally. All the legal papers say Victoria's Trunk because that's what I named it, so we need to fix that. You understand?" She dug a cigarette out of her handbag, then snapped it shut.

"Yes, ma'am," Mr. Blackburn said.

Anna Laurel patted Betsy's hand, pointed to the cigarette, shook her head no.

"I know. I'm not gon smoke it. I know better." Betsy held the unlit Virginia Slim in her left hand, and an opal ring slid up and down on a thin finger as she gestured. "Eva Clare, you can call it Victoria's Trunk if you want to, and we won't have to change a thing."

"I promised you I'd keep it Betsy's Trunk," Eva Clare said with a wink.

"Sir," Betsy said, shaking a long, arthritic forefinger at Blackburn, "the family wanted to keep their skeletons in the closet and pitched a fit over the use of Victoria's name."

"Yes, ma'am," Mr. Blackburn said.

"Eva Clare's letting all the skeletons out."

Mr. Blackburn nodded his head.

Betsy turned to Eva Clare. "I want you to call the store Victoria's Trunk. I mean it. I've always wanted that name. I couldn't do it, but you can."

"Okay. I'll do whatever you want. We'll make a new sign." She didn't care about the store name right now. She only wanted to complete the business transfer to her name.

Eva Clare and Betsy signed papers, and the deed was done. The three women headed back to the parking lot across the street. Betsy stopped in the middle of traffic to find her sunglasses in her purse and put them on. Eva Clare helped Anna Laurel nudge their elder along.

Eva Clare could barely contain her excitement over her entrepreneurial status. It gushed up out of her. She was a storeowner—a single-woman storeowner. She skipped a few steps, rocking Betsy's balance, and giggled. She was giddy, free, and happy. In the same day, she was released from her old life in Nashville and re-attached to old life encased in newness here in the Delta. The autumn sun smiled down on her.

The women settled into the car. "Can you stand the top being down, Miss Betsy?" Anna Laurel said.

"I got my silk scarf right here in my pocketbook." Betsy tapped the retro black purse. "I came prepared. I know you girls are wild and want to speed in the open air."

They headed back toward Highway 8 West with the top down, their hair blowing, except Betsy's. She had that big-flowered scarf wrapped around her head and tied under her chin. Betsy tried to put her cigarette between her lips, but the wind blew it out. Eva Clare caught and returned it.

"Put that thing in your purse!" Eva Clare yelled louder than the wind.

"Well, I'll swan, I guess I better."

"Hey, Betsy, we're having a bonfire and pier party to celebrate tonight at my house. You want to come?" Eva Clare shouted from the back seat.

"You gon let me bring my Scotch whisky?"

"Yeah, but if you're going to drink and drive, don't run your car into my lake."

Betsy's shoulders rocked with her laughter. Anna Laurel glanced over at Betsy, then with her brows lifted, back at Eva Clare.

That was a thing likely to happen.

RESURRECTION

Evening settled over the oxbow. A half-moon was rising, waxing gibbous.

With Roy and Lily's help, Eva Clare piled firewood in a heap for a bonfire by the lake and set up lawn chairs and a long table for the party-food.

Everybody started arriving around six, carrying food on silver platters, in McCartys Pottery bowls, and in CorningWare with glass lids that rattled as their carriers—Pete and Angie, Anna Laurel, Meredith, and Sunny—walked. An old Buick with Betsy at the wheel crept down the lane. A black Cadillac SUV rolled in, its shine gleaming pink in the sky's blush—Gerald and Jo.

Eva Clare greeted her guests on the thick carpet of Bermuda grass between the lane and the lake with a backdrop of evergreens, redswept trees, and dangling yellow leaves. She helped them place their dishes in order of salads, meats, vegetables, and desserts. Sweet-and-sour meatballs, spicy catfish tenders, and damn-hot fried chicken blended into a smorgasbord of smells with butter beans and ham hock and oniony corn pudding. The centerpieces she'd prepared offered a touch of October orange—bunches of small pumpkins and volunteer spider lilies in old Mason jars.

She took chips and dips out to the end of the pier and placed them on the cypress table where people could sit in the Adirondack chairs, eat, talk, and watch a brilliant rose, gold, and red autumn sundown. She lit the six torches on poles around the pier deck, then strolled back to the oxbow bank.

Anna Laurel clapped her hands for attention, welcomed everybody, and gave serving-line instructions to the eleven people gathered.

Eva Clare stood on the periphery watching her friends eat and talk. Roy approached her with a full plate. "Eva Clare, you are glowing. You look happier than I've ever seen you."

"I *am* happy. I'm glad to be home. Glad to be with these people of my past. These longtime girlfriends. Good old solid Pete. And Lily. What would I have done without her?" She watched Lily sit and put her plate on her lap. "Even Gerald. He drives me crazy, but I invited him, and he showed up."

"And me?"

"And you." She gently patted him on the shoulder, then held her arms out pretend-wrapping them around her clutch of friends. "In this clunky, dysfunctional mix of personalities, I've found my peace. In four months, I've built a whole new life here."

Sunny, holding a platter of hot chicken, a black satchel hanging from her shoulder, sat down beside Lily and crossed her ankles. "Try it," she said, holding the plate out. "C'mon, Lil, try my damn-hot chicken. It's getting to be a Nashville thing, and I made up a recipe to celebrate Eva Clare, you know, because she came home from Nashville."

"I get that connection." Lily picked up a piece. "Girl, this even feels hot to my fingers."

"Take a bite."

Lily bit into the meat. "Lord, have mercy!" She fanned her mouth and gulped soda.

"Good, huh? I'm thinking of making hot chicken pies to sell at the Pie Bird."

"With less heat than this, I hope." Lily panted. "You're gon need a side of sour cream to cut the burn."

"I can do that."

Sunny and Lily dived into talk about the food spread and the Pie Bird, and before Eva Clare could blink twice, Lily was offering Sunny her grandmother's muscadine pie recipe, and Sunny was thanking her in a fever pitch.

Sunny set the platter on the empty chair next to her, opened her satchel, pulled out a thick stack of papers, and held it up to Lily. "Here it is. The *real* history of Erin. It's all here—Victoria, Star, the quilts, the house on the Underground Railroad." She looked over at Eva Clare eavesdropping and motioned her over. Roy followed.

"It's authentic history," Sunny said. "I spent more time going through Betsy's trunk that Saturday after we sat in the front window like mannequins. I copied quotes and took pictures of documents. My manuscript is factual. I'm putting the truth out there." She handed the copy to Lily. "I made copies for both of you to review."

"I must say, I'm impressed," Lily said.

"And Eva Clare, I've got the answer for you," Sunny said.

"Answer to what?"

"I know what to do about the old public school's concrete foundation. You know, the place left behind after integration, the town's eyesore you're always complaining about."

"Ah yes, one of the ghosts on the oxbow. Dead, buried, but still hanging around. What've you got?"

"Make it a public park. The Coghlan-Steele City Park. Build a playground—a custom wood one. A pavilion, an outdoor fireplace. Paint grids on the concrete foundation for hopscotch, shuffleboard, giant-sized checkers. Something we can *all* use—the townsfolk and the country people."

"That's a great idea."

"We'll assign a committee and figure it out." She picked up her platter of hot chicken, offered Lily another piece, and went to sit by Meredith.

Anna Laurel popped open a bottle of champagne. Meredith and Sunny helped her pass out plastic flutes and pour the Korbel. Anna Laurel held up her glass to quieten the revelers.

"I'd like to propose two toasts, so don't drink all your fizzy on the first. Here's to Betsy Steele and Betsy's Trunk, a fixture in our town for fifty-eight years. Thank you, Betsy, for a good run, and congratulations on your retirement."

They cheered, then turned up their glasses. Betsy stood and because of her palsy, spilled some champagne trying to thank everybody.

Anna Laurel continued. "We have the past going out and the future coming in. One career ends, and another begins. Here's to Eva Clare Carlyle, the new owner of the Trunk. Congratulations on a beautiful remodel, a successful opening, and a good contribution to our town and economy. As of today, the store is named Victoria's Trunk. Thank you, Eva Clare. And here's to the future of Victoria's Trunk." She lifted her flute high.

They cheered, whistled, and sipped the bubbly. Roy struck a match to the pile of drunk wood, and the bonfire's flames shot high.

Anna Laurel signaled for attention. "Mister Mayor, would you like to say a word?"

Gerald choked on his fizzy and coughed. "No, no, I'm good. No speech." He waggled his hand. "Congrats to you both. Good job. Best of luck."

The half-moon shone, the fire blazed, and oldies music blared from a boom box. A whole lot of revelry went on. About nine, they started to pack up and leave. Betsy was first, after Pete turned her car around and aimed it up the driveway toward the road. She couldn't see a thing at night, she said. Pete and Angie claimed their bowls, carried them in totes, and before leaving, Pete put his bags down and collected Eva Clare in a hug so tight she could barely breathe. He released her and took her hands.

"I'm so glad you came home to Erin. You brought hope back to us. Thanks for bringing good change to our town and for getting us all together behind a good cause—saving Erin. You're our savior, Sweet Eva." He planted a kiss on one of her hands, then let them go.

Eva Clare wrapped her kissed hand around the hope charm on her necklace.

Gerald and Jo retrieved their dishes and started walking toward their Cadillac. Jo yelled a thanks and bye and blew a kiss. Gerald waved. "Appreciate the invite. We had a real good time."

She waved back. "Glad y'all came."

"Good party." Roy put his hands in his jeans pockets. "I'm going to head home, too. Good night, Sweet Eva." He kissed her on the cheek and turned to leave. She could feel the wetness stamped on her face, cool in the breeze.

Sweet Eva. She kind of liked that.

Anna Laurel, Sunny, Meredith, and Lily stayed for cleanup and watching the bonfire die down. The fun, food, and fizzy had filled them and made them drowsy. Their audible sighs gave away their sleepy status.

Buzzing from the champagne and the excitement of her new enterprise, Eva Clare started singing an old hymn and twirling around. "'Going to lay down my burden, down by the riverside.'" She clapped in rhythm—"'down by the riverside'"—then used her pointer fingers to tap the beat in the air toward the oxbow, old-river water. "Down by the riverside.'"

The others joined in, started dancing.

It felt right to belt out this song that Sweet Evelyn and Marthala used to sing together—this old spiritual dating back to before the Civil War. Marthala said it was a work song sung by slaves in the cotton fields. Now, it was perfect to describe Eva Clare's freeing.

She danced to the water's edge, singing, clapping, and the others followed in the glare of the bonfire and the dim light of the half-moon. She opened herself and finished the processing and letting go of her past—her husband, failed marriage, flood-damaged house, teaching career, church trappings, and the flawed aspects of her religion. Let go of the judgments she'd attached to the people of Erin for holding on to the old-ghost traditions. It wasn't for her to judge them, but to understand what was true and right and what was false and wrong. It was for her to examine herself and keep her own heart aligned with good and to walk away from a religion aligned with hate, racism, and intolerance. It felt good to lay down these burdens she'd carried around locked up inside her.

She pressed a closed hand against her heart, repented of her own mishandlings, opened her hand wide, and lifted it toward the sky, where she could see the stars between her fingers.

She walked to the end of the pier, got a lighted tiki torch, and held it up. So did the women following her. They danced back toward the bank, sang the chorus of the old spiritual. Lily moved up beside Eva Clare and took the lead on the next verse. "'Going to lay down my sword and shield, down by the riverside . . .'"

The women danced under the torch flames, marched by the bonfire, shuffled over the quilt of fallen leaves and under the branches of virgin

Coghlan trees. Eva Clare had never done anything like this before, especially in front of friends. The foolery empowered her and gave her a bond of closeness to the other women, this silliness that was something they might've done in the old, growing-up days, but didn't.

She could hear the thud, thud of her feet pounding against hard ground, her energy tamping the earth, filtering into it. All her life she'd pulled energy out of this fertile Delta dirt. Now, she was stomping it back in, giving of herself to her land.

The bonfire burned lower. Embers sparkled. The smell of woodsmoke hung thick in the air. Two pole lights gave definition. The procession wound through the cottonwoods, slash pines, and sycamores that stood in front of bald cypress trees at the edge of the Beulah oxbow. Eva Clare led the women to the patio, where she picked up a little cremation box. They nodded, aware of the contents.

The women marched across the yard to the lane, past the barn, to the rusty fence around the old family graveyard. They stopped, snickered like kids, then stood silent, held their breath, and waited as they did years ago for the ghosts to appear. No will-o'-the-wisps tonight. The women resumed their parade back toward the pier, slowing as they neared it.

After handing her torch to Lily and kicking off her sandals, Eva Clare opened the box and took out a bag of ashes. "It's time to let Sweet Evelyn go."

"Oh, honey, are you okay?" Meredith grasped her arm.

"I'm fine." But then, a let-down of tears. "At her funeral I promised to follow her course and work to build a community of love and acceptance." She glanced from friend to friend and nodded. "I think we're doing that." She looked at the bag, at all that was left of Sweet Evelyn, noted the bits of bone in the ash. Swayed, almost fainted.

Anna Laurel put a hand on her shoulder and gently squeezed. The others moved in close.

"I'm fine," she repeated. But her eyes filled, her chest felt hollow with a hitch in it, her legs were weak and buckling. She took a few wobbly steps down the pier planks over the lake, not sure of what she was doing. But going this way felt right.

She jumped. Right into the lake, the old Mississippi River channel. October nights in the Delta were mild, low seventies, but the water was chilly. She paid it no mind. She walked out until the water was up to her waist and she was accustomed to its coolness. Stood perpendicular to the downwind, held the bag in front of her, took off the wrapper tie, and tossed out a swirly cloud of Sweet Evelyn Carlyle.

"Bye, Grandmomma." Her voice caught. She quickly straightened her posture and held fast to her strength. Couldn't teeter here. Had to remain strong.

She ducked under the water, lowered herself to a squat, felt her feet pressing into the soft, squishy bottom. She opened her eyes, witnessed only blackness. Looking left, right, she couldn't see her hair floating about her, but could feel it against the skin of her neck and face. She couldn't see her own hands in front of her, but she opened and closed a hand and felt fingertips tapping against her palm. This was faith—not being able to see herself, but knowing she was there and whole. She'd hold on to her faith.

She planted her feet, pushed against the bottom muck, and sprang up from the lake, water gushing off her. "Eva rising!" she declared, pushing wet hair out of her face. "*Sweet* Eva rising!" A breeze blew across her wetness, but she was warm inside. "Rising to walk in newness of life!" Like she did as a child playing in the river, dipping under, coming up, copying her preacher after he dunked somebody in a baptism.

The other four women chanted, "Sweet Eva rising! Sweet Eva rising!"

"C'mon, girls," Anna Laurel shouted. "Let's go in." They capped their tiki torches, leaned them against a tree, kicked off their shoes, stepped into the water, and giggled like schoolgirls as they walked out from the bank, plunged themselves under, then sprang up, squealing. Except for Sunny, who didn't get wet from the elbows up.

All five came together, put their arms around each other's shoulders, and danced in a circle, singing, "'Going to try on my starry crown, down by the riverside . . .'"

A starry crown meant victory. Slave women of an earlier time sought a crown as they journeyed under these same sky-lights to freedom.

Above, the moon and a million stars hung for the beholding.

When the verse and refrain were over, Anna Laurel, Sunny, and Meredith trudged toward the bank, shivering, laughing hysterically, swearing—even pinky-swearing—each other never to tell a soul about this spectacle of behavior in the water.

Lily dropped back. Eva Clare, with shiny, silver-black water to her waist, looked up at the stars. Countless pinprick glimmers were pasted to a pitch-black Delta sky.

"What're you thinkin' about?" Lily looked up, too.

"That people are like the stars. Look at those tiny pinpoints of light. From our perspective, they've always hung in the same place—century after century. They form patterns that never seem to change—Orion, Ursa Minor and Polaris, the Big Dipper. Like the stars, some people are stuck to their positions in the darkness. They never seem to stray from their old prejudices."

"And you can't reach up there, get a pinch on one with your fingernails, and move it. You can't change people." Lily rubbed her arms like she was knocking back chill bumps.

"But star patterns really do change. New stars are born. Old ones die. Constellations move and change over time, over thousands of years."

"They change so gradually we don't see it in our lifetime."

"The stars will always be with us. So will the people stuck to the darkness. The fear of change will always be with us, too. But so will the fight for change."

Lily gave a hard nod. "We've come a long way, but we've still got a ways to go."

"How do we get there, Lily? How can a little boy like Gerald—following the example of a daddy who burned Black churches, beat people with his son's baseball bat, and helped murder three civil rights workers—grow up to be a man who embraces change?"

"I'm guessin' he can't. His heart is damaged. His hands carry the old traditions. His feet don't know a better way. Hate helped build his bones."

"Do we let hate drive us? Are we the one who says, 'Go away, there's no room at the inn'?" The water burbled as it lapped against Eva Clare, her slightest movements causing a stir. "Or do we open the door and say, 'Come in, sit at my table, sup with me'?"

"Like Catherine, Victoria, and Star. Like Evelyn and Marthala. Like you and me." Lily let out a soft sigh. "Each one of us is responsible for our own ignorance or awareness. You can't have your feet bogged down in hate while your hands hold a holy book and your heart claims a holy God."

Eva Clare stared at the stippled sky. Some stars were brighter than others; some twinkled more. "My hope is that the numbers of backward, wrongward minds will become fewer. The enlightened ones will strive to be bolder and outshine them." She stirred the riverwater slowly with her hands and watched the little ripples she created. "Change doesn't come in one wide sweep or one swift action. Change comes in soft pushes against the pressure. Change comes one willing soul, one discerning heart, one word, one action—"

"One apartment—" Lily held up a finger.

"One step at a time, walking forward, wearing down the high places, pulling up the low—"

"Making the crooked places straight." Lily pumped her fist in the air.

"I want to be remembered as someone who tried to make the crooked places straight in my little corner of the world. Someone who spoke up, pushed back on wrong, and treated everybody right. That's the least any of us can do. And the most."

They clasped hands, turned toward the bank, and walked out of the deep.

Oral History
Genealogy of Lily Greene As Told By Marthala Johnson

Handwritten in a Blue Horse Notebook

Goree-Hope (enslaved West African)
b. ~ 1760 West Africa
   m. Hercules

Carolina-Hope (enslaved)
b. 1775 Edgecombe County, N. Carolina
   m. Virgil

Luvenia (enslaved)
b. 1821 Edgecombe County, NC
      Master Andrew Coghlan

+Star (enslaved)
b. 1840 Neshoba County, Miss.
      Master Andrew Coghlan

++Riselle (freedwoman)
b. 1860 Bolivar County, Miss.
   m. Titus

+++Ellie-Rose
b. 1881 Bolivar County, Miss.
   m. Tom

++++Alight
b. 1906 Bolivar County, Miss.
   m. Henry

+++++Marthala
b. 1924 Bolivar County, Miss.
   m. Plez Johnson

++++++Josie
b. 1939 Bolivar County, Miss.
   m. Kenny Greene

+++++++Lily Greene
b. 1954 Bolivar County, Miss.

Original Coghlan Family Bible
Wellington/Prentiss
On the Beulah Oxbow,
Yazoo-Mississippi Delta

The Line of Evelyn Bounds Carlyle

Andrew Coghlan
1809-1861
married 1828
Eirinn Lafferty
1810-1859
↓

+Catherine Deering Coghlan
1844-1911
married John Amason
↓
↓
↓

++Annah Rachel Amason
1862-1934
married Joseph Tanner

+++William Patrick Tanner
1911-2000
married Brenda Smith

++++Gerald Tanner
1953-
married Jo Taylor

+Victoria Dove Coghlan
1846-1890
married Rufus Steele
↓

++Erin Rose Coghlan Steele
1863-1890
married Thomas Robbins

+++Emmaline Robbins
1889-1951
married William Bounds

++++Evelyn Bounds
1910-2010
married Lewis Carlyle

+++++Edward Carlyle
1929-1959
married Lucille Doak

++++++Eva Clare Carlyle
1953-
married James Roan

+++++++Lara Coghlan Roan
1978-

++Josiah Napoleon Steele
1867-1927
married Emily Woodward

+++William Jack Steele
1898-1950
married Lizbeth Martin

++++Dovey Elizabeth Steele
1923-

ACKNOWLEDGMENTS

I am ever grateful to the many people who have supported and encouraged me in this effort to write my debut novel.

At the top of the list, my deepest appreciation goes to Mary Catharine Nelson who cheered and rallied me on throughout the process and provided her support, talent, expertise, and services to bring this work to fruition, so kindly and graciously.

Early readers who generously gave critique and invaluable feedback include Mary M. Buckner, Colleen Speroff, the late Nancy Fletcher-Blume, and the late Neil O. Jones.

My two writers groups spent much time and effort in reading and critiquing chapters of early and final versions:

- Franklin Writers: Colleen Speroff, Terry Dunham, Chance Chambers, Jack Wallace, Jennifer Peterson Chambers, Susan Donovan Dunham, and the late Neil O. Jones
- Harpeth River Writers: Bill Woods (fellow Mississippian deserving additional kudos for solid advice and encouragement over and above group effort), Michael J. Tucker, Tom Wood, John Neely Davis, Catherine Moore, Micki Fuhrman, Sandy Ward Bell, Cindy King, and Judy Gregg

This list would be incomplete without a mention of my cocker spaniel, Edelheide Catherine Deering, "Heidi," heartbeat at my feet, editor at my elbow, who listened to this entire book read aloud and barked incessantly at imperative commands and voice inflections.

My research included numerous books read for historical details and foundation, wider understanding, and inspiration to tell my story. Of the many fiction and nonfiction accounts of the Delta and the civil rights era, I am particularly indebted to the following books and authors for their facts, truth, and honesty in writing: *The Most Southern Place on Earth*, by James C. Cobb; *White Privilege Pop Quiz*, by Molly Secours; *Coming of Age in Mississippi*, by Anne Moody; *Caste: The Origins of Our Discontents*, by Isabel Wilkerson; *The Steps We Take: A Memoir of Southern Reckoning*, by Ellen Ann

Fentress; *The Barn*, by Wright Thompson; *Killers of the Dream*, by Lillian Smith; *Magic Time*, by Doug Marlette; *John and Mary Margaret*, by Susan Cushman; *The Persia Café*, by Melany Neilson.

I offer brief quotes or paraphrases from authors of old books in my possession and old hymns in public domain found online, as follows:

Clemens, S. L., Mark Twain. *Life on the Mississippi*. New York: Harper & Brothers Publishers, 1874.

Cohn, David. *Where I Was Born and Raised*. London: University of Notre Dame Press, 1935.

"Down by the Riverside." Old spiritual sung by slaves before the American Civil War, published in 1918.

Hammett, Evelyn Allen. *I, Priscilla*. New York: The Macmillan Company, 1960.

Rowe, James. "Love Lifted Me." Hymn, 1912.

Shakespeare, William. *Antony and Cleopatra. The Complete Works of Shakespeare*. Glenview, Illinois: Scott, Foresman and Company, 1961.

Welty, Eudora. *On Writing*. New York: The Modern Library, 2002.

Woolston, C. H. "Jesus Loves the Little Children." Hymn, 1912.

— Kathy Rhodes

www.ingramcontent.com/pod-product-compliance
Lightning Source LLC
Chambersburg PA
CBHW020353110726
47899CB00006B/1712